SILVER FOX

To Llew

Book One

The Dragon Wakes...

*best wishes
Jenny Sullivan*

Jenny Sullivan

Wuggles Publishing,
Clydach, Swansea, South Wales.

Copyright © Jenny Sullivan
September 2010

ISBN 978- 1- 904043- 21 8

The right of Jenny Sullivan to be identified as the author of this book has been asserted by her in accordance with the Copyright, Design and Patents Act. All rights reserved.

No part of this publication may be reproduced, stored in a retrieval system, or transmitted, in any form or by any means without the prior written permission of the publisher, nor be otherwise circulated in any form or binding or cover other than that in which it is published and without a similar condition being imposed on the subsequent purchaser.

*To my wonderful husband Rob, who is, was,
and always will be my love and encourager-in-chief*

and also

*to my late, beloved father, Frederick Reuben Anderson
without whom I wouldn't be a reader, let alone a writer.*

Front cover design: Rob Sullivan from an original photograph
                               by Siân Ifan
                               Adapted by Arthur Perridge Photographic

Back cover design: From an original painting "Torchlight Fox"
                               by Paul D E Mitchell

To learn more about Owain Glyndŵr, contact
                 http://galwadglyndwr.blogspot.com

CHAPTER ONE

Elffin

'No, Master Iolo, please don't! Lady Marged will fillet me if I'm not back quick!'

Iolo Goch hadn't seen me. Owain Glyndŵr's household bard was pestering the child again. She was backed into a corner of Mam's stillroom, tears making clean runnels in the grimy face. I tapped Iolo on the shoulder, gently at first, then harder to get his attention.

'Leave the child alone, Iolo,' I said mildly, 'or I'll kick your bardic bloody arse up between your bardic bloody ears.' He glared at me without recognition, opened and shut his mouth and then turned and scuttled away, leaving Rhiannon to collect her spilled herbs. I tousled the unruly mass of hair and patted the grimy face. 'Run along, sweetheart, Mam's waiting. And look - don't let Iolo get you alone again, all right?'

She nodded. I swear her eyes were the biggest things about her.

Llewelyn

Chased out of the kitchens, clouted round the ear for thieving sweetmeats, glad anyway to be away from the bustling cooks, I took refuge in the peace of Sycharth.

Always golden, this place: I first saw it flooded with amber light, and I've loved it ever since. Five then, me, my father dead in battle against the bloody Scot, shoulder to shoulder with Owain Glyndŵr, and when he fell, Glyndŵr cradled him in his arms, my father's blood stained Glyndŵr's surcoat, and Glyndŵr grieved. Later, when Mam died of fever and my new sister with her, Glyndŵr had me and Rhiannon, my sister, brought to Sycharth. I remember him scooping me up, mail and leather armour harsh against my bare legs, telling me that when I grew up, I'd be a brave warrior. I rode before him on his horse to Sycharth, his arms protecting me. For that kindness alone, I'd die for him.

They say he has the powers of the Old Ones, which may be how he knew when Mam died. When *Tad* died, before, he brought her the news himself and when she wept and asked what would become of us, he reassured her.

He is *uchelwyr*, Owain Glyndyfrdwy, high born, a learned and honoured man. He once served the English court, but now he's retired to Sycharth, honoured for his kindness and generosity, his justice to his inferiors, and his patronage of bards and men of learning. He has Royal blood: he's descended from the old Princes of Wales, from Llywelyn the Last, foully murdered beside Cilmeri stream by cowardly *Sais* enemies.

This house is beautiful and welcoming, and because of Glyndŵr it's filled with laughter and music, and no one in need is ever turned away. He took my sister, too, when he didn't need to. Girls don't matter; after all, they're just a burden. But he'd promised *Tad*, my father, so he took her as well as me.

Iolo Goch would probably sing Glyndŵr's praises even if he weren't living in Owain's house, eating his food, drinking his wine and sleeping in his feather bed. Bed to himself, too, Iolo Goch. Bards are people to be respected, so Iolo doesn't share his with anyone - unless he wants to. Iolo sings like an angel, and his songs lift spirits - or cast them down, depending upon the occasion - but he's a wicked old devil, forever catching Rhian in corners and tickling and pinching her. Nothing she says makes any difference: no one listens to girls, but Iolo is old: his teeth are bad, and his breath smells like a midden. I found her crying, once, and promised that when I'm grown, I'll kill him for her. She said that by that time Iolo would probably be dead, six feet down and poking up daisies. I was hurt, because I was ten then, and almost grown. I'm tall as she is already, and she has no right to belittle me. I wanted to hit her, but hitting girls (even sisters, who don't really count) is not a knightly thing to do. How can a person comfort someone like that?

Elffin, my foster-brother hates Iolo. He's the youngest Glyndŵr and my elder by four years. At eighteen, he's a man, though his brothers tease him and call him stripling. Rhian is almost two years my senior and well enough for a girl. *Tadmaeth* could have sent her to a convent, but didn't. She'll be one of Lady Marged's ladies one day, and is being taught how to write and calculate, but she isn't as clever as me. She's only a girl, you see. She's thin as a twig, but she has pretty eyes. Elffin told Iolo that he'd batter him if he didn't leave her alone, which was plain enough even for Iolo, and Rhian's adored him ever since, which is just like a girl, although I doubt Elffin's noticed her. Not that *Tadmaeth* would let allow Elffin to marry her, even if he wanted to, which he doesn't, so she's wasting her time. She'll be found a husband some time. Girls are no use except to marry and get land and sons. And marry tidy where they're told.

Rhiannon

Fat Crisiant, the Lady's tirewoman, pushing wisps of damp hair back from her face, wheezing with the effort of walking downstairs to the buttery, leaned in the doorway of the cool room where I was supervising a servant girl skimming cream off the great, flat pewter pans. I loathe the ingrained sour smell and the sweet, greasy smell of the cream.

'Herself wants you, now.'

Whatever Lady Marged wanted, it would be better than this. Mind, whenever she sends for me it usually means I'm going to be punished. For the life of me, though, I couldn't think of anything I'd done wrong, and certainly nothing worth breaking into a busy Monday's tasks for.

'Tidy yourself, Rhiannon. Wipe your hands and for goodness sake do something with your hair. You look like a dandy-clock, child.'

'What does she want, Cris?'

She pursed her lips. 'You'll find out soon enough, I dare say. And if you done nothing wrong, then nothing to worry about, is there, *ferch*?'

I wasn't comforted. This was Out of the Ordinary. I don't like things that are out of the ordinary: I like my days smooth as cream, ordered and even. I've had a lifetime's worth of upheaval already, thank you kindly, and I don't want any more.

I left the cream to the dairymaid and scurried up the back stairs to my room under the eaves, ripped off my apron and wrestled my hair into a plait, which was all I could do to tidy it, then splashed my face with water. I took the stairs down three at a time, sprinted across the courtyard, skirts hiked, and up to Lady Marged's chamber. *Mamaeth* is usually calm, but she hates to be kept waiting. Sharply defined brows draw together over dark eyes, and twin grooves of annoyance appear between them when she's angry. We don't make her angry if we can help: not her husband nor her sons and daughters, grown though they might be, and married too, some of them. And most certainly not me.

I tapped at the door, waiting for the Lady's low *'Dewch i mewn,'* before entering as bidden. She glanced up, smiling. Nothing too bad, then! Perhaps she might praise me for once! Except that just as I couldn't remember doing anything particularly *wrong*, I couldn't remember doing anything particularly *right*, either.

'Rhiannon, sit down. I have some news for you.'

Don't like news, either. News means unpredictable. "News" can only mean change. She set aside her embroidery frame: I hooked a stool with my foot and thumped down on it, and she sighed.

'*Lift* the stool, Rhiannon, don't - oh, never mind.'

My face reddened under her exasperated gaze. She was probably deciding which bit of me to criticise first. When at last she spoke, it wasn't much of a relief, and in fact, things got rapidly worse.

'Rhiannon, Rhys ap Hywel, my husband's kinsman, has asked for you.'

My stomach lurched. 'Who? What for? I don't know him.'

'He doesn't know you, either,' she said, irritation in her voice. 'But he's heard of you and it will be a reasonable match and a good alliance for him. You won't want for anything.'

'But I don't *know* him!' I repeated, stupidly. I heard my voice rising. 'I don't love him,' I said, as calmly as I could. 'I've never met him! I can't marry someone I've never met!'

She took my hand in her cool fingers. I curled my own instinctively, so that she wouldn't see the bitten nails. Death on nail-biting, Lady Marged.

'You'll meet him, soon enough, and love isn't important. If there's kindness and goodwill, love usually follows - or at least an accommodation bearable to both parties. And when you have children -'

'Children?' My jaw dropped. 'I can't have children! I'm not old enough!'

'Nonsense. You're almost sixteen. You're small, but you'll grow, and I imagine Rhys will wait until you're ready. I'm sure he's kind, and his wife gave him two children before she died, so there's a son to inherit and a daughter too, so he'll be in no great need for more.'

'But I can't marry him! I -'. Recognising the expression on Lady Marged's face, I stopped. No use arguing.

'Your *Tadmaeth* and I have accepted his offer, Rhiannon. You'll be content enough when you've a household to run.'

She was implacable. The interview was ended and I was allowed to leave, fuzzy-headed and trembling. I managed to close the heavy door behind me before I collapsed. My knees gave way and I slumped onto the stairs. I thought I might vomit. I wanted to cry, but what would be the point? She never changes her mind.

She can never have loved as I love, or she would not do such a terrible thing to me.

How can I marry Rhys whatever-his-name-is. He's old and I don't love him. I love Elffin, but *She* wouldn't care, even if she knew. Elffin, my shining knight. I loiter near him when he eats, watch as he lolls beside the hearth in winter. Once, I found him asleep in the orchard, and crept close. I watched him for a long time. I dared to put my cheek close to his mouth to feel his breath on my cheek, dreaming, imagining his kisses. I would have stayed there forever, but then he snorted and stirred and I ran before he woke. But I dream, sometimes, that I stayed, and he woke, and he... Oh, what's the use of dreams? Something always shatters them. Most people think Elffin isn't as handsome as his older brother Madoc, but Madoc's eyes don't crinkle when he laughs, and it is Elffin's face that I see when I close my eyes and all that I ever wish to see when I open them. But *She* has decided
. Suddenly I heard feet on the stairs above me, so I slipped down the staircase, out the door and through the back entrance to the river bank, away from prying eyes. Alone, I could bawl until my eyes boiled red in my head, scream, howl, rage, turn the slithering brown river into a raging torrent with my tears. But, slumped on the riverbank, although the lump in my throat was big as a bolster, I couldn't squeeze out a single tear. Strangely, I couldn't feel my hands or feet: it was as if the warm day had turned to ice.

Unless I kill myself, I shall have to marry that man. Elffin doesn't know I exist. I'm only his foster-sister, so far beneath him that he doesn't even notice I'm in the same house. He'll marry some fine lady a hundred times more beautiful than me, and she'll be rich, and Elffin will probably love her, for men always love ladies who are beautiful and rich. She'll probably have breasts, too.

I must marry where I am ordered, but I'll never forget Elffin. Never. Perhaps I'll die instead.

Elffin

The buck crashed panic-stricken from cover and my arrow thudded into his heart. I slid off my horse, and slit the throbbing throat, then left the huntsman to gut him and bring in the prize. I set off home. It's not manly, I know, but I hate the bloody ripping of warm flesh from arse to throat, but if it's not done straight away the meat spoils. I do it if I have to, but I loathe the way it robs a beautiful beast of dignity, reducing it to nothing but bloody raw meat. How shall I feel when the quarry is human, as it surely will be some day?

The hunt itself was joy enough, and the buck a good size. I spurred Seren, my mare, my guts growling - breakfast was too long ago. Clattering under the wooden arches into Sycharth, I turned Seren over to Siôn Twp, then visited the kitchen to steal bread and cheese from under Bron's nose. She bridled and dimpled at me, and slapped at me playfully when I bent and kissed her. A fat old woman, behaving like a girl.

I ate sitting on the warm stone of the courtyard steps, watching doves wheel in and out of the cote, then doused my head with well-water before wandering inside. Mam is strict about her menfolk stinking of horse inside the house. The sound of a harp drew me towards the solar, where my father sat in the airy, sun-slipping chamber, playing for his own pleasure. He takes joy in the small things, my father: he's as often crawling on his hands and knees with one of Gruffydd's brood on his back as deep in some learned text. His music is his supreme joy, and why Iolo Goch is here, damn him. He looked up at my arrival, smiling a welcome, his long fingers drawing patterns of sound. I slumped into a chair opposite him, legs sprawled, eyes closed, enjoying the airy room and the music.

A commotion from downstairs stilled his hands, and exasperated, he glanced towards the door. 'Is there no peace?'

I grinned. *Tad* often complains that his retirement is anything but peaceful. We listened to the footsteps clattering on the wooden stairs, growing louder as the boots came closer. He cocked his head, then nodded, satisfied at having identified the intruder. 'Gruffydd.'

My brother's step is unmistakeable, though his heavy, purposeful tread is quite at odds with the humour in his face. He's like *Tad*, where I favour Mam, blessed with her straight nose and dark eyes, though my chin is square like Owain's, and my hair lighter and coarser. Mam says I'm stubborn as he is. I think I'm like Mam's brothers, but she says when I scowl, I'm Owain's image. I'll probably have his height some day, and I'm working on acquiring his dignity.

The door crashed open. Gruffydd was angry: the white grooves bracketing his nose betrayed it: Owain is the same, but he's slower to anger than Gruffydd.

'What?'

'Grey of Ruthin. His men have crossed our border - again. Taken Croesau, stolen cattle, burned a farmhouse. Killed the tenant, raped his daughter. For God's sake, *Tad*, enough's enough. De Grey shifts the border whenever the wind changes! Let me burn his bloody castle about his ears. I'll take back Croesau under our own terms.'

God, how I crave combat! I've seen no action, ever, because Sycharth has been largely at peace during my childhood, and I've always been kept out of any skirmishes for one reason or another, and it isn't fair.

'Let me come with you, Gruffydd?' I begged. 'I can fight as well as anyone, you know I can.' *Tad* raised a hand, quelling me, his eyes not leaving Gruffydd's face.

'What good would that do, Gruffydd? De Grey will retaliate, more people will die. No, my son, I'll try the peaceful way first.'

It's just as if I'm not here, I thought, *as if I haven't spoken*. I slumped back in my chair, chewing my thumbnail angrily. I'd show them, one day.

Tad stood, one hand fingering his light, forked beard. 'The peaceful way, Gruffydd,' he repeated, 'in law the lands are mine.'

'Welsh law. De Grey has scant regard for any law, and none for Welsh,' Gruffydd replied, the anger raw on his face.

'Under English law, Gruffydd. I swore fealty to England and I'll not break my oath because of de Grey. When Richard was on the throne I took a grievance to Parliament, and they decided in my favour. De Grey was forced to return my lands. Henry will do the same. Nothing's changed: Parliament still boasts honest men. Son, we must treat with England as equals, not take to the sword at every slight! We're civilised men. We'll ask for justice.'

'We won't get it,' Gruffydd spat. 'I won't bow my head to de Grey or the *Sais* Parliament.' The fury was fading, but Gruffydd was still angry.

'You'll obey me, Gruffydd.' *Tad*, ever the peacemaker, grasped Gruffydd's arm, shaking it affectionately, gazing into his face, smiling. 'When I die, I want to die in my bed, and my ambition is that my sons, in due time, shall do the same. *Diawl*, Gruffydd, no one wins a dispute over lands! Men die to gain a piece of dirt, and for months, years, their sons and their sons' sons die trying to keep it. No, I'll have peace, and I'll have justice, and I believe the English Parliament is the means of getting it.'

'The only justice de Grey understands is the point of a sword at his bloody throat.'

Tad raised his hand, silencing Gruffydd. 'Then he, and you, must learn another way. We'll go to Parliament. We've allies there: I fought at Henry's side in Scotland, and he was grateful. I trust him: I'll have justice from him. And don't forget St Asaph.'

Gruffydd's voice was derisive. 'You think Henry'll support Welsh against *Sais*? Not a hope. And a Welsh bishop? The one Welsh Bishop in Wales? What use is he against an entire Parliament of English?'

'We shall try, Gruffydd.'

Gruffydd hadn't given up yet: 'De Grey will say that the land runs between the two estates, like cheese between two bits of bread. If Henry must choose between two lords, he will choose English, not Welsh.'

Owain Glyndŵr shook his head. 'I've made my decision, Gruffydd.'

CHAPTER TWO

Llewelyn

Rhiannon, crimson-faced, shoved past me on the stairs, almost knocking me arse over ankles. I doubt she even saw me. I shouted at her, but she was gone. Lady Marged has probably caught her out and scolded her, and Rhian has never taken reprimands easily.

Ah, let her go. I've no time to waste on a girl. There's work to be done in the stables, and afterwards old Huw has promised to show me how to clean *Tadmaeth*'s armour. When I'm a squire, I'll need to do that, and keep my lord's weapons keen. I like working with Huw: he was Owain's squire before he got ancient, and went with him to Scotland and England and France, even. He knew my father, and the stories he tells make my heart pound and sing with pride.

Once, when Owain and he went with the Old King to Scotland, Owain was surrounded by a thousand heathen Scotchmen, and Owain fought until his lance shattered, and after that he used the broken lance like a dagger, laying about him until he was knee deep in Scotch blood, proud and undefeated. In his helm he wore a scarlet flamingo feather that fluttered and tossed in the wind, vivid as a sunset, Huw said. I do not know what a flamingo is, mind, but I expect it's a very fierce creature, since Owain wore it. Perhaps it's half-dragon. Glyndŵr was everywhere the fight was hardest, and men fell before him like grain before the reaper. And my father was at his side, valiant together like great Arthur and his liege man Lancelot until he was foully and treacherously stabbed through the guts by a Scotch savage. Did I say that my father died in Owain's arms? I expect I did. I'm proud of my father, and often tell what happened to him. I should have liked to have been there, to have seen them together, great heroes both, but I shouldn't have wanted to see my father die.

If I'd been Owain's squire then, I'd have tended their armour, and washed the blood from it, polished it until it shone like a mirror.

Huw is teaching me swordsmanship, and Elffin helps when he has time. Elffin is kind, though he teases me. Perhaps because he's the youngest he knows how it is to be a boy and at everyone's call. The others - the ones who live at home at Sycharth and don't have estates yet – they're too old to remember, I expect. Elffin has promised to teach me to use a lance, and he's promised that he'll ask his father for a horse for me one day. I'm learning to ride like a soldier, and I'm getting better - I haven't fallen off for two weeks and three days.

The hollow rattle of hooves on stone greeted me, and the warm, comforting reek of the horses. The stable is airy, lit with bright shafts of sunlight, dust-motes swirling at the open door. Most of the animals are out to pasture. When the weather's cold, they're brought in at night, not to take chill. Horses are big creatures, and the destriers enormous, their hooves like great feathery inverted bowls, their nostrils red and cavernous, their whiskery mouths full of square yellow teeth. But they are surprisingly quick to take chill, for such great beasts.

Siôn Twp had already begun shifting soiled straw from the stalls, piling it in an acrid heap onto the cart. Siôn always stinks: he doesn't wash very often, and he works mainly in dung, so the stink of horse-shit hangs about him like a cloud. One of his eyes watches the sky, the other his nose. He has a hare-lip and makes strange sounds when he speaks. He's mocked of course, and sometimes I join in, but only to show the other boys that I'm like them, in case they turn on me, instead. I wouldn't want that. But then afterwards I feel sorry for him because I tormented him, and guilt makes me go and steal food from the kitchens for him, to make him forgive me. I think he likes me a bit.

I don't mind working in the stables, though horse-piss steeped in the straw makes my eyes water. When we'd finished clearing the stalls, and had spread fresh straw on the ground and filled the mangers with fragrant hay, I left Siôn and went to find Huw. Perhaps he'd tell me stories, today.

Half-way, I tripped on the cobbles and fell, skinning my knees and muddying my breeches, but Huw won't mind. 'Clean clothes belong in the house, boy, there's honest dirt in stables,' he says.

But my knees hurt, and I sat picking dirt from bloody grazes so I was late, and Huw was ill-tempered and not in any mood to tell stories. Loved to talk, did Huw, and I loved to listen, so there, we were good workmates. Except when I was late and he was angry.

When I hobbled in today, he silently handed me a leather bridle and fatty paste to work into it to make it supple. He was putting a dull sheen on a piece of armour with fine, soft sand, and muttering to himself. I couldn't understand much of what he said, but I know that when he's in this mood, it is best to shut up.

I watched, instead, as he used the sand to rub rust from the armour he was working on: he wasn't in a mood to answer questions. Fatty stuff squished between my fingers, and I wiped them on a rag before using it to bring the leathers to a soft burnish.

Huw burst out suddenly with 'It will end in tears, mark my words. Bastard, stinking de Grey! And my Lord thinks a *Sais* Parliament will listen to him? We'll be laughed at, mark my words, and de Grey will take more and more, and where'll we be then? Glyndŵr is making a mistake, I tell you!'

I wasn't sure if I should speak or not. I wanted to stick up for *Tadmaeth*, who can do no wrong to my eyes, being both a hero and wise, but after rubbing away in silence for a few minutes I ventured a question.

'Master Huw. What's Lord de Grey done?'

Huw spat into the straw beside him. 'Taken Croesau, the border lands, where my cousin is - was - Glyndŵr's tenant. His men killed my cousin and raped his girl. Bastard. If I were twenty years younger I'd see to him. Rip his guts out with my bare hands, I would, aye, and dance on his entrails! Glyndŵr thinks *Sais* Henry 'll give him justice? *Sais* kings don't know what justice means! Bloody brigands themselves.' He spat again, for emphasis.

If my cousin had been killed, I expect I'd feel the same. 'If I were older, Master Huw,' I said, needing to let the old man know that I was on his side, 'I'd fight for your kin. If I could ride my horse properly, without falling off, I mean. When I can best Elffin in a swordfight. And lift a lance.' I slumped, miserably, hearing the hollowness of my words. He'd probably laugh at me. But he didn't.

'Ah, you're a good lad, Llew. You've a fine name, and your father was a brave man. Tell you what, I'll ask Glyndŵr about a mount for you.'

I held my breath, unable to speak. It was all that I wanted.

'The grey, perhaps. Sioned. She's gentle and obedient.' The old man's voice cracked into a cackle. 'All you need in a horse or a woman, boy!' Then his face collapsed into sadness again, and he returned to silence.

A horse of my own! I can't have the black stallion, and thank you, I don't want it: it half- killed Siôn Twp six months ago when Owain acquired it from his brother-in-law, John Hanmer. It picked Siôn up by his shoulder and shook him like a rat. He refuses to go near it now – he's convinced the horse is possessed by the devil. I don't think he is: I think he just doesn't appreciate people who stink, and shows his disgust in the only way a horse can. When I dream, I dream of riding the stallion, but to be honest, he'd probably crush me like the gardener kills a slug. I appreciated his fire, his beauty - but at a safe distance from his hooves and teeth.

The mare, Sioned, is better. She's my favourite: I never pass her stall, never cross her pasture, without an apple in my pocket. Best of all, though, she loves the minted sugar pieces that Bron makes. Bron turns her back, allows me to steal one or two bits, and I feed them to Sioned, her soft muzzle burrowing into my palm, her breath whistling with delight at the minty taste. Sioned reminds me of Bron when she's eating the mints. Bron tastes hot soup with just such a suck and whiffle, although Bron has better whiskers than Sioned. Bron wouldn't thank me for saying it, I expect, and I'd be grateful if you didn't repeat it, but it's true.   Bron is kind, except when she's busy. I don't go too close to her, though, if I can help it. She calls me "poor, motherless boy", and clutches me to her breasts, which is like suffocating between two sacks of flour. But when she's busy she's a demon. Her scarlet face shines with sweat, and she lays about her with her ladle and pans if she thinks anybody is slacking. I'm glad I'm not the pot-boy or the turnspit-dog, which howls pitifully when she puts red-hot coals under its feet to make it scrabble faster round its wheel.

I hurried, anxious to be free of Huw, to visit my mare. He clouted my ear. 'Do it well, boy, or do it over.'

So I hid my impatience, kneaded and rubbed and shined, and at last I was allowed to go. Bron piled my hands with fresh bread, cheese and apples: I must be back two hours before supper to practise in the tiltyard with Elffin, but until then, unless someone sees me and finds something else for me to do, I'm free.

Sioned was knee deep in buttercups, and buttercup pollen coated my bare legs as I approached her. I flatted an apple on my palm, and discovered that she is partial, also, to a bit of cheese. Up on her rough back, then and I laid myself along the length of her, my arms and legs dangling, the closest to an embrace I could manage, and breathed in her good smell. Then I saw my sister coming from the river, and sat up, waiting for her to come close, so I could tell her that this is now my horse (or at least it will be when Huw has spoken to *Tadmaeth*).

Rhiannon

I was tempted, instead of walking away from the river, to throw myself into it. It wasn't the thought of mortal sin that stopped me, or eternity frying in hell. I don't care what priests say, not now. I'm barely fifteen, forced to marry a man I cannot and will not love, whom I've never met, and if that isn't hell, what is? My life's over before it's hardly begun.

I reached the water's edge, gazed into the brown depths. One small step and I shouldn't need to worry about anything. One step and the merciful waters would end it all, and then, oh then Lady Marged would be sorry…

If the trees hadn't been quite so green, the drowse of bees in the long grass not so loud, and the river not sparkled as it did, I might certainly have thrown myself in, ended it all, forever, in one tragic gesture. But my mother taught me to be thankful for small mercies, and when I stopped to think about it, there were a few to be glad for. I tore up a stalk of grass and chewed it, counting reasons for living: I've had had six years of happiness at Sycharth, and have loved Elffin undiscovered for twelve months. I'll be mistress of my own house, which is some small consolation, since no one (except the man who would be my husband) would give me orders ever again, or make me sew until my fingers are sore, or skim cream. Oh, what it is to be a girl, and always under the control of someone else, usually male, or old, or both. It isn't fair. Elffin answers to no one except his father (and Lady Marged, though he'd never admit it), and one day, when he marries, he'll have his own estates, lording it over his wife and servants.

The thought of Elffin, especially married Elffin, renewed my misery. Who would he marry? For love? Or duty? I closed my eyes tightly and prayed, Oh, Holy Mary Mother of God, let it be duty! The thought of his lips on another woman's - still less a woman he might love, when he's never kissed me, nor is ever likely to, now, was altogether too much to bear. I wanted to grab the unknown woman and tear out every hair on her head, scratch out her eyes and kick her shins, whoever she might be.

Of course I knew, as I've always known, that Elffin is beyond me, and now will never, even by accident, be mine - or even know that I love him. I must be a realist, stop dreaming and make the best of it, the way Mam taught me. She always said "what can't be cured must be endured", and I can see the sense of that. Not that I'm an optimist, mind. I refuse to be. My life has been too full of sadness for that. I decided against killing myself. Instead, I selected a smooth stone from the river-bank, gave it Elffin's name, kissed it, and consigned it to the river, which swallowed it, settled it on the bottom with a thousand others like it, and flowed on, regardless. *This must be me,* I thought, *flowing forward, not back*. And, feeling suitably tragic, abandoned and hard-done-by, I left my love and the river behind. My heart was broken, but I'd live. Martyred and miserable until I die, but alive.

I climbed the small hill beside the river, and waded through thigh-deep grass towards Sycharth. And there was Llew, straddling a horse, a great stupid grin on his freckled face. Whenever he's gone from the house, he can always be found with the horses. I overheard *Tadmaeth* say to Lady Marged that Llew has a way with them, that he's a bright lad, and that he was of a mind to put him as a squire to Siôn, or even Elffin now he's old enough. I haven't told Llew this. He's swollen-headed enough as it is.

I'll be leaving him behind when I marry ap Hywel. But then, I see so little of him, what with my duties and his, and he's always with the men and I'm always with the women, that sometimes it seems strange that Llew is blood of my blood, and all that is left to me of my parents.

Meeting Llew, I was glad I hadn't cried and made my eyes red. I won't show him any signs of my unhappiness. He teases sometimes. He's not an unkind boy, but I'm his sister. Boys are always cruel to their sisters.

He sat up straight on the horse as I approached. He's grown taller, lately: baby fat lengthening into awkwardness, gawky arms and bloody grazed knees sticking out each side of the plump mare's back. I doubt he'll ever reach Elffin's height, for neither our father or our mother was tall, though my father was thick-set and strong.

From the look of him, Llew was imagining he was Lancelot du Lac sitting up there, or maybe King Arthur himself, but actually he looked like a scarecrow on a sack, straddling that fat mare.

'You'd best not let Huw catch you away from your work.' I was waspish with him, attacking before he could do the same.

Llew grinned. 'Huw knows, so there. Oh, Rhian, I'm having Sioned!'

Jealousy sparked, and my teeth clenched involuntarily. Not because Llew was to be given the mare: I didn't care about that. I could borrow any horse if I wanted to ride. I was angry because he's a boy, and free, and I'm a girl, and am not. He'll get all he yearns for, and I, nothing at all of what I desire with all my heart and soul.

Llew saw my feelings on my face, and his own face fell in disappointment. 'Aren't you pleased for me, Rhiannon? If I'm to be a squire one day, I must have my own mount. And Elffin has ~'

At the sound of his name the tears came. Mortified at my weakness, I was helpless. My knees gave way, I bowed my head on my knees, and howled.

Llew slid off the mare, knelt beside me, trying to tug my hands from my face, peering at me through my tangled hair.

'What's the matter, Rhian? Are you ill? Has Iolo Goch been bothering you again? I'll tell Elffin, he'll kill him dead. No, I'll kill him for you. We'll both kill him!'

Unable to speak, I shook my head, but hearing Elffin's name made everything worse. I fought to get the words out.

'Oh, Llew, I've got to marry Rhys ap Hywel, and I don't know him, and he is old, gone thirty, and old people stink, and he's got two children already. I am to take care of his brats and be his wife and I don't love him.'

Llewelyn's voice was bewildered. 'But you always knew *Tadmaeth* would get you a husband when you were old enough, and now you're fifteen, aren't you? Look, don't be afraid. He's Owain's kinsman, after all. I expect he washes sometimes. And he may be old but all his teeth are there. I met him in Llangollen with Elffin and Siôn last month, though he didn't mention, then, that he was intending to speak for you. He isn't too ugly, Rhian, even if he isn't young. Of course, he isn't handsome either, but he doesn't have crossed eyes or rotten teeth. You'll have to leave Sycharth, but you'll have your own home instead, won't you? Think of that, Rhiannon! Mistress of your own house!'

I couldn't help it: the words were out before I could stop them. 'But I don't love him!'

'Oh pooh, love! So what? I know you're greensick for Elffin, but he doesn't love you, you know. How could he, after all? Take my advice - forget him. Look on the bright side, Rhian. Ap Hywel is old, so he might die soon and then you'll be a widow with your own house and you can marry anyone you like! Except Elffin, of course,' he added hastily. 'He wouldn't want you.'

I resisted the urge to hit him into the middle of next week. 'Elffin's the only one I want. And some old men live to be eighty. Suppose he's one of those? Oh, God, Llew, think of that! I could be stuck with ap Hywel until I'm...'

I've never learned how to add and subtract in my head, though with a slate and enough time I can manage a sum that is often - well, sometimes - nearly right. 'Until I'm too old to care,' I finished miserably.

'Oh, come on, Rhiannon!' Llewelyn said, 'cheer up. Look, I'll let you ride Sioned for a bit if you like.'

I sighed. He is such a child. As if I could be so easily distracted. 'No, I'll walk.' I stood up, straightened my back. 'I imagine I'll survive. Maybe the world will come to an end before I have to marry ap Hywel.'

Llewelyn swiftly spat to his left and crossed himself. 'Don't say that! It's bad luck.'

I left him to his mare. My world had already ended. Llewelyn's was just beginning.

Elffin

Llew, attended by a strong odour of horse-sweat, was already in the tiltyard when I arrived. I stripped off my shirt before we began: there'd be a storm before nightfall. I flexed my shoulders, surveying the boy: he's sprouting fast. I don't think he'll be tall, but his shoulders are squaring out and his neck is already thickening with muscle.

I remember when he arrived here, riding in the circle of *Tad*'s arms, nothing but a chubby baby with round grey eyes and a tousled thatch of white hair, grieving for his lost Mam. Now his arms are near as long as my own, and he lacks but five or six inches of my height. When he fills out, he'll be a man to reckon with. I'm fond of him, though I don't show it in case he gets above himself. There's no malice in him, only dreams, which I expect life will soon put out. He's as honest as he's earnest, and I respect that - although his earnestness makes teasing him irresistible.

So I scowled. 'Why so cheerful, Llew? I haven't given you permission to be happy.'

At first, he looked bemused and guilty, then realised I was teasing. His grin split his freckled face. He rubbed a sweaty hand through his hair, making it stick up in straw-coloured clumps.

'I'm to have the -' he stopped, blushing as if he had said too much.

'Have what? The serving maid at the Bush? The pot of gold at the end of the rainbow? Bendigeidfran's severed head? What?' I sighted along the blade of the blunt practice sword, hefting the weight of it, testing the balance between grip and blade. 'What?' I persisted.

'Huw promised to speak to *Tadmaeth*,' he said, the words coming out in a rush, 'I'm to have the grey mare if *Tadmaeth* agrees. Sioned.' The smile broke through again.

'Does he now?' I spoke slowly, not looking at him. 'And what if I want Sioned? For myself?' He really was so easy to tease.

His face drooped. 'Then you'll take her, Elffin. She is yours.'

I relented, ruffling his hair. It was hardly fair to torment him. 'But I won't, Llew. She'll do nicely. She's gentle and obedient.'

'All that I need in a horse or a woman,' Llew said solemnly, and flushed scarlet at my roar of laughter.

'You know about women, do you?'

'Not really,' Llew admitted. 'Only my sister, and she -' Again, he stopped. His colour rose again, but he was grinning.

I sensed a secret. 'What?'

'Nothing, Elffin.' He picked up the other sword and sighted along it.

'And is the blade true enough for you, Sire?' I slapped his shoulder, making him stagger.

He rose to it, drawing himself up, raising his weapon threateningly. 'Aye, 'twill do, my Lord!' he snarled, and launched into the attack.

I could, of course, have disarmed him in seconds. He battered in too wide, flailing his sword like a hayfork. One flick and he'd have been helpless, my blade at his throat. But I was kind: I let him drive me back, parried and thrust as awkwardly as I could, and Llew's face shone with joy at his "besting" of me. Then, to put him in his place again, because one day he'd have to do this well or lose his life, I slipped the blunt sword neatly under his guard, bruising his ribs to teach him a lesson. The boy sat, clutching his side, but still grinning widely with the joy of it.

He'll be good one day, I thought, *if he learns caution.* And to come in fast and deadly and not like a woman threshing corn.

Later, I tried him on the wooden horse with a full-size lance; he hefted it, but the strain showed in the wobble of the weapon, the gritted teeth and the scarlet cheeks. But there were signs that he'd learn to balance it and to use it properly before long. Next time I'd give him a half-size lance, to let him get used to handling it on Siôned's back. He was already proficient with a long-bow cut to his smaller size, for he was that rarity - an individual with a natural, accurate eye. He could take a robin in flight any day, whatever the condition of the wind or weather. His eye was true to any mark, in motion or still.

My father asks often after Llew's progress: he's fond of him boy, and *Tad* has a graceful way that has built Llew's confidence, despite the fact that the boy and his sister are orphans and living on his charity. He has taken him and Rhiannon to home and heart. That's the true mark of Glyndŵr, my father. He is, when all is said and done, a good man.

'What were you saying about your sister?' I perched on an upturned barrel, wiping sweat from my chest and face with a rag.

'Nothing, Elffin.' But he coloured, so I naturally kept after him.

'If you don't tell me,' I threatened, 'I'll tell my father I want Sioned.'

'My sister is going to marry Rhys ap Hywel, Elffin. She's miserable because she doesn't love him. I told her she must do as she's told and make the best of it.'

'I'll bet that went down well!' I said, snorting with laughter. 'I'm amazed you're here, Llew. Ap Hywel asked for her?' I wondered what a man like ap Hywel would want with Rhian. She's all eyes and tangled hair, and great swarms of freckles, with no curve of breast or hip to mar the straight up and down of her. I'd have thought a man like ap Hywel would have wanted a woman in his bed, not a child.

Iolo Goch was after her, true, but then he's always liked little girls. A grown woman would laugh him to scorn and back for all his golden music and slippery words, and the village girls are wise enough to keep away from him. Only skinny Rhiannon, innocent and unknowing, didn't understand what Iolo Goch had been after. But I'd frightened him off.

'Ap Hywel's wife went and died, and he wants a new one to look after his children.'

'Well, Rhiannon will grow in time. In the meantime she can amuse his brats. I dare say she may even love him in the end. Women do, you know.'

'Do they? She's unhappy, now. I think she's afraid.'

'I expect she'll love him eventually.' I didn't know for sure, of course. Who can tell what women think? Or even if they do. 'She'll get used to him. Miserable, is she? Strange. I'd have thought she'd be glad of her own household to queen it over.'

Llewelyn glanced at me, his face alive with mischief. 'Trouble is, Elffin, and don't tell her I told you, but she's been like a sick calf about -' He stopped, suddenly. 'About someone else,' he concluded.

'She has, has she?' I sensed an opportunity to torment some other unfortunate. 'Who would that be, now?'

'Can't say, Elffin.'

'But you know.'

'I do. But I can't tell you.'

I could have pressed him. He'd have told me, in the end. But the day was hot and the river was calling.

CHAPTER THREE

Llewelyn

You'd think Rhiannon had been condemned to death! The Lady isn't going to relent, so Rhian's going to have to get on with it. I'm sorry she's unhappy, but she'll forget Elffin soon enough.

Duw, I almost let it slip to Elffin yesterday! He wouldn't want to know that some stupid girl thinks she's in love with him ~ especially not Rhiannon, who's bony as a broomstick and a temper that's hell on wheels. I almost feel sorry for ap Hywel. I'd rather have Sioned!

Oh, I wish my father had seen me in the tiltyard yesterday! I almost beat him Elffin, he was cringing from my flashing blade, and any second I could have pinked his ribs and finished it. But then he rallied, and my concentration slipped, and he thumped me and bruised my ribs. I'd have had him, otherwise. I can hold a half-lance now, and when I have Sioned, I'll be the finest warrior in the land, wait and see. Next time I'll definitely beat Elffin. I was *that* close to it yesterday.

I couldn't sleep last night thinking of it. It had felt so wonderful, beating him. Well, nearly. Naturally, I couldn't ever fight him with a sharp sword, it would be too dangerous for him. I'd never harm him, he's my friend, and perhaps one day I'll be his squire. Oh, how I long for a real battle! It will be so glorious. I'll hack my way through dozens of enemies, just as my father did, and Iolo Goch will sing songs about my bravery that will make tears gush like fountains from women's eyes and make children sit still with wonder.

Rhiannon's marriage it will be good, because it will give us the family we lack. Despite Glyndŵr's kindness we're without kin or prospects, except by his charity. It means I'll have a brother-in-law to support us if we need him. As John Hanmer is Owain Glyndŵr's brother-in-law, and bound to him by blood ties, so Rhys ap Hywel will be mine. It would be better if he were closer kin to Glyndŵr than he is, but if *Tadmaeth* respects him, then that's good enough for me. It ought to be enough for Rhiannon, too. Doesn't she want to be married and have a house of her own? If I were a girl, I should. I'm glad I'm not a girl, though. A girl won't ever know the joy of comradeship and the magical feeling of a sword singing in the hand. Rhiannon needs a man to mend her temper.

This afternoon Huw was teaching me how to oil armour and polish it without scratching. Except for brief border skirmishes with the *Sais* (they're always raiding, stealing cattle and land), life is peaceful here, but *Tadmaeth*'s armour must always be ready: he's Henry's liege man, and the English King is always having trouble with Scotland. The Scots harry the northern borders the way the English harry the Marches, despite the Marcher Laws ~ which, of course, were made by Marcher Lords. Even the King has little power there, and they are as often broken as obeyed.

I sat outside the armoury, the last of the day's sunshine warm on my shoulders, idly rubbing a breastplate in endless, circular strokes, at peace with the world and the rhythm of my task. I love Sycharth when a low evening sun pours like honey on the land. God knows I would have my father and mother alive and well, but if they had lived I shouldn't be here today. This is the finest place on earth. Glyndyfrdwy is beautiful too, and just as rich, but Sycharth is home. Here I came into the household, and I love it. Crossing the moat after a week - or even a day - away, and entering Sycharth through the graceful gateway is like slipping into paradise. The house stands on a small hill, and if I climb to the top of the tower I can see the evidence of *Tadmaeth*'s riches all around me: deer speckling the parks, the noisy flight of pigeons in and out of trees, and his lands stretching to the horizon and beyond. In the distance the river slides towards the sea, winding and curving and in places almost doubling back, is if it can't bear to leave. The loveliest sight in the world is surely a white dove with the setting sun painting its wings, wheeling over the yard before swooping into the cote and folding itself for the night.

You know, if I were struck blind, I believe I could tell this place by its smells and sounds: bread baking in the kitchens, the sweetness of crushed grass, dung in the stable yard; the clap of a pigeon's wings, the clash of metal from the tiltyard, the raucous yell of a rook, and by night the triumphant *kweek* of a hunting owl. But if I were blind, then I should not be able to see silken river slither over great mossy boulders, trout laze in shadowed water and assassin pike lurk in the depths. Follow the turn of the river between the trees, up towards the mountains, and there's a secret place where, beneath the trees in spring, bluebells flood, and the marriage of blue flowers and trees arching green brings tightness to my throat. I don't need Iolo Goch's ballads - my own senses sing the beauty of Sycharth, and a man would have to be deaf and blind not to appreciate it. Speaking of blindness, mind, the priest said last Sunday that God is everywhere. Therefore, dear, holy God, if You should be listening to me right at this moment, I pray You, do not strike me blind. Or deaf. Or dumb, or - oh, God, please leave me as I am, amen.

I suddenly felt sorry for Rhiannon, having to go away. I expect I'll miss her, a bit. I didn't hear *Tadmaeth*'s approach, and his voice startled me.

'Slacking, Llew? If the job isn't done well, I shall go into battle creaking and crumbling with rust, and it will be your fault.'

'Never, *Tadmaeth*. When I've finished it will be so bright it will blind the enemy, and they'll run like rabbits all the way to the Out Isles.'

He laughed, and pulled up a barrel to sit companionably beside me, leaning his tall frame forward, his forearms resting on his knees, squinting into the setting sun. 'Elffin tells me you're improving in the tiltyard. And Huw thinks it's time you had a mount of your own.'

He wasn't looking at me, and I couldn't bear even to breathe, for fear I should explode. What if he should refuse? I bit my lip, waiting.

'Elffin thought that Siôned would be right. She is -'

'Gentle and obedient, Sire. Just what -' I stopped, remembering Elffin's burst of laughter when I repeated Huw's comment. I didn't understand why, and so thought it best not to repeat it.

Glyndŵr's lips twitched behind the fine, forked beard, and at last our eyes met. 'So, what do you think, Llew?'

I took a deep breath. 'My Lord, Siôned would please me more than anything.'

'Then she's yours. You'll need something to occupy you when your sister has gone. You'll miss her, Llew.'

I shrugged. Men don't need sisters. And Rhian wasn't dying, merely marrying, and marrying quite well, considering. Mind, I wouldn't have *Tadmaeth* think me unfeeling. 'I suppose so, my Lord. But her husband will be kind her, I expect. And I'll see her sometimes.'

'Ap Hywel will be here tomorrow. You'll meet him then. Lady Marged believes he's right for Rhiannon. And who'd argue with your *Mamaeth?* I try not to disagree with her if I can avoid it!' He slapped his thighs, decisively. 'So then, Siôned is yours, Llew: yours to feed, to groom, and if she ails, yours to sleep beside. Huw will help you, but the responsibility is yours. A man's horse is more important than his sword, sometimes.' He chuckled. 'If all else fails, you can always run away on her.'

'You'd never run, my Lord,' I said passionately, 'and neither would I. I swear I wouldn't.'

'Sometimes running's not a bad idea. Dying unnecessarily's rather pointless, and not something you can change your mind about!'

I wondered if he was laughing at me.

'Sometimes, Llew,' he went on, 'it's an excellent idea to ride very fast away from your enemy - and give yourself time to consider your options!'

'I won't run. I am your man, as my father was, until I die.'

'As your father was, indeed. But if you're ever in such a situation, Llew, I hope you'll at least consider retreat? But thank you for your loyalty, my boy. Your father would be proud.' His bony face slipped momentarily into sadness and then, as quickly, brightened. 'Ah, yes. That's the other thing. There will be a *cymanfa* tomorrow. I think you should be there. Your sister's bridegroom is coming, and as head of your family, it's only right for you to represent your family.'

A *cymanfa*! My joy was complete. I tried to speak, but could not. A horse and a *cymanfa*, all in the same day! And me among the men, speaking for my heritage as a man should speak.

Tadmaeth slapped my shoulder as if I were grown, and rose, stretching. The light spun gold into his beard and his hair, which he wore unfashionably long - most soldiers favour the short crop that sits more comfortably under a helm. The evening light revealed the fine web of lines around his mouth and eyes. He's not a young man, although he's still strong, but he looked tired, and even before he'd entered the house I could tell he'd forgotten me. He was deep in thought, head down, brow creased, hands clasped behind his back.

What would trouble him? He is Owain Glyndyfrwdwy, master of everything. Except possibly, *Mamaeth*. I have difficulty calling her that, though not in calling Owain *Tadmaeth*. For all her good works there's a hardness in Lady Marged that is not in her husband.

Rhiannon

Crisiant, breathless with hurry, delivered Lady Marged's second summons.

'Herself wants you, Rhian. Look sharp, child, she hates to be kept waiting.'

'What does she want, Cris?' I was caught by a sudden spark of hope that she might have changed her mind, cancelled the marriage, but that thought was doused before it caught. Lady Marged never changes her mind.

Crisiant folded fat arms across her aproned front. 'How should I know? D'you think she tells me everything? If you're going upstairs, better do something with your hair, quick.'

Mutinously, I tugged a comb through. Crisiant reached out to take it from me, but I shrugged her away. Her ministrations are usually painful. Only the liberal application of oil could tame it, followed by tight braiding, but I loathe the oil, and Crisiant hauls my braids so tight I can hardly blink. My hair's like curly gold wire. God knows, I'm not vain, no one could accuse me of that: I've not much to be vain about. God wasn't generous when he made me. Except for my eyes, which are passable. I crossed myself hastily in case He was listening, and decided to punish me for my ingratitude by turning them permanently in opposite directions, like Siôn Twp's.

Good thought: I stared into the mirror, deliberately crossing my eyes. I looked like a witch. If I could do that all the time, maybe Rhys ap Hywel would take one look at me and change his mind. That would be good. But it was hard to stay cross-eyed: it made my eyeballs ache. However... I wasn't pretty. If I were, Elffin might have noticed me, so perhaps ap Hywel would take one glance at my thin body and mass of hair and shriek "Take her away! She's ugly!

She has no breasts! She's a scarecrow!" Well, I could hope. Perhaps if I ate nothing I might make myself even thinner.

Lady Marged was in her chamber, morning light flooding through the tall windows. The quality of her embroidery was famous, and the work stretched across the frame showed flowers so real I could almost smell them. Bright birds blazed in fantastic trees, and fabled animals twined through undergrowth and coiled round boughs. Lady Marged tried to teach me the complex stitches, the fine blending of colours, but I am not a needlewoman, and stabbed my fingers more often than not, so my work was usually blood-spotted and grubby from constant (enforced) unpicking. Sun filled the room, and the painted glass windows sent bright patches of colour sliding across the floors and walls. I'd loved these windows since I was small, and I'd spent hours sitting at Lady Marged's feet, watching the light slant through crimson and sapphire and emerald and purple. Those windows had earned me plenty of rapped knuckles, when I was distracted by jewels of light on a bare arm. Sycharth's windows were said to be as fine as some great church's in Ireland, though I can't remember which, and the ones in the family chapel were even more beautiful than these.

Meek before Lady Marged, I prayed for a miracle. Perhaps ap Hywel had fallen off his horse and broken his neck, or had a fit and died. Or even just changed his mind. I didn't wish him any harm: I just didn't want to marry him.

But no. Lady Marged had good news, she said. Somehow I doubted that.

'Rhys ap Hywel will be here tomorrow, Rhiannon. He's coming for the *cymanfa*. I hope,' she remarked, slipping her needle into her work and frowning, 'we'll have time to make you presentable before then. Your hair looks like you've been dragged through a hedge backward, and your hands are filthy. I shan't even look at your neck!'

I gritted my teeth and studied my hands, which were, I had to agree, somewhat grimy. But I'd been picking mushrooms, and the black juices had soaked into what was left of my fingernails. And my neck might not be spotless, but I'd bathed last week, so it couldn't be too awful. Besides, the last thing I wanted was to be "presentable". I didn't even want to be acceptable!

She took my chin in cool hands, turning my face this way and that in the light from the windows. She smelled of rosemary and spices, and suddenly all I wanted was to be folded into her arms, and told that I didn't have to marry anyone, that I could stay at Sycharth forever, yes, and be an old maid if that was what I wanted. Even in my imagination I couldn't see her encouraging me to marry Elffin, but I'd settle for old maid instead.

Lady Marged held me like that once, when I first came here, and was grieving for my Mam, though never since. Then, she said I could stay 'forever', but by forever, apparently, she meant only until a husband could be found so she could get rid of me. I scowled.

Lady Marged rubbed gently at my corrugated forehead. 'You have pretty eyes, Rhiannon, and good bones, but if you glare like that you will turn the poor man to stone. And oh, we must do something with that hair!' Her eyes glinted. 'I was right: your neck is filthy. Go and see Crisiant, tell her to find you something suitable to wear tomorrow night.' For the first time, she met my eyes. 'Are you happy, Rhiannon? Are you looking forward to being a woman married and in your own home?'

I should have kept my mouth shut, but my tongue's never in tune with my brain. 'What do I have to look forward to? I've never met ap Hywel, but I know he's old. Wouldn't he be happier with someone closer to his own age?'

Lady Marged's lips twitched. 'Thirty-four is not so old, Rhiannon.' She sighed. 'In fact, from the far side of it, it seems remarkably young.'

'But he's been married before.' Even as I spoke I recognised the stubborn note in my voice and knew it wouldn't help. 'And Crisiant says he's killed one wife already.'

She frowned. 'Crisiant gossips too much. His wife died of plague, Rhiannon. He loved her dearly, and has mourned her too long. He needs a wife and a companion for his children. And he's heard well of you.' She smiled, which made her severe face light up. 'I think Iolo Goch's song of praise to your eyes might have helped persuade him.'

'He's not like Iolo Goch!' *Oh, Holy Mary!* My skin crawled at the thought. Iolo Goch reduced me to the state of a rabbit confronted by a stoat.

'He's a man, and partial to a pretty pair of eyes. Rhys is not handsome, but he's pleasant enough ~ for such an ancient person.'

Oddly, I began to feel slightly better. Since no one could possibly be as handsome as Elffin, it didn't matter what ap Hywel looked like. But if he wasn't actually hideous and deformed, and wasn't in any way like Iolo Goch, then perhaps being married wouldn't be so terrible.

Lady Marged sat down again, motioning me to sit beside her, and I remembered last time and didn't hook the stool with my foot. Besides, I had a hole in my stocking. She drew the embroidery frame in front of her, and began work. I waited. At last, she cleared her throat. 'What of the duties of a wife, Rhiannon?'

Oh, *Duw*! Mam had drummed this into me since I was tiny. Then *Mamaeth* took over. Did she think I'd forgotten? I sighed. This was going to be tedious. 'I must order the servants - will there be servants, my Lady?'

She nodded. 'One or two, I imagine. Ap Hywel isn't poor. You will be comfortable.'

I screwed up my eyes, ticking off items on my fingers. 'I must see to the stillroom, brew simples, keep an orderly and pleasant house and ensure my manner is always pleasing to my husband,' I recited. 'I must see that my husband has fresh linen when he needs it, and always remember that his food must be hot and freshly prepared. I must order the servants and punish them if they do wrong, and dose them when they are poorly and need it, and see that the herb garden and the dairy are well kept. Oh, and see to the salting of meat and storing of food for winter.'

Lady Marged paid close attention to her work. 'And what of your duties of the bedchamber, Rhiannon?'

I took a deep breath, concentrating. 'I must tell the servants to change the bed linen at least once a month,' I gabbled, 'and put lavender and rosemary under the pillows and in the presses, air the pillows and if the bed has hangings, be sure they are brushed weekly with a stiff broom and wiped with a damp leather once a quarter. If the floor has rushes they must be changed weekly, and if it is wooden then it must be swept regularly.'

Lady Marged coughed. It sounded strange.

'Are you ill, Lady Marged? Shall I go now?' I was half off my stool, ready to run. 'Shall I tell Bronwen to fetch you a cordial?'

'No, Rhiannon, thank you. Sit down. My breath caught in my throat, that is all.' She took a deep breath and rummaged in her box for more thread. 'Your wifely duties, Rhiannon.'

What? I was lost. What else? What had I forgotten? Windows? Doors? Surely Lady Marged wasn't referring to the chamber pot?

Servants would see to that. I hoped they would, anyway. I stared at the Lady, wondering what on earth she wanted me to say.

'The marriage bed, Rhiannon?'

'I thought I'd mentioned that, my Lady. Change the bed linen -'

'Within the bed, child.'

'Within -?' Belatedly, I remembered overhearing Bron and Mari in the kitchens, gossiping about one of the village girls who was no better than she ought to be, they said. I'd asked them what they meant, but they only exchanged looks and sighs, and wouldn't say until I pestered them. Then they reluctantly explained that Anwen let men do things to her, for money.

'Do things?' I had asked. 'What, kiss her, you mean?' And then they'd laughed and turned their backs. Though I sometimes worked with them when there were guests, I wasn't one of them, and more often than not their gossip was mindlessly boring and I ignored it.

'Oh. Will he want to kiss me?'

'That and more.'

'More?' What more? Had Bron and Mari not told me the truth?

They hadn't. There followed an uncomfortable half hour, after which I fled Lady Marged's chamber, my face on fire and my brain tumbling.

My God, I thought, reaching the safety of the back stairs. I'd seen the stallion covering mares - but *people* did that, too? Holy-Mary-Mother-of-God. At least She'd never done that. Never had to, lucky for Her. It was hard enough imagining Lady Marged, but it was even worse to think of the Blessed Virgin doing that. I was both revolted and intrigued, understanding belatedly what Iolo Goch had tried to do. The foul pig! The thought of him doing - putting - ugh!

Did Elffin do that? Surely not. It was beastly, sickening. Elffin would surely do no such thing. Yet - Elffin. His lean, muscular back, the clean smell of fresh sweat when he came in from the tiltyard, the smell of leather and horse, was Elffin's smell. I felt a strange fluttering low in my stomach, and felt oddly out of breath. The trials of the morning had obviously made me hungry. I would think about this later.

Completely forgetting my resolve to starve myself, I begged bread and honey from the kitchen and fled to the orchard, apples hanging heavy in the green above me, and considered.

Lady Marged had said that sometimes, if a husband was kind and gentle, the bed thing was pleasant. Personally, I couldn't see how, or why it should possibly be, but anyway, it was only for getting foals and babies, so I doubt that I would need to put up with it very often. Even if I were to have ten babies, ten times in a whole lifetime isn't much. And since old women don't have babies, all that nonsense will stop when I'm about thirty, I expect. But the sad thought overcame me: if I have to do it, the bed thing, how much I would rather do it with Elffin. He would be kind and gentle. I laid myself down in the grass, wondering.

Elffin
Bittersweet, these *gymanfaoedd*, the stately ritual recounting of ancestries and kinship, the retelling of old battles, the singing of old songs, but they are necessary if we are to keep our Welsh identity.

My task, with Siôn and Dewi, was to construct the great beacon fire, to announce the *cymanfa* all over Wales. Let de Grey pick the bones from that. We'll have our land back from him, one way or another. My father has his heart set on English justice, but there's a small voice in my head that says he'll be disappointed. I hope I'm wrong, but I'm afraid I'm not.

Wood-gathering the fire-building is bloody hot work, dragging great branches around. The place where the *cymanfaoedd* are held is strange: some say it's where Nimue sealed Merlin, Myrddin Fawr, in the oak, and indeed a great tree stands just below the flat place where the beacon fire is made, in a great circle of bare earth sheltered on three sides by the jagged mountain, as if it had been scooped out, perfect for the purpose.

There have been *cymanfaoedd* here for centuries, Welshmen gathering to speak their ancestry, and it is always a strange thing to stand in the place where our ancestors stood, and speak of the dead as if they are still living, and to know for certain that in a hundred years' time when we and ours are dead and gone, our descendants will stand here and speak also of us. This is a haunted place, and I wouldn't come here alone at night for any price, even if the ghosts are our own ancestors. At night it is so dark it's as if light has never reached here, ever, and only the flicker of the great fire holds back the night.

Working beside my brothers, my mind drifted to Rhiannon. What will ap Hywel think of her? She's a skinny, prickly child, but

I'm used to having her about. She's always underfoot: every time I turn round, there she is, those great grey eyes blazing. All angles and eyes, that one.

That thought led to another. Will ap Hywel bed her? Surely not yet. She's so small, seems so young, that the thought of a man lying with her seems wrong, even if he is her lawful husband. Though she's near sixteen, which is older than many wives, I hope he'll wait. A willing woman is sweeter than one taken by force. Not that I have great experience in such matters, you understand, though I'm not totally without. I have my Anwen, in whose arms I lie whenever I can sneak away from the house. My father disapproves of his sons mixing too closely with the villagers (despite the existence of a good few bastard sisters and a brother, testament to *Tad's* youth) and Mam would fillet me if she knew. But oh, Anwen is so willing, and slipping into her welcoming body is like slipping into warm honey. She takes such a delight in small gifts I give her. I felt a grin spread across my face, remembering. It's so good, that man and woman thing, especially when the woman is both plump and agreeable. Lying with Rhiannon would be like lying with a fencepost.

That is not a good thought to have of my foster-sister, but there, she's on my mind, and I don't like to think of her unhappy. Yesterday I tried to raise the subject with Mam, but she told me to mind my business and leave Rhiannon to her. But I worry about the girl, and I'm fond of her - oh, in a brotherly way, of course. Still, as Mam says, none of my business.

When the wood for the fire was piled as high as Dewi, who tops two yards, and was as broad around as the duck pond, we flung ourselves down in the shade, drank the ale we'd left cooling in the stream, and allowed the cold liquid and the small breeze to cool our sweating bodies.

Dewi's fair-skinned like father, and the sun doesn't treat him kindly. His nose is already scarlet, and his shoulders will blister, being so close to the sun up here. Siôn's also tall, although not as tall as Dewi, and, praise God for His mercies, there are signs that I shall eventually outstrip them both. I've outgrown both breeches and jerkin again. Once, I was afraid I might be short, like Iolo Goch, and have to look up at all men and even some women, but then I put on inches almost overnight, and there's no signs of it stopping. Siôn, despite his fair hair, darkens quickly in the sun, and muscles slide under his skin as he moves.

I'm not stupid: I know Anwen lies with Siôn, and probably with Dewi too, but I'm worried about Anwen comparing us. One day I'll be as broad as Siôn, and probably taller than both, and if she should compare us they'll come off worse, poor things.

Her voice, gasping into my ear, *"oh, oh, Elffin, you are the best I have ever had, I swear, I swear"*. She says even thinking about me makes her thighs tremble. Thinking of Anwen's thighs reminds me of the savoury jellies Bron's making for the feast after the *cymanfa*, in honour of ap Hywel, who will soon take Rhiannon from Sycharth, and there I am forgetting Anwen and worrying about Rhiannon again.

My deep thoughts must have been obvious, for Siôn shook the last drops of ale from the bottle over me; splattering icy cold across my naked chest and making me jump and bellow.

'Deep in thought, *brawd bach*? Share them.' Siôn laughed. 'Or are they too obscene to share. Must be at least three days since you visited Anwen.'

I wish to God I didn't blush so easily: I try to control it, but blood, as any man will tell you, does as it pleases, and its rising causes problems in other places, too.

'No,' I protested, but Siôn and Dewi were already laughing.

'Then what, *brawd bach*?'

'I'm only thinking of Rhiannon.'

'Too late for that, she's spoken for. Anyway, Mam doesn't think she's good enough for you, in marriage or out of it.'

'I don't think of her like that! It's just - she seems so young. I hope Rhys ap Hywel won't use her unkindly.'

'He's a reasonable man.' Dewi rolled onto his stomach, idly shredding a dock leaf between long fingers. 'He'd have *Tad* to reckon with if he were unkind. Ah, likely he'll wait. She's a scrawny little thing, and he has two brats from his last wife. He'll be in no great hurry to get more. And,' he glanced up at me, grinning, 'as I'm sure you know, Elffin, good women are sweeter for waiting and there are always bad ones to pass the time.'

I'm not entirely sure I agree, me not being much for waiting where women are concerned. And then I was thinking of Anwen again and had to roll onto my stomach.

'Still,' I said, hiding my crimson face in my folded arms, 'I think someone should mention it.'

'Who?' Siôn was losing interest. 'How a man treats his wife is no one's business but his own. But *Tad* - well, Mam, anyway - chose ap Hywel for Rhiannon, and whatever Mam might think, *Tad* wouldn't let Rhiannon go to him if he thought he wouldn't be kind to her.'

Dewi was already asleep, his arm slung across his eyes, and since the job was finished, and returning home early would only mean that more work would be found for us, I too pillowed my head on crossed forearms, and slept.

CHAPTER FOUR

Llewelyn

I'd rather fight a dragon than speak tonight. This morning in the stables I was so tense I dropped clean harness, got a clout from Huw and had to start again. All day I've been trying to hammer my brain into remembering what my father taught me of our ancestors. But I was so young when he died, and there are so many Llewelyns, Siôn's, Rhodris, Gethins and Hywels that I remember one, then forget another and have to begin again. Oh, I know I'm going to mess it up, and I'll die of mortification in front of everybody.

The thought of the nobility listening to me scares me half to death. I tried sitting with my eyes shut, counting the branches of my family on my fingers, but the sun was hot, and I started to nod off, so then I tried walking the shady courtyard. If I go inside, someone will find me work to do. I must get this into my brain before tonight.

I was gabbling names and pacing when a group of riders arrived and I had to dodge to avoid being trampled. I recognised *Tadmaeth*'s horse, and leapt to hold its bridle while he dismounted. His hair was plastered to his skull and dark with sweat under his helm.

'Thanks, Llew.' His courtesy was unfailing. I left his horse with Siôn Twp, then scurried to the kitchens to fetch a drink for him, and carried it carefully to the solar. I loitered to try to find out what was happening, but my attempt to fade into the wall hangings failed. *Tadmaeth* frowned, and I was dismissed. I considered hanging about outside the door, but best not tempt fate.

I clattered out into the shady courtyard and started reciting again. From the corner of my eye I saw Rhiannon sneaking out. I considered (as head of the family) ordering her back inside, but I let her go. She probably wouldn't listen, anyway.

I was driven indoors by starvation, and as a result Bron made me carry and fetch between pantry, dairy and kitchen. I told her, 'I'm a man grown,' I said, 'and I have to speak at the *cymanfa*.'

'Man tomorrow,' she said. 'Today do as you're told.'

'I've got to rehearse, Bron! If I get it wrong -'

Hands on hips she gazed at me, damp hair curling in tendrils from her white cap. 'You don't know it now, boy, you never will. Your father dripped it into your lugs forever, I don't doubt. Milk from your Mam, history from your Dada. They do that, men, hammering in the past when they might better look to the present, let alone the future. You won't forget, Llew, don't fret. Now get from here and fetch me that butter. Now!'

I hoped she was right.

Rhiannon

Despite the tragedy that my life now is, I felt a leap of excitement when Crisiant brought the blue robe. It was slashed to show a cream petticoat, and tied at the waist with a creamy, silken cord and it was beautiful. I'm not allowed to wear it until tonight, but Crisiant let me try it on.

'Just as well you did,' she grumbled, reaching for her pins. 'I knew I'd have to take it in. Ach, more work for me.' She gathered a handful of fabric each side of the gown, and I surveyed my reflection in the looking-glass. The vivid blue made my eyes glow. Oh, when Elffin sees me wearing this, with the lapis lazuli necklace that's a shade darker, perhaps he'll fall in love with me, and demand that *Tadmaeth* lets us marry at once. Perhaps Elffin will fight Rhys ap Hywel for me, or abduct me and beg me to marry him. I wouldn't say yes straight away of course, I'd make him suffer a bit. I sighed. And pigs might fly. What use are dreams? A beautiful dress, but inside me, thin and plain. I was forced to bathe again, even though I was in the river twice since my last bath. Afterwards, shivering, I wrapped myself in a linen sheet and sat on a stool. Crisiant drew a bone comb from her apron pocket and assumed an expression of mingled martyrdom and determination.

My hair will be loose, and it's been washed in camomile water to make it shine. Crisiant, cursing, tried to tug the comb through it, hauling at wiry curls and stubborn knots. I screeched with pain until Crisiant, holding her own aching head, admitted defeat.

'If I had more time I'd oil it, try to put some shine into it. Men don't like girls with wild hair, and the devil's in this mop.' She threw the comb across the room. 'There's nothing I can do with it, look at it, like a great bush. And your skin's a sight. Your Mam must have *lived* on ginger pudding when she was carrying you!' Buttermilk washes had no effect on my freckles. 'And look at your arms. Covered, they are. Ladies' skin should be - aah, what's the use.' Crisiant knew when she was beaten. She sighed. 'There's not a soul could call you pretty, *ferch*, but those eyes do make up for what *yr Arglwydd Dduw* didn't give you,' she sighed. 'Now, see if you can keep clean and tidy until your man comes for you.'

'He's not my man.'

'Not yet, he isn't,' Crisiant retorted, puffing as she bent to retrieve the comb from behind the bed, 'but he will be, so better get used to the idea. Now, stay away from the stables, right? And the river. Sit nice and quiet, like a lady, and do something that won't make you mucky. Sew or something.'

When the door banged behind her, I wandered miserably to the window and looked out. It was going to be a long, boring afternoon. Llew was pacing the stable yard, his eyes screwed up, reciting our ancestry back to Adam and Eve. It infuriated me, watching him! I could do it as well as Llew if not better. I could still hear my father's quiet voice repeating over and over: 'You are Llewelyn ap Llewelyn ap Rhodri, ap Siôn Lawgoch, ap Gethin Du, ap Ioan Gwynedd ap Eifion,' ap, ap, ap - it went on for ages, but every true Welshman knows where he's come from, and is proud to tell it. Daughters know too, but we, being only female, are not allowed to recite, or even be present at their precious *cymanfaoedd*.

Elffin had also made himself scarce: probably off hunting. So not having even the small joy of watching him, there was nothing else to do but sit in the chamber waiting until after the *cymanfa*, when I'd meet my future husband. My stomach churned when I thought of it.

I slumped into the chair and picked up my sewing, but it's hard to sit still and sew at the best of times, and today I was miserable and restless, and in no mood. Lady Marged had loaned me one of her precious books, which was kind, but unfortunately it wasn't anything exciting or even distracting, but a worthy treatise on the duties of a wife written by some monk who should have known nothing at all about women. I thought about sewing, except I was stitching a bed gown, and when I picked it up I was overcome by the thought of having to wear it for Rhys ap Hywel. Part of me wished the coming night over, but then, that would only bring me a day closer to my marriage. I took a few wild stitches in the fine white fabric, then ran the needle under my nail. I took the Lord's name in vain, and hurled the bloody nightgown across the room.

A commotion in the courtyard distracted me and I rushed to the window, then stopped. It might be ap Hywel arriving early to view his acquisition, and I didn't want him to think I was eager. I peered cautiously out, hiding at the edge of the narrow window, so no one below could see me. I recognised Glyndŵr's mount amongst the sudden swirl of men and horses in the courtyard, and saw Llew take the reins and lead it towards the stables, while *Tadmaeth* disappeared into the house.

I wandered back to my chair, slumped back into it. Would I have to sit here, not allowed to move, until supper? I gritted my teeth, screaming softly in my throat with frustration. No. It was too much. My life was being ordered as if I was a brood mare. No, even less than that. Mares are mated with far more care than was being shown to me: mares, after all, are valuable, and I'm certainly not that. I'm just a burden, that's all. Tears burned the back of my nose and I sniffed. I *couldn't* marry ap Hywel. I'd run away, run off the edge of the earth if necessary, and disappear into nothingness. They'd be sorry then.

Second thoughts. I'd run, but be back by sunset, so that Crisiant can dress me in the blue gown. If Elffin sees me in that dress, sees how well it becomes me, how grown up I look, then perhaps...

I tugged off the clean shift and threw it on the bed, scooped the dirty day-dress off the floor, and slipped it over my head, hastily knotting the laces. Then I cracked open the door, listening for Crisiant's wheeze. The staircase was silent, so I crept down and out of the courtyard door, keeping close to the walls of the house, round the back to the tiltyard and stables, and, when Llew's back was safely turned, out the back way, down the slope behind the house to where the woods began.

I put my head down and sprinted into the trees, snagging my dress on a bramble. I didn't stop to untangle it, just wrenched it loose, tearing it, but I didn't care. I was free. Tonight I might be meek and obedient in the beautiful blue dress, but now I was free of Lady Marged and Crisiant. There'd be hell to pay rent to if I got caught, but I'd face that if it happened. Sitting in that chamber was like waiting for my own execution.

I twisted my hair into a knot so it wouldn't catch in overhanging branches. The sun slipped through the trees, spilling bands of light in my path: a magpie rattled out of a bush and I stopped to watch its clumsy flight. In the stillness, when it had gone, I could hear Afon Cynllaith sliding down to meet Afon Tanat, and coolness and solitude called me. There'd be trouble if Crisiant discovered I'd gone, and if Lady Marged finds out... She doesn't suffer disobedience in her own children, never mind me, and I'd be in for a beating. So what? If I'm lucky no one will find out and I'll be back before Cris knows I've gone.

The riverbank rises where the path joins it, and it's visible from the house. I'd only be fetched back if someone saw me. Instead, I headed upriver towards the hills. The sun was strong and the uphill path was rough. My skin prickled with sweat ~ I'd wash in the river before I went back.

A small weir, the water tumbling creamily over lichen-coated rocks, slithered into a brown pool. Fish rose to darting insects, their round mouths dimpling the glossy surface, and a heron gazed intently into the water. Kicking off my wooden clogs, and hiking my skirts to my thighs, I sat on the bank, my feet dangling in icy water. I'd been sitting for a while watching the hypnotic swirl of water, when something prickled my calf. I leaned over: a broken twig had caught between my leg and the bank. Reaching down, I tried to catch hold of the end. If I'd just moved my foot the twig would have spun away downstream, but instead, I leaned over to fish it out. Typical, my luck ~ if I do anything wrong, I get caught. I stretched just a little too far.

The pool was deep. I splash in the shallows when I bathe, but I've never learned to swim. My dress soaked up water, dragging me down. Icy water flooded into my mouth and shot up my nose, and strangling for breath I choked and fought, splashing and floundering, frantically feeling for solid ground beneath my numb feet. There was none: the river seemed bottomless, and I sank and sank, eyes open, bright bubbles of air floating past as I screamed underwater with the last of my breath. I was going to drown, and Elffin wouldn't see me in the blue gown unless they buried me in it.

Then my hair was grasped, my wildly thrashing arms pinioned by strong arms and I was towed to the bank and hauled out, choking, like a landed fish. When I stopped thrashing, heaving, panicking, I rolled onto hands and knees and vomited a gut-full of river water. My hair clung weed-like about my face, and my dress dragged down from the neck exposing my curveless chest. But I was alive. I opened my eyes to glimpse my saviour, and wished I was dead.

Elffin

Sycharth on a feast day, especially a *cymanfa* day, is no place for a man. I took my horse saddleless from the paddock, and carrying bow and arrows, faded away. Despite the bow, I'd no intention of hunting, but riding out empty-handed would cause questions, and I didn't want questions. I was off to see Anwen. I had a gift for her - a little pin shaped like a snarling fox I'd bespoken from a silversmith in Ruthin. Anwen's hair is fox-red, and I know she'll like it. She'll be grateful, too, and when Anwen is grateful... I rode through the trees to the back of her cottage, keeping out of sight of the main road. No point in causing gossip, and Anwen has her reputation to think of. Despite her liaison with me - oh, all right, and my brothers - I'm sure she's true to us. Anwen's no whore, just a simple village girl who's unfortunately found herself unable to choose between three such remarkable brothers. Fastening my horse to a bush a few yards away, I slipped silently between the trees towards the back of her tiny hut. I crept beneath the shuttered window, ready to slip round to the front once I knew I was unobserved. Then I heard Anwen, enjoying herself.

Wondering which of my brothers had beaten me to it, I stealthily crept closer, peering through holes in the wooden shutters. The inside was too dark to see properly, so I hooked a finger into a knot-hole and eased the shutter open. A shaft of light illuminated a pair of hairy buttocks rising and falling enthusiastically, and Anwen's bare feet waving in the air. Siôn? Dewi? I couldn't identify either of them from the arse. When I found out, mind, he'd never hear the last of it. Anwen shrieked and moaned and wailed, her dirty feet clasped now around the waist of her partner. Suddenly my mood changed. Anwen was enjoying herself - a lot, from the noise she was making. At last the bouncing buttocks collapsed, and the feet dropped back limply onto the bed. The man stood up.

It was neither of my brothers. I clenched my fists. This man, whoever he is, had taken advantage of Anwen's innocence. I was ready to break down the door and beat him until he -.

And then my brothers will laugh and say they knew all along that Anwen's a whore. Besides, the man was large, sweat rolling down his muscular back. I could beat him with a sword, no question, but with bare fists I might get thumped bloody and have to explain it.

I decided to swim: I was hot and sweaty. I was finished with Anwen, but sadly the urge remained. Cold water would be a cure, if temporary.

I crossed the river at the shallow point above the village, intending to head for the deep pool above Sycharth to wash off the sweat and horse-smell. Through the trees edging the river, I heard a wild splashing, and kicked my horse into a canter, wondering what creature would make such a noise. Perhaps I wouldn't return empty-handed after all.

A figure struggled in the water, hair plastered to a bony skull, a child from the look of it, and in trouble. I slipped off my horse, kicked off my boots and dived into the river, grabbing a hank of hair and hauling up. Once its head was above water I pinioned the flailing arms and I towed it to the bank, cursing my luck: my jerkin and hose would never be the same again, and it would be an uncomfortable ride home.

The child was small and thin, and water-dark tendrils of hair plastered a small pale face: a girl. A brown gown heavy with water drooped sadly from slight shoulders, exposing as far as the waist a chest flat as a washboard. She rolled over onto hands and knees and when she'd finished spewing river water from nose and mouth she wiped her face on her sodden gown and, shoved sodden hair from her eyes. Rhiannon. Oh, *Duw!* Had she tried to drown herself? Freckles stood out on her white face, and her teeth chattered wildly.

'S-s-second b-bath I've had today,' she commented, 'at least I'll be c-c-clean.'

I reached out and tugged a tendril of green weed from her hair. 'More or less. You're wet, anyway.'

'I suppose I ought to thank you,' she said, grudgingly.

'Don't bother, if you don't feel like it.'

'I don't.'

And the ungrateful brat stuck her nose in the air and set off along the bank for Sycharth, trailing sodden homespun and waterweed behind her. Dumbfounded, I caught my horse, which was cropping the grass a little way off, and set off after her. I drew level, slipped off to walk beside her, and offered her a ride.

'No.'

'You'll get back quicker if we ride.'

Her vehemence made me stagger.

'Why would I want to get back? I'm marrying someone I've never even met. I wish you'd let me drown. It's all your fault, anyway.'

'What?' I began to feel somewhat hard-done-by. I'd just saved her life, for God's sake, and now she was blaming me for all her troubles. It hadn't been a good day. Nevertheless, I remained calm and reasonable, despite her attitude. 'Ah, Rhian, Rhian. Women marry all the time! You'll get used to it. He's a good man, I expect. *Tad* wouldn't have agreed, otherwise, whatever Mam thought. Try to look on the bright side and marry him with good grace, that's my advice.'

At which point I found myself in the river again. When I'd scrambled out, she was gone.

CHAPTER FIVE

Llewelyn

'Come on, Llew, boy, eat something,' Bron said. 'Long night ahead, *bach,* and you're a growing lad. You want your belly rumbling?'

If I ate, I'd vomit. But - *Tadmaeth* thinks I can do it, and I must try, even if I fail. I longed for nightfall, simultaneously hoping that a miracle might happen and it would never come.

A swim might clear my head. If I sat around Sycharth much longer someone would find me work to do. I was crossing the tiltyard when a sodden Rhiannon came storming through the wicket gate. Her hair dripped in rat tails, her face was stark white except for a patch of crimson on each cheek. With hindsight I probably should have kept my mouth shut, but, well, she's my sister, and what sort of a man is afraid of his sister?

'You look like a drowned rat,' I commented. 'Where've you been?'

Her fist had her whole weight behind it, and only because I was caught unawares, you understand, she rocked me in my boots. She followed up with a kick at my shins and by the time my ears had stopped ringing, she'd disappeared indoors.

Next came Elffin, if possible even wetter, his face thunderous. He tossed a pair of clogs at me.

'Here. These belong to your lunatic sister. She left them by the river.'

I discarded the humorous manly comment I'd intended to make. From his expression he wasn't in the mood for levity. 'Why are you both soaking wet?' I asked instead, but I should have kept my mouth shut.

'Mind your own business. Rub down Seren and turn her out. And make sure you do it properly, or you'll feel my boot on your arse. I'll take Siôned tonight.'

My heart contracted. I'd hoped to ride Siôned myself, but if Elffin wanted to ride her, then that was that. I sighed. Ah well, I could always ride pillion behind Siôn or Dewi. But it wouldn't be the same. I led his mare to the stable, took off the saddle-cloth, rubbed her down and turned her out with the others. Siôned saw me and trotted over and I rubbed her nose, feeding her an apple, feeling the soft prick of her whiskers on my palm. I've felt more miserable in my life, but not often.

At the river I disconsolately stripped and plunged into the coolness. What on earth could Rhiannon have done to make Elffin so furious? I stood waist deep, my hair dripping into my eyes. Surely she hadn't told him she fancies herself in love with him? Oh God. I'd never be able to face him again if she had. I dragged my palms over my face, groaning. She'd gone and told him, and he was furious about it. Oh, *Diawl, diawl, Duw*. Damn Rhiannon. Bloody women! Could this day possibly get worse?

I clambered up the bank and sat naked in the sun, chewing nails and letting the warmth dry me. I wanted to slap Rhiannon, hard.

How could she do such a thing to me, especially with her betrothed visiting this very night. I had to make my peace with Elffin somehow, apologise for my sister and hope he'd forgive both of us. His pride was probably hurt that someone as stupid as Rhiannon could think of him like that. Ah, bloody, bloody women.

I dressed hastily and scurried back: better to get it over with. Elffin was in his chamber, combing the river weed from his hair, a linen towel round his waist. He wasn't pleased to see me.

'What do you want?'

'To apologise for Rhiannon, Elffin.'

'Ungrateful little -' He turned and looked at me, scowling. 'Women, eh Llew? Whores or half-wits, every one.'

'She's not a whore, Elffin,' I said, angrily, for despite everything, I had to stand up for her good name, 'and I'll fight any man who says she is.'

'Oh, not Rhiannon, you idiot. Anwen's the whore. It's her I'm angry with. Mind, this mad business with Rhiannon hasn't helped.'

I let down my hackles. 'Oh, everyone knows about Anwen. Rhiannon can't help being a half-wit, she's a girl, after all. They can't help where they fall in love, can they?'

Elffin unwrapped the towel from his waist to rub his hair. I averted my eyes from his nakedness, which unsettles me at close quarters. I'll have to overcome that if I'm to be his squire. But he's a grown man, and my eyes were dragged unwillingly back despite myself. A man makes comparisons, and they're not always flattering.

'What are you on about, Llew? Rhiannon in love? Who with, for God's sake?'

'What? You, of course.'

He stopped, the towel covering his face, then uncovered one eye. 'Me? Rhiannon?'

I could have kicked myself. Still, too late now. 'Aye. She's mooned after you for ages. Hadn't you noticed? The kitchen maids giggle about it. I expect it's because you saved her from Iolo Goch. Girls always fall in love with their rescuers, don't they? I'm sorry. She doesn't know any better, not having a Mam to advise her, but she doesn't mean any harm.'

Elffin looked thoughtful, and wrapped the towel around himself again. 'That explains a lot,' he said. 'I rescued her again, today - she was drowning herself. Small thanks I got for it, mind. She pushed me in again, straight away.'

'Why?'

'Why what? Why was she drowning herself, or why did she push me in? Who knows? All I did was offer her some brotherly words of comfort and advice. And then she shoved me in the river! But now...' Elffin sat on a low stool, water beaded on his brown shoulders. 'Poor Rhiannon. I wish I'd known.'

'Why?'

'Why, what?'

'Well, she's going to marry ap Hywel, isn't she? Isn't that what this is all about?'

'So she is.' Elffin stood, rubbing his hair with the palm of his hand so that it stood up in wet spikes. He grinned at me. 'I dare say she'll get over me. Eventually. Women, eh Llew?'

I sighed with relief. He'd forgiven me. 'Women!' I agreed.

Elffin leaned over, hooking clean hose from the bed. 'Tell you what, Llew. I'll ride Seren tonight. You ride Siôned.'

And so it was that I rode to the *cymanfa* on my own mare, in the pride of my manhood.

The great fire had been lighted: the leaping flames echoed the blaze of mingled excitement and terror that burned in my belly. My hands were slick with sweat on Siôned's reins, and I was afraid my legs might give way when I slid off her comforting back.

Forty or fifty men were gathered, firelight slicking their faces with amber, their grooms waiting in the edged shadows holding the horses. The fire would be visible for miles, even as far as Ruthin, where de Grey, if he had any sense, would be hiding and quaking. Ay, and the other Marcher *Sais*, too. Let them fear us. We've made a kind of peace, we Welsh, but we're not beaten.

Tadmaeth would begin, and the other men in order of their status, would speak after.

They were all there, Owain's brother Tudur, his sons, his brothers-in-law Rob Puleston and Gruffydd and Philip Hanmer. Bishop Hywel ap Madog Gyffin of St Asaph, Ieuan Fychan of Moeliwrch, Gruffydd ab Ieuan of Lloran Uchaf, Madog ab Ieuan ap Madog of Eyton, John Astwick and Crach Ffinnant, Owain's Wise One, the leaping flames illuminating their faces, and dozens more besides. Owain Glyndŵr raised his hand, and the low rumble of conversation ceased. I'd expected the traditional welcome, but - his language was courtly. His words were not.

'Kinsmen, friends. I asked justice from the King concerning de Grey's annexation of Croesor. The King knows me for a loyal man and ally, and knew my claim was just, but his Parliament ruled against me. Worse, my petition was shamefully dismissed. Despite Bishop St Asaph's intervention, the *Sais* disregarded him and derided me. They cared nothing for right or justice. They said,' - and here *Tadmaeth* briefly closed his eyes, drawing in a deep breath that swelled his chest. His voice was soft with menace and I was reminded that, despite his easy manner and gentle ways, he is a fearsome warrior. 'They mocked us - "bare-footed clowns" they called us.'

The silence was total, but lasted only a few seconds. Then a great babble of anger arose as the *uchelwyr* took in the insult, and snarled its response.

I heard a man behind me say, 'What chance had he in an English Parliament? Two Archbishops, one of them English, fifteen English bishops, nine English abbots and priors, sixteen English dukes and earls, thirteen English barons, seventy-four Knights of the English shires, and one hundred and seventy-three English burgesses. And of all of them only St Asaph to side with Owain Glyndŵr.'

Owain allowed the roar of voices to continue, his stillness stoking the anger. At last, his hand rose, and silence fell again.

'I am not a man lightly dismissed,' he began, 'and I've considered this matter in the course of a weary ride from London. When I've consulted my brothers and my sons, we shall meet again.' One or two muttered pieces of advice drifted from the assembly, much of it to do with the redistribution of de Grey's vital organs, but Owain, smiling, continued. 'In the meantime, my friends, I bid you *croeso,* welcome. My home and hearth are yours.'

And the *cymanfa* began. My heart still swells at the memory, and I can't find words to tell the glory of it. *Duw,* even Iolo Goch gained stature that night, standing close to the flames, the sparks cracking upward into the black sky, limning his frame with fire like a creature of legend. Iolo sang of ancient Kings and Princes, past battles, and his soaring voice raised the hair on the back of my neck, fetching tears to my eyes, so beautiful I almost forgot what an unpleasant old wretch he is. For such a voice, and such songs, I could almost forgive him.

And then it was Owain's turn to speak, his voice soft but clear, reciting his descent from the Lord Rhys of Deheubarth, Llywelyn Fawr ab Iorwerth, Prince of Gwynedd on his father's side, and Madog, Prince of Powys, four Gruffydds and Gruffydd Fychan, on his mother's. And I thought of the false *Sais* prince that they have forced on us, and wondered why Owain Glyndŵr should bow his knee to any man, and wondered who had a greater right to be Prince of Wales.

Rhys ap Hywel, as Owain's particular guest, spoke next, and I studied this man who would be my brother-in-law. He was old, of course, but that was good, because he'd be firm with my difficult sister. At first he spoke as if his mind were elsewhere, but gradually it gained in strength as he became caught up in his Telling. His lineage was old and worthy, but there were no great warriors like my father, grandfather and great-grandfather in his forebears. When he'd finished, the rest of the gathering, in order of precedence, spoke in turn.

One by one, sonorous voices rang above the crackle of the flames, Iolo Goch occasionally picking out a counterpoint to a particularly rhythmic or melodious voice with the pureness of his harp. One by one, one by one, one by one, and then - my turn.

My knees trembled, and I was afraid my voice might squeak and betray me, but thank God it held firm. I took a deep breath, the heart thudding in my chest, and heard Elffin's soft voice behind me: *'Go on, Llew. You can do it.'*

Speaking clearly, but taking Owain's example, pitching clear, not shouting, I began.

'I am Llewelyn, foster-son of Owain Glyndyfrdwy, but I am also Llewelyn ap Llewelyn Mawr. My Grandsire was Siôn ap Rhodri, ap Gethin ap Rhys Llew Mawr, ap Rhodri Goch, ap...'

I needn't have worried. I felt my father's soul prompt each word, heard his soft voice, and the voice of his father, and his father, and his father's father, helping me to remember them, each and every one, and was proud.

The last words, though, were not rehearsed. Perhaps they came from longing, perhaps they came from my father's soul; perhaps they were triggered by my earlier, darker thoughts. Perhaps it was just pride speaking, and if so, I am sorry, for it is well known that pride goeth always before a fall.

'I am Llewelyn, son of Llewelyn Mawr, proud and humble foster-son to Owain Glyndyfrdwy, greatest of men and true and rightful Prince of Wales.'

There was a sudden vast in-drawing of breath. And after, silence. Then, all round me, men stirred, muttering, and then a great shout went up, startling an owl out of the great oak, flapping crazily above our heads.

Owain didn't look at me. I was afraid he was angry. I knew my words were treason. I waited on my fate. But then I felt Elffin's hand gently squeeze my shoulder, and my knees, which had stopped trembling, began all over again, now that I had finished.

'Well done, Llew. You said what many men would have said. Should have said. God knows it's true.'

I caught sight of Owain's face, grim in the firelight. He looked at me, the fire reflected in his eyes, soberly, thoughtfully. And then, reluctantly, his lips curved in the sweet smile I had seen so infrequently lately. I smiled back, relieved that he wasn't angry. But then I saw the face of Rhys ap Hywel, who would be my brother-in-law, standing at his right shoulder.

Rhys was not smiling.

Rhiannon

I managed to reach the chamber without anyone else seeing me. Behind the closed door, I ripped off my sodden clothes and kicked them into the corner, and looked in the mirror. My hair clung to my face in tendrils, adorned in places with pieces of twig and duckweed. My goose-pimpled skin was mottled blue, and my teeth chattered. My nipples stood out from the almost invisible swelling of my breasts, making them look even smaller, and the ugly, sparse growth between my thin legs just made the whole effect worse. I didn't care how hideous I looked for Rhys ap Hywel, but I was miserable that Elffin's last sight of me as a single woman was half-drowned, half-naked in all my skeletal misery, spewing river water over his feet. I covered my face with my hands, hot with humiliation, and wished myself a million miles away. I pulled the coverlet off my bed and wrapped it round me, too wretched even to cry, utterly sodden with despair and cold and misery. I hiccupped, and spat out some more water. My nose ran, and I wiped it with the back of an icy hand.

Crisiant came back, bearing a tray with oat-cakes and a brim-full cup of mead, and she concentrated on steadying it, not looking at me until she had closed the door behind her and turned round. She shrieked, and the tray, the cakes and the mead became airborne. 'What in the name of God and all the holy apostles have you done to yourself? Look at your hair! I'll have to start again, you wretch. What's this?' She caught a strand of water-weed, and tugged it out. 'You've been in the river!'

I didn't speak, I just shrugged, and she lost her temper. She grabbed me and shook me until my teeth rattled. I think she'd have slapped me, but my covering sheet slipped off, and her face, unaccountably, softened. She took a deep breath, and calmed.

'Rhiannon, Rhiannon. You're going to be a married woman soon, *ferch*. You'll have to give up your wild ways then. Look, *cariad,* don't cry. We'll start again. The *cymanfa* is only just beginning so there's an hour or two yet, and God knows, it'll take every second of it to make you presentable. You sit, girl, and wait.' She bustled away. I noticed she locked the door behind her, though. I contemplated flinging myself from the window from sheer bloody-mindedness, just to spite her, but the window wasn't high enough to kill me. I'd just break my legs and be a cripple all my life, instead.

When she returned she had more food, and a cup of wine. 'Drink this, Rhiannon. It will warm you. You look like a drowned rat.' While I picked at the food and drank the heavy, sweet wine, she fetched warm water and washed me, sluicing my hair free of weed, finishing with a rinse from an earthen jug. I closed my eyes, bent over the basin, my wet hair hanging in a slick tail over my eyes. The liquid in the jug was cool on my scalp, and perfumed.

'What's that?'

'Oh, just a bit of rosewater. I'd been keeping it for - well, never mind. It'll make you smell nice, and give that great haystack of hair a bit of shine.'

I should have thanked her, I suppose, but what's the use of shiny hair if it isn't for Elffin? Crisiant combed, tugging the tangles down to the ends and pulling them out, until it waved down my back, as tamed as it ever would be. Why didn't I have hair like that Anwen? Hers was dark red, and shone in the sun like a fox-pelt. Mind, she's no-better-than-she-should-be, but her hair is beautiful. And she has breasts.

When my hair was dry, Crisiant fetched the cream undergown, slipped it over my head and tied the ribbons at the back. The soft fabric clung to my body, and I eyed Crisiant's vast frontage with envy, wishing I had - not all (God forbid, her breasts enter a room ages before she does) but some, at least, not the miserable bee-stings that I had. The blue gown, now altered to fit me, was slid up my arms and pulled over my shoulders. Crisiant laced it up the back, fetched a pair of blue slippers, too big but beautiful, and, hand at her mouth, surveyed me. Then 'Wait!' she said, and left me. There was a looking glass in the corner, a costly piece imported from France. The image was murky and greenish, as if the sea had got into it somehow on its journey. It gave me a wavery, underwater look, but was better than nothing.

My face was white under the goldwire hair, and freckles stood stark on my nose and cheeks. I could have been a corpse, except for my eyes. What would ap Hywel see? A thin girl with grey eyes. He wouldn't see the broken heart.

Crisiant appeared over my shoulder. She fastened a dark blue ribbon in my hair. 'There,' she said, smiling with satisfaction. 'No one could call you beautiful, Rhiannon, but with those eyes and a kind heart looking at you, you'll pass, you'll pass.'

The first horses clattered into the yard, the muted murmur of men's voices drifting through the open window, the deep sound oddly comforting.

'Now,' Crisiant said sternly, 'you stay *in by here*, Rhiannon. I'm putting you on your honour, *ferch*, understand?'

I sat, silently, not looking at her. Where could I go? I'd stay and meet my fate like a pig going to slaughter.

'Oh, child. Don't look so tragic! Marriage isn't that bad, and ap Hywel's nice enough, they say. He's kind, he's not ugly, and he's asked for you, so he must want you. Not like he was bribed to take you, is it? You afraid of your wedding night?' She gave me no time to reply. 'Nothing to be worried about, *cariad fach*! Indeed, it can be very nice, when the man's kind and takes a bit of trouble about, about - well, things.'

She had a strange expression. Surely Crisiant hadn't ever... But she was fat, and old, and - and not even married! What could she know?

She saw my face, humphed, and waddled away, her feet scuffing on the wooden stairs. Voices inside the house, now. I wondered how Llew's night had gone, if he'd come to tell me about it. Why couldn't I have been a boy? I'd have made such a triumph of the *cymanfa*. I gazed out of the window into the dark, not caring, not thinking. The voice behind me made me jump.

'I came to see if you're all right after your ducking.'

I turned, the blue dress swirling. Elffin stood in the open door, his face glowing from the cool night air, so handsome that my heart swelled.

'Why shouldn't I be?' I said ungraciously. I wasn't going to back down and be girlish, not when the humiliation of him seeing me half-drowned and half-naked was still fresh in my mind. He just stared at me, and I could see the soft beat of the pulse in his throat. I scowled.

'Ap Hywel's a lucky man,' he said, softly.

'What, getting a skinny, ugly girl?' This was the longest conversation I'd had with him in months, and I was spoiling it. Why couldn't I speak sweetly, make him want me, even now. Even now.

'You aren't ugly, Rhiannon.'

I wanted to believe him, but I'd seen, in the mirror. He was being kind. My spine was stiff as an angry cat's.

He stirred suddenly, and from the pouch at his belt took something small, wrapped in cloth. 'I've brought you a gift,' he said softly, and pushed it into my hand. 'A memory of me, for when you've gone from here.' Then his right hand cupped my cheek, his touch warm, his horseman's hand rough, and he was gone.

I stared after him, not breathing, tears blurred the room. I dried my eyes on the bed sheet and opened the package. Inside was a small silver cloak-pin, crafted in the shape of a fox's mask, perfect, lifelike, beautiful. Letting out a great, quivering breath, I pinned it to my gown. Inside, next to my heart, where no one but me would know it was there. It nestled cool and sharp against my skin. I could face anything, now. Elffin thought enough of me to buy me a gift. I raised my eyes to the wavering green mirror. My eyes shone, and my cheeks were pink. I almost looked pretty.

Elffin

I'm exhausted. I should be sleeping like a baby, but my mind repeats Llew's words, and inside my head I see my father's expression. Before that small smile of reassurance for the boy, there was a fleeting look of - what? It was unfathomable. The gush of sudden comment from all around us, the flood of red to Llew's face when he thought he had overstepped the bounds - all these are burned in my memory like scar tissue. And the great shout of approval that rose, after. He spoke only the truth, but *Tad* swore fealty to the English King, and he is no oath-breaker. But all the same there was something in his face...

And Rhiannon. I didn't intend to speak to her again, after this afternoon, but once Llew had told me - well, what man can resist a girl he knows is in love with him?

The blue gown became her, thin as she is, despite the scowl. Lord, she's prickly as a hedgehog, that one, when her pride is sparked, but then, so am I. Giving her the trinket I'd bespoke for Anwen was a thoughtless gesture meant kindly, but when I saw her face, I felt small and mean. She thought it meant more. Her face lit when I gave it to her, and her great eyes shone, and all for me. I was sure she'd wear the pin that evening, but she didn't. So much for my gesture. Still, the pin was only a small thing. A whore's trinket.

A cheap thing indeed against what ap Hywel brought her: a gold torc so old that perhaps once a druid wore it. He slipped it about her thin throat as a token of their hand-fasting. He could have her, now, if he wanted, not wait until after the wedding, but he won't. I saw his face when he first saw her: he hadn't expected a child. So perhaps she's safe from the marriage-bed, at least until she is older, and I needn't worry. But she's still my foster sister, and in that way, and that way alone, I care for her.

CHAPTER SIX

Llewelyn

Tadmaeth has been closeted with the family: his Hanmer brothers-in-law have been here too, and Hywel Cyffin, Dean of St Asaph and his nephews. Something's not right. Something's happening that I don't understand, there are secrets brewing. Sycharth is filled with soft voices behind closed doors. Conversations cease when I arrive with refreshment.

Crach Ffinnant in his monkish robe came, too: three days and three nights he stayed, casting spells. It's said he can foretell the future. He frightens me: he's silent and sinister, and *Tadmaeth* listens to him.

On the fourth day a rider in Arundel livery came with news from *Tadmaeth's* father-in-law, his mount skidding on the cobbles as he flung himself from the saddle, throwing his reins to Siôn Twp. He tugged off his leather helm, and turned to me.

'Where's Glyndŵr, boy?' His hair was plastered to his head with sweat, his face crimson. I took him straight upstairs then hurtled to the kitchens for refreshments, which initiative earned me a smile from *Tadmaeth*, but though I loitered, hoping to be allowed to stay, I was dismissed. I lurked at the foot of the stairs, out of earshot but waiting, though I couldn't say for what.

I learned nothing that day, but Lady Marged wept as she went into her chamber. Ill-tidings, then. I feared a death, yet there was no mourning black. Even so, a darkness haunted Sycharth. It was as if the household was grieving - but for what?

Elffin gave me the first clue: hooking me, Siôn Twp and three of the stable lads from Huw's clutches he set us to building a fire in the mountains. On the remnants of the last fire we piled brush and branches, hauled logs up the hill. Hard work, this: I had no breath for gossip, and Elffin was in no mood to talk. When the fire was ready for lighting, he slapped my back, sending me staggering. 'A good job, Llew, and in a worthy cause.'

'There's going to be another *gymanfa*, so soon after the last?'

'Oh, indeed, Llew. Tonight. A *cymanfa* to make all Wales listen. Aye, and the *Sais*, too.'

'Do I have to speak?'

'No, Llew. Ap Hywel won't be here.' Elffin scowled. 'He's -' He stopped.

'What?'

'Ah, never mind. You'll find out soon enough.'

'He's going to be my kin. I've a right to know.'

But Elffin shook his head and refused to say more. I was afraid I shouldn't be allowed to go, but Elffin took me, because he said I had a right to be there, which mystified me even further.

As the shadows gathered in the hills, a column of silent men rode out from Sycharth, where they'd been foregathering all afternoon. There was none of the merriment that had accompanied our last *gymanfa*, none of the bawdy joking, the friendly insults.

Tadmaeth's brother Tudur; my foster brothers; *Tadmaeth*'s brothers-in-law; St Asaph and his two nephews; and almost all the *uchelwyr*, the high born ones, many bringing kinsmen from further afield. But there were to be few speakers.

Hywel Cyffin in his clerical robes first, calling God's blessing on the gathering, and for good measure Crach Ffinnant added his incantations, throwing herbs on the fire which crackled and blazed blue, perfumed smoke billowing round us, though Dean Cyffin scowled. *Tadmaeth* said nothing, but stood in the light from the flickering flames head bowed, hands crossed on the hilt of his sword, like the carved figure of a knight on a tomb. Gruffydd spoke first, sharing the news the Arundel rider brought.

'I am Gruffydd, eldest son of Owain Glyndyfrdwy. As you know, the *Sais* Parliament decided against my father's appeal. Lord Arundel my grandsire informs us that the king's attention is on Scotland again. The King summoned my Lord Owain to join him. Owain Glyndyfrdwy does not hold lightly his oath of fealty, despite the recent dispute and harsh judgement. He would have obeyed the King's summons without delay. However, the King entrusted his summons to de Grey.'

A low growl of sound issued from the throats of the assembled *uchelwyr*.

'...who neglected to mention it to my father. When it was too late for my father to comply,' he continued, 'he reported to the King that Owain Glyndŵr had ignored his summons, and held his commands in contempt, has been the King's liege man, has risked his life to fight for his King. As a reward the King has declared him outlaw.'

The silence which greeted this news was absolute, broken only by the spit and crackle of the great fire. And then a hundred voices were raised in anger and protest. When the hubbub dwindled, Owain Glyndŵr raised his head for the first time, and spoke:

'I am Owain of Glyndyfrdwy, and my line descends from the High Princes of Deheubarth...' His recitation was heard in utter silence, and when at last the sombre, deep voice ceased, Gruffydd spoke again.

'I quote my foster-brother: "I am Llewelyn, son of Llewelyn Mawr, proud and humble foster-son to Owain Glyndyfrdwy, best of men and true and rightful Prince of Wales." What say you, friends? Does Llewelyn ap Llewelyn Mawr speak rightly?'

My face burned, and I joined in the mighty shout of approbation that rose from the assembly. Dean Cyffin, when the tumult had died away enough to allow his voice to be heard, tremulous with emotion, repeated Gruffydd's words: 'Best of men and true and rightful Prince of Wales."

And it began.

Rhiannon

Another *gymanfa*, barely a week after the last, though Rhys ap Hywel, thank God, won't be coming. The air seems charged with a kind of waiting silence. Only the scratch of Elffin's fox pin cheers me, that and the sight of him, his bent head, his long stride across the cobbled courtyard. I am desperate for these snatched glimpses, because by tomorrow night I'll be gone. I marry ap Hywel tomorrow in the chapel, and then I must leave here. His lands at Pentregoch border de Grey's: I hope I'll never see that man, because I'd spit in his face for his treachery, and then I'd probably be thrown into a dungeon forever.

At my betrothal supper, I was at the high table next to Gruffydd, and on my right was Rhys ap Hywel. Elffin sat nearby. I could hear his voice, see his brown hands, his long fingers as they lifted his cup, tore bread, cut meat. I couldn't see his face, and he made no attempt to look at me. But he gave me the silver fox. He thought of me, enough to give me a gift. Oh, if he'd done it sooner, perhaps I could have made him see how I feel, and it might have changed everything. I barely responded to ap Hywel's attempts at conversation, until Lady Marged leaned round Gruffydd and glared at me. I was so exhausted I ate little, just crumbled my bread and sipped wine, and during Iolo Goch's music when the cloths had been drawn I slumped in my chair, all but unconscious.

At last, *Tadmaeth* rose, and announced the betrothal to the assembled *uchelwyr*: not that they were interested. I'm nobody and great things are happening. But they applauded politely when ap Hywel rose in his turn compliment *Tadmaeth*, and to present me with his bride-gift, a great, clumsy golden torc. It bruised my neck as he slipped it on, and he caught a clump of my hair in his ring and tore it out. The torc is old and heavy, but means nothing compared with Elffin's silver fox. Besides, ap Hywel is marrying me, so however valuable it is, he's kept it in his family, hasn't he? It isn't really mine at all. After, ap Hywel took my hand and looked at me. I expect he was disappointed.

I saw an unsmiling man, taller than I, whose light brown hair is thinning at the temples, and whose eyes are a curious muddy colour, framed by colourless lashes. There are small lines around his eyes. I suppose he's ordinary rather than ugly. But he isn't Elffin. Despite my determination to make the best of it, I burst into tears, and was led away by Crisiant, who clucked over me like a mother hen, undressed me, folding the blue gown and cream kirtle into the cedar chest at the foot of my bed. Then she left me. As soon as she was gone, I got out of bed, opened the chest and unfastened the fox pin from the undergown. I slept with it under my pillow, and groped for it even before my eyes were open in the morning.

And then it was my wedding day: Crisiant wasn't taking any chances and locked me in my room, but I had no strength to run. Speech echoed muzzily in my ears and I hardly saw the preparations going on around me. When the ceremony was over, Elffin came with his brothers to kiss me and congratulate ap Hywel. His lips were cool. My hands slipped to my heart, where, beneath the stiff fabric of the new amber gown Lady Marged had given me, a silver fox pin nestled. My eyes followed him and almost as if he sensed that I was watching, he turned and our eyes met. But then he looked away, and went to speak to his cousin Margaret Hanmer, who is happy and lively, who wets her lips with her little red tongue. Who has breasts.

Llewelyn was puffed up with importance about something - to do with the *cymanfa,* apparently. He won't tell me what, just smiles irritatingly and says it's man's business. It would almost be worth marrying ap Hywel, just to get away from his smugness. Almost.

Elffin
So much has happened. I'm proud and terrified in equal proportions. My father, Prince of Wales! But ~ how can one small part of one small country stand against the might of England? Still, God is on our side, and we shall prevail, I know we shall.

Rhiannon is safely wed, thank God. Now I know how she feels, I wonder how I ever missed it. Her eyes are on me wherever I go: I turn and she's watching, and it's beginning to make me uncomfortable. A less honourable man might take advantage of the situation, might - but not me. I kissed the bride chastely on her forehead, and saw her colour rush and fade. Our eyes met, and I pitied her. But then I forgot her, because my cousin Margaret Hanmer is lively and pleasant company, and besides, Rhiannon would be gone before sunset. Once the wedding feast was over, ap Hywel put Rhiannon on the mare he'd brought for her, and they left for Pentregoch. She didn't look back.

Ap Hywel's land adjoins de Grey's, which might be why he refused to attend the second *gymanfa*. There's an old saying: "if a dragon sleeps in your courtyard, it is unwise to ignore it when making plans for your future". Reginald de Grey is one such dragon, but Owain is another, and this dragon is stirring. Still, honour demands Ap Hywel supports his kin, and now he's married to Rhiannon, he owes us a duty of kinship twice over.

The day after the wedding, de Grey sent a message that the King wished to agree terms. Even then, what followed could have been avoided, *even then*, but for de Grey. Owain Glyndŵr has never broken his oath of fealty throughout a long life of service to the King. Henry's message was that he was prepared to "forgive" him and rescind the outlawing. All *Tad* need do was repeat his oath of fealty. But again the message was entrusted to de Grey, who has treachery woven into the very fabric of his soul.

Tad agreed to meet de Grey at Sycharth, allowing him to bring no more than thirty unarmed men. But this was de Grey, and therefore *Yad* sent Iolo Goch to sit with his harp in the gallery overlooking the great hall. From there Iolo could see both the approach to Sycharth and the proceedings below, and our men were hidden in the surrounding woodland. We left the horses saddled and waiting in the tiltyard at the back of the house with Llew and some of the other lads. It's unwise to meet de Grey without an escape route.

Thirty of us, too: my brothers and myself, my uncles and other kinsmen. De Grey came clattering into the courtyard with his thirty men, and Owain greeted him as a guest and an equal, and not the treacherous reptile that he is. We brothers sat together, ordered to keep silent, but Christ it was difficult! My hand itched to punch that fat, self-satisfied face. I wanted to pound it to a bloody pulp and dance on it until my boots were red, and my brothers felt the same. But *Tad* had agreed to meet him in peace, and in peace we came.

We, *Y Meibion Glyndŵr*, the sons of Glyndŵr, stared at de Grey as if he were the Anti-Christ. Such a small, fat man, for one so venomous: we all tower over him. He took off his gloves and threw them on the table, lounging arrogantly opposite my father.

'His Majesty abhors your treachery, Glendower, but is merciful. You must admit your fault and renew your oath of fealty.' De Grey's eyes shifted rapidly to *Tad's* face, gauging his reaction, and flicked away again.

How *Tad* kept his temper I'll never know. He smiled. 'The delivery of messages, my lord, seems somewhat erratic, does it not? Perhaps His Majesty's envoy is not as efficient as he might be. While I'm grateful for his Majesty's generosity, I have not broken my oath of fealty, and therefore have no need to swear again. I remain, as ever I was, his liege man.'

'You are a traitor, Glendower, and should hang. I suggest you reconsider. The King will not remain patient for long.'

'Will the King restore the land you have annexed? Will you compensate my tenant for his losses? Will you punish your men for rape and murder?'

'I took what was mine, Glendower.'

'You took my land, de Grey.'

'Outlaws have no land.'

Dewi half-rose, his hand reaching for his dagger - which was not. Gruffydd caught him before arse left wood, but de Grey saw the movement and flinched, his small eyes slithering in our direction. *Tad* leaned back in his great chair, elbows on the arms, his fingers steepled before his lips.

Then from the gallery where Iolo Goch hid, we heard an *englyn* sung in our own tongue. Iolo Goch sang of the death of Ddinbych, brother of Prince Llewelyn.

'Think on Lleweni's chief nor slight
The murder of the Christmas night.
The blazing hearth in'Mwythig's keep
The burning heart's avenging leap'

De Grey, of course didn't understand it, but every Welshman there knew the signal meant treachery. *Tad* was instantly on his feet, the rest of us following, and collecting our weapons from an ante-room we left the house by the back way, leaping to the saddles of the waiting horses before de Grey's approaching army could see us, capture Owain. Though I doubt de Grey would have arrested him: more likely he'd have killed him, and claimed he'd broken truce.

Treachery is de Grey's lifeblood, and one day I'll bleed it out of him.

We returned to Sycharth when de Grey had given up and gone home. We gathered supplies and weapons, and fled outlawed into the mountains to wait.

CHAPTER SEVEN

Llewelyn
September is cold in the mountains. Beyond the comfort of firelight the silence and darkness are absolute, except when the wind howls down the valley. We huddle round a fire in bitter cold, eating what's left of our supplies supplemented by whatever we can hunt, biding our time.

I was outside with the horses while *Tadmaeth* and my foster-brothers and the others were inside. When they burst out of the door, I'd already turned the horses towards escape. De Grey, unarmed, dared not follow until his force arrived, and thanks to Iolo Goch's warning, we were long gone by then. Returning to Sycharth after dark when de Grey had slunk back to Ruthin, I rode pillion behind Elffin. Every tooth in my head was jarred loose by the ride back but I lost no time in saddling Siôned ready to go with them. Grabbing a satchel of food from Bron, I waited in the courtyard.

Gruffydd scowled when he saw me. 'He's too young. This fight is none of his.'

Tadmaeth's voice was calm. 'His decision. Llew?'

'I'm coming with you, *Tadmaeth*.'

'Elffin, look after him,' he said and I shook with relief not to be left behind with the ancients, the women and the babies.

'Just my luck, an infant to mind,' Elffin muttered, but a grin accompanied his words.

So here we are. We're too well hidden to be seen from below, even if de Grey was brave enough to venture into the mountains, which of course he isn't. He doesn't know the mountains as we do: where we can hide, he would be exposed. Gwyn Dafaden, named for the wart on his nose, sneaked down into the valley and killed a deer this afternoon, and a great haunch of venison is dripping fat into the flames, the smell making my stomach growl. *Tadmaeth* is in the cave with Tudur and Gruffydd, talking strategy, I imagine. We'll be at war soon, and at last I'll see a real battle.

Dafydd Hopcyn across the fire belched ~ and suddenly sat up, looking past me into the darkness. Nervously, he crossed himself, making the sign against the evil eye simultaneously with his other hand. I turned to see a shadowy shape, close enough for the firelight to crimson his face and beard. Crach Ffinnant.

Without acknowledging us, as if we - or he - were invisible, he glided silently past and into the mouth of the cave.

'How'd he get past the watch?' Elffin muttered. 'If Ffinnant can slip through, so can de Grey. They're asleep, damn them.' He went to check, returning minutes later, shaking his head. 'Wide awake and watchful. They swear they didn't see him pass.'

Dafydd spat into the blaze, crossed himself again. 'acourse they didn't. That ol' bugger, he's magic, he is. He do give me the creeps, aye. Still, at least he's with us. Good to have a bit o' magic on our side. 's well as God, I mean,' he added hastily, glancing heavenwards.

Wil Trefor leaned forward. Glyndŵr's got magic, too. Night he was born, they say his Da's horses was up to their bellies in blood in their stable.'

I felt my eyes grow round 'Is that true?'

'Aye, so they say.' Dafydd shifted his position, his eyes glinting in the red light. 'And what's more,' he went on, dropping his voice confidentially, 'there was a thunderstorm that night that split the heavens in two, and lightnin' so fierce it blasted trees for miles around. I had it from my father, who was Glyndŵr's grandfather's man. There's them what say Glyndŵr has darkness and light - aye, and the weather - at his command.'

Siôn, peevish at being left out of the council of war when his brothers were included, snorted angrily. 'Superstition. *Tad* isn't magic. Use your brain, Dafydd. A fierce storm, flashes of lightning, thunder like the wrath of God. And a dozen high-strung horses panicking, kicking with sharp hooves. Of course there was blood on their bellies!'

'Rivers of blood, Siôn lad, not a few drops from a couple of scratches. Hot red blood, deep as their bellies. And they d'say Glyndŵr cut his milk teeth on a sword-blade! Hanging over his cradle it was, like a rattle. Unless 'e 'ad it there, no way his Mam could get him off to sleep.'

'Ah, story-tellers. My father has no magic. Just God guiding his arm.'

'Then why's that Crach Ffinnant here?'

'Ffinnant advises him, no more, no less.'

'He casts bones, brews magic, seeks omens. Some say he summons spirits. And Glyndŵr listens to him.'

I lay awake in the dying firelight long after everyone else was asleep, my belly churning with excitement at the thought of battles to come. I, Llewelyn ap Llewelyn Mawr, fighting alongside my Lord, the True Prince of Wales, just as my father did. But I won't die. I'm invincible. I'm a swordsman, even at fourteen years old, able to best - well, almost - Elffin.

A faint yellow light gleams from the cave where *Tadmaeth* and his closest allies talk. I wished I could hear what they were saying. Was the Sorcerer summoning spirits? Part of me wanted to hide my head under my cloak, but I'm a man, and men don't hide. The cave entrance was still glowing when I finally slipped into sleep.

Rhiannon

Leaving Sycharth was the worst moment of my life. Except when my Mam died, of course. Elffin didn't even look at me. I'm another man's wife, now. But oh, if he'd made the slightest movement towards me, I'd have run with him to the ends of the earth, and been glad to be called wicked.

Rhys ap Hywel has hardly spoken to me. We left Sycharth as soon as the wedding feast was over, to be at ap Hywel's home before dark. Lady Marged kissed me on both cheeks and wished me well. I didn't look back. I kept my eyes fixed on the rump of ap Hywel's horse bobbing in front of me, and made my mind blank.

The sun was slipping behind the hills when we arrived, and the house was stark black against the crimson light. Pentregoch is quite large, but not nearly as large or as beautiful as Sycharth, although it, too, is built of wood on stone foundations. It's square, but has no graceful columns, no arched stained-glass windows glowing in its walls, no shady courtyards, no green-ness curving down to a silver river, no tangled darkness of woods. It's just a square, dark, three-storeyed house in a square, bare field stubbled from haymaking, and at the back of the house a small herb and vegetable garden, and beyond that a cobbled yard bordered by stables and a midden. No dove-cotes or pigeon lofts, and worst of all, no familiar faces.

When Rhys dismounted and came to help me down. The golden torc hung heavily on my collar-bones, symbol of my captivity. I belonged to him, now, and the slave-collar was the outward sign of that. He set me on the cobbles and stood awkwardly for a moment, holding my arms above the elbows, but I didn't look at him. He thinks he owns me, but he doesn't. He can't have my heart.

The serving man led the horses away, and ap Hywel strode before me into the house. The sun was almost gone, and I waited in the gloomy doorway smelling the stench of rushlights and boiled turnips overlaying wood-smoke and fresh rushes, and longed for the sunlight and sweetness of Sycharth. Then, as my eyes became accustomed to the gloom, a door opened at the far end of the room and a tiny, round woman bustled in, stopping in the doorway to throw up her hands in mock horror.

'Oh, Rhys, Rhys, back already, is it? I'd have lit candles to welcome you! There's a thing, coming into a dark house. And this must be Rhiannon.'

Numbly, I stared at her.

'Oh, look, *nawr te*. Bless you, *cariad*, you're exhausted, aren't you. Come in by here, my lovely, and take off your cloak. Rhys, you *twpsin*, you should have let her stay the night at Sycharth, not made her ride all that way today.' While she spoke, she undid the clasp at my throat and took my cloak. 'There's thin she is! Like a little bird. Never you mind, *fach*, we'll soon fatten you up.' Her plump hands brushed the heavy torc. 'Oh, look, that heavy old thing has bruised your neck. Let me take it off. Fancy making the child wear it, Rhys! Old as the hills, it is, and not even pretty.'

The weight was gone, and I rubbed the place where it had been. I wished I could shed my husband as easily. Surreptitiously I checked that Elffin's silver fox was still in place, and felt the comforting scratch of it inside my gown.

'Rhiannon,' Rhys muttered, 'this is my sister, Mari.'

My voice sounded creaky. 'Do you live here?' If she did, then perhaps I could go home to Sycharth, and she could look after him.

Mari chuckled. 'Oh, *Duw, cariad!* No, just visiting. Llangollen, I live, with my Edward and my boys. No, sweeting, I'll be gone from here soon as soon. You don't want me under your feet, you just married.'

Oh, but I did. She was a friendly face, and I needed her. 'Please stay,' I begged, 'you don't have to go because of me.'

She patted my face affectionately. 'Bless you, my lovely. No, I'll stay until you're settled in a bit, then my Edward will bring the children back and I'll go home.'

'Children?' In my misery, I'd forgotten I was a mother as well as a bride.

'With Edward and Tom and Rhys Fach for a week, while you get to know their Dada. You'll get on fine with them, don't worry. There's Ifan - he's fifteen, isn't he Rhys? Yes, fifteen. And Beti. How old's Bet, now, Rhys?'

'Nine. Nearly ten.'

'There. Little sister for you. That'll be nice.'

I didn't want a little sister. And I certainly didn't want a step-son almost as old as myself.

'Will you have something to eat?'

Rhys answered for me. 'No. She's eaten.'

'How about a nice hot drink, then? Some spiced wine?'

Rhys shook his head, but I wanted wine. It would help me sleep, perhaps, put me out of the misery of this terrible day. 'Yes, wine, please.'

'You sit by there, my lovely, and I'll fetch it.'

Obediently I sank onto the wooden settle. I was aware of Rhys standing awkwardly in the middle of the room, but I looked around at the furnishings, the shutters folded beside the windows, the beamed ceiling, the pewter-ware stacked on shelves, the iron pot on its trivet over the hearth, anywhere but at him. He stood a few minutes longer, and then as the door opened and Mari returned bearing a mug of steaming wine, he turned and left. Instantly, I let out my breath and my spine, which I hadn't realised was ramrod-straight, curved and slackened, so that I almost slithered off the seat.

Mari sat beside me and took my hand. 'Look, sweetheart. Don't be afraid of Rhys. He's a kind man, even if he is a bit awkward.' She paused, biting her lip, as if considering what to say.

'Do you know - well - ' she paused, sighing, then tried again. 'Men and women. Do you know?'

I nodded, too exhausted and miserable to speak. 'Lady Marged told me.'

'Don't be frightened, *cariad*. It isn't bad as that!'

It was the last straw. I burst into tears, and was totally unable to stop. In the end, they put me to sleep, alone, in a great bed. I woke up in the night, once, and I was still alone.

Elffin

Nine days after the second *gymanfa*, on the 16th day of September in the year of Our Lord 1400, my father, Owain Glyndŵr, was crowned Prince of Wales.

Tudur, his brother; Gruffydd; Mam's brothers Griffith and Philip Hanmer; *Tad*'s brother-in-law Puleston; Bishop Cyffin and his nephews; Fychan; ap Evan; ab Madog and Astwick, were all there.

The Bards did their work, as ever they do, slipping from manor house to hut to Abbey and monastery: singing the praises (aye, and likely embroidering them, too) of the new and rightful Prince of Wales.

And they came: eleven from Glyndyfrdwy; from Iâl nine; from Edeirnion six (none of whom was the man lately married to Rhiannon, which gave rise to much discussion). Priests, bards, peasants, and even an Englishman. Two each from Corwen and Bala, eighty-one Mortimer tenants. There were even eleven from Ruthin and one hundred and ten of de Grey's tenants rose to the call and followed Glyndŵr, although I wouldn't like to be in their shoes if de Grey gets to hear of it.

St Matthew's Eve. We came in across the hills, down towards Ruthin, and hid ourselves amongst the oaks of Coed Marchon, behind Ruthin Castle. Men rallied from all over: from Edeirnion, from Glyndyfrdwy and Penllyn, and we waited silently for sunrise. We were a strange assortment of warriors: ill-fitting armour handed down from father to son - ay, and grandson in some cases - and those who had neither sword nor bow and arrow armed themselves with what they had: small knives and rough spears. Two hundred and fifty more or less battle-ready warriors, bound together by a determination to punish de Grey. That we chose a Saint's Day Eve to do it was neither here nor there: de Grey is no respecter of religion, and Gruffydd told me that Crach Ffinnant had cast this day as auspicious for revenge.

Even the horses were silent, save for the sound of shifting hooves and the odd snuffle that waiting, restless horses make. Then, as the first birds began their sleepy calling and the yellow sun launched itself into the September sky, we crept down into Ruthin.

St Matthew's Eve Fair: the townspeople, swelled in numbers by traders from all over the North, English and Welsh mixed had gathered in the marketplace, though Welsh traders are handicapped by *Sais* laws. In many of the border towns we aren't allowed by English law to sell or even barter. Many had stocked their stalls overnight by the light of guttering flares, and had slept beside them all night, guarding their wares.

The town gates swung wide and we slipped one by one inside, disguised as peasants, in rough, dung coloured clothes, and mine itched. I followed Dafydd Huw past the sentries on the gate: Llew, tight as a bowstring with excitement, was doing as he was told for once. Llew had seen less conflict than I had, and *Tad* entrusted him to me and me, in my turn, to Dafydd. Before we began to drift from the woods down into the town, I warned Llew to stay close. His eyes shining, he fingered the grip of his sword and nodded.

'I mean it, Llew. Do as you're told, right? Or your first battle may be your last.' I could see he didn't believe me: he thought he was invincible. It took a scratch to my thigh in a tilt-yard scrap with Gruffydd when I was fifteen to convince me that I was mortal, but it was a cheap lesson, and I learned it well. Llew stumbled as we passed the sentry, and I clouted him hard on the ear to take his mind off his nervousness. 'What was that for?' he complained, but the blow relaxed and settled him a bit.

The streets were full of bleating goats, panicky sheep, angular, phlegmatic cows, and the smell of their dung mingled with the smoke of the cook-shop fires, spitting fat, bread baking, the perfume and spice-sellers' stalls, and the stench of unwashed bodies. People jostled, pushed, shoved, shouted, laughed, screamed at pickpockets and men and women pissed where the fancy took them, which is no way to behave. Mam would have been mortified if she had seen it. I wondered where de Grey was. I wanted the sword that skewered him to be mine.

We filtered into the crowds, weapons hidden, our manner unthreatening, until we were in the shadow of Ruthin's vast red castle. Casually, I fingered cloth on a dyers' stall, bought sweetmeats I didn't want, squeezed fruit for ripeness, all the time listening, listening. Eventually I found myself at a silversmith's booth. At the front of his green display cloth were several small silver fox-mask pins, like the one I had given Rhiannon. He'd copied my design, and was selling it.

'Rogue,' I muttered, and the man grinned, showing a rotten tooth in front.

'Silver trinkets, my lord? For your lady-love?'

Llew and I moved on, waiting for the signal. He was quivering again, and I thudded an elbow into his ribs. 'Calm down, Llew,' I whispered. You're as nervous as a chicken on a feast day.'

'I'm not n-nervous,' he stuttered. 'I'm excited, that's all.'

'Well, you shouldn't be getting excited about a simple fair-day.'

'But it's not a -'

'Shut up, Llew.' He subsided, but I wasn't sure how long I could contain him. He was likely to give us away, if the wait continued much longer. But then I heard a faint whistle that was picked up and echoed across the teeming, bustling square, and shortly after all hell broke loose. Many a Welshman fell, but the attack was so sudden, so terrifying, there was no resistance, and no time to enquire after loyalties before striking. Memories of the attack come in flashes: the silversmith scooping his trinkets into the skirt of his tunic and tripping, spilling the lot into the slurry of shit and mud, in which he knelt, weeping; a stampede of cows, goats and sheep beaten through the town gates towards the woods, where they were encouraged to join us in the mountains. A small boy sitting on a sloping roof, cheering on the battle with complete disregard for his own safety, and a young woman, her skirts scooped into a bundle around her waist, showing more than her heels to the pair of young men pursuing her.

Llew windmilled his sword and wounded one man, but for the most I kept him behind me, so he wouldn't be harmed. I tossed him a blazing torch, and he danced around like a madman, touching fire to thatch and cloth, yelling hysterically as the flames bit in and flared up, dancing to the next roof, the next stall, until he was a wild shape limned in fire, leaping like an imp of hell.

And all through the looting, burning, killing, I felt only the steady crash of my heart and the joy of rising up at long last from beneath the heel of the *Sais*. The one *Sais* we wanted, though, Reginald de Grey of Ruthin, he hid inside the walls of his castle like the coward he is, and watched his town burn. He was not hurt, except in his pride and his pocket, and the latter was painful to the tune of £12,000, they say, and when we left only three buildings in Ruthin were untouched, and one of those was his castle.

Though there were casualties among the enemy, none died, unfortunately. For ourselves, we lost fourteen killed or captured, among them Gwyn Dafaden whom de Grey put to death with seven others, but there are ever losses in battle, and Gwyn was a man of unpleasant personal habits and an untruthful tongue.

And then, as swiftly as we came, we withdrew into the mountains.

CHAPTER EIGHT

Llewelyn
I killed a man, I did, honest! I ran him through and he squealed like a pig! That was Ruthin, mind, five days ago, and since then we've put half the North to fire and sword. Denbigh and Fflint, Hawarden and Holt. Oh - and Rhuddlan - *Duw,* nearly forgot Rhuddlan! Then we slipped along the border to Oswestry and fired that and Welshpool, too. Men are coming from all over North Wales to ride under Owain's banner. Wherever we go our sacred Red Hand pennant flutters overhead.

We *should* have taken Shrewsbury, but Hugh Burnell of Welshpool mustered the militia and beat us back. I know we're not invincible, but if we hadn't been fighting on the banks of the flooded Fyrnwy, I know we'd have won.

After we'd attacked Ruthin, *Tadmaeth* was quiet and sad as if he were mourning. What's to be sad about? "Welch doggis" Henry's damned *Sais* Parliament called us, but they'll be thinking again now. We can't take on Henry right now, but later - well, who knows? When I think of what we've done, I can hardly believe it. No going back now: Wales has risen. Well, Gwynedd, anyway. Tomorrow, perhaps, all Wales will rise to the One True Prince.

Yesterday Elffin and I were hunting: discreetly, since de Grey's men are everywhere: twice we had to hide while his men passed by. When they'd gone, we killed a boar. We were taking it back to camp when Elffin grabbed my arm, jerking me to a stop and signalling me to silence. We hid and waited.

Two strange figures were stumbling up the rocky, hidden pathway towards our encampment. They looked a little older than I, perhaps seventeen or eighteen and both wore threadbare black gowns so that they resembled a pair of moth-eaten crows. One had a long sword at his waist, in which his feet and gown constantly tangled so he often tripped: the other had only a small dagger and an unwieldy bundle that he found as awkward to manage as his companion's sword. They weren't de Grey's men, from the look of them: de Grey's men were nervous in the mountains, afraid Glyndŵr might be behind them. Not once did this pair look back. We strolled behind them openly in the end, grinning to see them pant, puff and trip up the path. At last they collapsed and the one with the bundle sat on it and put his head in his hands.

'We're never going to find him,' he moaned. 'Why did I listen to you?' We should have stayed where we were safe ~ and my feet weren't mostly blisters.'

'If Owain Glyndŵr has risen, we should be beside him,' the sword-bearer answered. 'Anyway, how safe would we be, Welshmen at Oxford, if Wales is rebelling against the crown? They're already suspicious of us - Meirion was accused of spying for Glyndŵr, and Gwydir was tortured. Mind, Gwydir would've talked if they'd tickled his feet. God knows what'll happen to him now. Anyway, who wants to be a student when Welshmen are fighting for their freedom.'

'Haven't seen much fighting, have we? Couple of singed hovels, a burned cornfield or two. Unless you're counting the man-eating sheep that attacked you. Maybe the uprising improved in the telling. It's all rumour, I tell you. There's nothing happening, no bloody rebels.'

Elffin's voice was mild. 'Here's two. Your business with Glyndŵr, gentlemen?'

They jumped as if they'd been stuck with red hot needles. The one with the pack started so violently that he fell off it Stumbling over his sword, the taller of the two attempted a bow, but was standing on a downhill slope and was too off-balance to manage much more than a brief pecking movement like a chicken.

'Gwilym of Hawarden. Student. Oxford University. At your service, my lord.'

His companion, whose long-lashed eyes made him pretty as a girl, was still glowering suspiciously at us. Elffin shifted his attention to him. 'And you?'

'Not that it's any of your business. Tomos ap Tomos of Ynys Môn. Also student, late of Oxford University.'

'And your business?'

'Damned if I know,' muttered Tomos, and turned his back, but Gwilym slapped his vast sword dramatically. His sweaty face was earnest. 'We've come to support Owain Glyndŵr. Do you know where he is?'

'I might. But then, you might be English spies.'

Gwilym's face reddened. 'Damn you! Do I look like an Englishman? Is my tail forked? Do I have horns? Loyal a Welshman as ever lived, me, Welsh from my back teeth to my toenails, and if you accuse me of being English again, I'll kill you.'

He'd probably need to stand on a box even to draw his sword. However, he'd now gone too far. 'You'll need to kill me, first,' I growled, my own sword half-drawn.

Elffin punched my arm, chuckling. 'Easy, Llew. Let them live a bit longer. There are Hawarden and Ynys Môn men with us: if they are who they say they are, someone will know them.'

I was inclined to believe they were genuine, although already I preferred the round-faced, earnest Gwilym. We relieved them of their weapons to be on the safe side, and the bundle too. That was as far as charity went, however. Siôned was burdened with boar, and Elffin had no intention of sharing Seren with either one of them. So we made them walk ahead of us, stumbling over roots and stones, protesting every step of the way.

When we got close, Elffin blindfolded them and we took them a roundabout way into camp. Time enough to show them the easy way when we were sure of them. The smoke from the fire made them both cough, but I shoved Tomos of Ynys Môn ahead of me through the clusters of men stringing bows, sharpening swords, throwing dice. The boar we'd brought was rapidly butchered and spitted over the fire, and the smell of roasting pork cheered us all. Besides, it had been taken from de Grey's lands and would taste twice as sweet because of it.

Gwilym was recognised by a Hawarden man with back-slapping and loud laughter, but as yet we had only one Ynys Môn man with us. He stared at Tomos, and walked around him as if he was inspecting a cow before purchase, but didn't recognise him, which increased my suspicions, though *chwarae teg*, it's a big Island and it's possible they lived at opposite ends of it and had never met. But

Tomos claimed to high birth, so he should have been recognised. Something didn't ring true. He was Welsh, at least, because he spoke our tongue - but only time would reveal his loyalties. He was too handsome, and I didn't like him.

Rhiannon
I hardly saw my husband that first week. Mari stayed, and I met Jack, Rhys's man, and Gwenllian the kitchen girl, and Elin the maid-of-all-work, and got to know my new home. There's a big, stone-flagged kitchen, with a great hearth and a turnspit dog that I shall get rid of as soon as I can: I can't bear to see the little creature's misery and blistered, tender pads. Three other rooms on the ground floor: a small but fashionably furnished parlour in which I sensed the hand of my predecessor; and a smaller, cosier room with wooden settles grouped round a fire and a scrubbed wooden table where the family eats when there are no guests. There's also a dining hall with a long, polished wooden table and carved chairs. Upstairs, four rooms, one for Rhys and myself, one each for his children, and a guest room. The servants climb a ladder to the attics to sleep and Jack sleeps over the stables. Under the house there's an earthen cellar for storage, and I'm never going down there if I can help it: it's dark and there will be rats and spiders. There are several out-buildings, dairy, barns, and a midden well away from the house. It isn't nearly as grand as Sycharth, but I suppose Pentregoch isn't too bad.

Despite my homesickness, a small part of me knows that Lady Marged has finagled a good marriage for me. I like the thought that this is my domain: it will be good to be in control of my own life at last, with no one to lecture me on my shortcomings - except Rhys, of course.

Mari showed me the dairy where great shallow pans of milk stood, the cream rising thick and yellow to the top. She picked a speck of grit from one pan and Elin, who was in charge of butter making and skimming the rising cream, had her ears boxed for not covering the pans properly. Elin has a runny nose, and I resolved to introduce her to kerchiefs. Her sleeves will be better for it.

Mari had made the servants work before my arrival: my bedroom was spotless, as were the kitchen, best-room, dining-room and little parlour. But the lack of a wife's touch was everywhere else: Mari hasn't had time to organise the still-room, and the first wife's collection of herbs hanging from the roof-beams has crumbled almost to dust. I have Lady Marged's own book of recipes, her bride-gift to me, and I'll try to use it. I'll have plenty to do, organising and controlling such a house: still, the more work the better: it will help pass the time. If I'm busy perhaps I won't mourn Sycharth and Elffin quite so much.

The day before Mari left we had horses saddled and rode around ap Hywel's land. There is more of it than I'd thought, and along its borders on two sides lies de Grey of Ruthin's land, for all it had been stolen from Welshmen to give to him. It's uncomfortable having *Tadmaeth*'s enemy so close, closer, even, than I'd realised: Rhys also tenant-farms for him. Still, his first loyalty will be to his kinsman, Owain Glyndŵr. That's what families are for, isn't it?

I saw Rhys usually at dinner, when he's polite: while we eat I slither sly glances at him. He's old, but not so old that his hair is white, and he has his teeth, all but one, which shows if ever he laughs, which he doesn't often, and then usually at something Mari has said. He mostly ignores me. He has no blemishes or pox-pits, but he isn't handsome. If he weren't my husband I might possibly like him as a friend. He's done me no harm.

But he is my husband and I don't know what to say to him. Nor he to me, apparently, since he's hardly spoken except for "pass the bread" and "did you sleep well?" since we arrived here, and even that has dwindled.

I do sleep well, because he hasn't bothered me, thank God. Perhaps he won't want that: he has two children already, so perhaps he won't want any more. I can just be his housekeeper, his children's companion and substitute mother, and he'll leave me alone to dream of Elffin. Perhaps I can be a little bit content here, if not happy.

The night before Mari was due to leave, we three sat about the table in the dining hall, candles lighted because the nights were drawing in, and Hywel spoke to Mari of the mare that would foal within days, of the red cow that had kicked Elin that morning, of the crops stowed safe in his barns, and I ate and half-listened, because I was imagining myself sitting just so at supper with Elffin.

Gwenllian brought us good cheese: white, crumbly, moist, which we were eating with apples instead of a sweet dish, when a rider clattered into the yard. Rhys rose and looked through the window-glass - greenish, thick, not clear and fine like the glass in the windows of Sycharth and Glyndyfrdwy.

'Iorwerth,' he said shortly, and left the room. We'd finished eating, Gwen had cleared the remnants of the meal and Mari and I, by the time he returned, had moved to the cosy back parlour. Though a fire burned in the hearth I drew my woollen shawl around my shoulders; it was a windy night for September, and draughts found their way in under doors. I sat on the high-backed settle gazing into the fire, seeing castles in the embers, and shooting stars and strange faces, nodding in the warmth and the glow, dreaming as always that I was elsewhere.

Eventually Rhys returned, dropping onto the settle opposite me. Mari, her hands never idle, was stitching at an embroidery frame, but she would have to stop soon, because the light was too dim for her to see properly and her eyesight was already poor.

'What news, Rhys?'

He drew a deep breath and glanced under his pale lashes at me. 'The worst. That fool Glyndŵr has sacked Ruthin - during the St Matthew's Eve fair. He hit Rhuddlan, Flint, Hawarden, Holt and Denbigh, too. Henry will react, now. There's no going back for Glyndŵr. He'll end on a scaffold, mark my words.' He ran his hands through his hair. 'Damn him!' he burst out, 'why couldn't he leave well enough alone?'

My stomach clenched and the dinner rose to my throat. *Tadmaeth* had attacked Ruthin? What of Elffin? Llew? I opened my mouth to ask the question, but commonsense for once kept me quiet. My voice thick in my throat, I asked, carefully, 'Is my brother safe? *Tadmaeth*? My foster brothers?' He couldn't see my hands clenched so tightly in my skirt that all feeling was leaving my fingertips.

Rhys nodded. 'Aye. Apparently. For the time being, at least.' He stood, running his fingers through his sparse hair. 'The fool, the bloody, bloody fool. And I'm burdened with his damned foster-daughter. God help me if de Grey tars me with the same brush as Glyndŵr. Dear God, I'm his kin, and if that weren't bad enough -' he glanced at me, and stopped. 'If de Grey holds that against me, I'm finished. I never took Glyndŵr for a fool, but now -'

Mari had stopped stitching, had slipped the needle into the fabric and sat back watching her brother. 'Owain wouldn't rise without good reason, Rhys, you know that as well as I do. Distant kin, true, but blood is blood. He'll have good reason, mark my words.'

Rhys made an exasperated gesture with his hands. 'Aah - de Grey annexed some of Owain's scrubby land. Might have been Owain's, once. But what we Welsh hold, we hold only in the King's favour. Glyndŵr took his case to the King, and the King sided with de Grey. *Sais* with *Sais*, of course. How could Glyndŵr think it would be otherwise? De Grey has the King's ear, and Glyndŵr's lost.'

'God will be on *Tadmaeth*'s side,' I declared. 'God won't let de Grey win.'

Rhys ap Hywel pulled a disgusted face. 'God sides with the biggest army. Which Glyndŵr does not and will never have. He's finished. I hope to God I don't go down with him.'

I crossed myself quickly at the blasphemy: I'm not one to take risks where God is concerned. Mari patted my knee, half-comforting, half-quieting me. 'Will you join him, Rhys?'

'Join him? Are you mad? Not only has he sacked Ruthin - which might have been forgiven, since his quarrel was with de Grey, and some might say had some justice in it - he's also declared himself Prince of Wales, which is treason whichever way you look at it. Henry won't appreciate that! No, I'll stay neutral as long as I can. How can I support Glyndŵr? De Grey's my neighbour and my landlord. It's bad enough, God help me, that I've taken Glyndŵr's ward to wife.' He pressed both hands to his face, like a man in pain. 'I'd be dispossessed before I had time to blink. I saw the way the wind was blowing when my idiot brother-in-law let his tongue run away at the *cymanfa*. I should've cut my losses then, despite the dowry Lady Marged dangled.'

My eyes prickled. I knew what Llew had said at the *cymanfa*, it had been the talk of Sycharth and I was proud of him. I bit my lip: it was hard to have to sit there and not stick up for my brother. Rhys's words also made it clear that I hadn't been married for anything other than expediency - and money - whatever Lady Marged had said. As my pride absorbed this blow, it also swelled - *Tadmaeth*, Prince of Wales! - followed swiftly by terror. Battles, men dying, and Elffin in danger. And I'm married to a coward and a traitor to his own.

Angry words rioted in my head. I fought them down. Instead, 'Good night,' I said, and left the room. Mari didn't follow me.

Gwenny was drowsing on the stairs, and I prodded her awake to unlace my gown. When she'd gone I crept into bed, clutched Elffin's silver fox and prayed for Elffin's safety and *Tadmaeth*'s, and all my foster brothers. At least Llew would be safe - he was surely too young yet, to ride with Glyndŵr? But it was a long time before I slept, and when I did I dreamed of burning fields and bloody battles and pile upon pile of shattered bodies.

Elffin

It makes me proud, the way Welshmen rally to my father. They come in ones and twos - like the Oxford students Llew and I found yesterday - and in large groups bound by kinship. The great lords, however, at least those not linked to our family by blood or marriage, are slow to commit, but they will, soon. When they see we're winning despite the odds. There's nothing like victory to attract waverers to a cause. Even old Huw has left Sycharth and tottered up the mountain to join us: mind, he has personal reasons to hate de Grey since the slaughter of his cousin and the rape of his niece. Concentrates a man's mind, a thing like that. Old and doddery he may be, but he's a good man for all that.

The King knows: he's hurrying south from the Scots campaign. Thank God for the Franciscan houses, whose network of spies is better than the King's. Monks travel faster than soldiers, because they don't stop to skirmish and burn along the way, and are usually let pass unhindered - and often with a good meal inside them, for friars bring news!

Shrewsbury is strengthening its defences: the Welsh in the town are looking over their shoulders, and those traders who value their livelihood are wringing their hands and protesting their loyalty to the English crown with every breath. No matter. When we want Shrewsbury, we'll take it. Right now we're lying low in the foothills of Eryri, but tomorrow we return to Sycharth, which, being moated, can be defended as well as any place, except perhaps a castle. The doorkeeper will have work to do for once. It will be good to be at home again, to sleep in a bed. Llew misses Sycharth. Strange: it isn't really his home, and yet I think he loves it better than I do. Maybe I take it for granted, but for Llew it's heaven on earth, to hear him talk.

I saw a fox, today, slipping through the sunlit woods like a streak of flame, and I thought of the wiry gold of Rhiannon's hair, and wondered how she fares. Knowing that she cares for me, I worry about her, and remember the strange, tight-strung look of her when she left Sycharth. Llew, heartless little wretch that he is, has put her out of his mind, he's so caught up in talk of killing and battle. He's convinced himself he killed a man at Ruthin, but he didn't. He mustn't get over-confident, for that way lies disaster. And enthusiastic though he is, he'd be no match for a real warrior, who'd finish him off and eat dinner at the same time.

Admittedly, I've six inches on him in height, but I can beat him with ease. I occasionally let him to win, to encourage him: he'll learn in time, but I fear for him in real battle. I fear for myself, too, because I haven't had much experience either. But I'm older and stronger and taller. God grant we both have time to grow up, and in one piece.

When I'd finished thinking of Rhiannon and her brother, I thought about Anwen. Faithless she may have been (oh, all right, she's a whore) but all the same I miss her warmth and her laughter - yes, and her other assets too. Perhaps soon I'll pay her a visit, if I can get away.

CHAPTER NINE

Llewellyn

We're going home! Three weeks we've been hiding here, but soon it will snow and travel will be impossible not only for us, but for our enemies as well. We *should* be at home! Owain Glyndŵr is Prince of Wales, and he shouldn't have to hide like a criminal. England may have outlawed *Tadmaeth*, but to us - and all true Welshmen - he's our Prince. The order to break camp had just been given when old Huw, bristling with elderly fervour, tottered up the mountain to join us. Never mind, I'll give him a ride down on Siôned.

Last night we sat, a great circle of comradeship, around the fire and Iolo Goch sang a new song. He crouched on a log, firelight glinting on his harp-strings, and delighted us with the vision of de Grey cowering behind his castle walls while Owain, a great golden eagle, tore the town in his talons, and swept up to Eryri with his spoils. He sang that we were heroes all, that our swords howled like demons in the air, blades running crimson, and behind us we left nothing but death and ashes. It's true!

To pass the time until we left, Elffin and I sparred. Hefting the sword is easier, lately: my neck and shoulders are getting stronger, and I don't ache so much after practice. I'll never be tall as Elffin, but I'll be strong as him some day. He'll need to be careful, mind - I've killed a man, now.

I attacked fiercely, though I didn't want to hurt him. By sheer luck he managed to catch the hilt of my sword, and ripped it out of my hand ~ probably because I was holding back, which would have been fatal in other circumstances, of course. He grinned in that irritating, superior way he has. I threw up my hands in mock surrender and retrieved my weapon. 'Sorry, Elffin, wasn't paying attention. Shall we try again?'

'Do you want to?'

'Of course.' This time I thought I'd teach him a bit of a lesson. We circled round each other for long seconds, and I looked for the slight drooping of his left shoulder as the muscles of his other arm tensed, the tell-tale sign that he himself had taught me. The shoulder dropped, I leapt to the left to throw him off balance, and swung my weapon, intending to miss, of course, or strike him a gentle, glancing blow on the shoulder or arm.

But as I leapt to the left, he went to *his* left, and I stumbled and twisted, feeling clumsy, because he wasn't where he should have been. Then, suddenly, his sword was prodding my Adam's apple.

'Not ready again, Llew?' he asked, kindly, although the grin wasn't far off.

'I was ready,' I said, a bit sullenly. 'You beat me fairly. But you cheated. It wasn't skill, only trickery.'

'Little brother, expect tricks, or you'll get your throat slit.'

'I survived Ruthin, didn't I? And Hawarden, and Holt, and -'

'You did.'

'I killed a man at Ruthin, didn't I?'

'No, you didn't. You only wounded him. Besides, he was too old and creaky to get away. It was like spiking a slug.'

'That's a lie! He was a grown man, and strong -' I stopped. Elffin lifted an eyebrow. 'Oh, all right. Perhaps he was a bit old and slow. Perhaps I didn't kill him altogether.'

'No, you just killed him a little bit, right Llew?'

I felt the grin tug at the corner of my mouth and ducked my head so he wouldn't see it. 'Iolo Goch called us heroes with howling swords, so it must be true, mustn't it?'

'It's Iolo's job to make us believe we're invincible - ready for the next time we stick our necks out. While we're risking our gizzards, he's off composing something stirring for after.'

'Aye,' I said. But oh, Elffin, I *want* to be invincible! I'm ready to die for *Tadmaeth*,' I said passionately.

'Yes,' Elffin conceded, 'me, too. But not yet, all right?'

'I'd rather not die at all, if it's all the same to you,' I admitted ruefully. 'Could we practise some more, please?'

We battered at each other for another hour, until I was covered in bruises and wheezing like an old man. Elffin thrashed me again and again, until I knew to expect the feints, the tricks, the mock-stumbles, and was watching for them. And waiting for them, so that I could do the opposite of what he expected me to do. And almost - almost, almost, I beat him. I'll say no more than that, but I think learned a little. Not least to be less boastful in future.

When we'd done, and were standing, swords drooping from aching arms, chests heaving, Elffin threw me a water-bottle, and I poured the brackish water down my throat and over my sweating head. My chest hurt and my legs trembled.

'You did well, Llew. Do twice as well in a real fight and you may survive.'

I scowled. 'Twice as well? I thought I was getting better.'

'Oh, you are.' Then, with a fast move that I missed entirely, he hooked my feet from under me and I was flat on my back again.

'But never, ever, lose concentration, Llew.' He grinned, and his teeth gleamed in his brown face.

Oh, it was good, even aching all over, to go home! Huw clung like a cripple's hump to my back, muttering at the way I rode, nagging that I sat Siôned like a sack of flour, and that the bones of his arse were murdering him: I should have let him walk. But I hardly heard him. The setting sun flooded the sky with crimson, doves fluttered into the cotes as we crossed the moat. I looked down at the still water - and shuddered, for the dying sun had turned the moat red as blood. I shoved the thought away. I don't believe in omens, not even those surrounding *Tadmaeth*'s birth. He's rightful Prince, and none can deny it or attribute it to omens, stars, luck or chicken entrails.

Lady Marged, holding her skirts above the mud, ran from the house. I've never seen her run anywhere before. She clung to *Tadmaeth*'s stirrup, smiling up at him. I looked instinctively for

Rhiannon, before remembering that she wasn't there. I missed her then, and wished I had a girl who would run to meet me, her white ankles flashing in the dusk, even if she was my sister. It would be better to have a girl who loved me, mind. Siôn Twp told me that Anwen in the village will - you know - if you give her a bit of money, but I don't want a girl who'd do it with Siôn Twp. But still, heroes should have maidens waiting for them, though with me around they won't be maidens long!

I wandered into the kitchens and Bron got me, pressing her breasts up against me like soft battering rams. I extricated myself and gave her a kiss. In return she gave me a heel of a loaf and a hunk of meat to tide me until supper, and I sat at the scrubbed table and munched contentedly. I told her how brave I'd been, and about the man I had fought. I didn't say I killed him, honest, although I may have hinted it. Sal the scullery girl was loitering in the corner, listening. I peeped at her from the corner of my eye. She's younger than Rhiannon, but she's got breasts like little apples, and her eyes are bright as a bird's. Bron clouted her and sent her to build up the fires, because Lady Marged would be calling for food any minute.

I stored Sal away in my mind for future reference.

Rhiannon
Perhaps I'm safe from the bed business, Rhys being so old. Perhaps I can just look after his house. I can do that: after all, Mam and Lady Marged have lectured me on the subject since I was small.

I woke one morning, opened my eyes and yelped: a pair of blue eyes, only inches away, gazed into mine. I sat up. A tiny girl - so thin that she seemed just an arrangement of sharp bones, topped by a triangular cat-face, knelt on my bed. She grinned, showing small, white teeth.

'She's awake now, Ifan.' I looked over her shoulder. In the doorway a youth as long and colourless as two-yards of pump-water slouched. He had his father's straw-brown hair and muddy, suspicious eyes: The girl, in contrast, had black hair and inquisitive blue eyes. She bounced on the bed to get my attention.

'I'm Beti, and I'm nine, nearly ten. That's Ifan, he's fifteen and you are our new Mam.'

I scratched my head and scrubbed the sleep out of my eyes. 'I suppose I must be.'

'You're not very old, are you?'

'I'm nearly sixteen,' I retorted.

'That's not very old. Ifan's fifteen. That means he's almost the same age as you.'

I struggled upright, clutching my bed gown to my neck, still half asleep. 'Look,' I said, 'I've never been anyone's Mam before. But I'll do my best, all right?'

Beti nodded solemnly. 'All right.' She turned to her brother.' Is that all right, Ifan?'

He scowled. 'She can do what she bloody wants. *Tad* married her for the dowry, not because he wanted her. She's nothing.' He slammed the door behind him as he left.

Beti shrugged. 'Ifan's rude, isn't he? He didn't want Dada to get another wife, but I expect he needs one to look after him. My Mam died of the sickness. I didn't get it, but Ifan did. He nearly died, but not completely.'

Unfortunately, I thought.

'Will you get up, now?'

I flung back the covers and got out, splashed my face with water from the ewer, and dressed. I unplaited my hair, combed out a few of the snarls with the bone comb that Lady Marged gave me at Christmas last year, then twisted it into a rough coil at the nape of my neck. I turned to straighten my bed: Beti was holding my fox pin.

Resisting the impulse to snatch it from her, I said as calmly as I could, 'May I have that, please?'

She held it up. The silver gleamed in the morning sun.. 'It's pretty. You're my new Mam, you should give it to me for a present, to show you like me.'

'No.' I softened my voice. 'It's mine. My -' I thought rapidly. 'brother gave it to me.'

'You've got a brother?' She bounced, excitedly. 'That means I've got a new uncle, as well as a new Mam, doesn't it? What's his name?'

She had forgotten the pin in her excitement, and I took it from her fingers. 'That's right,' I said. 'Llewelyn. Llew. He's almost fourteen. He isn't as tall as your brother, but he's wider.' And less pale and droopy, I thought, and more intelligent, and probably braver and certainly more polite. At least sometimes, I amended, being honest.

'Can he come and see us?'

'Oh, I expect he will, one day.'

'When?'

I was beginning to get exasperated: I like to wake slowly and not be interrogated before my eyes are properly open. 'I don't know. Sometime.' I went downstairs, leaving her to follow, slipping the pin into my pocket until I could hide it.

Mari's husband was there, a round, white-haired, scowling man.

'Not much of her, is there?' he growled. He spoke English, and I bristled, not keen on *Sais* so close.

'Now, Edward, Rhiannon will suit Rhys nicely. She'll get on well with the children, and once she starts having babies, she'll plump up lovely, I'm sure. We all do, you know!' she said ruefully, patting her hips.

I'm going to stay thin, then, because I'm not having any babies, ever.

Eventually, Mari and Edward left, and I was left alone with Rhys and his children.

I stood in the middle of the yard, waving until they were out of sight, and then looked up at him, wondering what I should do next. Should I ask him? He didn't stay long enough for me to do any such thing: the stable boy brought his horse, and Rhys swung into the saddle.

'Back at supper-time,' he said shortly, and kicked the mare into motion. He didn't look at me. Right, then: I must decide what to do myself.

First, I helped Beti unpack her belongings and stow them in the press in her room, but decided Ifan could do his own. He made no attempt to do it, and I certainly did not intend to do it for him. He slumped in the corner, sullen eyes following me. The fond image I'd had of two biddable little angels was rapidly disappearing: what with his sulks and Beti's ceaseless chatter, I already felt like screaming.

I'm not used to children. Llew was the youngest at Sycharth, and being my brother I could usually shut him up if I needed to, either with sarcasm or brute force. I went into the kitchen, where Gwen was scouring pots with fine sand, her face red, her sleeves rolled up.

'What shall we have for supper, Gwen?' I asked, brightly.

'Couldn't say, Mrs Rhiannon,' she said, turning her back on me.

'There's cold mutton left, isn't there?'

'I 'spect. If it ain't been et.'

I knew it hadn't been. Gwenny was apparently testing my mettle now Mari had gone. 'Then we'll have that,' I said firmly. 'And you'll need to bake some more bread,' I suggested, peering into the earthenware crock where it was kept, 'there's hardly any left.'

'Can't bake bread, Mam.'

'What? Then who baked this?'

'Mrs Mari, Mam.'

'And where did you get bread before Mrs Mari was here, Gwen?'

'Man in the village baked it, Mam. But Mrs Mari said it weren't nice. There was bits in it, like. Grit and such.'

I'd never baked bread. I got out Lady Marged's recipe book. Yes, there were the ingredients and instructions for bread. In the pantry were flour and yeast, and I wrapped an apron around myself and set to. It seemed a very long process, but it was quite interesting to see the way the dough got bigger and bigger when it was put by the fire, and battering and thumping it improved my spirits. Besides, Beti soon got bored with watching, and took herself and her chatter off to play with her doll. I should teach Gwen how to do it, if this batch tasted good. I slid the loaves into the oven and turned to speak to her. The girl's back was towards me, her shoulders hunched. I hoped she'd stop sulking soon. Now Mari was gone, I seemed to have a choice between Beti's chatter and a sullen silence from everyone else.

Determined to keep busy, I visited Elin in the dairy, gave her a bit of rag and showed her how to blow her nose. She shoved it up her sleeve, after, and I had horrid visions of it falling into the cream.

The herb garden Rhys's last wife had planted was scruffy but still visible behind the house, so I took Lady Marged's useful little sketch-book of herbs, and tried to identify what was there. It was badly overgrown and needed weeding, but some of the plants were still recognisable. I gathered those in the best condition and made them into bundles to dry.

I told Gwen to set the table, and though I'd intended to wait for Rhys, he was so late that we ate without him, helping ourselves to the cold mutton and new bread, which tasted as good as it smelled. I felt quite proud of myself. Beti went quickly to bed when the sun went down, but Ifan sat, silent and hostile, with me in the small parlour while I mended one of Rhys's shirts. He didn't speak: he slouched, whittling at a bit of wood, his lank hair falling over his forehead. Beti was a chatter-box, though sweet enough, but I might find it difficult to love my step-son. Perhaps I could charm him somehow, try to make him like me. Briefly, I wondered where the old, rebellious Rhiannon had gone. Here I was, baking bread, mending, worrying about my step-son's hostility, conforming: I was learning to endure, as Mam had advised.

Elffin

Six months back I might have thought that sleeping under the stars would be fun, but now I know it's bloody cold and the ground is hard, so to hell with stars! Mam is fussing over *Tad*, who doesn't notice, because he's wrapped up in planning and intelligence and meetings with the world and his neighbour.

A couple of days after our return, Gwilym and Rhys ap Tudur, our kinsmen, took Anglesey in Glyndŵr's name, but since neither has sworn fealty to him, and since they're great opportunists, this bit of business may have been entirely self-interest. However, they stirred up the King, who was at Northampton, good and proper. If reports are true, he almost demolished his lodgings around himself in fury when he heard. Anglesey goaded him into action: he crossed into Wales, burned out the Franciscans at Bangor, then went for Beaumaris, burning, looting and raping as he went. They say there isn't a cow, sheep, virgin or barn left standing between the border and Beaumaris, but we should have done the same if it had been us. Except for burning out the Franciscans, of course, because they're for us. They believe King Richard is still alive and Henry a usurper, though Richard's dead, of course, and sensible folk know it, since his bloody corpse was exhibited in London on a cart. Loyalty to a dead man is not a lot of use, but the Franciscans didn't see Richard's body, so consequently they're convinced he's still alive. Sad for them, but good for us.

Henry didn't have it entirely his own way, however: Gwil and Rhys caught up with him near Beaumaris Castle, and put the fear of God into him. The King holed up behind the walls, losing more than his dignity, for this success brought many more to Owain's cause, and there was a flood of Anglesey men swearing fealty to Glyndŵr as a result.

Tomos Oxford Student has finally been recognised by a Moelfre man who came in after Beaumaris. He vouched for Tomos's family (although strangely, not for Tomos). Young Llew may not be much of a swordsman yet, but he's a good judge of character, and Llew disliked Tomos on sight. He doesn't trust him an inch, and I'm inclined to agree.

I haven't been near Anwen: why should I? There's a girl here who's been fluttering her eyelashes at me since the day I got home. Her name is Angharad, she's my mother's tiring-woman, and she's round and willing. She's prettier than Anwen, and mine until I get tired of her. God grant I don't give her a child. It wouldn't worry *Tad* overmuch, he has plenty of bastards of his own, but Mam - well, I don't want to even think about that. But the nights when Angharad creeps to my bed (three other girls share her chamber) are worth the risk. Mind, in the middle of it all the other night, as I was thrusting into the softness of her, and she was gasping beneath me, strangely, I found myself thinking of Rhiannon. I thought *does Rhiannon do this?* The thought put me off completely and I was totally unable to continue: I had to pretend I had a cramp in my thigh. I clutched my leg and moaned, pretending I was in agony. No matter, though. In minutes I was hard again, and at Angharad as if nothing had happened. Strange, Rhiannon of all people - well, I'll take care not to think of her again when I'm busy!

Henry has confiscated all the Hanmer's lands, as well as our own. His half-brother Beaufort has them now, in title if not in fact, so they have been given to a bastard by a bastard, royal or not, yet neither bastard can lay hands on them, nor ever shall, if I have anything to do with it!

Winter will be peaceful, please God, though we'll still attack the borders to keep ourselves in practice and the enemy off balance. We need grain, cattle, sheep, and even a small flurry of horsemen raiding a farm - English preferably, or Welsh if the farmer has neglected to declare for his Prince - can carry off plenty.

The King is back in Shrewsbury, so we are safe from him for a while. There'll be snow soon, and Henry won't attack in winter, so we can rest and relax. But next spring, he will have to act. No matter: we have right on our side, and by then all Wales will be under our banner.

CHAPTER TEN

Llewelyn
It's hard to believe that we're at war, though we live behind strong walls and reinforced gates. Sycharth is on a hill and if riders are seen, the alarm is raised and the guard alerted until visitors have been identified. Our porter was once the idlest man here because the gates were always wide to guests, expected or not. But times change, and we must be ready for attack even at Christmas and the season of goodwill to all men. Except de Grey, of course.

So many are crammed into Sycharth that the walls are bulging! There are even men sleeping in the stables, much to Huw's disgust: in his opinion stables are for horses, and snoring, farting men unsettle his precious beasts.

We won't see de Grey until Spring: deep mud is no encouragement to warfare. Still, we can't quite relax - unless we get snow. What a Christmas we'd have then! Lady Marged has invited Rhiannon, her husband and his two children here for the festivities, so, though I pray for snow, I don't want it to come until Rhian's here, then we can have mountains of it.

Then I can tease Sal, eat my fill and enjoy Christmas with my sister here to make my happiness complete. She and ap Hywel live a bare three hours' ride away, with a good road between the two estates is fair. They've been allocated a room in the guest house because Rhiannon's old room currently accommodates seven men. Strange to think of Rhian as a respectable wife, when only yesterday she lay beside me on the river-bank tickling trout, hooking them flapping onto the bank. She was better at it than I was - she had more patience for that at least.

The tiltyard has been cleared of snow, straw laid and braziers lighted to stop us freezing while we practise. Even at Christmas we must be battle-ready. I practise with Elffin sometimes, but more often with the other boys and some of the more patient and obliging men. This is good: each one has his own tricks, his own style, his own habits. In war my opponents will be strangers, and variety helps me learn. I beat Tomos yesterday: good, because I don't like him. He fawns on me because I'm Glyndŵr's foster-son, but I don't trust him. Elffin matched us, and I let Tomos think I was unskilled. His contempt of me was obvious, but I drove him back until he tripped and fell full length in a pile of filthy, sodden straw at the edge of the yard. His friend Gwilym laughed until he cried. Gwilym's a good friend, though he fancies Sal. But she has eyes only for me. I have a Yule gift for her, a handful of bright ribbons, and I hope this will make her willing.

On the subject of willing girls, Elffin is bedding one of Lady Marged's tiring women, and is as smug as a cat in a dairy. I'd heard talk, but when *Tadmaeth* sent me to Elffin's chamber with a message, I had proof. The door was locked, but I hammered on it until he opened it. He tried to block my view, but I saw Angharad, bare as an egg - and in the middle of the day, too! She grabbed the bedcovers and squeaked, Elffin turned me about, shoved me out and slammed the door, but I saw her breasts, which were very nice indeed. Since then, whenever I see her about the house, I can't help looking for the outlines of her bareness under her clothes, which causes a problem in my breeches.

Later, Elffin came looking for me. I was in Siôned's stable, eating an apple. He sat silent beside me.

'What you saw today, Llew,' he began.

I made big eyes at him over the apple. 'What was that, Elffin?'

He grinned, sheepishly. 'Angharad -'

I scratched my head. 'Lady Marged's woman, you mean? Haven't seen her for days.'

He patted my shoulder, relief on his face. 'Good, Llew. Our secret, eh?'

I almost choked on the apple. 'Our secret?' I hooted, 'Oh, aye? Ours and every tiring woman and kitchen maid and scullery girl and stable lad and -'

His look of horror was comical. 'They know? How can they?'

I tossed the bitten core in my hand. 'Let me see. Angharad told Bethan, Bethan told Gwyneth, Gwyneth told -'

'All right, all right.' He put his head in his hands, ruffling his hair. '*O Arglwydd Dduw!* Why can't women keep their bloody mouths shut?'

I clasped my hands around the apple-core and fluttered my eyelashes. 'Ooh, Bethan, Elffin's soooo wonderful! Strong and fierce as a bull, he is, and so gentle and handsome, and his co-'

He clapped his hand over my mouth. 'Hush, for God's sake, someone will hear you!'

I pushed him away, laughing. 'You mean there's someone who hasn't heard? What if she has a baby, Elffin? Then you'll catch it!' He looked so worried I took pity on him. Well, sort of. 'Rhian's coming home for Christmas. How will she feel, the man she loves mooning after some other girl?'

He grinned. 'Ah, she's forgotten all about me by now. She's a married woman. She won't care what I do - or who I bed.'

I stood up and palmed the apple core for Siôned to take. 'Maybe she's having a baby herself. She's been married three months, now. Women have babies quick after they're married.' The devil nudged me again. 'And some before, as well.'

Oh, you should have seen his face!

Rhiannon

Home for Christmas! All of us, Rhys, Beti and me. And Ifan, more's the pity. At first Rhys didn't want to go in case de Grey found out, then he realised that it's just as dangerous to offend Owain as de Grey. I almost pity him, trapped between them - but a man who ignores his duty to his kinsman and Prince doesn't deserve pity. At last he said that if the roads were clear, we could go. He probably prayed for snow to keep us at Pentregoch, but I prayed ten times as hard, and twenty times more often, that not a flake would fall until we were safely home. Then it could snow until Doomsday, for all I'd care. Since I'm still a virgin, and virtuous (at least in body) perhaps God's more likely to listen to me than to Rhys ap Hywel, who isn't a virgin at all, and must have vast numbers of sins on his soul, being so old.

I longed to see Elffin. I'd wear the silver fox pin. He'd know, then, that though I'm ap Hywel's wife, I still think of him. Nothing can come of it now that I'm married, but - just to see him.

We were to leave in time to be there for Christmas Eve and Mass in the family chapel when candles flicker on the coloured glass of the windows, and the space is filled with warmth and light and smiling faces. The day before I kept peering anxiously at the sky, terrified it might snow, but though it was bitterly cold and the sky threatened, it didn't. I was afraid to sleep that night in case sleeping-not-praying let it snow, but eventually I did.

Will Elffin recognise me? I've gained weight and have breasts, now, though not as big as Crisiant's, thank God.

Morning was cold but dry, and I flew about packing last minute things: gifts I'd made for Llew and *Tadmaeth* and Lady Marged, small gifts for Rhys, Beti, even my step-son. I wish I had something for Elffin, how could I give it to him? We almost didn't go, because Rhys sent Jack to scout around the countryside before we ventured out, to check that none of the Fat Toad's men were about. De Grey will hear of it somehow. He has eyes and ears everywhere. What if he does? I'm going home to Elffin and Llew and *Tadmaeth* and Lady Marged if I have to walk every step of the way through neck-deep snow.

At last we set off, Beti riding pillion with her father, Ifan and I on our own mounts. Jack rode with us, but there was little danger of attack so close to Christmas. The wind rose as we left, and I wrapped my cloak tightly round me, but the chill cut to the bone. I didn't care. I was going home.

Beti was warm enough *cwtched* into her father's back, but Ifan complained over and over that his hands were numb and his feet were frozen - until his father told him to shut up. I didn't care if he froze solid. It's hard to like Ifan, let alone love him. He may be my step-son, but he's given me nothing but sullen looks and insolence since the day we met.

Oh, that first sight of Sycharth! My heart lifted, and overcome by delight I kicked my mare into a gallop to be first into the courtyard, but the wicket gate was closed. Once, it was open day and night, but now a Prince lives within the walls, and treachery takes no account of holy days.

By the time the gate was opened, the others had caught up, but I was still first into the courtyard, the mare's hooves clattering on the cobbles. I looked around, longing to see Elffin or Llew, or any familiar face, but there was only a thin, dark youth who stared at me. I stared back haughtily: he was handsome, but he wasn't Elffin. And then Llew was there, bursting from the house bellowing a welcome, swinging me down and hugging me until I was breathless. I was astounded to be looking up at my little brother.

'Llew! You're huge!'

'I know,' he replied, smugly. 'Welcome home, Rhian.'

I hugged him again, so happy I couldn't speak. I was about to ask for Elffin, but stopped myself in time: my husband and his children were dismounting, and Jack was unloading the pack-horse. Too many ears…

I'd assumed I'd sleep in my old bedchamber: it was a shock when we were taken to the guest lodge instead. Even worse: Rhys would share with me. Beti would sleep in a dormitory with the other little girls visiting with their families, and Ifan would bed down with the youths, but Rhys and I had to share.

'But -' I began, looking from the great bed to Lady Marged's tiring woman, who had ushered us into the chamber. Rhys gripped my upper arm, and his look silenced me. I looked round, frantically. There was a chair in the corner. He could sleep in that. Or maybe on the floor, on a pallet. If he would not, then I should. I couldn't share a bed with him, not with Elffin so close, I couldn't.

A fire burned in the hearth and the room was wonderfully warm after our freezing ride. While Angharad, the tire-woman, unpacked my bags, I gazed out of the window. It was snowing. I hoped it would snow forever. Soon it would be time for supper.

And I would see Elffin.

Elffin

After so many nights in the mountains, home is so normal, so wonderful that it doesn't seem real. I should be the happiest man in the world, except for what Llew said, yesterday. If Angharad and I are common talk, then my mother might find out. She knows everything, eventually. What if Angharad's pregnant? Dewi heard, and he says there are ways to stop a girl falling pregnant. I hadn't given a passing thought to babies, then: but now, God help me, they're with me waking and sleeping! I dream of them, bawling and stinking, great heaps and stacks and piles of babies everywhere, all of them fathered by me! Dewi would tell me if I asked, but I don't want to show my ignorance. Anyway, he'd only torment me, after. Brothers are like that. I wish I'd taken the opportunity then, when he said, and not pretended I was wiser than I am. I don't want babies with Angharad or anyone, yet.

My sister Catherine is home too: she's been living with the Hanmers, learning to be a lady. She's beautiful, Catrin: the bards call her "*Gwenllian of the Golden Locks*", and I was wary of her at first, she seemed so elegant. Then this morning she threw a bit of bread and honey at me, picked up her skirts and ran away shrieking. I chased her, caught her and rubbed honey into her hair to teach her a lesson, and now we're as we were, brother and sister. She'll marry soon, I expect, when Mam finds the right man. *Tad* thinks it's up to him, but it's Mam, really, has the final word. *Tad* deals with the world beyond the household, Mam with everything else! Then Catrin will have babies, because when men and girls go to bed together - no. I don't want to think about babies any more.

Christmas Eve my brothers and I went hunting. The snow made tracking easy, our breath smoked on the air, and only the warmth of the horses and the exercise stopped us freezing to death. We stopped for cold meat and bread at noon, and Siôn and Dewi ambushed Maredydd and Llew with snowballs, and the four of them went down in a flurry of snow, laughing, punching, kicking, wrestling. When we'd brought down a good size stag and Maredydd had been scared by a boar that hurtled from a thicket and surprised us and Llew had shown off by hitting a running rabbit clean through the eye with an arrow, we set off home, arriving just in time to change and get to the great hall for supper. Mam would have skinned us if we'd been late, and we only just made it. My arse had hardly touched the bench when they came, hand in hand, to their seats on the dais. My brothers and I were relegated to the lower tables that night, except Gruffydd and Maredydd, because there were so many guests. I was starving, and crumbled a bit of bread while I waited for the pages to serve the fat pike, stuck with rosemary and glistening with butter. I glanced at the top table. Ap Hywel was on Catrin's right, but where was Rhiannon? I looked again, not finding her, and then, disbelieving, back at the woman on ap Hywel's right. The mass of bright hair was unmistakable, but this girl was lovely in dark green, cut to show off a small, creamy curve of breast. Skinny, plain *Rhiannon?*

Sensing my eyes on her, she looked up. My jaw was hanging like Siôn Twp's. I couldn't look away, and then her gaze shifted to the person next to her, who was speaking to her behind his hand. Was this really little, angry Rhiannon? She turned her head, gracefully acknowledging the page who was serving her with fish, and something pinned to the front of her gown glinted in the light. My heart thumped: I knew what it was.

I don't know how I felt, then. Wistfulness at having missed out, and a strange feeling of premonition: as if a space were opening in my heart to admit something troublesome. Or was it just that Angharad was watching me?

She, of course, was lower down the table, but her eyes hardly left me. She wore Christmas finery, but my eyes strayed to

Rhiannon, time and time again. Sometimes the great grey eyes saw me look, and she bent her head to her platter or turned away, her cheeks colouring.

There was entertainment, after, and Iolo Goch sang a new song about the birth of the Christ child. Mummers performed an amusing play with a bumbling king in it (dubbed Henry, of course, and driven with sticks and yelling, from the hall), and some village men balanced other men on their shoulders, and still more men balanced atop them, and then the topmost men fought with blunt swords, with their heads in the roof beams. Of course they all collapsed in a heap, and we laughed until the tears ran down our faces.

Later, there was Mass to welcome the Christ child, and we crowded into a chapel filled with candlelight, and I stood with my brothers behind our parents. And all the while I was conscious of Rhiannon close behind me. I could almost feel the warmth of her body, and I was hard put not to turn and smile at her.

Afterwards, we said our goodnights, wished for peace (and victory, of course), and went to bed. I'd drunk enough wine to make me drowsy, and was exhausted from the day's hunt, but couldn't sleep. Because of the number of guests, Siôn and Madoc were sharing my room, so even if I'd wanted her, Angharad couldn't have visited me that night. And I didn't want her.

Rhiannon kept me wakeful, and I couldn't say why. There was a hollowness inside me, but also a warmth and delight that filled my soul. The only truly identifiable emotion was amazement: amazement that she had grown so beautiful in so short a time. Amazement that, despite being wed for three months, she wore the trinket I'd so carelessly given her. Amazement that she still seems to have feelings for me.

I stretched in the bed, grinning in the darkness, then turned onto my side, my face pillowed on the palm of my hand. Dawn lightened the sky outside the small window. And eventually, smugly, I slept, dreaming of little breasts, warm in the palms of my hands, and a pair of great, smoky eyes, watching me.

CHAPTER ELEVEN

Llewelyn
I found the bean in my piece of plum cake: I chose Mali to be my Lady of Misrule. Not being immodest, but I was very humorous! Elffin kept filling my wine-cup, and everything I ordered anyone to do, they had to do it. And I had to kiss Mali, and everybody cheered. She went scarlet and wouldn't look at me, but later, as we sat side by side on our mock thrones, her hand crept into mine. I looked at my foster-family, and our neighbours and allies, and felt such affection for them that I had to bite my lip. Perhaps the wine made me sentimental.

Elffin kept looking at Rhiannon, and I thought of ordering him to kiss her, but ap Hywel wasn't joining in the fun so I didn't, for fear of causing problems. But I thought of lots of other amusing things to do: the more I drank, the funnier I got.

I made Gruffydd walk everywhere on tiptoe until midnight on St Stephen's Day. Every time he was caught flat-footed he had to drink some wine, and he was very drunk by noon, when he fell over and had to be put to bed. He was also very sick. Rhiannon laughed until she cried at the sight of sober Gruffydd tottering and blinking like Siôn Twp. Best of all, though, I made Iolo Goch Royal Scapegoat and forbade him to eat anything but bread and water for the whole of Christmas Day. He'll get revenge later, I expect, but it was worth it to see his miserable face as the rest of us feasted on spit-roasted peacock, still in its feathers, and roast goose with quinces and pears. It was a repayment for his treatment of Rhiannon.

She seemed so pleased to be home, at first. I don't think she loves her husband yet. She doesn't hold his hand or touch his sleeve the way Mali does to me, but at first she seemed happy. And then, suddenly, she was not. The day before Twelfth Night she changed from shining girl to silent ghost. Perhaps Gruffydd and her husband quarrelling has upset her. Perhaps she's pregnant. I don't know. All I know is that her joy has gone.

The argument, thank Christ, happened away from *Tadmaeth*'s ears. He would have been furious at such discourtesy to a guest. We were in the solar: Elffin, Siôn and I tossing dice, Gruffydd (now sober) playing chess with ap Hywel; Madoc, chin on hands, watching the game. Ap Hywel won the first bout, and was setting up the board for a second when Gruffydd spoke. 'If you can beat me again, Rhys, I'll give you my horse. If not -' he stroked his chin, as if considering, '- you swear fealty to my father.'

Elffin, stopped the dice-cup in mid-rattle. The silence bristled.

'Easy for you, cousin. Your horse against my lands, my livelihood and likely my life. I'm de Grey's tenant, and I won't risk what I have on hopeless dreams.'

Elffin slammed down the cup. 'Hopeless? Man, we've hardly begun. You're a kinsman twice over! You of all people owe him your support.'

'I owe him nothing: we're distant cousins, that's all. I took the girl for her dowry and because your mother wanted rid of her. I'm here purely because I didn't want to antagonise Glyndŵr. If de Grey finds out, I'm ruined.'

Gruffydd leaned across the table menacingly, scattering chessmen. 'Perhaps you're spying for de Grey?'

'Should de Grey ask me questions, I'll answer - truthfully.'

I thought Gruffydd might hit him: he lurched forward, upsetting the table and making ap Hywel flinch, but Madoc stepped in. 'Whatever his loyalties, Gruffydd, he is our guest and our kinsman -' he glanced at ap Hywel '- however lightly he regards us. In the end he answers to his own conscience, as we all do.'

It would have been better if they could have left that same day, but snow was still falling, and the drifts were high around Sycharth, so they were trapped until the thaw.

Once Christmas was over, *Tadmaeth* got down to business. Hour after hour they talked, he and those of his allies under his roof, and sometimes Crach Ffinnant was there with his spells and smoke and sinister predictions, although no one saw him come or go. Rhys ap Hywel was not included.

I caught Elffin with Angharad in the stables yesterday. Elffin shares a room, as I do, but he shares his with his brothers. I, for my sins (which are not as many as I'd like) have to share with ap Hywel's brat, whom I dislike almost as much as Tomos. At least Tomos takes on my duties so that I can chase Mali: Ifan is a lout and a coward. If he's beaten in the tiltyard he sulks, so none of the other boys will fight him, and I caught him burning the turnspit dog's arse with a coal when Bron wasn't about, while the poor creature yelped and scuffled and rattled the wheel round. I let it out, after I'd clouted Ifan and made his nose bleed, and took it to Huw to heal. I found Bron another little dog, although I wanted to stuff Ifan into the wheel instead. I feel sorry for Rhiannon, living with him.

Sorry for her for other reasons too, though I don't know what they are. The argument between Gruffydd and ap Hywel is common knowledge now. Maybe she's torn between her husband and Gruffydd. Perhaps that's why she is miserable.

Rhiannon

Rhys and Gruffydd have quarrelled, and Christmas is over. I sit at table and Rhys sits sullenly beside me, eating little and drinking a great deal, and I'm afraid of him. I'm afraid of him because he sleeps in my bed. I scramble into my bed gown and hurry under the covers before he comes in, and lie frozen waiting for his breathing to take on the slow rhythms of sleep. Then I relax, though I dare not sleep. I'm so tired that twice yesterday sitting with Lady Marged I dropped my needlework. She stopped in mid-sentence and frowned at me.

'Rhiannon, go to your chamber and rest. Your eyes are near shutting with tiredness. Go, child, now.'

Gratefully, knowing ap Hywel was elsewhere and I could sleep, I dragged myself up the stairs, my head buzzing with exhaustion. I closed the shutters, took off my gown and left it where it fell, and sank gratefully onto the bed. I slept so deeply that there were no dreams, and I knew nothing more until I awoke in the middle of the night to darkness and a groping hand.

I opened my mouth to scream, smelled wine-heavy breath and knew. His hand sealed my mouth while it lasted, and it was shame and pain and humiliation and horror. My flailing hand found the little silver fox under my pillow. In the morning I had deep cuts on my fingers from the sharp metal. Morning was a long time coming: I lay aching beside his snoring body and wondered how I could still live. I hated him and prayed for death before the sun rose.

But rise it did, and me with it, breakfasting in bruised silence, going about my duties, such as they were, since I am a guest, finally creeping to sit with Lady Marged and stitch and prick my fingers and wish for death. At least Elffin would never know. I wouldn't come back here, ever. I'd never see him again. It would hurt less that way. I'd spoken to him twice in the last few days, careless, casual words of friendship, and once he'd touched my hand. Warmth rushed through me and left me trembling. I'll take care he doesn't find me alone again. It would be more than I could bear.

Lady Marged tried to include me in conversations, but my mind wouldn't work and my voice sounded strange when I spoke. At last, she dismissed everyone but me.

'What ails you, child? Are you pregnant?' she asked, bluntly.

I shook my head. 'I don't know. I might be. But not yet.'

She looked puzzled, but did not pursue it. 'Rhys is kind?'

What could I say? He *wasn't* unkind - except that he had used me as I supposed all husbands used their wives, but there had been no affection in it, no care for me. So much for the reassurances about the bed thing: she and Crisiant had lied to me. So I pleaded homesickness. I'd be better when we were home, I said, knowing that leaving Elffin would finish me, and also that I couldn't stay, not now.

'Well, the weather is improving. And when you leave, you shall take Angharad with you! I've spoken to Rhys, who has agreed. She will be your tiring woman.' She smiled with satisfaction at a blessing bestowed. 'What do you think of that?'

What did it matter? I'd still be living with Rhys ap Hywel. But at Pentregoch, perhaps he wouldn't want to sleep with me any more. Perhaps I could talk about home with Angharad when no one was listening. I picked up my sewing again. The needle picked in and out of the fabric, the winter sun through the window was warm on my back, and I heard the slow drip of melting snow.

Elffin

Mam sent for Angharad this morning. I hid in the stable and quaked. Later, when Angharad told me she was being sent to Pentregoch as Rhiannon's tiring-woman, my knees almost gave way with relief. Angharad howled and wailed, and I patted her, but all I felt was relief. I'm safe: Mam doesn't know anything. When Angharad's gone, I'll be more careful. Angharad isn't speaking to me, but she follows me anyway, glaring accusingly from reddened eyes.

I'll miss her when she goes, I expect, but soon I'll be too busy for women. When the roads are open the King will be about again, and we'll probably find ourselves in the mountains once more - where there are no women anyway!

That old rogue Gruffydd ap Dafydd has joined us. De Grey called him "the strongest thief of Wales", after Gruffydd raided his lands and appropriated a sizeable portion of de Grey's stables - the pride of which is currently residing here at Sycharth. The King's gift to de Grey, the stallion is being pampered by Huw like some fabulous unicorn. De Grey threw an almighty tantrum at his loss, hurling goblets and candlesticks at his stewards, overturning chairs, all the while cursing Gruffydd and promising to burn him out and hang any man that supported him.

Gruffydd's reply was hardly conciliatory: "as many men as you kill, and as many houses that you burn for my sake, I'll burn and slay for your sake, and I don't doubt I'll fill up on your bread and ale into the bargain". Crusty old bastard that he is, he's a man after all our hearts, and he's looking for a leader. And *Tad* is it: a thousand like him and we'll carry Wales - *Duw,* and England too!

The snows are melting: after a bitter December, it's now unseasonably warm, and where once there were unbroken fields of white, each day more green appears. The river has burst its banks, but when it subsides Rhys ap Hywel will be gone and the air will be cleaner for his absence. I'll miss Angharad, but I'll miss Rhiannon more.

The first few days she was here, her eyes followed me, and I managed to talk to her once or twice, but now she seems to be avoiding me. I don't think I've upset or offended her, and it bothers me. Perhaps ap Hywel is too old to please her. I admit, thoughts of bedding her occurred more often than were good for me. I began to look for her - just to talk, mind - I'm an honourable man, and ap Hywel is our guest despite everything.

Ah, she'll change, I dare say, once she has a baby - she'll get fat and dote on the brat, forget all about me and probably never wear the silver pin again. Anyway, she's going and so's Angharad too, thank God, so I can stop fretting that Mam will find out. Once she's gone I'll talk to Dewi and ask him how not to get babies on women.

What will this year hold? Henry, bothered by Scotland, won't want an expensive war with Wales too, and perhaps if *Tad* gave in and surrendered Croesor to de Grey, the King might pardon him. But in my heart I know he won't surrender anything, especially not to de Grey. Anyway, de Grey is hell-bent on revenge, so we must stand up for our rights. Mind, there's pride here, now, where before there was none. Men stand taller, and their names lengthen daily as ancestors are disinterred from distant memory and added to their heritage.

When Angharad has gone I'll rid myself of the ridge of fat that Christmas has left. Llew's mooning after Mali. I'll hook him out, give him some exercise. Perhaps it will stop me thinking of Rhiannon.

CHAPTER TWELVE

Llewelyn

I miss Rhiannon, but Sycharth is a happier place now Rhys has gone: after the quarrel the atmosphere was unpleasant. Maredydd and Madoc, to their credit, did their best to hide their feelings, but Gruffydd, Siôn and Elffin left any room ap Hywel entered.

Ifan tattled to Bron that I'd stolen her turnspit dog, but I'd already told her and found her another poor creature to twirl her roasts. She boxed Ifan's ears and threw him out of her kitchen. She doesn't hold with cruelty, she said, which made me hide a grin, because she's none too gentle if her meat's burning, but a person who causes pain for enjoyment is no sort of person at all, to Bron's way of thinking, and I agree with her.

Before they left, as Rhian's brother and head of the family I had a word with Ifan. He's older than I and taller, but I'm broader, stronger - and braver, if I say it myself. If I could scare him enough, perhaps Rhian would have an easier time living with him. Besides, I have a personal score to settle. He's been lurking round the stables trying to catch Mali and me - well, you understand. I grabbed him by the scruff of his scrawny neck and marched him behind the stables, where I clouted him. 'Right,' I said, after, 'upset my sister and I'll wind your guts round your ears and knot 'em under your chin, understood?' Instead of quaking in his boots, however, he smirked.

'Your sister! My father'll fill her belly soon and if she dies in childbirth, who cares? She's can be replaced. Like Elffin's whore. I'll fuck her, soon, and you can tell Elffin that, if you like.'

'Angharad? You? My boy,' I said loftily, from the great height of my personal experience, 'find a snake and practise on that. Angharad's out of your league.'

His face flamed. 'Watch out, you. My father's got you sister's dowry and he doesn't need her now. I expect he'll get rid of her soon.' He chuckled. 'Might even kill her. You might suspect, but you'll never know. Accidents happen, and who's to know?'

I didn't think ap Hywel would harm Rhiannon, but Ifan was another matter. He was capable of just about anything. He saw my face, then, and ran.

Next day, they left. Rhian clung to me, wordless, while her husband stared stonily ahead, the little girl, Beti, clinging to his back. Ifan gazed down at us from his mount, a smirk twitching the corners of his mouth while Jack, their foreman, loaded the pack-horse.

Angharad slumped on her mare, face blotched with tears, nose running, looking for Elffin, who, wisely, had taken himself off. What did she expect? He's a man and she was willing: that's all there was to it - at least according to Elffin!

But Rhian's my sister, and I hated to see her unhappy. All I could do was help her mount, and stand helplessly watching as they rode away. There was a lump in my throat fit to choke a pig. I watched their dark shapes dwindle, and then, as the party reached the ford, Jack, ap Hywel's foreman, cantered back, reining his horse in beside me. He's well-mannered for a servant, which is probably why Rhys uses him as escort: strong enough to protect, a handy swordsman, and yet civilised enough not to cause offence in a great household like our own. He'd hardly spoken to me while he was here, but I'd seen him around, and noted his behaviour. He gave the impression of having been born to better things than his present position.

'Give me a coin, Llew,' he said, holding out his hand.

'What?'

'You lost to me at cards, Llew. You forgot to pay.'

I stared at him. I'd never gambled with him in my life. But something in his eyes made me fumble for a coin. He tossed it in his big hand.

His voice was soft: 'I'm Glyndŵr's man, Llew, to the death. I'll protect Rhiannon as if she were my own sister. Some things I can't prevent, she's ap Hywel's wife, damn him, but Ifan won't harm her while I have breath, I promise.' Wheeling his horse, he spurred it on, catching up with the fast disappearing riders.

My attention was taken by a hand clutching the back of my neck in a grip that was relentless, if (for Dewi) reasonably friendly.

'Llew, lad,' he said, shaking me like the barn cat. 'Just the person I need.'

I racked my brains to try to remember what I hadn't done. His boots were oiled, his sword honed - I'd even groomed his horse this morning, which wasn't my job but had taken my mind off Rhiannon. Silence was best: excuses when I knew what I'd done wrong. He propelled me round to the back of the stables, where he released me and leaned against the wall, eyeing me. 'Mali,' he said, amiably.

My heart sank into my boots. 'Mali?' The word came out as half croak, half squeak.

'Have you fucked her yet, Llew?'

'God, no, Dewi!' I squawked, my face flooding hot.

'Not for want of trying, Llew.'

'I haven't - I didn't - I w-'

'Oh, spare me! You're fifteen, with a cock, and the girl's willing. But Mam will fillet you if she falls pregnant. You'll end up supporting the brat, at the very least.'

I'd been trying to bed Mali since Christmas Eve, it was now well into January, and I was feeling fairly confident of imminent success. Babies hadn't crossed my mind.

'God, look at your face. There are ways, my boy, for a man to take his pleasure and not concern himself with the results...'

And in a few brief sentences of a practical nature, involving something that was so simple that I couldn't understand why it hadn't occurred to me, he enlightened me.

Feeling manly once more, I shook my head, admiringly. 'However do you know stuff like that, Dewi?'

Dewi chuckled. 'I was told, little brother, just as I've told you.'

'Does Elffin know?'

His grin grew wider. 'I don't know. I did broach the subject, but he said he knew everything there was to know, and probably more. You know Elffin. Perhaps you should tell him, just in case?'

I felt I might enjoy educating Elffin.

Rhiannon
Half-way home, I lost my temper. I was leaving the home I'd loved since childhood, my brother and my love, and I was dry-eyed. And there was Angharad howling and snotty and bawling like a banshee. She'd sniffled and hiccupped and sobbed, and I'd had enough. I pushed my hood back so she'd be in no doubt about my feelings.

'Shut up,' I hissed. 'There's no one on this earth as miserable as I am. Am I weeping and wailing? No, I'm not, and if you don't stop I'll give you something to cry about.'

Her mouth fell open. I'd never spoken to anyone like that before (except possibly Llew. And Elffin, once), and it shocked her to silence, which, apart from odd stifled sobs, lasted until we reached Pentregoch.

Jack helped me dismount, as always, but then, unexpectedly, he gripped both my forearms in his and squeezed, sharply, before releasing me. Startled, I looked up. His face was impassive, but his eyes were, without question, friendly and compassionate. I felt a sudden sense of comfort: was he on my side? Someone to talk to if despair threatened?

Inside, the fire roared in the kitchen chimney, and Gwen had broth simmering. We sat around the wooden table, and by the time the hot, thick liquid had disappeared from the bowls, the colour had returned to Beti's cheeks and even I felt better, especially since Jack sat opposite me and, although his face was turned resolutely towards his food, his presence warmed me as much as the broth.

Angharad would be tiring woman to both Beti and me, and when we'd eaten and Gwen was clearing away, I took her upstairs to the attic room where she was to sleep. She carried her belongings in, and I left her. I had no patience with her: how dared she? I had far more right to be miserable than she. I had a horrible feeling I might have to share a bed with ap Hywel that night, and he would want to do That again. He seemed to want to do it every night. At least it didn't hurt so much, now, and when he'd finished he turned his back to me and snored, so I could sleep a little then.

It didn't take long for me to realise that my nightly ordeals were far from private: Ifan's chamber was next to ours and I knew he listened while his father grunted and heaved on top of me. I felt humiliated, shamed, and his knowing look told me he knew it.

We'd been home a few weeks when we heard that the English Parliament had discussed the "Welsh problem". Some of *Tadmaeth*'s erstwhile allies have accepted Henry's offer of clemency and escaped punishment: his brother Tudur chief among them, and Hywel ap Madog Cyffin of St Asaph and even Crach Ffinnant, the sorcerer. Crach Ffinnant is a slippery old devil, and is forever saying one thing and doing another, so he'll swing in the wind like a weathervane. Parliament, though, is uneasy: the Marcher Lords are worried, and Rhys rubbed his hands with satisfaction when he heard of the measures in place to curb we Welsh in our own God-given land.

We Welsh may not hold high office; Henry's castles are to be strengthened and their keepers will be *Sais,* not Welsh; the people of the Marches have the right to vicious reprisals against Welshmen - no proof required. No Welshman may marry a *Sais* wife, or get wealth from the *Sais,* or even live in England. This will drive out the remaining Welsh students at Oxford and Cambridge, which will swell *Tadmaeth's* numbers - but with such sanctions, can we survive? Maybe they'll have the opposite effect and people will be so incensed by it they'll flock to *Tadmaeth*'s side. Perhaps these restrictions will be Henry's downfall.

Ap Hywel was content, but I was furious. I hid it, of course. But I was in the still-room one morning, fetching dried fennel to settle Angharad's queasy stomach, when Jack appeared in the doorway. We shared a few moments of companionship and indignation against the *Sais* and I felt better for it. Angharad is crying again, and I wish to God that Lady Marged had kept her.

Elffin

The King has offered pardons to Anglesey, Caernarfon and Merioneth, but not to *Tad,* or Rhys and Gwilym ap Tudur of Penmynydd. They're family, though they're opportunists, and being against the *Sais,* they are, however tenuously, our allies. Henry thought he had us under control, but then Rhys and Gwilym struck - hard - when it was least expected. That they chose Good Friday is neither here nor there, though there are some who say that it's mortal sin to attack on the most sacred day of the Christian calendar. Rhys and Gwilym, however, are not men to be dictated to by either Church or chivalry, and they laid their plans so well that a certain unholy joy stirs, sin or not. Anyway, with a price already on their heads, what did they have to lose?

John Massy of Cheshire is custodian at Conwy - or was, for his King descended on him like the wrath of God for his negligence, outlawed him and stripped him of his lands. Massy held a garrison of fifteen men-at-arms and sixty archers, well prepared for a siege with food and water. Masons were about like ants, strengthening Conwy's walls and defences, but Massy is a pious man. He and all but five of his men were on their knees in church when our sinful kinsmen struck. A "harmless carpenter" knocked politely at the castle gate claiming he'd been sent to do some urgent work inside. And they let him in!

He overcame the two gatehouse guards and opened the gates to Gwilym, Hywel and forty others. Rhys Ddu of Erddreiniog and the rest of the band infiltrated the area around the castle and the streets of the town, and by the time Massy had got off his knees, the town was ablaze from end to end and the castle was taken. The King was at Denbigh when they told him he'd lost Conwy. He's besieging the castle, but he'll never get it back.

Daily, small bands of men ride out from Sycharth; we burn and steal, but this is war, and a man not for us is a man against us. As always the poor suffer, and the foot-soldiers that fight while their lords hide behind castle walls. Sooner or later the time will come when Henry visits Sycharth, but by the time they get here we'll be long gone. These are our mountains, and they'll shelter us.

I keep busy: to be honest I'm missing Angharad: she was willing, and here, and now she's not. So deprived did I feel in that department last week that I was all but ready to visit Anwen, but there's a rumour that she gave Elis Hairless the pox. Therefore I was in no mood for Llew the other day (though I was grateful for the information because now I shan't need to ask).

I had to pretend I already knew, of course. I arranged my face in a tolerant expression, but let him talk. Mind, it's damned annoying to find this out now Angharad's gone. She's probably barren, since what we did should have given her babies by the dozen. Still, now I know, I'll be more careful in future.

I think of Rhiannon sometimes, and wonder how she is. I hope she isn't pregnant: childbirth is dangerous. Besides, ap Hywel's a traitor, and I'd rather Rhiannon didn't bear his brats. The thought of her sleeping with him disturbs me: I don't think she loves him and the idea of them together is unpleasant.

Last night I couldn't sleep. I went out to walk in the courtyard despite the cold. The gate was unlocked and the gate-keeper snored on his cot, a flask of wine hugged to his chest. I clouted him awake and stood over him as he locked and barred the gate, then I clouted him again for his carelessness, and pointed out that in the event of a visit from Henry or de Grey, his guts would be the first ones spilled since he would be most convenient. Much later, I wondered where the wine had come from: gate-keeper's pay doesn't run to luxuries. I lay awake then for another hour, with a mouse scrabbling in my brain wondering if someone had bribed our gate-porter. I slept eventually, none the wiser, but I'm on my guard now.

Rhys ap Hywel's man Jack is for *Tad*, Llew says. He'll be some protection for Rhiannon, and may bring news of her sometimes. And Angharad, of course. Perhaps I'll ride over with Llew. But - given the unpleasantness at Christmas, probably better not.

Women are strange: here we are preparing for all-out war, and Mother is trying to marry me off to my Hanmer cousin Elizabeth! I'm not ready for marriage. Time enough to settle down when I'm old, and *Tad* rules all Wales and we are at peace again.

CHAPTER THIRTEEN

Llewelyn
They call him "Hotspur", and he seems to be everywhere, and Gruffydd says he's a worthy opponent. The King, however, is disinclined to pay for the war Hotspur is trying to win for him, which is poor reward for a hero.

Hotspur is currently busy recovering Conwy from Rhys and Gwilym ap Tudur, though we temporarily distracted him by attacking Dolgellau. We were all but finished when he caught up with us. The fight was short, but we gave as good as we got and drove him off. Dolgellau and its environs are ours, and even Hotspur is lost when there are valleys and hills and rocks and forests for us to hide in, and strike from.

So he withdrew to Denbigh, and *Tadmaeth* and those closest to him took refuge in the mountains. Some speculate on why *Tadmaeth* hasn't helped the Penmynydd brothers at Conwy, but he has kept his own counsel on that. His reasons will be clear in good time.

After Rhiannon left, a brief thaw turned snow to slush and rivers to icy torrents, but after, a hard, bitter January brought great hillocks and billows of snow that froze, and then more snow again, so that travel was impossible. *Tadmaeth* and my foster-brothers thrashed and paced in frustration, driving Lady Marged wild with their restlessness and muddy boots.

Crach Ffinnant arrived just before the snow. I think he's a traitor for accepting Henry's pardon, but he's constantly at *Tadmaeth*'s side. *Tadmaeth* spends time on his knees in the Chapel, but also seems to need the Crab, with his potions and incantations. I don't know if I'd want to see my future - what if I saw my death? As far as I'm concerned the future can take care of itself and I'll worry about it when it happens.

I don't like Crach Ffinnant. His wintry eyes skewer me. I avoid him, mostly, in case he can read my mind - I'm afraid of what he is, and sees, and knows.

It was March before we could travel, and Easter before any significant news reached us. In between I practised with my sword, or at the butts (I am still the best archer at Sycharth) or straining to heft the full-size lance Elffin gave me, slithering around a straw-strewn tiltyard. The first time I picked it up I thought my eyes would pop out, but it's getting easier, and my shoulders don't ache much any more. Now I have Sioned, I'm better at riding and controlling my weapons. She's so easy: a slight pressure of knee, a twitch of a rein and she responds. I haven't fallen off for ages. Sometimes I dream about riding her into battle, my sword singing in my hand, cutting down the enemy like ripe corn. Like my father, in Scotland with *Tadmaeth*.

Also in those short, snow-burdened months, when I was not in the tilt-yard, I was with Mali. I shouldn't like this to get around, you understand, but I've done It at last! Spring was in the air and I gave her a ride on Sioned. My arms went round her waist, her hair tickling my face, and when we came to a secluded spot in the woods I tumbled her off and we did it in a bed of snowdrops. Mind, I put down my cloak, first, so she wouldn't have wet grass under her, and it took me a bit to persuade her, but she let me, in the end. She cried, after, but I *cwtched* her and told her I'd look after her, always, and said she definitely wouldn't have a baby, because I did what Dewi said, although it was difficult. I gave her a red ribbon Rhian left behind. Mali earned her love-token, and Rhiannon won't miss it.

Mind, she's different, now, Mali. Though it was *me* that took *her*, I can't help feeling she took something from me, too. It's as if she owns me - or thinks she does. I belong to no one except *Tadmaeth* for whom I'd gladly die - though I hope it won't come to that.

It was a relief to head south: the lowland men are ready to join us, but Glyndŵr needs to go South for it to happen. We're camped at Pen Pumlumon Fawr, which is easy to defend and well hidden. From here we can strike easily north and south.

At night I look up at the immensity of the sky - and of what we are doing. We're few, but we're Welsh, and one Welshman is worth a hundred *Sais*.

Our camp is above Cwm Hyddgen, where two nights ago *Tadmaeth* made a covenant between the *uchelwyr* of the North, his kinsmen and those few from the South attracted by a Wales free of England. No turning back, now: *Tadmaeth* is outlawed, as are we all, and capture will mean death - at the very least. Some deaths are merciful: others are not.

Five hundred of us here, and at night fires glow, illuminating faces as they shift and turn. There are a few women, but they aren't Mali. She may be only a kitchen girl, but I miss her.

We'd been in the mountains a few days when Jack brought messages from Rhian and also news of de Grey's movements. He spoke with Elffin privately, since when he's been in a filthy mood, God knows why. I don't think it's fair to be cursed when I'm only making a joke.

I accompanied Jack a little way when he left, his horse ambling beside us. He's a powerful, taciturn man, but his manners let me speak without guarding my words. 'Is she happy, Jack?' I asked, hoping Rhian was settled in her new life.

'No. I imagine ap Hywel beds her, but she'd not welcome his child. She's homesick, and it's a loveless marriage. Besides,' he continued, his hand rasping across his whiskers, 'If her man supported Glyndŵr it might make some difference, but knowing he's de Grey's is more than she can bear. Ifan plagues her, ap Hywel is irritable or indifferent, and she is lonely.'

'She has you.'

'And how much use d'you think I can be?' He gazed down the valley. 'I'm nobody, Llew, just a Jack-of-all-trades. Rhiannon's better off than some. I came through the remains of a village on my way here, after de Grey's men had visited, and there was a girl there with a look of Rhiannon about the eyes. She'd been raped and she was half mad with it. Rhiannon, thank God, is spared that.'

'It's part of war, Jack.'

'I've seen war, Llew. Why make miserable people even more miserable?'

He left, then, carrying messages for Rhiannon from me, and I didn't see him again until afterwards...

Rhiannon

Now I understand why Lady Marged gave me Angharad. I don't know why I didn't guess sooner. She vomited every morning all January and half of February, only I was too preoccupied to put two and two together. Or one and one and make baby, which is what's actually happened. It's due late summer. Hywel's furious: Lady Marged has given him another problem.

'Slut!' he shouted at her, and went to hit her. 'No man to take you off my hands - and none likely to want you.'

She cowered, but he didn't follow through. He slammed out of the house, rattling the pots on the dresser. I feel sorry for her: she doesn't want to be here any more than I do, and it's bad enough having to do the bed thing, without getting pregnant into the bargain.

I asked her who the child's father was.

She turned away. 'I'm sorry, Mrs Rhian, I can't tell you.'

Perhaps she didn't know. Perhaps she did it with more than one man! Why would anyone *want* to do that? At least now everyone knows, she's stopped crying. Little Beti is taken with the idea of a baby: but Ifan, predictably, sees not the coming child but the act that made it, and touches Angharad when he thinks no one's watching. Yesterday I caught him trying to put his hand inside her bodice. I threatened to tell his father if he didn't leave her alone, but he sneered.

'D'you think he'd care? She's a whore.'

'She's not, Ifan.' I could feel my temper rising to explosion point. 'She's a woman as your mother was, as I am, and as Our Lady was, and you should respect her.'

He spat, the gobbet landing on Angharad's skirt. 'She's a filthy slut, and so are you.'

Angharad wrestled the soup ladle away from me: sadly, I only managed to clout him once, but you would have thought I'd half-killed him, the way he screamed. He told Rhys, of course, but his father was preoccupied and ignored him.

Next morning when I woke, ap Hywel had gone. I washed his smell from my body and went downstairs. The kitchen door was wide into the garden, and dust-fairies danced in the shafts of sunlight streaking the flagstones. Perhaps I should have thought "spring-cleaning", and set the servants to work, but instead I thought, "air" and "sunshine". I left Angharad to supervise Beti, Elin and Gwen, and went across the cobbled yard to the stables. Jack was checking the mare's hooves for stray stones.

He turned his face towards me, the mare's foot braced against his thigh. His smile was genuine: at least one person here was pleased to see me. 'Mrs Rhiannon?' he said.

'I can't stay inside in weather like this, Jack,' I said, tying my hair back with a ribbon. 'I thought I'd ride in the woods for an hour.'

He straightened, releasing the mare's foot, and leaned on her broad back, his face ruddy with cold air and exertion. 'Ride?' he frowned. 'On your own?'

'Why not? What's going to happen to me, ap Hywel's wife and Glyndŵr's foster-daughter. I cover both sides, don't I?' I said bitterly.

'Men don't bother with introductions before they rape. If you ride, I go with you. Your husband would kill me if anything happened to you.'

'I doubt that. Delighted to be rid of me, more likely.' I'd been silent too long: my tongue was off and running.

Jack frowned. 'Is life so terrible?'

I kicked a loose cobblestone across the yard. 'No. It isn't terrible. It's just not particularly worth living at the moment. And for God's sake, Jack, call me Rhiannon.'

'If ap Hywel heard me so familiar with you -'

'Then when he can't hear, Jack. Please?'

'Rhiannon it is, then.'

It was partly the joy of being in the open air; being away from Pentregoch; delight in the company of someone uncritical, that made that spring morning memorable. We rode through lakes of bluebells, dew splashing my skirts to the knee; disturbed rabbits and alarmed deer, and rode for miles through the rolling lower slopes of the mountains. I was delirious with Spring. We stopped at the edge of a coppice. My hair had come down, and I laughed as I shoved it out of my eyes. Suddenly, Jack clapped a hand across my mouth, simultaneously grabbing the bridle to pull the mare back into the trees.

A small war-party in de Grey livery was riding up the hill. We slid silently to the ground, holding our horses' muzzles to stop them betraying us, and backed further into the trees. The men seemed in no particular hurry: their pace a fast walk rather than a canter. When they were out of earshot Jack gazed after them, frowning.

'Heading for Glyndyfrdwy. I must warn them, but - ' he glanced helplessly at me. I understood at once.

'Go on,' I urged. 'You go. I'll be all right. *Go on!*'

He hesitated a moment before galloping down the hill to get to Glyndyfrdwy before the de Grey's men.

When I reached home I turned the mare out into the paddock before going inside. Jack or the stable-boy would see to it later. Angharad, hands on hips, was standing over Gwen, who was half-heartedly scrubbing the flagstones. Beti was "helping" Elin make bread, her face spattered with flour. Ifan was nowhere to be seen, happily: the less I saw of my step-son, the better.

I stank of horse-sweat, so I washed and changed, careful to remove the silver fox and hide it before hanging my soiled gown on a bush in the garden to air.

Ifan, smiling, appeared beside me like a malignant spirit.

Now *that* worried me.

Elffin

My father's cousins, Gwilym ap Tudur and Rhys Ddu of Erddreiniog, the brothers of Penmynydd, have shamed us all. We cheered when they captured Conwy, even if they did it on Good Friday ~ but they betrayed their comrades to save their own skins. They handed over nine of their own men, shackled like criminals, to Hotspur. The brothers escaped with their miserable lives while nine brave Welshmen were drawn and quartered for Henry's entertainment. My father is incandescent with anger.

De Grey is about again: Jack, apparently, made it to Glyndyfrdwy ahead of a raiding party, and as a result de Grey's men were beaten off and we lost only a few sheep.

Llew said he'd known Jack supported *Tad* since Christmas. He said he'd promised to take care of Rhiannon. I had a powerful urge to box his ears for his smug grin, but I sleep better now I know she has an ally. Though Ifan's a snake, and ap Hywel himself is dangerous, tied by tenancy to de Grey and yet with a kinsman's foot in our camp.

It's hard to know who are friends and who not: I don't trust Tomos of Ynys Môn, for instance. He's fond of lurking behind doors. In face he's offered to take my duty at *Tad*'s door so often I refuse him on principle now.

One man of whose treachery we are sure: Hywel Sele of Nannau, who has allied himself with Hotspur against his own. Nannau once belonged to my ancestor, Cadwgan ap Bleddyn, Prince of Powys, but Sele has it now. He's Welsh, but doesn't support us. We'd waited to see which direction he'd go: Hywel Sele values his own skin above all else. Then we learned he'd invited Hotspur to Dolgellau! In June, Hotspur's army arrived, and we were there to welcome him, battling in the shadow of Cader Idris, and neither side gave quarter. Hotspur's powerful, and if he weren't English, a man I could admire. Once, *Tad* was surrounded and might have been captured, but my brothers and I went in like fiends to get him out of it. We gained no advantage, but neither did Hotspur. It's possible he's tired of fighting us, because he's gone off to Scotland, so for a while we can forget him.

Once he'd gone, we wasted no time at all in sorting out Hywel Sele. *Tad*, my brothers and I visited Nannau and captured him. On the way back I was riding side by side with Dewi; Llew on Sioned trailing a little behind us, singing softly to himself as we crossed the narrow stone bridge at Dolgellau, the sun warm on our backs. Our prisoner was neatly parcelled, the butt of much well-meaning advice from his captors, and then the day turned from triumph almost to complete disaster because we were too relaxed. Thank God Llew was in the rear, because the man immediately in front of us took an arrow in the throat and crashed off his horse, eyes bulging, blood staining his jerkin.

Sele's son-in-law, Gruffydd ap Gwyn, had chosen a good place for ambush: he had two hundred men, and surprise. He trapped us in the confines of the bridge, our party riding single file across it. They shot half-a-dozen men before we could react, and the subsequent skirmish was fierce and bloody. I personally killed eleven men, and when we left there were nearly a hundred dead and many more wounded, including Dewi, who has a wound in the thigh, not serious, thank God, and it's clean, but he won't ride for a while.

At the end, we still had Sele. Not a happy man by any means, but I dare say he'll be ransomed soon enough. He might even change to our side, but probably not. He's a stubborn old bastard, and believes we'll fail. We won't. More and more are joining us, and almost the whole of North Wales is ours as well as parts of mid Wales.

I should be a happy man, sleeping like a hog in a sty, smiles for dawn and dark - except for the other news Jack brought. I was sitting on the riverbank, and the roar of the river hid the sound of his approach. He touched my shoulder and squatted on his heels beside me, rubbing the side of his nose with his forefinger. He was silent for a good while, and I glanced at him enquiringly.

'Looking for a bit of peace away from the women?' I asked, grinning.

'There's something you need to know, Elffin. Not sure you'll be glad to hear it, mind.'

My mind leapt instantly to Rhiannon. I was wrong.

Briefly (and without the hint of a grin, fair play) he told me that Angharad is pregnant. I opened and shut my mouth because I couldn't think of anything useful to say.

'Do you think it's mine?' I ventured at last.

'Come on, Elffin! You had her seven ways from Sunday before Lady Marged got rid of her. She didn't have time to go with anyone else, even if she'd had the inclination!'

'Oh,' was all I could think of to say. 'Thanks for telling me, Jack.' Though I wished he hadn't.

When he'd gone I wondered who else knew. Rhiannon, of course, which made me cringe. Ap Hywel and his brat. Mam? I offered up fervent prayers for Mam's ignorance. Fortunately we were soon away from Sycharth and even if she found out I wouldn't be there for her to be skewered by my lady mother's tongue...

CHAPTER FOURTEEN

Llewelyn

Outnumbered three to one, taken by surprise in the worst possible place. All four hundred of us should have died in Hyddgen's green bowl, our main force oblivious to our fate. It might have been different, and would have, if I hadn't quarrelled with Elffin and taken myself off to sulk.

He's touchy as a wasps' nest lately. I made a little joke - man to man - about Angharad, and he erupted!

'Mind your business, Llew and grow up. *Cae de geg,* keep it shut, all right?'

My temper was up as fast as Elffin's. 'I'm as much a man as you. You had Angharad, I've had Mali, so there.'

Then I thought it might be wise to leave, because Elffin had that look in his eyes that meant pain if I hung around. I caught Sioned, and made myself scarce.

So, there I was, sitting overlooking the valley, the camp tucked in its hollow half a mile back, nursing my woes and thinking of incisive remarks I might have made if I'd thought of them in time.

At first I thought heat haze was distorting my vision, but then I saw the unmistakeable glint of sun on metal: a large force was approaching. I didn't wait to identify them: who they were didn't matter. There were four hundred men in the camp, relaxed, thinking themselves secure. I'm a bad judge of numbers, but even I could tell that there were more of them than us! Sioned, peacefully cropping the grass behind me, was surprised into a half-rear by the thump of my arse hitting her back: I kicked her into a gallop and she stretched her neck and went. I rode into camp shrieking and waving my arms: Elffin stared open-mouthed as I hurtled past him. *Tadmaeth* was in his tent, Rhys Gethin and the Crab with him: they looked up, startled, as I burst in.

'Coming,' I gasped out, 'up the hill.' I wasn't making sense, but the right words wouldn't come.

'Who is, Llew?' *Tadmaeth* asked kindly, forefinger stroking his greying beard.

'Army!' I croaked. 'Huge army! Coming fast!'

Then they were gone, raising the alarm, buckling on swords and strapping on armour as they ran. Men tumbled from tents and leapt from where they'd been lazing: we shouldn't have been ready, but we were as ready as we could possibly be given the time we had.

My hands shook as I buckled on body-armour, tugged on my helm, the leather snug against my skull, and strapped on my sword. My bow was strung, arrows protruding from the cloth bag across my back. We were armed and ready, but also trapped. Every man recognised that we were doomed. And every man fought like a demon anyway.

The Flemings (foreign wool-weavers that infest Benfro, Caerfyrddin and Ceredigion) had the high ground. Their lands and benefits *Sais*-granted, they chafed at the prospect of losing them. Determined to rid themselves of Owain Glyndŵr, they thought to make a surprise attack on us. We were surrounded, and any military tactician worth his salt would have sucked his hollow tooth and pronounced us dead. They were a thousand and a half, by Elffin's estimate, and we were less than five hundred. We should have been slaughtered, but we fought. How we fought!

The battle is a blur, and I remember only flashes of it. Uphill, the closing ring of mailed men, sun glinting on swords and shields. My heart pounded. I'd vowed to die for *Tadmaeth*: looked like I'd be doing it sooner than planned. *Tadmaeth* had told me to run if I had to, but there was nowhere to run to. We were surrounded by men on high ground, and we should have been easy targets.

I rammed a dozen arrows into the turf, ready to snatch up and fire. I should have waited for the order but I didn't. I notched one, drew back and back and let fly: mine the first blood. I can see the Fleming now, his gauntleted right hand at the shaft protruding from his throat. He hunched forward, swayed back, his mount nervous under him, and fell. Mine, all unwitting, was the signal. The enemy, implacably, began to close the circle. They might kill us, but by God they'd know they'd been in a fight.

Later, I remember slashing my sword into some man's face, turning even before he fell to face the next. Sioned, bucking and skittering sideways at the noise and the stink of blood, her eyes rolling. Elffin, a man demented, face smeared crimson; stench and shrieks and an ear-tearing cacophony of metal on metal. A two-edged spear in my peripheral vision, and a twist of my body as instinctive as it was impossible, to avoid it. The spearman, off-balance, lurching forward, his own body's weight driving him onto my blade.

Tadmaeth, Rhys Gethin and Elffin, sweat pouring from them, rallying our men into a mad charge. We had nothing to lose and somehow we broke through the encircling enemy. They, knowing their advantage was lost, fled. Two hundred of them dead when the battle was over, and as many Welshmen. Two hundred of my comrades, two hundred husbands and fathers and brothers and sons. *Tadmaeth* grieves for every man lost. Only Crach Ffinnant was impassive as we buried our lost ones above the waterfall at Mynydd Bychan. Many of us hid tears: we'd all lost friends and every man of us counted himself lucky to be alive.

Among the dead was Gwilym of Hawarden. I grieved for him and his gentle earnestness; as honest as his friend Tomos is sly. Gwilym was my friend. We suffered together at sword practice, swam together afterwards, and were close, though he was older than me. Pity Tomos hadn't died instead, with his handsome face and his creeping, sly ways.

Rhiannon

From scraps of news Jack brings, *Tadmaeth* and a few hundred Welshmen have gone south to Pumlumon, leaving the greater part of the army in Snowdonia to harass the English. Rhys spits and snarls as each bit of news arrives. I know the signs now, and keep out of his way when he rides in, tosses his reins at Jack and slams into the house.

He'll never support Glyndŵr - he's de Grey's man, and if his Lordship calls I must stay in my room until he's gone. My husband doesn't want de Grey reminded that he's married to Glyndŵr's foster-daughter. Good: I couldn't occupy the same room as that slimy toad, still less be polite to him. God knows, I try to be as good a wife as I can, but it's hard. Disdain during the day and invasion at night. And in the morning, Ifan, smirking.

Half way through April I felt ill, aching from head to foot, hot as hell, and I tried not to think about my Mam's death from plague. Then, when I thought I'd recovered, the sickness shifted to my stomach, and I began to vomit. Each morning I stumbled out of bed to vomit into the chamber-pot. It lasted so long that I began to wonder if I'd been poisoned. But the sickness was gone by mid-morning, and I was able to get on with my tasks. I didn't suspect a thing until Ifan made me understand.

We were beside the fire after supper - Ifan, Beti, half-asleep, her head resting in my lap, and Rhys, studying his accounts, scowling at the figures. Angharad, her pregnant belly vast now, waddled into the room, one hand massaging the small of her back.

Ifan shifted suddenly. I glanced up, distracted from my sewing. He was staring at Angharad's great stomach, a half-smile twisting his face. Then he looked pointedly at my own, and smirked.

Then, I realised - oh, God! - that I was pregnant. Blood flew to my face. Oh God, oh God, no! I'd been so ill that I hadn't thought... How many months since I'd bled - one? Two? Oh, God, oh God, Ap Hywel's child. Lifting Beti aside I stood up. 'I'm tired. I'm going to bed.' My voice sounded strange and Angharad glanced at me, startled. I rarely went to bed early, avoiding the place where I was most vulnerable to my husband. Who didn't even look up.

Ifan's eyes narrowed with dislike. I couldn't see why: any child I had would have less claim to ap Hywel's estate than he. Rhys would follow English inheritance laws, not Welsh, and Ifan would have it all when his father died. It wouldn't be divided equally between the sons in Hywel Dda's old way.

Angharad followed me, lumbering up the steep stairs to unlace my gown. I still didn't quite believe it. 'Angharad,' I began, as her fingers fumbled at my back. 'How did you know you were pregnant?'

She laughed. 'When I started spewing every morning, and kind words made me cry. But mainly the vomiting. Every morning my head down the privy, dreading Lady Marged finding out. She did, of course. Ears everywhere, her Ladyship. That's why she sent me here. Bloody Crisiant and her clattering jaws.'

I faced her, shaking my head. 'She can't have known! She'd have made the father marry you if she had. She made Elinor wed Dai One-tooth when she was having a baby.'

Angharad laughed. 'Oh, no, no, no.' She laughed until the tears ran down her face. 'Not me. Never me.'

I scowled, not seeing anything funny. When she stopped for breath I said 'I think I'm pregnant too.'

She sobered then. 'Oh, Mrs Rhiannon -'

'I don't want to have it. If I do, I'll never get away.'

Angharad sat on the bed, her eyes narrowed. 'There are ways, my lady...'

'What do you mean? What ways?'

'There's a woman in the village. She knows things. Gwen says she has stuff to abort a woman.'

'Why didn't you take something like that?'

'I thought the father loved me. Even if he couldn't marry me, I thought he'd still be kind and love me and the baby, even if he had to marry someone else. Stupid, really. He doesn't even know.'

I didn't care about her. I had my own problems. 'Can you get something for me?'

'Me? Ap Hywel would kill us both! I'll tell you where she lives, the woman, but I daren't help you. If he didn't kill me he'd turn me out, and I'd die in a ditch having my baby. Don't make me, please?'

Later, in bed, I lay on my back and touched my stomach. It felt rounded, and my breasts were tender as boils. How could I now have known? I visualised my body swelling, as Angharad's had, and shuddered. I couldn't run away then even if I wanted to. I'd imagined that, if it all became too terrible, I could at least run away. I hadn't thought where, just that I could, if I had to. But now I was trapped. No. I couldn't do it. I wouldn't. Not his child.

I'd find the woman, make her help me. I'd have to sneak away on foot, because taking a horse meant Jack going with me. He'd disapprove, I was certain, even if he is my friend. He's a man, and men don't understand. They don't have to bear brats.

Next day, I cornered Angharad in the bedchamber. 'Tell me where that woman lives,' I demanded.

She'd obviously had second thoughts. She backed away, shaking her head. 'Don't make me tell you, Mrs Rhian,' she moaned. 'She's a witch. She'll want money. The master will kill me if he finds out.'

'*I don't care.*' I lips felt stiff. 'I want it gone. I don't care how. Tell me, or I'll kill you myself.'

I probably wouldn't have, but it did the trick. Right then she was more afraid of me than of ap Hywel. She told me.

Elffin

Hyddgen was a turning-point. Our reputation has grown, men have come from the South, from Cardiff and Monmouth. Glyndŵr is seen as a man who took a near-disaster and turned it to triumph.

Llew did well. If not for him we'd have been slaughtered, trapped as we were. It's a miracle we weren't: whoever heard of a tiny army, totally surrounded by a force three times its size, battling *uphill* out of a ring of enemies and not only surviving but winning?

We lost friends, some I've known since I was a child, some new, including Gwilym of Hawarden. But Hyddgen has turned the tide for us. Wales is rising to Owain Glyndyfrdwy.

Except. We buried Gwilym, his arm almost severed, his face unmarked but for a small cut on his cheekbone, and as we laid him down it occurred to me that I hadn't seen Tomos all day. I helped fill the grave then stood, easing my back, looking for him. He was missing, was Master Tom. When we'd buried our dead, I asked questions. Tomos was not well liked: too many men grimaced, or spat at the mention of his name. No one had seen him, and he wasn't in camp. I visited the look-out posts (new since the battle: we'd believed ourselves safe in our hollow) and told the men to keep their eyes open, and tell me when Tomos reappeared,.

He slithered into the camp just before dawn. I was half-dead with exhaustion, and it took the look-out a while to rouse me. I sat up, swiping the sleep from my eyes.

'He's back.'

I nodded, and tugged on my boots. Tomos sat by the fire. His nose was buried in a leather cup, and he eyed me over its rim.

'Tomos,' I said as pleasantly as I could. 'We looked for you.'

He lowered the cup, frowning uncertainly. 'For me, Elffin? Why?'

'We were worried,' I lied. 'After the battle we couldn't find you with either the living or the dead. So, where were you?'

He didn't ask 'what battle'. He set down the cup and glanced sideways at me, firelight glinting on his face. 'Llanidloes, Elffin. I didn't even know about the battle until a minute ago.'

I folded my legs beneath me, and sat beside him, the warmth comforting. 'How fortunate for you. Why Llanidloes, Tomos?'

He grinned, the long lashes shadowing his smooth cheek. 'You need to ask, Elffin? A woman of course, mad for me, she is.'

I'd give him the benefit of the doubt. He was as pretty as a girl, and some women like the type. I slapped his shoulder. 'Lucky man. Wish we were all as lucky as you: if you'd been here you might have died. Like Gwilym.'

'Gwilym's dead?'

'I buried him myself.'

Tomos hid his face on his crossed arms. 'If only I'd been here. Perhaps I could have saved him.'

I was silent, waiting until he looked at me. There were no tears for his friend.

I went back to bed, but couldn't sleep. Perhaps he did have a girl in Llanidloes. From now on, I'd watch him.

CHAPTER FIFTEEN

Llewelyn

My feet are cold, and Elffin moaned and spoke in his sleep last night. Most likely a nightmare: I have them sometimes, though I'd never admit it. Once, I ached for the glory of battle, sighed for the taut song of the bow. But glory doesn't last. Memories last, and they're terrible.

After Hyddgen men came to us from everywhere, North, South - aye, and England, too. England's no place for a Welshman today, not if he values his skin.

After Hyddgen, we crossed Wales, leaving fire and blood and desolation. My dreams of chivalry are a bit battered these days. Perhaps if my father had lived he'd have told me the truth about war. I suppose heroic stories are what boys want, not arms hanging by bloody sinews and guts spewing purple from slashed stomachs, and the stink of blood and shit and fear, and the screams of men and horses.

Once there was a sweet pattern to summers hazy with heat and plenty: days of regular meals and ordered tasks. Summer evenings when I rioted and rolled with the other boys, hurtling naked through dusty air into the coolness of the river. I learned my letters, waited at table. Days when I sat indoors sweating over a slate or a parchment when I longed to run free in the honeyed green of Sycharth.

I've been gently raised and I was taught to be courteous to priests. Respect was due to those who gave their lives to God. You'll understand, then, that I found it strange to attack an abbey, especially the Abbey where the last Prince of Wales had been laid to rest. My conscience got up on its back legs that night!

Elffin says the Cwmhir monks were mostly *Sais*, and guilty of betraying Owain, so they deserved to have their abbey burned.

Perhaps he's right, but my conscience twinges and I wonder what God thinks about it, and if He is still on our side. English or Welsh, they were still holy men.

We attacked New Radnor the same week. I thought I was hardened, but my mind clenches like a fist at the memory of *Tadmaeth*'s execution of sixty defenders and the mutilated corpses on the castle walls. He fought with my own father, side by side, and though enemies must be taught a lesson, I was sickened by the blood and cries and stink of fear. I thought I knew *Tadmaeth*, and didn't believe he could do something like that. After the executions, mind, when the bloody corpses had been hauled upwards, the job done, he was silent, withdrawn. He bent his head to hide his face as we rode away and spoke to no one.

Dreaming, my mind plays tricks on me, showing *Tadmaeth* as he was, gentling a grandchild, playing his harp, stooped over a chess-board. Is this the man who sat stone-faced as blood flooded cobblestones?

Then, Montgomery Castle, where we made no impression on it or its defenders. The town, however, was a different matter. Hardly a house was left standing, and we were laden with plunder.

We were stopped at Welshpool: John Charlton held the castle against us and chased us as far as Llyn Peris, and in the subsequent fight we lost too many. Almost as bad, he captured our sacred banner. They say it has been sent to Henry, who has had nightshirts made from it for himself and his son. Curse him for his disrespect: may the skin the sacred cloth touches, burn and boil and rot.

Instead *Tadmaeth* has adopted Uther Pendragon's banner. Lady Marged has sewn it, mingling the golden silk with threads of red Welsh gold from Dolaucothi. He kept it secret until the first time it was unfurled, and when I saw it snap free, the great red-gold dragon writhing and cracking in the wind, my heart swelled. I'll never forget the low roar that came from *Tadmaeth*'s followers: it is burned into my brain and I shall hear it until I die.

Some called Welshpool defeat. But when we left, the greater part of it was in ruins, and most of us were alive to fight again elsewhere. Next time, we'll succeed.

Oddly, this "defeat" has worked in our favour. According to our spies Henry was planning to invade again, but since his informants told him how disastrously we'd been routed at Powys, he thought we'd been subdued and so he went home! As if one setback would finish us.

At Welshpool, I understood Owain's advice at last. His words crossed my mind at Hyddgen, but at Welshpool I saw them for the gift they were, and now I agree that sometimes it's wiser to retreat and live to fight again than stay and be killed. Glory is all very well, but once a person is dead he isn't much use any more, is he? We didn't run, mind. We regrouped, and we'll march again.

The poor people are rising to *Tadmaeth,* waving wooden pitchforks and sticks, clamouring to fight for Wales and Glyndŵr and Uther Pendragon. The lesser squires come too, from a mixture of patriotism and fear. At New Radnor they saw how Glyndŵr treats enemies, so perhaps it was a good lesson after all. England's boot has been on Welsh necks for too long.

Duw, Gwynedd men are madmen in a skirmish! They even frighten me when they charge, screaming and shrieking, baring their teeth and waving their spears, and I'm on their side! Henry must be furious that "his" Welsh longbowmen shoot at Englishmen these days. And a longbows will go through padded hauberk, through armour, through a man's thigh and still have force enough to pin him to his horse!

To hear the talk around the campfires, we're invincible and totally fearless, but in the darkness there are small sighs and moans of troubled dreams. I dream too, sometimes, of battles and bloodshed, but mostly of Sycharth, where it's always summer. I lie on the hard ground watching the sun crimson the mountains, and think of Rhian, and wonder how she is. I hope she's safe and happy. And oh, I think often of Mali, and what we did together. Does she think of me? Most of all I dream that one day we can go back to Sycharth and everything will be as it was. Except of course *Tadmaeth* will be Prince of Wales, and Henry of England will be back in his kennel. Elffin is snoring again.

Rhiannon

Luckily, the day was warm and I could wander nonchalantly out of the house, avoiding the stable yard and Jack, and sneak into the woods. I unpinned Elffin's silver fox and hid it in the linen press for safety: it didn't seem right to wear it, me pregnant with ap Hywel's parasite.

Beti was crooning to her wooden doll, and Ifan, thank God, was out with his father. I could hear Jack whistling in the stable yard, and Angharad, knowing where I was going, had shut herself away in the dairy. I think she was afraid I'd make her go with me, but I didn't want her. I wanted to go, do what had to be done, whatever it was, and have it over.

I rarely went to the village, and never alone. I was forbidden to leave the house without an escort, and there would be hell to pay if ap Hywel got wind of this, or Jack for that matter.

I found the house easily enough, if it could be called a house: it was barely a hut, mud plastered in the cracks between rough-cut log walls to keep out wind and rain, wooden shutters covering the window holes, and plumes of smoke rising from a gap in the thatch.

I thumped on the door. At first there was silence, and then someone fumbled with the door latch. I'd expected a wrinkled, bent old crone, but this woman was young, only a little older than me from the look of her: perhaps twenty, straight and slim. Black tangled hair hid her eyes until she shoved it back: then I saw suspicious hazel, and her parted lips showed even, strong teeth. I'd expected an ancient I could bully, and it unnerved me.

She leaned in the doorway, arms folded, eyes assessing, insolent. 'Well, now,' she said, 'and what might you want, lady?'

My mouth opened and shut, but nothing came out. Nausea roiled, and I put a hand over my mouth, heaving helplessly. The woman's eyes widened, and she stood back.

'You'd better come in.'

I followed her, retching anew at the stench of mutton-fat rushlights. It was clean, at least, and the wooden furniture well-finished, but there was little comfort in it. Bundles of herbs hung from the roof-timbers, and a blackened pot hung from a fire-dog.

'Pregnant, is it?' she asked. I nodded.

'Not married? Don't want a bastard to spoil your chance of a good match to some unsuspecting lad?' There was almost a sneer.

I shook my head, stung by her hostility. Then I found my tongue. 'I'm married. But I don't want the child.'

'Bit of fun with a stable-boy, lady?' Her knowing grin irritated me, and my temper flared.

'It's my husband's child. I don't want it. I won't have it.'

She stared, eyes narrowed. 'Who are you?'

'Rhiannon,' I said wearily.

'Rhiannon who?'

'Just Rhiannon. Now, will you help me, or not?'

'If your husband finds out? Why should I take the risk? Could bring trouble to my door. Who's your husband, then?'

'No one important,' I lied. 'Look, just give me whatever it is and tell me what to do. Please? I've got money. I can pay.'

The insolent stare held a while longer, then she silently turned, took a cloth bag from a small wooden box, and dangled it in front of me. I made a grab for it, but it was whisked away.

'Money.'

I opened the purse dangling at my waist and gave her a silver coin I'd taken from Rhys's money chest.

From the way her eyes widened I knew it was too much. Still, too late now. She grabbed the coin and tossed the bag my way. Off-balance, I missed it, and had to stoop and retrieve it from the earthen floor. 'What do I do?'

'Make yourself a strong infusion, Lady. Drink it twice today, three times tomorrow, and three times the day after, before you eat. If the babe doesn't quit by then, come back and I'll give you savory.'

'Will that get rid of it if this fails?'

She laughed. 'If this fails, a tisane of savory will give you an quicker labour.'

Outside, I clutched the bag, feeling a rustling dryness inside it that echoed the dryness in my mouth. It had to work. Head down, I hurried through the woods, anxious for it to be done, so preoccupied I forgot to skirt the stable-yard, and was stumbling on the cobbles before I remembered I wanted to avoid Jack. I jumped at the sound of his voice.

'Where have you been?'

'Out,' I said, shortly.

'I can see that. Where?'

'Leave me alone.' I tried to push past, but he caught my wrist, gently restraining me. I dropped the cloth bag: he picked it up.

'What's this?'

'Nothing.'

He untied the drawstring, bent his head and sniffed. His frown was sudden and fierce. 'What is it?'

I shrugged. 'Something to - to settle my stomach.'

'There's mint for that. And fennel and aniseed and clove-pink. You've a cupboard full of cures. What's this?'

The nausea returned with a vengeance. My stomach heaved, and I bent over, splattering the cobbles.

His arm was round me in an instant. 'Rhiannon, you're ill!' He raised his voice and shouted. 'Angharad! Where are you?'

The door opened and through gut-wrenching retching I saw Angharad approach. Her face was a picture of guilt.

Jack looked from Angharad to me and back again. I didn't need to tell him, he knew. 'You're pregnant?'

I nodded, dully.

'And this?'

Again, I shrugged. Angharad covered her mouth with her hands. 'I didn't want to tell her, Jack!' she wailed. 'I told her it was dangerous. I warned her. But she made me.'

'All right. Get inside, Angharad,' he ordered. I pulled free of his arm and tried to follow. 'No, Rhiannon. You stay. I want to talk to you.'

He tugged me after him into the stable. The little mare was in there, due to foal any day. Everyone and everything was at it. Maybe it was catching, like the plague.

I pulled my wrist free. Jack glared at me. 'Are you mad?' he hissed. 'Don't you know what this stuff can do?'

'Get rid of it,' I said, mutinously. 'I don't want his child. If I don't have a baby I can still get away. I can go home.'

'Home where? This is your home now.' Jack shook his head. 'You think Lady Marged would have you back? You're married. You made a vow before a priest, and you're stuck with it, like it or not. And if Rhys sleeps with you, sooner or later you'll fall pregnant. That's life, Rhiannon: get used to it.'

'I can get rid of it.' My eyes were shut, my teeth gritted.

'And what about the next one? And the one after that? If, of course, you survive aborting the first.'

'Survive?' I looked blankly at him. 'Why shouldn't I?'

'Why? Because this stuff -' he waved the bag under my nose '- this stuff will twist your womb in knots and make you bleed. You'll get rid of it, all right. And once it's gone, then you have to hope the bleeding stops. Because if it doesn't, it'll get rid of you, too. That what you want? You want to bleed to death?' He closed his fist round the cloth bag and shoved it inside his shirt. 'I promised your brother I'd look after you, Rhiannon. And like it or not, I'm keeping you safe.'

'You promised -? What business is it of yours?'

'Oh, Rhiannon. I know how unhappy you are. I - I know.'

'If I have the baby I might die in childbirth,' I said mutinously.

'You might. But there's a much, much greater chance of dying if you swallow this stuff. Do you really want to kill his child? And possibly yourself?'

I had no answer. I didn't want the baby. But I didn't want to die. Not before I'd seen Elffin again.

Elffin

The respite after Welshpool is over. Henry reached Worcester in September at the head of a hundred thousand, and his son captains Chester and Hereford men. He won't rest, he says, until he's destroyed Owain Glyndŵr. He's going to be tired, then. It's a long, hard road for an invader, and ap Gruffydd Fychan of Caeo didn't help much. Did you hear about that?

A gentle old soul, Gruffydd, Welsh as the day's long, and still the king didn't suspect! "Trust me," the old man said, "I know where Glyndŵr's hiding! Follow me," he said, promising to show him the place in the mountains where, he swore, Glyndŵr could be captured. And Henry wanted so much to believe him that he followed without a murmur.

The king's men wore their legs to the knees trudging after ap Gruffydd through forests, stumbling over branches and slashing brambles; floundering through bogs, scrambling up mountains and tumbling down them. Their shins were bloodied by rough rocks, their feet drenched and aching with cold from wading streams, their clothes soaked and their teeth chattering from icy rivers. For five long days he led them, until the English were dropping in their boots. Then, as the poor bastards rested their weary bodies at Llandovery before setting out again, ap Gruffydd, in that gentle voice of his, told them all about his sons. Singing their praises, he was, and no mistake, brave they were, and mighty, and both of them sworn to Glyndŵr...

As you can imagine, Henry was not particularly entertained by this revelation, and he showed ap Gruffydd exactly how unamused he was. The old man's quartered remains went from Llandovery to the four corners of Wales. A lesson, I suppose, but one that will hone the desire for revenge in every man who knew ap Gruffydd. His sons are grinding their teeth and sharpening swords, for it was a cruel, traitor's death for a gentle, if mischievous, old soul. Henry will pay one way or another.

The King's revenge didn't end there, because next he attacked Strata Florida Abbey where eleven of our Princes are buried, evicted the monks and left the abbey a smouldering ruin. He stabled his horses before the high altar, and Strata Florida's sacred treasures are long gone, chiming and bouncing in *Sais* saddlebags. Agreed, we sacked Cwm Hir - but they were all English spies there, and so it was justified. What he did at Strata Florida has harmed the King, because it's alienated many of those who might otherwise have supported him.

Henry sent troops out, searching in vain for Glyndŵr, who was safe at Pumlumon Fawr, knowing Autumn in Wales: the weather would do more for our cause than a hundred battles. This has increased the rumours of Glyndŵr's supernatural powers, and naturally the bards are stirring the pot, much to *Tad*'s amusement. Crach Ffinnant muttered and burned handfuls of sparking stuff on the campfires, and waved his skinny arms, but who knows if what the Crab did was effective or if it was the highest power of all?

All I know is that the heavens opened, thunder crashed day and night, lightning seared trees and sizzled on mountainsides in Henry's wake. There was even snow, and Henry's troops were half-starved, soaked to the skin, their armour rusting and their boots sucked off in the bogs, when they tottered back to England thoroughly beaten and demoralised.

Henry's hundred thousand men achieved only some homeless monks and the destruction of one of God's most beautiful houses. Except - when they left they took with them a thousand weeping, frightened Welsh children to be their bond-slaves - the child of any Welshman suspected of being loyal to Owain.

Mind, while old Henry was wallowing thigh-deep in good Welsh mud, a small band of our men swooped on young Henry's baggage train, and from under the terrified noses of its escort, carried the arms, horses and tents of the false Prince off into the mountains.

God is doing his best to convince Henry whose side He's on!

CHAPTER SIXTEEN

Llewelyn
I was day-dreaming. I slopped hot broth on my leg and swore. Elffin's face was drawn. He's touchy as a man with a boil on his arse lately. When I heard what he wanted, it was a relief that for once I wasn't in the shit with him. I felt a bit proud, and pride is a sin, but this is something I do well.

'Llew,' he said, his arm across my shoulders. 'Be Tomos's shadow.'

'Be his friend?' I asked, 'or follow him?' I hated the Anglesey man, although these days he ignored me unless I was with my foster-brothers.

Elffin grinned. 'Follow him. See where he goes, who he talks to - even the most casual conversation. You'll need to be careful, mind. Stay out of sight - but don't lose him. Can you do that?'

'Can birds fly?' I said, drawing myself up so that I was almost equal to him in height. 'I'll walk with him, ride with him - I'll even go with him to piss!'

'*Iawn,*' he said, laughing. 'There's dedication!'

'Why, Elffin? I loathe Tomos: he makes my skin crawl. But -'

'I don't like him any more than you do. Tomos is nothing like Gwilym was, and I've disliked him since I first saw him. There are people like that: some you like instantly, and they're friends until death. Some you don't, and nothing will change your opinion.'

'The only thing that'll change my opinion of Tomos is if God Himself arrives on a cloud to argue his case. Even then I'd think hard about it.'

'He wasn't at Hyddgen,' Elffin went on, 'with some woman in Llanidloes, he said, but -'

'Women look at Tomos as if they want him served up on a plate,' I said enviously. 'Maybe there is a woman.'

'We need to know, Llew. If it's true, then all's well. Perhaps then I'll trust him. But we'll see.'

I'm a very good follower, even if I say it myself. I learned from Huw, who taught me to move silently over all sorts of terrain. I can cross a wood without cracking a twig, an open field without disturbing a rabbit, and I can keep so still that a fox can pass within a yard and not see me. Following Tomos would be easy.

He didn't go to Llanidloes. I stayed with him for four days: I could tell you when he farted, when he scratched, when he slept and how loud he snored. I trailed him, he trailed *Tadmaeth*. I saw when he hid in the trees to avoid Elffin. I knew when he stole half a rabbit from Bychan's campfire and blamed it on the dogs, and I knew where he tossed the bones when he'd eaten it. I slept with one eye open, and just as well I did. He slipped out of camp before dawn one morning, slithering behind a tree on the edge of the camp as if he meant to piss. But he kept going, and nobody saw but me. He led his horse quietly down into the woods, waiting until the watchmen's backs were turned, for they of course were watching for incomers, not for someone sneaking out. Once out of sight he mounted and rode towards Machynlleth.

I caught Sioned and saddled her, took a short cut, so that I could catch him up without him seeing me. He didn't ride into Machynlleth, and it almost caught me by surprise when he left the road and hid himself in a small copse of trees halfway up the hill.

At first I thought he might have seen me, and was waiting for me, but he wasn't looking in my direction. I slid off Siôned's back and waited, my hand on her nose to silence her. The sun flooded the hillside with cold, primrose light, but my breath steamed on the air and I wished I could stamp my feet to warm them. Next time we sacked a market town I must try to liberate some felt boot liners: my own had worn through long since.

I watched and waited, and the drip on the end of my nose was an icicle by the time I saw movement on the Machynlleth road. A lone rider cantered towards us. I wiped my nose on my sleeve and stared. I knew him. But who?

And then he reached Tomos and dismounted. I was too far away to overhear, but I recognised the rider. My brother-in-law.

My first instinct was to show myself, ask after Rhian - but this wasn't two friends meeting by chance. Tomos hardly knew ap Hywel. At Christmas they'd spoken occasionally, which was one more reason to despise them both: who would want either of them for companionship?

Had ap Hywel had a change of heart? Perhaps he wanted to change his allegiance to Owain. No. Rhys knew who buttered his bread, and it wasn't Glyndŵr.

So, Tomos, secretly meeting my brother-in-law. Elffin was right: Tomos was a traitor. How much did he know, how much damage could he inflict? He was never at strategic meetings, but his habit of spidering around doorways would inevitably have caught him scraps of information. A small bag changed hands and disappeared inside Tomos's padded jerkin. A true Judas, then.

Fury and terror cramped my belly. A member of my family - my own sister's husband - spying for the enemy. It was bad enough that ap Hywel didn't support *Tadmaeth*, but to actively work against us! My shame was a cold, sick thing.

No wonder Tomos hadn't been at Hyddgen if he'd known of the attack in advance. Tomos, who listened at camp-fires, who lurked beside tent-flaps and cave-openings. Tomos, whom we - Elffin and I - had brought into our ranks. Who could betray us all.

We'd opened our arms to him and he'd betrayed us. How could I tell Elffin that ap Hywel was working against us? Did Rhiannon know? Surely not. Even if she'd come to love the man, she would never betray *Tadmaeth*.

If she'd known, what could she have done? She's only a girl. *Oh, God,* I thought, *what am I to tell Elffin?* If I lie, tell him that Tomos was sniffing a skirt in Llanidloes, he'll betray us again. If I confess that my brother-in-law is de Grey's spy, how can he trust me? I'd be tarred with the same brush as ap Hywel and Tomos.

My mind in uproar, I waited until they left, then followed Tomos back to the camp. I should have gone straight to Elffin, but what could I say? I am betraying my friends.

Rhiannon

So. I'm going to have a child. I haven't told Rhys: I don't care if he'll be pleased or not. The nausea, thank God, is passing. Angharad looks ready to burst: she lumbers about, her belly thrusting, her legs straddled to help her balance. She puffs and sweats and whines until I want to slap her, and when I look at her I see myself in seven short months. Oh, God, I don't want to look like that. I don't want to have this child.

Jack watches me outside, and Ifan watches inside. Ap Hywel is never here, and Beti prattles all day. She's a sweet enough child, and means well, but she's driving me slowly insane. Did I ever, even at her age, spend hours asking my mother her favourite colour? Favourite flower? Favourite, for God's sake, *smell*?

In the end I told her my favourite, favourite, *favourite* thing was silence, and would she please shut up. She was hurt for a minute, but soon forgot and began again. She's like toothache.

Angharad has been talking to Elin, who's been talking to someone in the village. The war is going *Tadmaeth*'s way, they say, but that news was old when I heard it, and anything could have happened since. He could be dead and we wouldn't know. I pray for him every night, and for Llew and for Elffin. For Elffin. Oh, God, keep them safe, don't let them be killed, or hurt, or captured, or anything bad. When I pray for Elffin I clutch the silver fox that he gave me like a crucifix, and hope I'm not blaspheming, and that God won't punish me by harming him.

I don't pray for ap Hywel at all. At supper last night he said he'd be away for a few days, and despite everything my spirits rose.

Needing to be polite, or perhaps just to fill the silence that is always present when Beti is in bed, I asked 'Where are you going?'

He threw his spoon on the table and glared at me. 'Why?'

I gritted my teeth and managed to speak softly. 'I'm your wife. May I not ask?'

'You're also Glyndŵr's foster daughter. The less you know, the better. Who can say what goes on in your mind? Aah.' He rubbed his face with his open hands. 'Why did I ever marry you?'

'I could go,' I said, trying to keep my voice neutral, my clenched fingers hidden in my skirt. 'If I'm so inconvenient.'

'Indeed you could.' He looked at me speculatively, and my heart leapt. He was going to send me home. Oh, please God, please God, please...

'Why not send her to de Grey, *Tad*? She'd be safe there,' Ifan said.

De Grey? I'd kill myself rather than live in that man's household. Glyndŵr's foster daughter, inside Ruthin Castle? My life would be hell. Surely he wouldn't send me there. Rhys's next words, delivered on the back of a wry laugh, made me sag with relief. 'De Grey? Don't be stupid, Ifan. How could I? No. My problem. Unfortunately. Unless Lady Marged...'

'Oh, she can't go back to Sycharth.' Ifan nibbled a lump of cheese. I had never noticed his resemblance to a rat before. I wished I'd thought to poison the cheese.

'Why? I could say that it was for her safety.'

'But then you'd have to send Beti with her, wouldn't you? You could hardly save your wife and not your daughter.'

My husband shrugged. His face said that it would be a bargain. Beti, after all, was only a girl.

'But you can't send her back, can you? Not now.'

I knew what he was going to say and glared at him, willing him to shut up, not to betray me. Rhys would have to know some time, but not yet.

Ap Hywel stared at his son and raised his eyebrows.

'Shouldn't a pregnant woman be with her family, where she belongs?' Malice was written all over his long, pale face.

Ap Hywel's gaze slid to my belly, then to my face. 'It's true?' His voice was soft, but I couldn't tell if it was emotion or anger.

I nodded, still hoping that perhaps he'd send me back. If I could go home to Sycharth, I would see the child was taken care of. When it was born I could give it to someone else to look after: there were always wet-nurses in the village, and when it was weaned Lady Marged would know someone clean who could bring it up. Perhaps if I could make her understand what it had been like for me, she might take pity on me. Perhaps once the child was born Rhys's sister would take it.

His face flushed. He stared at me, and I knew he was angrier than I'd ever seen him. 'When were you going to tell me? Why do I find out from my son? How did you know, Ifan?'

'Listened to her spew, *Tad*. She howled into her chamber pot regular as a rooster every morning.'

His eyes came back to me. 'It's mine?'

'What?' My mouth fell open. Did he think I'd do *that* if I didn't have to? 'Of course it's yours! Whose else?'

'Then you stay. No son of mine will be tainted by Glyndŵr.'

Elffin

Llew returned an hour after sunrise. I hadn't seen him go, but Tomos was missing too, and I realised Llew would be with him. I raised an arm to him, but he ducked his head as if he hadn't seen me, and wandered over to the cook-tent to find breakfast. Tomos was already back, lolling against a boulder outside *Tad*'s cave.

My head aches. All I can think of is Angharad. She's there when I sleep and when I wake. I don't love her, but I feel responsible for her. I made her pregnant. She's with Rhiannon, at least, who's kind enough for all her foul moods. She'll take care of Angharad and the child. I doubt ap Hywel will be happy about Mam palming him off with a pregnant servant. Not that Mam knew, of course. Coincidence. It must have been.

What can it be like to give birth? I know it's hard, because I heard a woman in labour once. *Duw*, it was like she was being tortured. But then, as soon as the child was safely out of her and *cwtched* in her arms she was all satisfied smiles, the pain forgotten. I'm glad I won't be there, knowing it's all my fault. It will be a son. I wonder if Mam knows? I don't want to even think what she'd say. I'm brave as the next man in battle, but Mams are different.

Perhaps Angharad will have an easy time of it. She's a big girl, strong. Perhaps it will be quick for her, and over soon. I hope so.

There's so much to worry about. I look at *Tad* sometimes and wonder where the gentle man has gone, whose doors were open to all comers, and whose heart found room for two orphaned children. Often his expression is bleak, and except for inconsequential things, he speaks only to Gruffydd, who speaks to us, and we each speak to the men in our groups. And he speaks to Crach Ffinnant, who appears from nowhere in his monkish robes, his eyes veiled. And *Tad* listens. Everywhere are rumours of Glyndŵr's magical powers. Perhaps that's a good thing: a leader who can handily summon thunder and lightning if a plan goes awry is a good leader to follow. But some mutter that dabbling with dark forces leads only to hellfire and destruction. Sometimes I look at *Tad* and think that, wherever hell is, he's already there.

When winter comes, perhaps we can go home. It would do *Tad* good to see Mam. And I long to lie in a bed in a snow-bound stronghold watching whiteness reflect on the ceilings and winter sun dazzle through stained glass, and listen to the sound of a household waking up and going about its business. I know Llew would be ecstatic to be at Sycharth, but he'll be just as content at Glyndyfrdwy.

He'll be anxious to make up for lost time with his Mali, also. I won't have Angharad, but there's bound to be other girls. If I'm careful and don't let Mam find out, I can make the most of my opportunities. I haven't been altogether deprived, I admit: there are always women around any camp, but I don't use them often. I don't want a woman every man for miles around has had. Some of our number rape when a town or a village is sacked, although *Tad* punishes them if he finds out. But I can't. I think of my sisters and know that it's wrong, just because a man can, because he's bigger and stronger, and his cock is hard because of the violence and the stink of blood. It is strange, that. Before, I'd have thought that the last thing on a man's mind would be women.

Henry's at Shrewsbury, having been sent furious and humiliated home. But he'll be back when he can.

Tomorrow, although it's November and the campaign all but over for the winter, we attack Caernarfon. They won't expect an attack this late and with luck, we'll be inside before they even know we're there.

CHAPTER SEVENTEEN

Llewelyn

A grey dawn broke. I should tell Elffin, but if I do, perhaps he'd think me like ap Hywel: *bradwr,* traitor to family and comrades. Could I have misunderstood what I saw? Did ap Hywel and Tomos simply pass the time of day? Why shouldn't they meet? It's no good. I know I'm pissing in the wind thinking that way. I saw what I saw: one selling information, the other buying. But the longer I waited, the harder it became to confess.

All over the camp, drowsy men strung bows and packed saddlebags, preparing to hunt, some sharpened weapons, preparing for the ahead. And then we were summoned to our groups. Elffin leads ours and despite his youth commands respectful silence: he is of Glyndŵr's blood. Every man, restless yet longing for rest, was happy at the prospect of action, if only to break the boredom. Today we take Caernarfon. Every man happy, that is, but me. Conscience nagging, I prepared for battle: then, from the corner of my eye I saw a figure sneaking away. Tomos. This time he'd bloody well fight, I'd see to that.

He slithered from tree to tree, surreptitiously making himself scarce, but I was behind him. Just as he was about to disappear entirely, I shouted, 'Tomos!' Then again, louder. 'Tomos of Ynys Môn!' Men turned, curious.

He looked back, his face reddening. 'What?'

'Where are you going? Take care you aren't left behind.'

'Jesus! Can't a man even take a shit in peace?'

'The latrines are that way.'

'They turn my stomach. I prefer to use the mountain.'

'Your stomach's weak, isn't it? At Hyddgen you couldn't fight at all.' Behind me the men fell silent, listening.

'I was at Llanidloes when the Flemings attacked.'

'So *you* said. Lucky, that, all things considered. If you hadn't been in bed with your woman, you might have protected Gwilym, and he might have lived. But you were busy and he died. Tell you what: we'll ride together today. We can protect each other. I can beat off all the rampant females so you can fight.'

'Not a problem you'll ever have, Llew,' he muttered, beginning the climb back up the slope.

Tomos was pinned down, but that didn't solve my problem. When we'd taken Caernarfon, then I'd tell Elffin. I'd be able to explain why I'd kept my brother-in-law's treachery secret. I could hardly distract him now. Whatever information Tomos sold to ap Hywel, it had nothing to do with Caernarfon. Tomos couldn't have known about the day's plan, so he couldn't have betrayed us. Today we had the element of surprise, and we'd take Caernarfon easily. Despite everything, my muscles were tense with anticipation.

The closer we got to Caernarfon, the worse I felt. I wasn't afraid, but there is always a strangeness before battle. My heart thumped and I felt sick, but all that disappears as soon as the battle starts.

Glyndŵr halted us just beyond the few houses huddled under the castle walls. Caernarfon is English, and its five hundred or so inhabitants unlikely to support us. But surprise is worth a thousand men. The castle squats like a toad: they say a warren of passages runs inside it so that a man needs not stray into the open for the entire circuit of its walls, and was virtually impregnable. I struggled against a feeling of foreboding. We slipped silently into the town.

Rhiannon

Elin crept into our room to fetch me without disturbing Rhys. I was awake anyway: there's no way out. I'm married, pregnant, and trapped. In summer I might have run away and thrown myself on Lady Marged's mercy. But now I'd freeze to death. I'd never reach Sycharth, and *Mamaeth* wasn't likely to be sympathetic anyway, especially to a runaway pregnant wife. By next spring my belly would be too big to go anywhere. I had no option but to stay with Rhys ap Hywel at least until the child was born. It would just take longer than planned to get away, that's all. I contemplated suicide, but decided against it. After nearly coming to grief in the river, drowning had no romantic image of gentle waters closing over a willing head. I'd fought and gulped and thrashed and it had been horrible. Mind, if Elffin had let me drown I shouldn't be looking for ways to do away with myself now.

Some plants are poisonous, but which? Lady Marged's book of simples didn't cater for suicide. Some of the recipes were labelled "Beware! Will cause scouring and griping". I've done enough scouring and griping, thank you. I don't want to suffer. I'm not in favour of that at all. So I was contemplating my options (slitting my wrists and bleeding to death, or slinging a rope over a beam and jumping off a stool) when Elin came to fetch me.

'Quick, Mrs Rhiannon! She's having it. Oh, come quick, will you?' Her whisper was husky with panic.

I slipped out of bed, put on a shawl, and hoped Elin knew how to deliver a baby, because I didn't. All I knew was that it hurt and soon I'd have to go through it myself. Whatever Angharad suffered, so should I.

She was sitting bolt upright on her pallet, her bed gown wet with sweat. 'Oh, Rhiannon,' she wailed. 'I don't want it.'

'Bit late for that,' I said, sitting beside her, trying to smile.

'I want to go to sleep and wake up when it's all over. It hurts!'

Elin sniffed. 'It'll hurt a lot more before the *babi* do come, look. My sister near died with her last, she did!'

I glared. 'Thank you *very* much, Elin! Go and get a shawl for the baby, and find a basket to put it in. Bring water for Angharad. Is there anything else we need?'

The maid shrugged. 'I dunno, Mrs Rhiannon? I've never had no *babi*.'

'But you've seen them born. You've helped.'

Elin shook her head. 'I never. My Mam used to send us away when she was at it, and my sister do live over Llangollen so I never seen her, neither. Terrible, it is, she says, like torture, she says. Goes on and on, feels like f'rever. Felt like she was being torn apart by wild horses, she said.'

Angharad let out a shriek and clutched my hand. 'I'm going to die. I am, I am.'

'No you aren't. I'm here. I'll help you.'

'Oh, oh, oh, it hurts! Ow, ow, Aaaaah!' She screwed up her face, ground her teeth and yelled. The tendons on her neck stood out, her body thrashed, and sweat ran down her face. When it stopped, she slumped and cried pitifully.

'Come on, Angharad. Just think! Soon you'll have a lovely baby.' I hope, I thought.

Her expression was fiendish. 'I don't want a bloody baby. I just want this to stop!' she hissed.

It was a long night. The pains grew steadily stronger, and I felt increasingly helpless. How long did babies take? As long as this? I sent Elin to find Gwenny to ask if she knew anything about babies, but she knew less than Elin, although naturally she had a dozen theories and old wives' tales from her Mam. The best she could suggest was a bit of hair from a mare's mane tied round Angharad's big toe.

'You just has to wait, Mrs Rhiannon,' Elin said. '*Babis* do come when they're ready, Gwenny says.' So much for Gwenny, then.

By dawn, I was beginning to think that there was something seriously wrong. Nothing was happening, yet the pains got worse. She'd even stopped screaming, which was just as well, because she'd already woken Rhys, Ifan and Beti. Rhys stuck his head in the doorway, grunted and stamped out of the house long before the sun was up.

The intervals between the pains were growing shorter, and the pains themselves seemed to last longer and longer. Angharad was grey-faced and weak, grimacing and whimpering with the onset of each pain, and opening her mouth in a soundless scream as each pain peaked. She had no voice left to yell. She'd stopped thrashing, and was curled round her belly as if to protect the pain. The morning sun slanted through the window and she turned her face to it. 'I can't do it any more,' she whimpered. 'I'm tired. I don't know what to do. Let me die.'

There was no one I could turn to. And then I remembered. I shouted for Elin, who crept reluctantly up the stairs. 'Sit with her, Elin. Hold her hand. Make encouraging noises, but don't you dare tell her again how your sister nearly died, or your Mam's eyes popped out and had to be poked back in, or I'll kill you myself.'

Sulkily, Elin took the stool I'd vacated. I sped down the stairs and into the yard. 'Jack!' I yelled, and he appeared, shirtless despite the bitter weather, in the stable doorway, mopping his chest with a towel.

'Bad, is it?' he said, shaking his head. 'Poor Angharad. Still, it'll be over soon.'

'There's something wrong. Nothing's happening and she's in awful pain. She's going to die. No one else knows anything about it and I don't know what to do.' I suddenly realised I was holding him by the arms and shaking him.

He freed himself, ran into the house and up the stairs. Angharad was twisting weakly, her whole body focused on her swollen belly, one hand clutching and tearing at Elin's, who was screaming at the pain of crunched bones.

When the pain had passed, Jack turned Angharad onto her back and felt her belly. Elin ran before she was asked to do anything else. I should have been embarrassed at Angharad's nakedness, but I didn't care that Jack was a man and was putting his hands on Angharad. It didn't matter. He pushed her legs apart and looked between them. Angharad didn't care.

'The baby's big,' he muttered. 'She's exhausted. If she were a mare I could do it, but my hands are too big. We need a woman.'

'Don't look at me!' I begged, backing away. 'I couldn't. I don't know how. There must be someone else, please, Jack.'

'There is,' Jack said. 'But if ap Hywel finds out, there'll be hell to pay rent to. Make sure Elin and Gwenny keep their mouths shut - threaten them if necessary, pay them if you have to, but it's her only chance. Stay with her.'

He crashed down the stairs, and moments later I heard the clatter of hooves on cobblestones. It seemed hours before he came back, but at last he was there. And with him was the witch-woman.

She approached Angharad, winding her hair into a knot to keep it out of her eyes. 'Get me water,' she ordered. 'And butter.'

Butter? Elin, loitering outside the door, hurried downstairs. The woman scrubbed her hands, then knelt by the pallet and, parting Angharad's legs, gently slid her fingers inside her.

'*Duw*, the dada must have been a size!' she exclaimed, slapping Angharad's thigh, smiling reassuringly. 'Big as a calf, it is. Boy, for sure.'

Elin came back with the butter, and the woman rolled up her sleeves and greased her hands. 'You,' she said, nodding at me. 'You prop her right leg up and talk to her. 'You, useless,' she said to Elin, now wailing in the corner, 'bugger off.' 'You,' she nodded at Jack, 'get behind her and support her back.'

She knelt between Angharad's thighs and got busy. At the next pain, Angharad suddenly took a deep breath and began to push, screaming hoarsely and pushing her foot against me, hard.

'Stop that!' the woman said fiercely. 'No noise. You need all your strength to push. No screaming. Put your head down on your chest and get on with it, woman.'

The next pain came: Angharad, veins cording on her neck, heaved, and the woman's hands slipped into her body. After, Angharad panted and wept.

'No more,' she pleaded.

'Oh yes. A couple more.' She rested her hand on the blue-white swell of Angharad's belly and grinned. 'There's a lucky girl, aren't you! All that fun nine months back, and now you're paying for it. But still, you get a baby, don't you! There's a prize! Come on, here comes another one. This time push as if you were shoving its bloody Dada off a cliff.'

Angharad held her breath and pushed, grunting with the effort, her face crimson. A tiny, dark protuberance appeared in the V of her thighs. It looked as if her body was turning itself inside out, and I swallowed back nausea. And then the protuberance surged forward and became recognisably a head, facing down towards the bed sheets.

'Stop pushing!' the woman commanded, untangling a purple, fleshy rope from around the baby's neck. 'Right, you. One more push and it's here.'

With the next pain, the baby's shoulders, one after the other, slipped out, and then the rest of it slithered from Angharad's exhausted body, tiny, unmoving, the hideous purple rope attached to its belly. Blue. Dead. All that effort for a dead baby. All that pain.

The woman tied the cord in two places and bit through the rope between the ligatures. She picked up the body by its feet, slapped the tiny blue buttocks. A coughing wail echoed into the silence. Miraculously, the baby turned pink and screamed, weakly.

'Bit worn out,' the woman said, 'but he'll do, he'll do.' She wrapped the baby in a cloth and passed it to Angharad, who opened her arms and gathered it in.

'Put it to the breast,' the woman advised. 'Help stop the bleeding. More he sucks, quicker you'll be out and about. Well, now. Was he worth it?'

Angharad was in no doubt. 'Oh, yes!' she sighed, her eyes flooding. 'Look at his little fingernails!' Then she slipped her wet shift to her waist and put the baby to the breast.

'Another bloody man,' the woman muttered, but her face was gentle when she said it. 'No lying in bed, either. Up a while tomorrow, and move around. Don't want to lose you to milk-fever.'

Instructing me to tell Elin to wash Angharad and then let her sleep, the woman turned and left. I followed. Downstairs, she eyed me, her hazel eyes bright.

'Still got it, then?'

For a minute I couldn't think what she meant. Then I remembered that soon I'd suffering the same ordeal. I nodded, miserably.

'Just as well, considering who you are,' she commented, unknotting her hair and fingering it around her face. 'If you need me when your time comes, send for me. Ceridwen, I am. If your man will let me in the house, of course. Some will, some won't.'

I found money and gave it to her. Jack went through the door, and she turned to follow him, but then stopped. 'I know things,' she said suddenly.

'What? What sort of things? The future?' I asked, blankly, too tired to care if she knew God and all His angels.

'No. Some say they can, but not me. I can judge the future, and sometimes I judge it right, but that's different, isn't it? No. I keep my eyes and my ears open, and I learn things. You're Glyndŵr's *maethferch*.' It wasn't a question, it was a statement.

I nodded.

'You'll be for him, then.'

'Of course.'

'Then watch your man. He's not.'

'I already know that. He's de Grey's man, inside and out.'

'And d'you know he's meeting with one of Glyndŵr's? Secret, like, in the woods on the Machynlleth road. Don't know who, but he's a pretty lad. And then your man rides to de Grey as if his saddle was red hot.' Then she was gone. Snapped out of my exhaustion, I went to find Jack.

Elffin
They said there were only twenty men-at arms and eighty archers in Caernarfon. They said. It doesn't matter. They were expecting us. When we rode through the town, the place was empty, which should have warned us, but it didn't. Perhaps with hindsight, which is always perfect, we were arrogant, believed ourselves invincible.

The market cross jutted up, and great tubs of water stood on each street corner against the threat of fire. Most of the shops were shuttered and the townspeople were inside their homes. The tollbooth was unoccupied, which again should have warned us. Only a blacksmith was at work, and he didn't so much as glance up as we passed. English, of course.

John Bolde is Caernarfon's keeper, and he was waiting.

We sent a great wave of men, hoping to fight our way into the castle ward before they realised they were being attacked. But the garrison charged out to meet us, and there were more than twenty men at arms, and many more than eighty archers. The garrison had been reinforced. The information we had was wrong, or old, or both.

And while we were ripped apart by a rain of arrows from the castle, and fought hand to hand with pikes and swords, the town behind us came alive. The townspeople, English to a man, and with no reason to love Glyndŵr, attacked us from behind and almost destroyed us. Three hundred of us died. We were slashed to ribbons, but they at least knew they'd been in a battle, because we destroyed their bloody town before we left. Despite the tubs of water we torched it, shattered it, and killed many, all in the shadow of those sinister, implacable castle walls.

Three hundred good men, lost. But the fighting is over for the winter, and every man thanked God for it. No more, now, until spring. There's no more energy, no more determination, no more longing for blood and battle. Only exhaustion remains, bone-weariness and a longing for home and hearth and family.

We carried our wounded, but, God forgive us, left our dead. My brothers are safe, thank Christ, and so is *Tad*, and Llew. We had been betrayed. But by whom?

CHAPTER EIGHTEEN

Llewelyn

Thank God I'm alive to see the end of another year. What I said to *Tadmaeth* once about dying: stupid. There's nothing glorious about dying; the only thing that's glorious is the way a man dies, but if no one sees, who cares if it's glorious or not? I'd still give my life for *Tadmaeth*, but now I understand the value of the gift. Before the snows come, we'll go home. *Tadmaeth* thinks Glyndyfrdwy is safer and more convenient than Sycharth, and it's a good second-best.

First, we've wounded men to be healed, or if they're too badly injured they must be cared for until they die.

Crach Ffinnant came as the chill sun slipped behind the mountains, streaking the snow-clad peaks with crimson. Men crossed themselves as he brushed past them, the bloody sun outlining him, making him seem from another world. They say he has a secret cave lit by elf-shine. Whatever, he came when we needed him: he knows more than our surgeons. Oh, Wil Potions slaps on holly bark and mallow mixed with lard and wine. His dirt-ingrained hands plaster the stuff on wounds to stop them festering. If rot's set in, he has linseed and bean meal to mix with a coloured cow's milk - if we can find one, but Crach Ffinant looks, and knows if a man will live or die.

When he'd inspected the wounded, there were eleven who got nothing but poppy juice to aid their passing. The others Wil treated, and their groans echoed through the camp and made me want to cover my ears. Healing isn't always gentle.

Throughout the battle, I'd attached myself to Tomos like a limpet. I stayed with him, saw how he avoided the thick of it. Once, when he was trapped by a Caernarfon man whose sword was poised above his head, Tomos turned in the nick of time, shouted. The man turned away. We'd been betrayed, and I knew who'd done it. Retreating, Tomos was in the forefront, not assisting the wounded, waiting for nothing and no one. By the time the main party and the wounded returned he was wrapped in his cloak beside the fire, apparently asleep.

Elffin is closeted with his father, brothers and uncles. It's too late now for talk. Every bone aches with exhaustion, but still I can't sleep, knowing what I know. At last I got up, fetched Elffin's armour and worked grease into the stiff leather and, because no one was watching, wept as I worked, for old Huw is also dead. Not in battle, he was too ancient for that, but from being old and sad. I wept for myself, too, because I knew I had to tell Elffin that the deaths of three hundred good men were my fault.

At last he came out of *Tadmaeth's* cave, white with fatigue and grief. I fetched him cheese and bread and a cup of ale, and wrapped my cloak round his shoulders. When he'd eaten, he put his head back against the boulder, and closed his eyes.

'Elffin...'

'Can it wait, Llew?' His eyelids were dark in the flickering firelight. 'I'd love to talk, but I'm so tired my bones are crumbling.'

'I'm sorry, Elffin.' My voice was a whisper. 'If I don't tell you now I'll die.'

He opened one red eye.

'We were betrayed, and I knew, and I didn't tell you.' I twisted my hands together, anguished.

He sat up, eyes guarded. 'What do you mean?'

'I followed Tomos yesterday and he met someone on the Machynlleth road. I didn't tell you.'

'Why?'

'I thought you'd blame me. And you should. We lost three hundred, and it's my fault.'

'Who did he meet, Llew?'

I couldn't answer. I sat silent.

He gripped my arm, hard enough to hurt. 'Listen. Whoever he met, Tomos couldn't have betrayed our plans for today. No one knew. It was only decided this morning, and against *Tad's* better judgement. He let Gruffydd talk him into one last strike before winter. We betrayed ourselves. If we'd looked, we'd have known Caernarfon had been reinforced. Common sense would have told us that English townsfolk wouldn't help us. Gruffydd's desolate, and Owain is taking all responsibility himself, which is making it worse for Gruffydd. So whoever Tomos met, it had nothing to do with today. So tell me. Who?'

Despite my relief, shame kept me silent. He shook my arm, mock-roughly, then released it. 'Come on, Llew. Who was it?'

I let out breath, clouding in the frosty air. 'Ap Hywel, Elffin. Rhian's husband.'

'Ah.' he said, softly. 'Why doesn't that surprise me?'

'I'm so sorry,' I said.

He stared at me. 'Why?'

'He's my kin, Elffin, and he is a traitor.'

Elffin snorted. 'He's no kin to you. He married your sister, that's all. Did you arrange the marriage? No, Mam, did. You did well, little brother. I'm proud of you. Keep watching Tomos, see who else he meets.'

'Don't you want to kill him? I do. I hate him, the filthy *bradwr*.'

'Yes, I do. But he's more useful alive. At least for a while. We'll bear his stink meanwhile.' He got up, groaning at his stiffening muscles and headed for the cave where Owain was closeted with Crach Ffinnant.

I put his half-cleaned armour aside. My hands were shaking. *He didn't blame me.* I closed my eyes and thanked God. Then I opened them, and fixed them on the slumped, firelit shape of Tomos of Ynys Môn. Closer than his own shadow, I'd be, from now on. And if he betrayed us again, I'd kill him myself.

Rhiannon

Beti has abandoned her doll and is cooing over Angharad's baby. Angharad is besotted. She wraps the infant to her breast in a great shawl, curled like a small animal. She says that it's the most beautiful child in the world, although all babies look the same to me, like wrinkled, old, ugly men, only smaller.

'Is it like its Dada?' Elin asked, when she was allowed to hold it.

Angharad blushed, and took the baby back. 'A bit,' she admitted, peering besottedly at the contorted little face.

'If I knew the father's name,' I said, slyly, 'then I might be able to agree with you. Or not.'

Angharad glanced at me. '*I* know who he is,' she said quietly, 'and that's what matters, isn't it?'

Sometimes, when ap Hywel and Ifan were away, she put the baby bare on sheepskin near the fire, and let it kick, the plump little legs waving wildly. I bent over it if I was passing, searching its tiny face, but babies' faces have no character until life stamps it on, and I could see no resemblance at all to anyone at all.

I can't fasten my skirt properly, and have had to sew on two strings to make the waistband bigger. With Angharad's help I worked out that the baby would come in February or March, and I keep telling myself how far off that is. But one night, with Rhys lying beside me, I remembered Angharad's labour, and terror crept over me. I'd wanted to die, but not in childbirth. Angharad had suffered terribly, and yet hadn't died. How much worse did it have to be for a woman to die? I shuddered, turned over and tried to sleep. The sensation took me unawares, and I shifted, thinking it was wind. It was the child, kicking. I turned onto my back, and spread my hands across my belly. The baby moved again, a definite kick this time. Suddenly I realised that the faint fluttering I'd felt for months now had been the child's early movements. Now it was making its presence felt.

My mind turned in on itself. My body wasn't mine any more, I'd been invaded. This wasn't my child: it was Rhys's, planted in my body against my will. But my body, willy-nilly, was feeding it, caring for it, helping it grow, and something in my head was making me feel - what? Protective? I hoped not. I'd already decided that once it was born, I'd run away from here, and it, and ap Hywel, who could find a wet-nurse for his brat. I'd take my chances with Lady Marged. She'd be furious, but perhaps she'd let me stay. All I had to do was wait until it was warm enough to leave, then I'd walk away from this house for ever.

Next day, well wrapped against the raw November air, I crossed the courtyard to the dairy, where Elin was supposedly churning butter. But the rhythmic sound of the churn had stopped Suddenly, I heard a low whistle, and forgot about Elin and the butter. I looked round. Jack was half-hidden behind the stable door. Glancing over my shoulder to make sure Ifan was elsewhere, I went in.

'News, Rhiannon,' he whispered. Glyndŵr attacked Caernarfon two days ago, but they were beaten off, and lost many men. He survived, and your brother and Glyndŵr's sons with him, but they were routed. It's a bad way to finish the year: he'll be hard put to rally his men for the new year's campaign.'

'No he won't,' I said fiercely. 'They'll rally because he's their True Prince.'

Jack shook his head. 'We'll see. What about you, Rhiannon?' His great hand reached out, hovering over my stomach as if he was going to touch it.

I shrugged. 'It will come. Nothing I can do about that. As you said, that's life.' I didn't realise that I was crying until he stretched out his hand and wiped off a tear, gently, with his rough thumb.

'Is it so bad, Rhiannon?' he asked, gently.

I nodded. 'Oh, Jack, I want to go home.'

Both of us jumped at the voice. '*This* is home, step-mother, remember?' Ifan appeared in the doorway. 'Have I interrupted a secret tryst with a servant? For shame!'

Jack's fists were balled, and I spoke fast to shut him up. 'Tryst?' I said as lightly as I could manage. 'What are you suggesting, Ifan? What a murky little mind you have.' Wrapping my shawl tightly across my breasts, I swept past him with my head up.

Ifan followed me inside, leaning in the doorway and watching as I fetched my work-basket and settled to mend Rhys's shirt. He was making me uncomfortable, but I refused to be intimidated: I ignored him, threading my needle and stitching calmly at the worn elbows. I was getting used to sewing: my fingers were almost puncture-free these days.

Eventually, he went upstairs. His father was away, but Rhys never told me where he was going, or when he'd be back. We'd fallen into some sort of truce, I suppose, because we had to live together, but he knew that I didn't love him, and that I never would, and he, certainly, didn't love me or even particularly like me. There was no kindness, still less respect. I was Glyndŵr's foster-daughter, he was de Grey's man, and if Glyndŵr fell, and he was sure that he would, I would drag him down.

I thought about Caernarfon, and shuddered. "A great many" had been lost, according to Jack. How many was that? A hundred? Two? I thought of my little brother earnestly learning how to use a sword and a lance in the tiltyard, his freckled face pink with excitement, his arms waving like windmills. If I saw him now, would I recognise him? I looked down at myself and grimaced. Would he recognise me? My breasts were swollen, and my waistline was gone. I looked like Crisiant. Thank God Elffin couldn't see me!

Suddenly, I remembered Christmas last year, when I'd worn Elffin's brooch. I hadn't realised how much I'd changed until I saw it in his eyes. The green gown became me, I knew, but the sudden flash of interest when he saw me sitting beside Rhys was unmistakable. And then his look had risen from my breasts to my face and he'd recognised me. I tried to recall his expression, but couldn't. Sometimes I even had difficulty picturing his face. I put aside my sewing, closed my eyes, tried to see Elffin in my mind's eye. I put my hand to my bodice, feeling for the hardness of the fox pin inside my bodice. It wasn't there. Frantically, I patted myself, feeling for the brooch, held my clothing away from my body and shook myself, but nothing fell out. I went out to search the yard, but didn't find it. Perhaps it was upstairs. Perhaps I'd just forgotten to pin it on. I hurried inside and clambered up the narrow stairs, my bulk making me wheeze, frantically rummaging under the pillow, in the piled bedding. Nothing. I sat on the bed, my hands covering my mouth, feeling my lips quiver. It was gone. My last link with Elffin.

Angharad, sleeping baby wound tight against her body, came in carrying linen for the press. She saw my face and stopped, her arms full. 'What's wrong?'

'I've lost something. A - a silver pin. Shaped like a fox's mask. Have you seen it?'

She shook her head. 'No. It'll turn up. Things usually do, if you don't look too hard. Don't worry, you'll find it.' She put the linen away and went away, humming contentedly to herself. Now that the baby had come, she was happier, more settled. It seemed to have given her life a focus, somehow, something that took her away from her own miseries. For days, I looked for my silver fox, but it had gone.

A week or so later, on a bright morning, Angharad left her baby asleep and went into town with Jack to the Christmas Fair, taking Beti and Gwen with her. Elin was in the dairy, my husband had ridden to Ruthin and would be away overnight - hatching some plot with de Grey, I thought bitterly, but the house was peaceful. I was sitting in my room, brushing my hair when the door opened and Ifan came in, without knocking.

'What do you want?' I said, coldly.

'I've got something of yours.' He held up my silver fox.

'Oh! Yes! It's mine. Oh, thank you! Where did you find it?' I got up and reached for it, delighted to have it back, prepared even to smile at him for finding it..

He held it out of my reach, grinning. 'In your bed. Under the pillow, where you always keep it.'

'What were you doing, looking in my bed?'

He pulled a face. 'Your bed? My father's bed.'

'Whatever. I sleep in it. Sons don't usually rummage about in their father's bedding.'

'I do. What will you give me for it?'

'Nothing. It's mine. Give it back at once.'

He shook his head. 'No. You've got to give me something for it. Perhaps - oh, let me see. What about a kiss, step-mother?'

'I'd sooner kiss a diseased rat,' I said coldly, stepping past him onto the small landing at the top of the stairs. I heard him hiss, and then his shove hit me in the small of the back. I crashed down the stairs, tumbling and rolling, hitting wall and stair, until I reached the bottom. I dimly remember Elin's voice, screeching, and then nothing.

Elffin

Tad called us together, my brothers and I, and to his credit included Llewelyn in the gathering. He's been quiet since Caernarfon. I told *Tad* about Rhys and Tomos of Ynys Môn. Siôn was all for cutting Tomos's throat to teach him who to talk to and who not, but Gruffydd thought he'd be more use if he was unaware that we knew of his treachery. False information in the right place could be useful. Even Siôn saw the sense of this.

'I'd quite like to kill him when the time comes,' Llew said. 'I'm fed up to the back teeth with watching him piss and shit.'

In *Tad's* cave a lantern was hooked on a metal spike driven into the rock, and a brazier glowed, smoke finding its way out of the door with difficulty. Before the meeting I sent Tomos to the other end of the encampment on sentry duty. He'd suffer if he left his post, and the other lookouts would know if he did, though as yet they knew nothing of his treachery. He wouldn't be alive, otherwise.

'Caernarfon was a disaster,' *Tad* began.

Gruffydd interrupted, his voice low. 'My fault, Sire. My plan. You just agreed it.'

Tad frowned. 'Do you rule me, Gruffydd? Or do I rule you? I the father, you the son, I the Prince, you my liege. My decision. My fault. I should have known the defences would have been reinforced. Anyway, over now. We learned a lesson. God will sort out blame, if there is any.' He straightened his back, easing it on the low, rough bench. 'I've been in contact with Northumberland.' He raised his hand, smiling, as Gruffydd started to protest. 'Never mind how, Gruffydd. I've promised to swear fealty to the King again, if he allows me to return unmolested to my lands and grants a free pardon for us all.'

Llew went still as stone, and Gruffydd's eyes glittered. 'And Northumberland's reply?' he asked softly.

'He asked what my intentions are. If I submit unconditionally to the King's mercy, then he'll ask for my life. He promises nothing else. I refused to go to England to plead my case. Strange deaths have occurred on English soil, with or without the King's knowledge.'

'Now what?' I asked.

'We wait.' *Tad* replied. 'If I can treat with Northumberland - and perhaps Mortimer, who seems a reasonable man - then I'll end this. There've been too many deaths, and I'm afraid I'll lose all I hold dear if it continues. I can bear to lose my lands, but not my sons.'

Llew had been silent, his eyes wide, flicking from *Tad* to my brothers. 'We can't give up!' he burst out, suddenly. 'You're Prince of Wales! God is on our side. We'll win!'

'Llew. Ah, Llew. We talked, once about horses. I told you that sometimes a horse is better than a sword, because a horse can remove you from danger.'

Llew nodded.

'If we end this now, before it goes any further, then you keep your sword, your horse, your life. If we continue, my next step may be your last.'

I didn't notice Crach Ffinnant in the shadows at the back of the cave until he moved, his sudden appearance making Llew start. He looked round at us all: Gruffydd, Madoc, Maredydd, Tomos, Siôn, Dewi, Llew and I, gazing into our faces as if searching for something. I expected him to spout another of his predictions, but instead he thrust his hands up his wide sleeves, bowed his head and glided silently from the cave.

Llew's breath whistled out of his lungs. He does not like the Crab and won't even look at him in case the wizard can read his mind. I think Ffinnant's a fraud. He has no magic, only the ability to convince people that he has tricks with herbs to make a person see strange things and a very good spy network.

That thought led to another. And another.

CHAPTER NINETEEN

Llewelyn

I scattered the ashes of the campfire, the last task before we left Pumlumon, with a grin on my face as broad as Crisiant's arse. We were leaving later than we should have been, but our wounded made travel impossible. The snow held off, but the cold was a thing as tangible as rock. When I stuck my head out from my cocoon each morning, my eyes watered and my head ached. Men weren't meant to sleep outside in winter. Riding down the mountain, ice crackled under Siôned's hooves and her nostrils steamed like dragon breath.

Glyndyfrdwy is not Sycharth but it's still home. It was a slow journey, because of wounded men in litters. Despite poppy-juice, hisses of pain at the jolting turned quickly to groans. De Grey should have been snug at Ruthin for Christmas, but all the same we were alert for ambush, outriders everywhere, with Wil Sharpeye riding ahead. But I ached to put Sioned into a mad gallop for home.

Four miles off, the first fat flakes of snow fell, and it was that magic hour when it is neither light nor dark, but a strangeness in between: someone said once that Frenchmen call it 'the hour twixt dog and wolf'. Snow drifted and the air had an eerie blueness. At last, Glyndyfrdwy appeared, a dark shape in the distance, but closer, we could see candlelight glowing behind jewelled windows. Elffin rode beside me, and like me, he was gazing at Glyndyfrdwy as if it were the Holy Grail.

Lady Marged was waiting, her eyes on her husband and sons, and Crisiant wept when she saw Elffin, and again when she saw me, and held up her arms. Luckily, being taller these days, I'm no longer in danger of suffocation between her breasts. The top of her head fits under my chin, now, and I can almost get my arms all round her - if I stretch.

'Oh, *Duw*!' she said, swiping wet from her eyes. 'Look at the size of you! Big as trees, the pair of you!' Then the soft weight of her was pressed against me again, and more tears were shed. Over her shoulder, I saw Mali, the red ribbon I'd given her in her hair, and her eyes filled with light. I had to ignore her, of course, except for a small smile, but I'll make it up to her, later.

The wounded were taken off to be fussed over, and the rest of us were enfolded by the household. Soup and bread and meat were brought, and the fires banked up and it was so good to be within four walls again that I almost died of contentment, nodding off by the fire like a cat, every bone giving off a small, glad ache.

Two weeks to Christ's Mass, and Lady Marged was Preparing. Great boughs of holly and fir stood in the courtyard ready for Christmas Eve (bad luck to bring them inside before). The woodpile stood higher than I did, cut ends leaking fragrant sap, and the Yule log, a great trunk of gnarled apple-wood, was drying in the barn, ready to fill the house with the spectre of long-gone fruit.

The rich odour of apples stuck with cloves, the fragrance of new rushes and the sweet smell of yellow wax candles brought back memories of last Christmas at Sycharth, when Rhian had been with us. I'd miss her, this year, but at least I shouldn't need to be polite to my traitorous brother-in-law and his odious son.

I wondered when - or if - I'd see Rhiannon again. A visit would be virtually impossible in current circumstances. Both rebel and outlaw, I could hardly go calling on ap Hywel. He might decide to hand me over to his master. I'm not important enough to warrant a ransom, of course, but that mightn't stop him. It's a sobering thought, that I may not see my only blood kin ever again.

At supper I sat with the family: no longer waiting at table myself, but being waited on by admiring small boys. I watched Mali circle the tables, bringing meat, and later a dish of onions and cream, which she held for me while I helped myself, her face modestly lowered. I replaced the spoon in the bowl and slid my free hand up her skirt. She jumped a foot into the air and squeaked, drawing eyes to us. I scowled at her, so that I shouldn't be blamed, but winked also, which made her blush even more.

I want to be with her. I'll burst if I don't have her soon. God knows when, though. I'm sharing a bed with Elffin, and the chamber with two others, most of the rooms being full of guests and the wounded, and if I lay a finger on Mali in daylight Bron will have me for it, since she doesn't agree with such goings on.

Iolo Goch sang afterwards, his voice wreathing like smoke and ringing like crystal. If you don't look at him, you might think it was an angel singing, although angels wouldn't sing the bawdy songs that he launches into when Lady Marged isn't there!

Midnight was long past when the men dispersed and fell into bed, although Elffin, having drunk even more than I had, slept instantly, snoring face down in feather pillows.

Strange, sleeping in a bed. I almost wanted to put my cloak on the floor and sleep there, being more used to the hard ground, but the floor was occupied already, and I was better off in the bed. I wasn't sleeping next to Tomos, either, which made a welcome change: he snored and farted in his sleep, but he was billeted in the stables, and with the snow still falling he wasn't going anywhere.

We hunted next day, Elffin, Madoc, Siôn, Gruffydd and me, riding through great billows of snow, the horses hating the drifts but breasting them because we asked them to. We found a stag with a fine rack of antlers, and it was my arrow that brought him down. We gutted him, and put him across one of the horses, and set off home happy in the knowledge that for a few short weeks at least, there'd be no more fighting. We'd sleep easy in comfortable beds, there'd be drink to make us drowsy and content, food that was cooked on spits and in ovens, not scorched on a smoky campfire, and best of all we could let down our guard and relax.

And there was Mali...

Rhiannon

Elin had stopped screeching when I came round, but was weeping instead, snot from her blob of a nose running down her chin. She was bending over me, fluttering like a chicken. Ifan had made himself scarce.

'Oh, Mrs Rhian!' she said helplessly. 'You fell downstairs! Oh, are you dead?'

Fairly obviously I wasn't, but I was in pain.

'Oh, Mrs Rhiannon,' the girl sniffled. 'You hit your head a terrible crack, you did!'

As if I didn't know. I tried to sit up, but a fierce shaft of pain in my head, echoed by one in my lower belly, put me on the floor again. 'I don't think I can get up by myself,' I whispered.

'Oh, Miss, whatever shall we do? The Master's away, and Jack won't be back for ever so long. Oh, Miss, fancy you falling all the way down the stairs like that!'

'I didn't fall,' I said shortly. 'Ifan pushed me.'

Elin stared at me, and her hands came up to cover her mouth. 'Oh, Mrs Rhiannon!' she blurted. 'Don't say that! Master Ifan wouldn't do that!'

'Yes Master Ifan would,' I said through gritted teeth. 'He did. Look, help me up. If I can get to a chair perhaps I'll feel better.'

She half-carried me through to the little parlour. I slumped painfully on the wooden settle and took a careful inventory of my bits and pieces. Nothing seemed to be broken, I could move all my arms and legs, but my head felt as if it was splitting open, and there was a dull ache in my belly and back. I put tentative fingers to my head and found various lumps. Despite the way I felt, my brains were not actually trickling out of my ears. I might survive.

Then shock set in and I began to tremble. Ifan had pushed me! I might have been killed. I'd goaded him, but did he hate me so much? He was spiteful, malicious - but did he want me dead?

Probably not, I reassured myself. Perhaps it was my fault. But if I'd died, and if it looked like an accident - only my word to say that I'd been pushed - then he probably wouldn't be too sorry.

Elin brought me a soothing tisane. I sipped it, trying to keep my shaking hands from spilling the hot liquid, but I felt clammy and cold, and couldn't stop shivering. I became gradually aware that the pain in my back was increasing, growing gradually in intensity and then, to my relief, dying away again, and at the same time I felt my belly cramp. After a minute or two, the pain came again, stronger this time.

Then Elin shrieked again, looking at the floor under my seat. 'Oh, Miss,' she moaned, 'you're bleeding something awful.'

I saw a dark pool spreading across the flagstones. My head swam, and I knew I was about to faint again. In an emergency - which this was proving to be - Elin would be useless. I'd die while she ran about bumping into furniture and wiping her nose on her sleeve. Summoning strength from somewhere, I said, as firmly as I could manage, 'Elin, fetch Ceridwen, quickly.' Then, just as Elin was shaking her head nervously, I felt myself slipping into darkness again. 'Fetch her!' I muttered.

I opened my eyes to pain. I was lying on my bed, the coverings stripped off, my feet propped on pillows. Ceridwen, her sleeves rolled up, was stirring something in a steaming beaker. Seeing me move, she sat beside me, and lifted my shoulders.

'Here,' she said. 'Drink this. It will help stop the bleeding.'

I sniffed the liquid suspiciously. 'What is it?'
She rolled her eyes. 'Does it matter? Horse-mint, tansy and ale.'
'Is that all?'
She nodded and I drank it. I've tasted better, but there was a comforting warmth to it. When I had finished it I sank back, my head swimming again.
'Why am I bleeding?'
'It looks like you're going to get your wish.'
'Wish?'
'Baby's coming. It'll die, I expect. It's too early. The air will be too strong for its lungs. A bit later, it might have a chance, even if it is winter, but now...'
I stared at her, not understanding. 'It can't be the baby. It isn't due until -'
She patted my hand. 'I know. But babies don't take kindly to mothers who jump down flights of stairs.'
'I didn't jump. Ifan - Rhys's son - pushed me.'
It was her turn to stare. 'Really, Rhiannon? Ifan pushed you?'
I nodded, and watched her face change. Then a pain crept up on me, swelling and swelling until I thought my back would break in two. It was too powerful for screams, but I grunted like an animal and arched my back.
'There, there, now' she wiped my face. 'Won't be long now. It'll get worse, but it will end, I promise.'
And so it did, but not before I'd wailed and howled and wished I was dead a hundred times, all the time knowing that I was suffering one-tenth of what Angharad had. But it came, and it was alive, but only just. Ceridwen took the tiny creature as it slithered out of me, its head no bigger than an apple, wrapped it and put it in my arms. It was breathing, just, and it was a boy. I traced a cross on its forehead and named it Owain, after *Tadmaeth*. When his soft, moth-light breathing ceased, I kissed him, not because I loved him, but because he was tiny, and mine, and his life was over before it had begun. He'd relied on me. I'd let him down.
Then 'Oh shit.' The obscenity coming from Ceridwen seemed inappropriate at that moment of birth and death, but then I saw that I was still bleeding, and bleeding and bleeding.
The lifeless child was tugged from my arms and dropped on the bed, and Ceridwen got to work to try to stop the flow. She screamed for Elin to fetch dried yarrow from the still-room.

I swallowed the yarrow, and still I bled. When Ceridwen threw her shawl about her shoulders and headed for the door, I stared in terror and amazement. 'Ceridwen!' I wailed, 'don't leave me!'

She turned, and glared. 'Don't be stupid. As if I would! I'm going to fetch something from home. I'll be back as fast as I can. You,' she jerked her head at Elin, indicating the baby. 'Wrap that up and take it outside. Put it somewhere safe where the dogs can't get at it in case her man wants to see it before it's buried. Then stay with her.'

I heard her thump barefoot down the wooden stairs, then the clatter of her clogs as she tore across the cobblestones. Elin stared at me, tears trickling down her face, wringing her hands and shifting from foot to foot. Then she pulled herself together, took a cloth from the press, picked up the baby and wrapped him, hiding its tiny face last of all. I watched her leave, and wondered whether soon we'd be buried, my son and I, in the same grave. Blood seeped warm.

And then Ceridwen was back in a gust of cold air, flinging her shawl into one corner and forcing open my mouth, tipping a bittersweet cordial down my throat so that I choked back to consciousness, and spluttered and coughed.

'That's it,' she said. 'That has to work. Don't you dare die on me. Come on, Rhiannon, concentrate. Don't go to sleep, now. You need to stay awake. Elin, put another pillow under her feet. Stop bleeding, Rhiannon, stop it, now.' Her face was fierce, the dark brows drawn together in concentration, as if she could keep me there by sheer will-power. Maybe she did.

When ap Hywel came back, the bleeding had stopped, and I was being fed broth to get my strength back, and red wine to make more blood to replace what I'd lost. He stood at the end of the bed, his face expressionless, while Elin backed away and fled, her banshee wails floating back up the stairs. Ceridwen, though, stood her ground, arms folded, her eyes glittering.

'Got rid of it, did you?' he said, not taking his eyes from my face. 'And the witch helped you.'

'Your son pushed her downstairs,' Ceridwen said softly. 'And Rhiannon was close to dying.'

His eyes flickered to her. 'Ifan? You're lying.'

Ceridwen frowned. 'Your son, ap Hywel. You know him best.'

'Get out. One word of this to anyone and you'll hang for the witch you are.'

She shrugged, and lifted her shawl up to cover her hair. 'I'll leave you the rest of the cordial,' she said, straightening the bedcover across my stomach. 'If you bleed again, get word to me. I'll come, I promise. No matter what he says.'

I grasped at her hand. 'Thank you. I won't forget you.' And then she was gone.

'Where is it?'

'I don't know. Elin took it. She's kept it safe. It isn't buried yet.'

'Did it live?'

'For a few minutes.'

'What was it?'

'A boy. I named it, and made the sign of the cross on his forehead so he'd go to God.'

'What did name did you give it?'

I wasn't stupid. 'Rhys,' I lied, crossing my fingers under the bed linen.

He turned and left, and I didn't see him again for more than a week, although he was in and about the house.

I asked Elin if he'd said anything to Ifan, and she shook her head.

I turned my face into my pillow. Rhys ap Hywel would believe his son before his wife.

Snow came that night: slow, heavy flakes silencing the world. I didn't cry again until ap Hywel was away and Jack stole up to see me. He held my hands and I told him what had happened.

'What if I start another baby?' I wept. 'I have to get away, Jack. Ifan pushed me down the stairs. What if he does it again? I'm frightened. I want to go home.'

He bent and I felt his warm lips in the palm of my hand. 'The snow's too deep, now, Rhian, but I promise, when you're well again, I'll get you away from here.'

'Keep Ifan away from me?' I begged, 'I'm afraid of him.'

'Are you sure he pushed you?'

I told him about the fox pin, and Ifan finding it and refusing to return it, and demanding a kiss. 'I told him I'd rather kiss a diseased rat.' I admitted, and watched Jack's face crease into a grin.

He shook his head. 'Oh, Rhian. Your tongue'd slice mutton at twenty paces. Please, curb it, especially with your step-son.'

'He had my brooch!' I said indignantly. 'And he's an evil, weasly little slug.'

'Is the brooch so important to you?'

'It was a gift from - one of my foster-brothers. It's all I have left of home except Lady Marged's recipe book. Which is dry as dust. I wear the pin always. But now it's gone.'

Jack came that evening, and silently handed me the silver pin. I cried when I saw it, tears of weakness trickling off my nose, salt in my mouth. When I looked up, he was gone. He left late that night, despite the snow, without saying goodbye or telling anyone where he was going. But I thought I knew.

Elffin

My father's bid for peace didn't succeed. It could have, and thereby saved the English crown humiliation, suffering and money, but while Northumberland was advising Henry to treat with Glyndŵr, he was also, good military man that he is, advising him to garrison the Pole and reinforce Chester and Harlech.

It might have worked, but there are those who don't want Glyndŵr pardoned, who would prefer him dead. De Grey, of course, but also Beaufort, who has Glyndŵr's lands. He won't release them willingly. Indeed, why should he?

De Grey apparently suggested that Northumberland and Mortimer should meet *Tad* near the English border: then Glyndŵr could be killed, ensuring the instant collapse of the rebellion. Treacherous bastard. I might respect him more if his treachery occasionally benefited his King, but it doesn't, and never will. Northumberland, for all his sins, and to his eternal credit, refused, and the opportunity passed.

But we're at Glyndyfrdwy, and no sooner do we sit than food is pushed into our hands and the fire built up. We're warriors, but we could grow soft on this, and never want to leave again.

Ten days before Christmas the day dawned clear as crystal, one of those perfect winter days when sun flashes diamonds on snow and dazzles the eye, and icicles send clear drops to plop on the heads of the unwary. Just after noon there was a commotion at the gate. I was in the solar with Madoc, Gruffydd and Siôn, all of us full of food, and I was the only one energetic - or curious enough - to get up and look out of the window. The door-keeper and another man were carrying someone inside, while a third man led a trembling, blowing horse into the courtyard.

We were downstairs and in the yard in seconds, opening doors and making room by the fire, shooing dogs and drowsy men out of the way. The newcomer was propped in a chair, and hot ale brought, for he was almost unconscious with cold and weariness. When he raised his face from the mug, I recognised him.

Llew, who has been trying desperately to get Mali alone since the day we came home, wandered into the hall, recognised the visitor and ran to him, gripping him by the shoulder.

'Jack? What's happened? What in God's name brings you here in this weather? Is it my sister?'

No sane man rides any distance in deep snow. My thoughts leapt to Rhiannon, and then, belatedly, to Angharad.

'Rhiannon, yes,' he muttered. 'She lost her child yesterday and near bled to death.'

'Rhian?' Llew's face had lost all its colour. ' Is she all right?'

'She'll live. She fell downstairs and the baby came early. It died. She almost joined it.'

Llew put his face in his hands and I realised how fortunate I was to have my family. Other than Rhiannon, he has no one.

'If she'll live, then why come?' Blunt Madoc always spoke his mind. 'Couldn't you have waited until the weather broke? Where's the urgency?'

Jack leaned towards the fire. 'She was pushed.'

I dropped to one knee, looking up into his face. Who did it?'

'Ap Hywel's brat. He stole some trinket from her, and tormented her with it. Asked for a kiss for its return, and when she refused - a bit waspish, being Rhiannon - he lost his temper and shoved her. She should be taken from there before he tries again.'

I was afraid I knew the answer, but I asked anyway, as lightly as I could manage. 'What was it he stole?'

Jack shrugged. 'Nothing much. A silver pin, shaped like the mask of a fox. A gift from one of her foster-brothers, she said, but precious to her.'

Llew pounded his fist on the back of Jack's chair. 'That little, rat-faced bastard! I'll tear his head off his neck and stuff it up his -'

Mam, alerted by the commotion at the gate, appeared behind him, speaking softly. 'Perhaps you'd better not finish that sentence, Llew! I am sure we all appreciate your distress.'

He subsided, blushing. 'Sorry, *Mamaeth*,' he muttered. 'But ap Hywel's son pushed Rhiannon downstairs and nearly killed her. He killed her baby! Jack came to tell us, or we wouldn't know.'

The Lady sank onto a settle, concern disturbing her habitual calm. 'Oh, poor child! How is she, Jack?'

'Recovered in body, my Lady, but low, low in spirits.'

'It is hard to lose a child.'

Jack shook his head. 'Forgive me for speaking, Lady Marged, but she didn't want ap Hywel's child. She doesn't love him and he resents her for who she is.'

'Who she is?' Mam's face was puzzled.

'He's de Grey's man, Lady Marged, and afraid that marriage to Glyndŵr's foster-daughter will be held against him. He gives her no love, and little of his company, although he shares her bed. She wants to come home to the only family she has.'

Mam was silent for a few moments. Then: 'She is married to ap Hywel.' She was implacable. 'His wife in the eyes of God, and she must stay with him. He is her family now. It is her duty to bear his children, even if she doesn't love him. She may not come here. It would be wrong to come between a man and his wife.'

'And if she dies, Lady?'

'She is in God's hands.'

None of us had seen *Tad* come into the hall. 'She was once in mine. She should come home, my love.'

My mother met his eyes. Her back was sword-straight and her voice unwavering. There was more steel in her than in many a soldier. 'Rhiannon was ever one to over-dramatise. She stays where she is. If we take her back against his wishes, it might be all that de Grey needs to attack us, here at Glyndyfrdwy, or even at Sycharth. Abduction of a wife? We are in enough danger here already, husband, without courting certain disaster.'

Owain Glyndŵr, Prince of Wales, turned on his heel and left the hall. Mam was right, of course, but I pitied Rhiannon. Then I saw the small smile of satisfaction, so fleeting that I might almost have imagined it, on my mother's face.

CHAPTER TWENTY

Llewelyn
It was so easy to let Rhiannon go. Her happiness hadn't been important in my new man's world. I'd been so certain she'd learn to love her husband. But she didn't, and no blame to her. Her stepson has tried to kill her, and her husband feels nothing for her. And I, her brother and only blood kin, can change nothing.

I raked my hair in frustration. 'I can't disobey Lady Marged,' I told Jack. 'Even *Tadmaeth* won't do that: Prince of Wales, he is, but she rules the household. If I could get Rhian away, I would, but where could I take her? A nunnery? She'd empty it in a week and the nuns would take up devil worship as the safer option. If I brought her here, would Lady Marged relent?' No. Rhian would be back at Pentregoch so fast her feet wouldn't touch the ground.

'Rhian's been miserable since she left Sycharth, but now she's afraid too.' He paced, head down. Then he stopped. 'However -' he shook his head. 'No. Too dangerous.'

'What?' I grabbed his arm. 'Anything. Tell me!'

'You could see her. You'd need to be careful, mind, stay well away from the house. If de Grey caught you, meaning no offence, Llew, he'd kill you out of hand. You aren't worth ransoming!'

'Where? There must be somewhere.'

He rubbed his jaw, fingers rasping on stubble. 'Somewhere far enough from Pentregoch but close enough for her to get away. You couldn't travel in this weather, anyway.'

'You came, though. So, where, Jack? Just for an hour.'

'If that, in case she's missed. He smiled, although it didn't reach his eyes. 'Ceridwen's hut. She saved Rhiannon's life. Some say she's a witch, but she just knows about herbs and physics to cure what ails. I'll ask her. If she'll risk it, I'll get word to you. When you're there, I'll bring Rhiannon. Tell no one, Llew, or it could be the end of me. If ap Hywel or de Grey learn that I've been here, I'm good as dead. Worth the risk: it will do her good to see you.'

'Thanks, Jack. When I can come, I'll leave early: I should be there around noon. How do I find the place?'

'It's about a mile away from the house, right on the edge of the village, which is good. Too many eyes, nowadays, too many clacking tongues. Here.' He grabbed a piece of charred wood and sketched a rough map on a flagstone. 'Here's the house. Leave your horse here and go on foot. Ceridwen will come for me and I'll bring Rhiannon.'

'What if you can't get away?'

'I'll manage somehow, though you might have to wait. You'll be safe enough, if you're careful.'

I was like a badger with arse-ache after Jack left at mid-day, hoping to reach Pentregoch after dark.

Later, Mali cornered me in the shadows near the kitchen. I kissed her, quickly, and disentangled myself. 'Not now, Mali,' I mumbled. 'I'm busy.'

'You said you loved me.'

'I do. But right now I've got things on my mind.'

She pouted and folded her arms, which pushed her small breasts together at the top of her bodice. I might have weakened except Bron arrived, boxed Mali's ears and sent her to scour some pots.

'And you,' she said, wagging her finger at me when Mali, had run away clutching her ear, 'you leave her alone. She's got work to do, and she can't concentrate with you sniffing at her skirts all day.'

'Me?' I protested, 'what have I done?' I shouldn't have asked.

She folded freckled arms and glared. 'Want me to go into details, is it, Llew? Next time you put your hand up her skirt while she's serving, you'll be for it, right? I'll beat you black and blue, big as you are. Keep your trews done up, is it? She's not a bad little worker when you're not around, but when you are she's useless. And if there's a baby, we'll all know whose fault it is, right?'

Well. Imagine, a servant speaking like that! Long after
Bron waddled away I thought of some very sarcastic remarks that would have reduced her to shreds, but right then I couldn't think of anything, much. I just stood like a half-wit, opening and shutting my mouth. *And* she clouted me for good measure. I slouched off to my chamber to try to think of something to take my sister to cheer her up.

I was sitting by the fire, trying to decide between a pretty silver ring I'd looted at Rhuddlan, and a more expensive but less attractive gold cloak-pin I'd liberated at Holt, when Elffin slumped beside me. He was not happy.

'Your face,' I said, 'looks like a slapped arse.'

'Shut it, Llew,' he said, 'or I'll shut it for you.'

'Look,' I protested. 'I've got problems too. No need to have a go at me.'

'Problems?' he said, 'you haven't got problems. You don't know the meaning of the word.'

'My sister's living with a man she hates, with a step-son trying to kill her,' I protested. 'And I've got to try and get -' I stopped. Ooops. I shut up.

'Get what?'

'Nothing.'

He hauled me off my stool. 'What are you up to, Llew? Tell me or I'll drop you out of the window, head first.'

'You and what army?' I blustered, but I knew he could do it. I just wasn't sure if he would.

'Just me. Now, tell me.' He gave me a shake that rattled my teeth.

'I'm going over to see Rhian,' I said, sullenly. 'Jack's going to bring her somewhere safe.' He dropped me, and I rearranged my jerkin.

'Is he, now. When?'

'As soon the weather's cleared. If I can just have an hour with her, perhaps it'll help. I've got to see her, Elffin. She's my sister and she nearly died. Even if Lady Marged won't let me bring her back, I need to see her. Don't tell anyone.'

'Don't worry, Llew, I won't tell. I'm coming with you. Less suspicious that way, right? We'll say we're going hunting. Or say we've been hunting, after. I'll get Bron to give us some food to take with us.' He'd lost his miserable expression.

I half-heard a sound outside the door, but that wasn't unusual, and I forgot it at once. Whatever Elffin's motives, I'd be glad of his company. But it would be hard, waiting.

Rhiannon

Rhys is sleeping in Ifan's room, thank God, because I'm still bleeding. I miss Jack. If he's really gone to tell Llew, surely he won't leave me here? Unless he is too busy with war to think of me. In the meantime all I can do is wait.

I don't know what happened to the baby. I expect it was buried: it lived and died, and only I cared, and I didn't care enough. What if it had lived? Would I have loved it?

One morning I woke to find ap Hywel standing over me. I stared back, knowing that if I didn't face him he'd assume I was guilty of something. Did he think I'd killed the baby? I could have, once, but

I'm glad Jack stopped me. I was beginning to lose my nerve and was tempted to look away, but then he spoke.

'You must apologise to Ifan and make your peace with him. He swears before God and on his mother's life' (*Ha!* I thought. *Bit late for that! His mother's been dead for years!*) 'he didn't push you. You tripped, and he tried to catch you. Perhaps you dreamed it. But I forgive you for accusing him.'

Why argue? My word against Ifan's. The sneaking, murderous little rat. I won't give him an opportunity to try again.

Angharad brings my food, but I see no one else. Even Beti's been kept away. Perhaps she'll go to her Aunt when the roads are clear. I enjoy the solitude, the sun on the snow filling the room with light, and I drowse and wake, drowse and wake. Sometimes I cry, but not often, because I can't bear weakness. Crying changes nothing. I'll still be married to Rhys ap Hywel, and I expect he'll want to sleep with me, and then this will happen again.

He doesn't know I named the baby for *Tadmaeth*. That secret's mine. There is nothing else to cheer me. At first I wished I'd died, but when I grew stronger, my spirits rose. Winter sunlight blue on snow has a way of lightening burdens.

Angharad brought me bread and cheese for breakfast, and I ate it all. Afterwards, she took the platter away and brought her baby. She's named him Gethin. I tried to remember a Gethin at Sycharth, but the only one that came to mind was old, toothless, and unlikely.

The baby was *cwtched* on my raised knees, and I held his flailing fists and made conversation. I don't talk nonsense to him: if he's to be intelligent he should be spoken to properly. Angharad, however, blows bubbles, and calls him "*Cariad sidan fach*" and talks such drivel I'm surprised the baby doesn't go to sleep in disgust. When I talk to him, his bright eyes never leave my face, and he sticks out his pink little tongue, blows bubbles and makes excited noises. I don't like babies, mind, they're messy and smelly, but this one I will make an exception for. I told him all about Sycharth, where his Mam came from, cheering myself up and making myself miserable, all at once, when Gethin pulled a face I recognised. He was so like someone I knew! But who? Whoever it was, recognition had been instant. But then he made a huge farting noise with his lips and spattered me with spittle, and Angharad came and took him away to feed him, and I was so tired I fell asleep myself.

It was dusk when I woke to the gentle creak of the door. I lay still, feigning sleep in case it was Rhys. The room was in shadow. A dim shape at the door, a darker patch against the gloom. Then it came towards me, and through slitted eyes, I recognised Ifan. My heart hammered.

He bent over me. 'I know you're awake,' he whispered, his sour breath in my face. 'Sorry about your accident. I'll do better next time, I promise.'

I clamped my eyes shut. I wanted to scream, but knew it wouldn't make any difference. Perhaps when he killed me, ap Hywel might believe me, and Ifan would be punished. Wouldn't do me much good though, would it?

Elffin

Whenever Jack comes, he brings news that turns my brain to porridge. This time, I knew what he was going to say. I couldn't understand what was so urgent, and I was almost relieved when he went to Llew, not me. But now it was my turn.

He rubbed the side of his nose. 'Congratulations,' he said, a grin twitching his mouth. 'You have a son. Gethin.'

'Has she told anyone -'

'No. Unless she's told Rhiannon, but I don't think so. She had a hard time of it. If not for Ceridwen - who also saved Rhiannon - she'd have died. The lad was a good size, and she's not broad in the hips. But they're both fine.'

'Does she need money?'

'Women always need money, Elffin. But in the way you mean it, no. She's cared for, though she came in for some abuse when ap Hywel learned he'd been landed with a servant with a full belly. He'd throw a purple fit if he knew he was harbouring Glyndŵr's grandson. Lucky the lad's strong: when he's older he'll be put to work.'

'But -'

'But what? He's your son? He's a bastard you got on a servant. That your Mam got rid of.'

'Mam didn't know.'

'She did.'

'She didn't. She couldn't have!'

'Servants talk, Elffin. Your Mam has as good a network of spies as your father has - possibly better, given the Caernarfon fiasco.

She knows everything that happens, everything - sometimes before those involved know themselves! She'd spoken to Angharad, who admitted that she was pregnant. Angharad didn't need to tell her who'd done it, your mother knew already. So she was neatly dispatched with Rhiannon.'

I grabbed my hair, despairingly. 'Mam can't know for certain.'

Jack grinned. 'You underestimate her, Elffin. Women know a lot more than we give them credit for. And *Duw*, if she met the boy, she'd be in no doubt at all.'

'Like me, is he?' I could feel a grin creeping onto my face.

'The spit. He's got Angharad's little nose and is dark-skinned like she is, but he'll be rangy as a colt by the time he's four, and stubborn as a mule already.'

Pride swelled. Me, a father! 'Jack, if I give you some money, will you give it to Angharad if she needs it?'

He laughed. 'How do you know I won't steal it?'

'You're Glyndŵr's man, Jack. You wouldn't steal from his son. Or his grandson.'

'No. There's times when I could shake your mother until her teeth rattled, but your Mam would give de Grey a time of it if they went head to head. She's as manipulative as he is, and no one should underestimate her. Lady Marged doesn't lie - but there's times when she's economical with the truth.'

I scowled. 'My mother's -' I began. Mam had disposed of Rhiannon, removed Angharad, and stopped Rhiannon coming home. I knew she was right, that if we brought Rhian here it would give de Grey and ap Hywel excuse to attack us, but still, Rhiannon was trapped with someone who hated her enough to shove her down a flight of stairs.

Jack raised an eyebrow. 'You were saying?'

'Never mind. And stop grinning. Maybe Mam does arrange things to her own advantage, but she's still my mother.' *Duw*! How pompous I sounded.

I had to ask. 'The pin Rhiannon lost - the one Ifan took. It was a silver fox, you said?'

Jack nodded. 'Just a cheap thing.'

'She treasured it, though.'

He nodded. 'She said it was her last link with home.'

That didn't help, either. I watched Jack mount and wished I had something I could send Angharad besides money. But what?

Certainly not affectionate messages. I didn't want to raise her hopes. All right, she'd had my son, but I didn't love her, could never marry her. I couldn't even acknowledge my child. If Mam suspected, I didn't want to confirm it. If she knew for definite, then God help me. Christ, she'd hang me by my heels and flay me alive. Money was safest. I wanted to send something to Rhiannon, too, so she wouldn't cling so fiercely to the cheap trinket I'd so casually, thoughtlessly given her.

CHAPTER TWENTY-ONE

Llewelyn
One pale, icy morning, we left. The gate-keeper fumbled at iron bolts, eyes half-shut, muttering about being got up early on a cold morning.

The air was so cold my chest ached, but when the sun came up branches dripped rainbows off their tips, and light dazzled on swollen rivers. We made good time and before noon were near Pentregoch. The muddy track to the house stretched empty, ice stippled in ruts. We branched off between the trees: it was colder in the shadows, and I was glad of my fur-lined cloak.

We hid the horses and made our way towards the hut. When the woman opened to our knock, a stink of mutton-fat rush-lights and wood-smoke greeted us. She scooped black hair from her face. 'You'll be the brother,' she said. 'You've the look of herself about you. Mind, she's prettier.' She draped a shawl round her body, and slipped wooden clogs onto bare feet. 'Hot broth in the pot,' she said, indicating the cauldron steaming over a fire-pit. 'If she can't get away, you'll have to wait, won't you? Perhaps until tomorrow.' She slipped out, closing the door behind her.

'God, I hope not!' Elffin muttered. 'If we're late back we'll catch it. The gatekeeper thinks we're hunting - if they have to send out a search-party the fat will really be in the fire.'

I shrugged. 'If necessary I'll stay, you go back. She's my sister. You don't need to be here. Mind,' I added hastily, 'I'm glad you came, Elffin.'

'No need. Want some of this stuff?'

'I suppose it *is* broth?' I said, peering into the pot. 'It smells all right, but she's witch, isn't she? We might turn into toads.'

'You'll be all right then,' Elffin said. 'Definite improvement where you're concerned.'

I swiped at him with the ladle, then slopped some broth into a wooden bowl. I tasted it. 'This is good!'

Elffin tasted and raised an eyebrow. The bowl was emptied in moments. 'I wonder what that was,' he said, thoughtfully, as I finished my own. 'Venison. Or rabbit. Not like either, though.'

'Better off not knowing,' I said. 'Maybe hedgehog. Or squirrel.'

'Or rat.'

I shuddered. When we'd finished we sat beside the fire and waited, lulled into silence by the warmth of the fire.

It was mid-afternoon before she came back, by which time we'd run out of conversation and Elffin was wrapped snoring in his cloak stretched out on a bench in the corner. I was drowsing on a settle by the fire. Jack came in, a woollen cloak wrapped round him, and behind him, smaller, thinner than I remembered, her great grey eyes almost filling her face, Rhiannon. He hadn't warned her, and her jaw dropped, her eyes widened, she flung her arms wide and rushed towards me, squeaking with delight.

'Shh, Rhiannon,' Ceridwen warned. 'Ice on the ground, sound travels.' She piled twigs on the fire, and the rich smell of burning brambles filled the hut. 'Take off your cloak, *cariad*. You won't feel the benefit when you go, otherwise.' She hitched her skirts to her knees and rubbed life into bare, purpled legs.

Rhiannon let go of me, her hands reaching for the fastening of her cloak. She stared past me. Her face lost all colour and I realised that she was going to faint, and caught her as she fell.

Elffin shifted awkwardly from foot to foot as Ceridwen patted her face and burned feathers under her nose and brought her, choking, back to consciousness. Her eyes opened and fastened on Elffin. She'd forgotten I was there. Whatever feelings she'd had for him before, she had still.

'Elffin,' she said, her voice a sigh of longing. I patted her hand, kissed it, knelt beside her, but she didn't notice.

Was this a way to bring her home? If Elffin - but Lady Marged wouldn't stand for it, and there was still ap Hywel. Anyway what would Elffin want with my idiot sister?

Elffin was silent. I stared at him. Elffin? Rhiannon? Surely not. And then we were all distracted, because Jack's cloak heaved and screamed.

Grinning, Jack shrugged the cloak off his shoulders. In his arms squirmed a fat, red-faced baby, furious at being woken. It screwed up its face and wailed. Rhiannon held out her arms as if she were glad of the distraction, and Jack put the baby into them.

'Poor Gethin,' she crooned, kissing the downy head. 'Half-smothered under Jack's cloak, and woken too early, and all for no good reason, is it, *cariad fach*?'

'But your baby died,' I said, stupidly.

'Yes,' Rhian said, calmly. 'This is Angharad's. Jack said he needed some fresh air.'

I swung round, staring at Elffin. Now I knew why he'd come with me!

'You sly bastard!' I howled. 'You got a son on Angharad and you didn't so much as hint!'

Rhiannon

Jack persuaded me to go walking with him. 'The sun's out,' he said. 'The trees are full of demented birds, and you've been stuck indoors too long. Come on. It'll do you good. We'll take Gethin, give him some fresh air and his Mam some peace. He won't be cold inside my cloak.'

Gethin was teething, and irritable as a boil. He shrieked when Angharad picked him up, and shrieked louder if she put him down. He didn't like me, that day, either, and I hoped Jack's loping stride would rock him to sleep. Angharad handed him over gratefully, and within minutes of setting out Gethin was a limp bundle against Jack's chest.

Jack didn't warn me, though I quickly realised we were heading for Ceridwen's hut. I didn't mind. I wanted to thank her - she saved my life, and now I have two allies at Pentregoch. She hadn't seen Gethin since he was born, and I was eager to show him off.

The trees were winter-skeletal, sun dappled gold on the damp earth. The hut was dark inside after the brightness. And then I saw my brother, tall as a tree and broad-shouldered, even bigger than last Christmas - a man, now. Hope swelled. Perhaps he'd come to take me home!

Common sense asserted itself: of course not. How could he? I was married to ap Hywel and nothing but death - his or mine, God grant it was his - would change that. But it was so good to see him! My eyes blurred with tears so that, when I stopped hugging him and stepped back to take off my cloak, at first I didn't see the other figure in the shadows.

And then I saw the beloved face. He looked older, and inside his jerkin there was muscle. He was a good six inches taller than Llew, and Llew was close to six feet. But he was still Elffin. My breath seemed to stop, and then blackness came.

I came round spluttering from the stench of burning feathers and realised I wasn't dreaming. Elffin was here, with Llew, in Ceridwen's cottage. If the world ended that instant, I'd die happy. I stared, struggling to find something to say, something witty, clever, something Elffin would remember later, and smile. And then Gethin woke and bawled, and I took him from Jack to comfort him, glad to have something to do with my hands, a place to hide my face.

Even before Llew shouted, I knew. Elffin was Gethin's father. I clutched the baby closer. When Elffin had gone, Gethin would be a blood-and-bone link with him. I could cherish him and lavish all the love I had on him, instead. My eyes met Ceridwen's, and her lips twitched. My brother, God bless his guileless heart, was blissfully ignorant of the undercurrents, and clouted Elffin on the back.

'You sod, you!' he bellowed happily. 'No wonder Lady Marged got rid of Angharad!'

Elffin's eyes were fixed on his son's grumpy little face. He wasn't seeing Gethin at his best, and so I sat, propped my feet on a bench, laid Gethin along my knees, held his hands and his attention, and chatted him into a good humour. Then, when he was smiling (his father's smile) I turned him to face Elffin.

'There,' I said. 'Go to your Dada, Gethin.'

Elffin reached out uncertain arms and accepted the wriggling armful. He poked him uncertainly in the stomach and Gethin gurgled and reciprocated by inserting his forefinger up his father's left nostril. Eyes watering, Elffin gazed fatuously at us all. 'Is he like me, d'you think?'

Jack laughed. 'Peas in a pod,' he said.

Llew stuck out a finger and Gethin grasped it firmly, inserting it into his mouth. I covered my mouth with my hand, remembering Gethin's new tooth. Llew grimaced and removed his finger rapidly. My brother wasn't used to babies, either.

I had an hour to delight in my love and my brother, enjoying the sight of Elffin and his son, knowing that Gethin is mine in trust. I had a reason to live, now, a reason to keep going. I had part of Elffin with me, to take care of.

Elffin
She is beautiful. Thinner than a year ago, when the sight of her at the top table beside her husband stopped my breath, but there's sadness in her, now. The great grey eyes dominate her face still, but the mouth is womanly, her neck is long and white, and the childish freckles are barely noticeable across her nose. She's slim as a flower, but her breasts are high and rounded. But she's another man's wife, and I was there to see my son. Who had not arrived, from the look of it.

And then Rhiannon fainted, and I would have gone to her, except Llew got there first, and Ceridwen was ministering, and no one noticed me at all. My legs shook when, as her eyes opened, they sought mine and fixed on my face.

But then my son bellowed, and was unwrapped, and Rhian took him and played with him until he was better-tempered. Then she gave him to me, and her touch burned as she placed him in my arms.

I don't like babies, as a rule. They're loud and damp, and they stink, but this is flesh of my flesh, and I wish I'd got him on Rhiannon and not Angharad. He has *Tad's* light hair, and I think his eyes will be the same colour as mine. He's sturdy and has two little teeth, sharp as knives (as Llew found out) and no respect for his Dada whatsoever. He bounced in my arms and stuck his fat finger up my nose and in my ears and finished by pissing all over me.

And I stood daft as a girl while Rhiannon spread her knees and laid my son across them, took off his wet cloth and replaced it with another. Well-endowed, my son, which is to be expected. My mind was set. 'I'll take him back with me,' I declared. 'When Mam sees him she'll melt. Bastard he may be, but he's mine, and she'll take him because of it.'

'No.' Jack's voice was cool and quiet.

'What? He's my son!'

'Angharad's, too.'

'Didn't know she was pregnant. If I had -'

'Angharad carried him despite being cursed by ap Hywel and abused by his son. She nearly died when he was born, and she loves him to the last breath in her body.'

'Ap Hywel mistreated her?'

'Aye. He was hard with her at first. What would you expect? If he'd known she was breeding he'd have left her at Sycharth.'

'Ifan?'

'Ifan thought that because you'd taken liberties with her, he was entitled to do likewise. Angharad stood up to him, but he made her life miserable. So. Your son he may be, but this is his home.'

'What if ap Hywel finds out whose grandson he is?'

'Then he'll have a hostage to fortune, won't he? But he won't find out from me or Angharad.'

'Or me.' Rhiannon's voice was small. 'You can't take him, Elffin. He's all I have, now.'

'Since you lost your own child,' Ceridwen said quietly, a hint of warning in her voice, but her face was impassive.

'Yes,' Rhiannon agreed, her eyes not leaving mine. 'I'll take care of him, Elffin. I'll tell him who he is, when he's old enough to learn and keep it secret. I'll tell him, the way my Dada did Llew, so that he can stand up a free man at the *cymanfa* when he's grown up and speak his ancestry as you will, as your father does and his father did before him.'

They were right, of course.

I played with Gethin for almost an hour, but then Llew reminded me that time was running on and that Rhiannon and Jack must return to Pentregoch before they were missed. I gave my son to Jack to wrap in his cloak, my heart torn at the way his fat hands grasped Jack's shirt and he snuggled against him.

Rhiannon embraced her brother, and then turned to me. I should have kissed her hand, perhaps touched her cheek, not betrayed to anyone how I felt, but it was beyond me. My heart was in pieces, and I took her in my arms. I felt the heat of her, felt the beat of her heart, steady, strong, felt the press of her breasts against me. I wanted to kiss her mouth, but contented myself with a brush of my lips on top of her wild hair. I doubt she even felt it.

I left then, striding through the woods towards the horses, tears coursing down my face, completely unmanned.

Llew caught up quickly, striding beside me in silence. Where the woods thickened, I turned back, hoping for a last glimpse of Rhiannon. I could still feel her hair beneath my lips.

CHAPTER TWENTY-TWO
Llewelyn
We rode north-west in darkness. We wouldn't be home until close to midnight. Travel was slower in the dark, despite the moon illuminating the patchy snow.

I was preoccupied, head down against the cold, and Elffin equally silent. I was too worried by Rhiannon's plight to give much thought to Elffin. I'm glad I wasn't born female. Imagine leaving *Tadmaeth's* house forever. Home was a beacon of light in the darkness and cold of the mountains, and though I missed Sycharth I knew that I could go home when winter came. I remembered a freezing night, shivering under my cloak, my feet blocks of ice, teeth clattering. And I pictured Sycharth in late summer, the grass burned yellow by long suns, the sky blue deep enough to drown in, remembered the dust of hay-making coating my skin and sweat trickling down my face. It didn't make me any warmer outside, but *Duw*, how it warmed my soul!

I'd let Rhian be sent into a cold and comfortless marriage, without love or even honest lust within it. Though there'd been a child, so lust at least on his part - either for my sister or for the children she could give him. For some men the lust for one is as strong as the other. If she'd died in childbirth and left a living son he might have been content.

But these were dangerous times, and ap Hywel - who had been involved in nothing but minor skirmishes since the uprising began - could die in battle, or even in a fall from his horse. And Rhiannon would be free. But what if he died, and I didn't know? Then she'd be under Ifan's control. I wanted to kill him.

Suddenly, there were dark shapes beside us, and I shouted. 'Ride, Elffin!' but it was already too late. Less than five miles from Glyndyfrdwy, but our horses were tired, and we were on the lower slopes of the Berwyns when they intercepted us, their hoof beats muffled by snow. They surrounded Elffin, and though he fought like a fiend, wounding two of the attackers, he'd been taken by surprise, and in minutes was ringed by armed men. I had two choices - I could ride like hell for Glyndyfrdwy and raise the alarm, or I could try to rescue Elffin. Naturally, I chose wrong. I charged, even though there were a dozen of them, older, more battle-hardened men. I took one man down because I surprised him, and was wildly hacking at another, but they were too many for me, and Elffin couldn't help. Something hard connected with the side of my head and I was unseated, Siôned's panicked arse disappearing in the distance. They wouldn't kill Elffin, he was Glyndŵr's son, and valuable. They didn't bother with me, perhaps didn't recognise me, and if they had, probably still wouldn't have bothered. I was clubbed again from behind and fell, my face breaking through a crust of icy snow as I hit the ground.

When I came round, my blood dark on whiteness, I was alone in a circle of trampled snow. I rolled over and sat up, my head pounding. I could barely feel my fingers, shoved them into my mouth to warm them. Something moved in the trees, and I leapt to my feet, looking wildly about for my sword, but to my relief it was only Sioned. I think she looked shame-faced, but it's hard to tell with a horse. She trotted up, shoving her muzzle into my neck in apology.

'All very well,' I scolded, collecting the trailing rains and clambering stiffly into the saddle, 'but I needed you. *Tadmaeth* says a horse is more valuable than a sword - but not if the bloody horse leaves before its rider, Sioned.'

She looked back along her shoulder, blew a warm cloud of steam at me, and waited. In the almost-darkness, I gazed at the blackened, churned circle where Elffin and I had been ambushed. The moon painted shadows on the snow, but away from the trees it was almost as bright as day. My sword had been left where I'd dropped it, and I slipped off Sioned to retrieve it. Then I followed the trail of hoof prints leading away from Glyndyfrdwy. Perhaps I should have raised the alarm instead, but if I could find out where they'd taken Elffin, then I could fetch his brothers to rescue him.

Stars sang in the still air and I huddled inside my furs, head down, following the trail until at last I smelled wood-smoke.

In the mountain's shadow I could barely see the line of dark hoof-prints. Ice crackled underfoot, and when I heard voices I slipped off the mare, tied her securely to a tree and went on foot to a small hut, backed against an outcrop of mountainside. A dozen horses were tied on the sheltered side, and a single lookout stood guard, huddled inside his furs, stamping his feet and shrugging his shoulders up about his ears to keep warm. He was looking, yes, but not in the right direction. I was behind him, surprise on my side, a knife in my hand. He wiped his dripping nose on his sleeve, grumbling to himself about the lucky bastards inside, and then his throat was gushing blood and he died.

A window, nothing more than a square hole in the wooden wall on the valley side, was covered by tightly stretched leather, light barely visible at the edges. I made a tiny hole in it at eye-level with the point of my knife, and peered through. I saw part of a room bare of furniture, and men sitting or lying around a small fire, eating. I couldn't see Elffin but he must be there somewhere. Somehow, I had to get the men out of the hut. If I had tinder, I could set it on fire. But I hadn't and anyway Elffin was inside and he probably wouldn't appreciate roasting alive.

A horse stamped and blew, and suddenly I had it. I dragged the dead man into the shadows and crept towards the line of horses, untied one and walked it clear of the others, hitching it to a tree lower down the mountain. And then I untied the others, leapt and yelled and clapped like a wild thing, and they rolled their eyes, reared and stamped, whinnied and screamed, and took off - fortuitously in the direction of Glyndyfrdwy.

The door of the hut flew open and men poured out, cursing the cold, and ran shouting after the horses, which being sensible beasts, tucked in their tails and ran faster, furiously pursued by their owners.

I was inside in an instant. Elffin lay bundled in a corner, tied securely, his mouth stuffed full of filthy rags. My knife slit hide thongs, then we were outside and two up on the horse I'd tied to the tree, and off we went to Sioned. We didn't go straight home, we carefully detoured round the gaggle of men floundering through the snow. We caught up with the horses, though, and invited them back to Glyndyfrdwy.

We didn't talk about what had happened: we both knew that we'd come to it in time, but now was not it. We put our heads down, and put distance between ourselves and recapture as swiftly as possible. If they caught us again, they wouldn't leave me to freeze to death, they'd kill me straight away.

The gate-keepers had changed shift: the replacement was just as friendly as his early morning counterpart. 'Where you been, Master

Elffin?' he grumbled, 'you're for it, goin' off like that. Her Ladyship've been takin' on like nobody's business, she have, and your brothers is gettin' ready to go lookin' for you. Lady Marged thinks you're likely lying dead and cold in the woods, she do.' He glanced at the milling mass of horseflesh we had driven into the courtyard. 'Where're we expected to put all them extra horses?'

Elffin dismounted and tossed his reins to the watchman. 'Find somewhere,' he said, shortly, and disappeared into the house. I made myself scarce, went to find Bron and get my bloodied head looked at, something to eat and a peaceful seat by the kitchen fire, where I could think. Then Crisiant's unmistakable bellow stopped me in my tracks.

'Llewelyn! Upstairs.'

I knew that tone, and thought I might run.

Away.

Rhiannon

I'm as content now as I'll ever be: I can look at Elffin's son each day, see Elffin's face in Gethin's, and remember the pressure of his body against mine, his lips touching my hair.

When we got back to the house, the door burst open and Angharad rushed out. 'Where have you been?' she yelped. 'You've been gone all afternoon. Is Gethin all right? He must be starving! Oh, my sweetness!' She took him from Jack's arms and rushed indoors, untying her bodice as she ran.

I stood and watched her feed him, his fat hands starfished on her breast, his eyes closed, grunting like a piglet, and wished I could do it instead. She glanced up and caught my eye.

'The walk's done you good. Your eyes are bright and there's a bit of colour in your cheeks.'

I opened my mouth to tell her I'd seen Elffin, seen Llew, but the words died in my throat. I didn't dare talk about it.

She'd loved him. Lain with him, night after night, and he had done with her what ap Hywel did to me. What had it been like? Had she enjoyed it, or had it been as awful for her as it was for me?

I'd find out, somehow. The getting was horrible, the birth unspeakable. What woman would deliberately suffer such miseries - unless there was joy in it somewhere? Unless babies are the joy.

Ap Hywel came in for supper, rubbing his hands against the cold, followed by Ifan, whose eyes darted to Angharad's exposed breast. Sensing his eyes on her, she drew her shawl close about her, raised her head and looked defiance.

Rhys seemed in good humour, which made a change. I made an effort to respond, not to rouse his suspicions. God help me if he found out where I'd been.

He grabbed a loaf and tore it, swabbing sauce from his plate and shoving it into his mouth. 'Take more bread,' he urged me. 'You must eat more, get strong again. You're looking better, Rhiannon.'

'Her walk agreed with her,' Ifan put in, his eyes on his plate. 'She was out today.'

Rhys frowned. 'Alone?

I shook my head. 'With Jack. You forbade me to leave the house alone.'

'Jack's always with her,' Ifan said softly, lifting his eyes to mine. 'He follows her everywhere, have you noticed?'

Rhys put down his bread and looked at his son and then at me, eyes narrowed.

'He's an excellent bodyguard, and I am grateful to you for allowing him to escort me, Rhys,' I said swiftly.

He slowly began to eat again, but Ifan hadn't finished yet. 'He's your faithful slave, step-mother, isn't he?'

'He's a servant,' I snapped. 'That's all.'

But the poison had been administered and I - and Jack - would be watched in future. He was my only link with Elffin and Llew, and without him I was lost.

Elffin

Iesu Grist, I ache! It was a rough ride, face down across a saddle, and a couple of hours tied up in a freezing hut didn't help, either. Thank God I wasn't there much longer. I'd have frozen to death.

I'm furious that I let myself be captured. If not for Llew (and God, I owe him a debt I can never repay) I might be in a stinking hole in Ruthin Castle waiting to be ransomed - or hanged. Probably the latter, me being the youngest son and not worth much.

A year ago Llew would have been crowing because he rescued me. But he's not. He's subdued. I believe he's thinking. He doesn't do that often. When we got home I was summoned to the solar, where Mam and *Tad* waited, Mam fretting, *Tad* thunderous.

'If you must hunt in this weather, for the love of God take someone with you,' he bellowed. 'And be back before sunset!'

'Llew was with me.' I tossed my gauntlets onto a footstool. 'We'd have been back long before sunset, except de Grey intercepted us.'

'What?' *Tad* sank into his chair, his eyes fixed on my face.

'We were on the low slopes of the mountain. A dozen of them and two of us. They left Llew for dead. Me, they took with them. Look on the bright side, *Tad*,' I said, trying to inject some levity into the conversation, 'at least you don't need to pay a ransom to get me back. Wouldn't have been a big one, mind.'

Mam's face was grey with shock.

'How did you escape?' They spoke together, and neither noticed.

'Llew, thank God for him,' I said. 'He followed their tracks, created a diversion and got me out. And here we are, a dozen horses to the good, since Llew had the sense to encourage them in our direction. You can be proud of him, *Tad*. I owe him my life.'

'Crisiant,' Mam said softly, 'fetch Llewelyn, please.' Crisiant levered her bulk off her stool and went to the chamber door. Her voice echoed off the walls. *Tad* winced.

'I could have shouted, Crisiant,' he said mildly.

Crisiant's face went pink. 'Sorry, my Lord,' she said, 'but it's hard, up and down these stairs all day. I get such a twinge in my knees and my back is -'

Llew arrived, looking guilty, saving us from Crisiant's miseries. To my horror I realised we hadn't bothered to get our story straight. *God!* I prayed *don't let him blurt out the truth*! I racked my brains for a way to forestall him.

'A whole day's hunting,' I said swiftly, trying to divert his terrible honesty, 'and not so much as a rabbit to show for it. Eh, Llew? Just a lot of bruises, right Llew?'

He caught my drift, thank Christ and all his Apostles. 'Oh. Right, yes. Bruises, yes. No rabbits, no. Not even the sight of one. Must be the cold, keeping them indoors.'

He was babbling, and I wished he'd just shut up.

Tad put both arms round him, tightly. When he let go, Llew's face was pink with pleasure.

'No need to worry, *Tadmaeth,* honest,' he blurted. 'We were all right, we -'

'Llew.' *Tad* raised his hand and Llew stuttered to a halt. 'Llew. You saved Elffin. How can I thank you?'

My heart lurched. If he said "bring Rhiannon home" there'd be blood around the moon. Mam'd never agree, hero or not. Worse, what if he included Angharad and Gethin, too? I needn't have worried. Before everything, Llew is both romantic and single-mindedly loyal.

'He's my brother, *Tadmaeth*,' he said simply. 'My father fought beside you, and I'm proud to be your foster-son. I don't want anything else, thank you, Sire.'

'Llew, Llew boy. Not my foster-son. My son, in all but blood.'

Duw, I thought he'd burst with pride.

Bit different later, though, when Bron got at us.

'God knows,' she panted, hacking lumps of bread and finding cold mutton for us to eat, 'Lady Marged's got enough to worry about without you two *twpsins*, you two daft oafs deciding to disappear until near midnight, getting yourselves caught by that fat little turd from Ruthin and nearly killed. Feed you?' she said, shoving steaming mugs of mulled ale and piled platters in front of us, 'feed you? I'd like to take all the skin off your backsides, I would. And what about me, still in my kitchen at this hour? Thoughtless, you.' And she clipped Llew's ear, although I think it was mostly affection. I ducked, so she didn't get me, but it dimmed the stars in Llew's eyes and bent him to his meat.

'Listen,' I said, after, when we were side by side in the big bed, the firelight flickering on the walls and the dawn busily getting up outside the window. 'For God's sweet sake don't say anything to anyone about fetching Rhian home. I'll do it if it kills me, somehow or other, I promise.'

I saw his head turn towards me in the half-light. He was grinning broadly. 'Oh, I know you will,' he said. 'I know!'

CHAPTER TWENTY-THREE

Llewelyn

I'll remember *Tadmaeth*'s words until I die. Mind, if he or Lady Marged knew the truth, the sky would fall on our heads. It is a difficult thing, lying. Tell one, and five minutes later you have to tell another.

We realised straight away - well, Elffin quicker than me, being older and possibly wiser although personally I'm not convinced - it was unlikely a dozen men had lurked about on a freezing night on the off-chance that one of Glyndŵr's sons might trot along. They knew we were coming. However, no one but Elffin and I knew our plans. We'd ensured that gatekeepers and kitchen maids knew we were going hunting. Someone had eavesdropped. Jack couldn't have betrayed us: he didn't know in advance when we'd come. Anyway, I trusted Jack, and while Tomos of Ynys Môn is around, there's an obvious candidate. No proof, of course, but there, considering Tomos - which we have, at length - we don't need any.

I'd hoped for a long rest at Glyndyfrdwy, but before Twelfth Night the snow melted and the watch had to be doubled to make sure we weren't surprised by attack.

Tomos seemed to be everywhere we didn't want him to be. I was all for cornering him on a dark night and slitting his throat, but Elffin disagreed.

'We'll give him some rope, Llew,' he decided. 'And then we'll hang him with it'

At the beginning of January we attacked Ruthin, partly because Elffin's brothers were upset at their little brother being roughly handled (I'd been even more roughly handled: the egg on my head still hadn't gone). Ruthin - and especially de Grey, if he was at home - needed a bit of a lesson, and besides, Ruthin's handy and a successful attack would be a good start to the new year.

We meant to take the watch unawares and capture the castle, but, like Caernarfon, Ruthin was expecting us. Bowmen lined the walls and there was a brief but bloody battle. Only a few of our men died, thank God, though a few were wounded: I got an arrow in my left arm which bled rivers but healed quickly. It's left a small but immensely satisfying scar.

But we'd been betrayed. De Grey had known, so we set about discovering - well, to my mind proving – who'd done it. Then Aled, a pragmatic Ceredigion lad who'd been run off his Oswestry master's land for siding too loudly with Owain Glyndŵr, complained that he'd looked for Tomos the night before, but that he'd disappeared. Then, we knew for certain. But we bided our time.

The Year of Our Lord 1402 made even the least superstitious of us thoughtful. On a January night when the stars were icy pinpricks in a clear sky, Elffin and I were in the courtyard, visiting the privy before bed, having done our best to drink the household dry. We stood companionably side by side, feet braced. I looked up, tottered slightly and soaked Elffin's feet, then stood open-mouthed at the miracle happening overhead.

Arcing across the night like a fiery dragon was a great comet, trailing a glowing tail. Awe-struck, we stared, Elffin even disregarding his drenched boots. By the time it disappeared behind the trees, our delicate bits were getting frostbitten so we hastily tucked them away.

'What'n Goss - Godses's name was that?' I whispered, as if the star-struck heavens could hear.

Elffin blinked, blearily. 'Thass, thass a sign. You mark my words, Llew, thassa sign.'

The wine sang in my head. 'Sign? Wassorta sign?'

'Buggered if I know.' He hiccupped. 'But issa good sign. Def'nitely a good sign. Def'nitely.'

Who was I to argue? He was older than I, and wiser, wine-and piss-soaked or not.

It was there again the next night, and the next, and each night more and more of us waited for it to appear, watching its blazing, miraculous passage across the night sky. The clergy (naturally) were certain it was a Sign from God, but couldn't or wouldn't say exactly what God had in mind when He sent it. According to Crach Ffinnant and probably the entrails of a black cat and the smoke of the fire and the way the thaw had come early and the mistletoe had been thick with fat white berries, the comet was a good omen. It represented Glyndŵr, rising in the dark night of English oppression, and by its light Owain would lead his Welsh flock out of darkness into the light of freedom.

It's a happy thought. I hope he's right, but who knows? The comet disappeared each night, even if it came again the next, and most nights were clear enough to see it flash across the arc of darkness, putting the stars to shame. But if it doesn't appear? What are the omens then? I prefer to believe it's just an accident of nature. Safer that way, than looking for omens and such, though I admit that before a battle I always put my right boot on before my left and cross myself if I hear a crow.

Meanwhile, omens or not, there was Tomos. We knew he was the one who'd betrayed us, and eventually we took our suspicions - tidied up, of course, with no reference to our visit to Pentregoch - to our brothers, and together decided on a course of action.

Action, unfortunately, had to wait, because the weather, from being mild, turned suddenly as foul as it had been friendly. When the comet finally disappeared from the skies it took the sunshine with it. It rained so hard the river broke its banks and when the rain stopped the winds began, gusting and howling round Glyndyfrdwy day after night after day, ripping off thatch and felling trees. Then the snow returned, and until the weather cleared we could do nothing at all but sit by the fire and grumble.

Secretly, Owain's council planned a second attack on Ruthin: at least, part of the plans were secret. The rest we discussed loudly, ensuring Tomos was within earshot, which he usually was. Glyndŵr himself would lead the attack, we said. Tomos listened. All Glyndŵr's sons would be with him, bent on revenge, we said, and because we knew that the gates would be open for trade, this time we'd have the element of surprise. Twenty men could easily take the castle, we boasted, and Tomos listened.

And then again I became Tomos's shadow, and when he slipped away from Glyndyfrdwy, thinking himself unnoticed, I followed. Once again he rode to the copse: this time, however, it was Ifan he met. I was tempted to kill him for what he did to my sister. One body more or less would make no difference, and certainly no one would blame me. But then our plan to trap Tomos might go awry, and we'd risk another betrayal, and more men dead. So, though it hurt me to do it, I let Ifan go to Ruthin to report to de Grey. I pictured him posturing before his Toadship, acting the man of the world and the master-spy, and grinned. I doubted he'd be popular with de Grey tomorrow, if all went to plan.

Owain, Gruffydd, Siôn, Madoc and a dozen men rode for Ruthin next day. Tomos went with them, wearing a saffron jerkin as conspicuous as a seagull in a flock of blackbirds, so de Grey's men knew who not to aim at. When they were out of sight, Elffin and I, with fifty more men rode like demons to reach Coed Marchon before the first group reached Ruthin. Each of us had brought an extra helmet and a stick, which we sank into the soft ground on the far side of a small rise. On top of each stick we placed a helm. Then, just as we had in our first attack on Ruthin, we hid in the trees and waited. Our look-out reported that the castle gates were open, but a glint of steel within the gatehouse betrayed that they were waiting, forewarned and forearmed. Tomos again.

Tadmaeth and his party attacked, creeping as obtrusively as possible up to the gates of the castle. They were ready when the defenders emerged at a run, brandishing swords, roaring their triumph, certain that they had the advantage of surprise, eager to take Glyndŵr and his sons and chieftains. The attackers fell back as if beaten (and I regret to say, Siôn and Gruffydd will never be actors) and retreated, leading their pursuers towards where the rest of us were hidden. Tomos circled helplessly on his horse, having carefully positioned himself at the rear of the raiding party, now finding himself somehow at the front. He didn't know whether to fly or die! The defenders followed on horseback or on foot, sure they'd routed Glyndŵr, eager to capture him. So eager that Reginald de Grey himself, at the head of some thirty prematurely triumphant defenders, charged after the fleeing rebels into the heart of the wood.

Then they stopped, spotting the line of helmets peeping from above the earth bank, and (as we'd hoped) took them for Owain's men making a stand. De Grey's force obligingly gathered in a tidy group to discuss the situation. But they were well into the wood, and they weren't watching their backs. Our second party led by Elffin filtered through the woods, surrounded the tight little knot, and de Grey's line of retreat was gone.

Duw, I'll treasure the expression on de Grey's face until the day I die! Triumph to panic, in an instant. His men tried to fight, but we had the advantage and apart from one or two that managed to escape, all were killed. Lord de Grey was very courteously offered Glyndŵr's hospitality. His arrogance led to his ruin, and only one man amongst us didn't rejoice...

We took de Grey to Dolbadarn Castle, looming foursquare over the wintry sheet of Llyn Peris. Llewelyn Fawr built it to guard the Caernarfon road, and built it to last. De Grey won't be comfortable there, but he'll be treated more honourably than he deserves. It will cost him ten thousand marks for his release, six thousand to be paid within four weeks, which will be painful to those who have to empty their pockets to find it. And his eldest son, among others, will be security for the balance.

De Grey swore an oath (eventually) never to stand against Glyndŵr again, but then, he's never been particularly trustworthy and personally, I'd kill him and be done with it, but Glyndŵr is both chivalrous and honest, and besides, alive, de Grey is worth money!

We have yet to deal with Tomos.

Rhiannon

The weather's been so bad I've been trapped inside while rain fell in sheets, and howling winds demolished ancient trees. Ap Hywel, muffled in an oiled-wool cloak, is rarely here, and since these days he takes Ifan with him, more often than not I'm left with just Angharad, Beti and the serving women. And Gethin, my joy.

He's crawling now, his fat rump waggling comically, and he pulls himself to his feet on furniture and friendly legs. He's so like Elffin I can hardly take my eyes off him.

I rarely speak to Jack: it's dangerous. I won't risk his safety now Ifan has planted suspicion in his father's mind. I leave rooms as Ifan enters them, try to stay near Angharad or Beti or Elin or Gwen. I spend as much time as I can in the dairy and the still-room, places he can't go without making it obvious that he's following me. I can't fight him: he's Rhys's son, and I'm only the wife Rhys doesn't love. But I can avoid him.

Ap Hywel sleeps in my bed again, so I get little sleep. I can't bear the thought of him touching me.

But there's news: Rhys came home last night, his face black with fury, bellowing for Ifan.

Glyndŵr attacked Ruthin again,' Rhys said. 'And - '

'I know!' Ifan smirked, his eyes sparkling. 'It was me who warned de Grey. I got it from-' - his eyes flicked to me - 'our friend. I went straight to His Lordship because you were away.' He smirked, proud of himself.

'Shame,' his father snarled, 'because I'll have to answer for it. I wish to God you'd minded your own business, you bloody fool.'

Ifan's face fell. 'What?'

'What? Glyndŵr attacked Ruthin, that's what, and because *someone* had warned de Grey, his Lordship thought he could cover himself in glory by capturing Glyndŵr and his sons.'

'*Tadmaeth*? Taken?' The words were out of my mouth before I could stop them.

Rhys glanced at me. 'No. On the contrary, de Grey's in Dolbadarn, and Glyndŵr wants ten thousand marks for him.'

Ifan's voice was high with panic. 'But I warned them! I told them Glyndŵr was coming! Why weren't they ready?'

'Because your informant didn't tell you everything. Maybe Glyndŵr knows there's a traitor in his camp. Perhaps you were seen meeting him. He knew Glyndŵr was going to attack Ruthin, but not that a trap was being laid elsewhere. Attacking the castle was a trick to pull de Grey out of it. He was ambushed and taken. The king will be looking for someone to blame.'

Ifan sank down onto the settle, his eyes wide. 'They know about Tomos?'

Ap Hywel's voice was harsh. 'They know. And you can bet that Tomos Turncoat will be turning again, before long. On the end of a rope, probably.'

Ifan's hands were clapped over his mouth, and he just made it outside before he vomited. He knew that if Tomos had been seen, then so had he, and whoever had seen them would have told my foster-brothers - and my brother. I hugged myself with joy. Ifan would be punished. Soon, I hoped. And now I knew the name of the traitor in Glyndŵr's camp.

Elffin

Iolo Goch sang until he was hoarse, and we emptied more than one cask of father's good wine in celebration - it isn't every day you capture an enemy so easily. And when our heads had stopped pounding next day, we dealt with Tomos of Ynys Môn. We had him watched, to make sure he didn't escape. Easy enough: he hid in the stables most of the day. Llew and I went to talk to him.

'Tomos! That was a fine yellow jerkin you had on yesterday.'

'Very nice,' Llew agreed.

The traitor smiled uncertainly. 'My lady-friend made it for me.'

'Oh yes?' I raised an eyebrow. 'The one in Llanidloes or the one in Machynlleth? You've got so many, Tomos, if they got in a tidy queue they'd stretch from here to Cardiff.'

'Was it the Pentregoch woman sewed it?' Llew asked.

'Pentregoch?' Tomos looked puzzled. 'I haven't got a woman there.'

Llew scratched his head in mock puzzlement. 'Really? Well, then I must be mistaken. I followed you once, and you met someone from Pentregoch then. Mind, come to think of it, it didn't look much like a woman. That was the day you said you were visiting your Llanidloes lady.'

Tomos's handsome face paled. 'You followed me?'

'Well,' I pulled up a keg and sat next to him. 'You managed to escape without a scratch at Hyddgen, when Gwilym died - then again when we attacked Ruthin. You lead a charmed life - you even wore bright yellow into battle! How brave is that? We couldn't work out how you came through battle after battle unscathed. Even Llew's been wounded, right Llew?'

'Right,' Llew agreed. 'So I've been keeping you company,' Llew said. 'When you went to bed, I was nearby. When you got up, I got up too. When you shat, I followed.' He shuddered. 'Not pleasant, but somebody had to do it. And I was right behind you when you met ap Hywel's brat, the day before yesterday.'

'Now, ap Hywel's de Grey's man,' I pointed out, tapping Tomos's head to attract his attention. 'And so is his son, so, Tomos, what business did you have with him, I wonder? Hm?'

The handsome face was white and sweating. 'I just - I met him by accident, I swear! He, he - asked about Llew for his stepmother's sake.'

'Now that I doubt,' Llew commented, eyes glittering. 'Until recently, my sister had no news of me for months. Is it possible Ifan - and ap Hywel, of course, you accidentally met him, too, didn't you? - have such poor memories they forgot to tell her?'

Tomos was sweating now, despite the cold. 'How should I know? Perhaps he didn't want to tell her. She's no use to him, is she, being Glyndŵr's foster-daughter. Perhaps it pleases him to keep the news to himself.' He knew he was babbling.

He looked past me, and his eyes widened as one by one my brothers entered the stable. He scrambled up, backing away.

Gruffydd, his arms folded, looked steadily at him. 'You betrayed your friends, Tomos of Ynys Môn. *Bradwr!*'

Tomos shook his head.

'You did,' Madoc agreed. '*Bradwr!*'

One by one my gave their verdicts. Traitor he was, and as a traitor he would hang. Gruffydd was for making it public to discourage anyone tempted to do likewise, but we trusted the rest of our men. Word would spread, anyway. Llew thought we should hang him from a tree in the copse. When ap Hywel or Ifan next went to meet him, they'd find his dangling corpse. We locked him in the stable to consider his future - what there was of it - but during the night he escaped. Llew muttered that probably some woman had helped him. Whatever. He was gone.

Owain Glyndŵr, rightful Prince of Wales, was never betrayed by one of his own again.

CHAPTER TWENTY-FOUR

Llewelyn
The air's fresher without Tomos about, even if we didn't manage to hang the bastard. He'll pay one day. Ifan and ap Hywel go unpunished, but their time will come.

I think of Rhiannon more than I ever did when she was here. She has no one but Jack. There's Angharad, of course, but she's probably more powerless than Rhian, and also has her baby to think about. Gethin will be her priority, and she'll do whatever's necessary to keep him safe. Rhiannon is alone.

Mali's no comfort, she's too afraid of Bron to come near me. Mind, she looks at me cow-eyed, sighing, but if I catch her alone, she ducks her head and runs away for fear of Bron, which is annoying. Damn Bron and the eyes in the back of her head!

Around noon today, there was a commotion at the gate: servants ran in all directions, and *Tadmaeth* was fetched, which was strange, a Prince summoned to his own gatehouse! But the visitor was important: His Humbleness the Abbot of Cymer, bent on a Holy Mission, determined to reconcile *Tadmaeth* and his cousin Hywel Sele. Now personally, I think Sele of Nannau should be damned and set fire to, since it was he who invited Hotspur to Dolgellau in the first place. We almost lost *Tadmaeth*, then, and it was pure luck we managed to net Sele instead. Sele isn't mistreated. He eats well and is accommodated comfortably; but captivity chafes and he isn't at all happy.

The Abbot is one of those hollow-eyed Christians who probably wears a louse-ridden hair shirt under his habit like Becket did; takes ice-water baths and beats himself three times a day with nettles just for the fun of it. He arrived uninvited on a sway-backed mare with an escort of miserable monks. Bron, of course, turned the kitchens into a frenzy of yelping spit-dogs and weeping kitchen-maids to feed them. She half-emptied the fishpond and wrung a peacock's aristocratic neck in his honour, but the Abbot ate only bread and salt and drank water, Adam's apple bobbing, his bare, bony feet side by side under the table, tidy as a mouse. His monks, mind, as thin as the Abbot, but obviously less happy about it, launched into the food as if they hadn't seen anything like it for years. They probably hadn't: poor bastards were walking twigs.

The Abbot is on *Tadmaeth's* side, but has a bee in his bonnet about Hywel Sele. When the meal was over, he spoke to *Tadmaeth* and Gruffydd, who gave us the conversation second-hand, after.

'Bloody old God-botherer,' he muttered. '"Cousins," saith the Abbot, steepling his fingers and casting his eyes heavenwards, "should be friends."'

Cousins, apparently, should not lock each other up, no matter what Sele had done to *Tadmaeth*. It is Christian to forgive, the Abbot said, and even if Hywel Sele had been misguided enough to invite *Tadmaeth*'s enemy into *Tadmaeth*'s neighbourhood, and that enemy brought a large army, and even if Sele didn't support *Tadmaeth*'s rule, well, all over now, isn't it? All forgotten, and anger had run its course, and past times were past times, and all in all, the Abbot desired nothing more than to see Owain Glyndŵr, his Prince, and Hywel Sele, his Prince's own cousin, united in friendship. Oh, and Sele turned loose.

Gruffydd poured himself a beaker of wine and leaned back in his chair, one booted leg propped on the knee of the other. 'Our parent finds it hard to refuse a priest. Personally, I think Sele would be best in a hole six feet by two, but you know *Tad!*' He scratched his thigh, absent-mindedly. 'While we've got Sele, we know what he's up to. Once he's out, there'll be trouble. *Tad* may forgive, but I don't, and Sele won't, either. He'll want some sort of revenge.'

All the same, the Abbot left next morning, letters of safe-conduct in his pocket, Hywel Sele smugly at his side. The Abbot, hair standing up around his tonsure like a dandy-clock, a self-satisfied smile on his face, watched while *Tadmaeth* and Sele exchanged a brief - and insincere - cousinly embrace. *Tadmaeth*'s expression was unreadable, but Sele's was all too clear.

Then the Abbot, overcome by success, made Glyndŵr promise to visit Sele at Nannau as soon as possible, and (somewhat unenthusiastically) Sele endorsed the invitation.

'Like a spider inviting a fly,' Gruffydd said, setting down his wine-cup.

"A little hunting," the Abbot suggested, "and a pleasant meal taken in brotherhood, and all will be well."

Tadmaeth, I think, trusts Sele about as far as he could hurl him, but he'll go to that God-forsaken place half-way up a mountainside above the Wnion Valley, just to please the damn Abbot. Still, we'll be there to take care of him.

Rhiannon

I was woken by someone hammering at the front door. Ap Hywel, his thin hair on end, leapt out of bed and stumped downstairs. The voice was vaguely familiar: I couldn't put a face to it, but knew instinctively it was no one I wanted to see. I crept to the top of the stairs and listened.

'In Christ's name, man, are you mad? Why come here?' Rhys's voice. 'What if you were followed?'

'No one followed me this time. Your brother-in-law has been spying on me for weeks, apparently. He saw me with both you and your son, and they were going to hang me, but I escaped. I need food and a fresh horse, mine's half-dead.'

My husband was less than sympathetic. 'You're the spy: if you'd been a better one de Grey wouldn't be in Dolbadarn and I wouldn't be neck deep in shit.'

'I told what I knew in good faith. If de Grey was taken it's not my fault.'

Tomos of Ynys Môn: the spy. He'd escaped. I wished there was something I could do, but I was helpless. They'll find him eventually, God will see to that, and then they'll hang him. And after, I hope they'll throw what's left to the pigs.

He ate, took a fresh horse and left. Rhys didn't come back to bed, thank God, and I stood at the window and watched the traitor go, ill-wishing him every day from now until the end of the world.

I'm happier here now I have Gethin to love. Angharad wasn't curious about my sudden devotion: she's his mother and convinced he'll charm everyone eventually. But one day I let my tongue run away with me.

I promised Elffin I'd teach his son what he needs to know. He's too young yet to understand - or even speak - but little boys must begin to learn as soon as they're old enough to listen, to make them remember. It's amazing how at first all they can do is eat, howl and shit, and within a year they're on their feet and beginning to talk.

Gethin is bright, and I love to teach him pat-a-cake and sing him rhymes.

'You, little one, are Gethin ap Elffin,' I whispered, holding him on my lap so that I could look into his face, happy just to be able to speak his name aloud, 'ap Owain Glyndŵr, Prince of Wales, ap -'

'What?' I hadn't heard Angharad come into the room. 'What did you say?'

'Oh! You startled me, Angharad, I -'

'What are you saying to my baby?' Her face was white, and she snatched him from me arms.

'Nothing!'

'What did you call him?' She clutched the bawling child as if I'd threatened him.

I tried to look innocent, but I don't think it was successful.

'Rhiannon, I'm not stupid. What have you been saying? What did you call him?'

I picked guiltily with my fingernails. 'I called him Gethin ap Elffin.'

'Why?'

I jumped in with both feet, tired of keeping the secret. 'Because he's Elffin's.'

She backed away, holding Gethin so tightly he squeaked and struggled. 'No he isn't! He isn't! Who told you that?'

'Angharad, he looks exactly like him.'

'No he doesn't. He's nothing to do with Elffin. Nothing, you hear me? His father was - someone else.'

'But -' I stopped.

She was calmer now. She sat opposite me, Gethin balanced on her knees. 'Listen, Rhian,' she whispered, looking behind her to make sure there was no one to hear, 'if Ifan suspected Gethin might be Elffin's - which he isn't - what do you think his life would be worth?'

She was right. I'd endangered Elffin's son.

'If I can come into a room and overhear you, do you think Ifan can't? He spends so much time lurking in corners his arse is triangular!'

'I'm sorry,' I mumbled.

'He's no one's but mine, Rhiannon, until I can get him away from here. He's just my bastard child.'

I went cold. 'Get him away? What do you mean? You can't!'

'Not yet. But when I can.'

'Where?'

She shrugged. 'God knows. Not Sycharth, that's for sure. No welcome there. Maybe my sister at Caernarfon. But remember, if Ifan finds out who Gethin is, his life won't be worth spit on a hot griddle.'

A few days later de Grey's agent sent for Rhys and Ifan, who rode off as if they were going to their executions. I quite hoped they might be, but despite de Grey's capture Ifan had acted with the best of intentions. I'd have liked to be a bug in the rushes when they tried to explain, however. ..

When they'd gone, I could at last talk to Jack, though first, I found tasks for Elin and Gwen to keep them well away from the stables, then ensured Beti was with Angharad, playing with Gethin. The day was dry, though lacy traces of ice clung to the mud between the cobblestones. Jack was shoeing, the horse idly tugging hay from a net while he wrenched nails out of the old shoe.

'I wanted to ride today,' I said, leaning in the doorway. A nail came free, and was dropped in the dirt at his feet.

He looked up, grime smudging the planes of his face. 'Later, perhaps, Rhiannon. I've got to shoe this lady first, and then there're are other jobs your husband wants done.'

'But I probably can't get away this afternoon.'

'Then you won't ride today, will you?'

I was startled by the anger in his voice. 'What?' I'd expected him to drop everything and saddle two horses.

'You won't be riding, Rhiannon.' He straightened, looking me straight in the eye. 'Don't you know how much danger you're in?'

'No more than usual.'

He shook his head. 'You think? Ifan knows we met Elffin and Llew the other day.'

'What? How?'

'Who knows? Perhaps he followed us.'

'Why hasn't he told Rhys, then?'

Jack shrugged. 'Maybe he has.'

'No. Rhys would have said something.'

'Then Ifan's keeping it until he needs it.'

'If Rhys finds out, he'll be furious.'

'You're his wife. Why shouldn't he be?'

I locked my hands together, to stop them trembling. 'Jack, I've got to get away. When the weather changes, I am going.'

'And Angharad? Gethin?'

'I'll take them with me. Jack, will you come too? *Tadmaeth* will find you a place in the household. Or even in his army if you want to fight.'

He turned to the forge, working the bellows. Fire glowed white and sparks flew, making the mare shift uneasily. 'I don't know, Rhiannon. I don't know. Perhaps.'

I had to be satisfied with that.

Elffin

When the Abbot appeared on our doorstep I knew he'd be trouble, but I couldn't begin to know how much. *Tad* had promised that he'd be reconciled with Hywel Sele, so reconciled he would be, no matter what advice his sons gave him, and we gave him plenty.

So, on a warm April day we set off, my brothers and I and a small escort of men, to Nannau to dine with Sele. Madoc and Gruffydd spent tense days trying to convince *Tad* to wear mail beneath his finery: for once, thank Christ, he listened.

Sele met us at the gates with a smile so vast I mistrusted it immediately. We were invited into the great house the Prince of Powys had built three centuries ago, were fêted, fed, and wined. When we'd eaten, Hywel Sele invited *Tad* to walk with him to resolve their differences. Man to man, he said.

Gruffydd made to accompany them, but Sele raised a hand. 'Alone,' he said, smiling his too-wide smile. 'We'll put our differences behind us, and be friends as long as we live.'

Fine talk, but when they'd left the room, Sele's arm linked cosily through *Tad*'s, at Gruffydd's nod I excused myself, and followed them. I kept out of sight, but watched Sele.

It's a useful thing, a suspicious nature! Sele collected a bow and arrows at the gate: *Tad* was unarmed except for his small dagger, but knowing there was chain mail under his tunic, I breathed more easily.

Tad loosed himself from Sele's clutching arm as soon as they were outside. They spoke so quietly I could hear only the low drone of their voices and Sele's occasional high-pitched laugh.

Once, when *Tad* stumbled, Sele extended a solicitous hand to help him. *Tad* spotted the stag first.

The beast stood, great head raised, breathing the still air, half-sensing the two men. *Tad* touched Sele's arm, silently nodding towards the creature, as if he were saying "There now, there's a worthy target!"

Sele raised his bow and fitted an arrow, sighting carefully along it; drew aim on the stag, but as he loosed the shaft he turned, firing directly at my father's heart. Thank Christ is - was only a small hunting bow: a longbow would easily have penetrated the mail shirt and he'd have died: however, Sele was close enough for the force of the arrow to make *Tad* stagger and fall. Thinking he'd killed him, Sele bent over him. And then *Tad* recovered himself, and Sele ran for his life.

I ran to intercept him, the terrified stag crashing past me in the opposite direction. Glyndŵr reached him first. A short dagger was all he had, and all he needed. Sele hadn't worn mail: in any event his throat was bare above his tunic, and Sele died. *Tad* thrust his blade into the earth to clean it.

'What'll we do with him?' I asked. 'We ought to leave him to rot.'

Tad looked around, his face calm. 'There.' He'd expected treachery, and was unsurprised. We lifted the lifeless body between us, and dropped him into the trunk of a hollow oak, crammed his bow and his quiver on top of him, and left him there. There was just a smear of blood on the ground, and rain would soon take care of that. Sele could stay there and rot: Christian burial was too good for him.

'Elffin - go back, tell your brothers what's happened. If I'm seen without him his men will suspect.'

I was reluctant to leave him, though with Sele dead he was safe enough. I ran back to Nannau, where our escort idled outside ready for our departure. I took a moment to warn them.

My brothers were still at table. For all their apparent ease, they were taut as bowstrings. Servants cleared platters, and hounds snapped at bones in the rushes. When Gruffydd saw me return alone, alarm bloomed in his face, his hand darting to his sword. I took my place at the table, smiling to calm Sele's men, leaned towards Madoc and whispered. Madoc spoke to Gruffydd, Gruffydd to Siôn, and so from brother to brother, man to man until all were aware, and then we rose, drawing swords. There were as many of Sele's men as there were of us, but they died. Llew, his face grim, herded the household's women and children outside: Sele's treachery, not theirs. Then we burned Nannau.

The fire took hold, and the thatch caught with a crackle and hiss, sparks leaping, the flames a beacon. When the news circulated that Glyndŵr had survived - and avenged - an assassin's attack, rumours of his indestructibility would increase his mystery, fuel the talk of his charmed life.

It was a tedious ride back, made more so by Gruffydd and Madoc.

'We were right all along, weren't we? Once a traitor always a traitor, and sod the Abbot,' Madoc crowed. *Tad* told him to shut up or he'd throw him off the mountain.

'All very well,' Gruffydd said, nodding wisely. 'But if we hadn't insisted, day after day until we wore you down -'

With a roar, *Tad* spurred his horse, leaving us to follow.

I should have thought *Tad* would celebrate Sele's defeat, but he and Lady Marged seemed sad. Cousin or not, a traitor's a traitor, and with luck it will be a hundred years before Sele's rotting remains see the light of day.

CHAPTER TWENTY-FIVE

Llewelyn

Some say Glyndŵr wasn't at Pilleth, that he couldn't have been, that Rhys Gethin alone took Edmund Mortimer - but he was there.

I was with him on the mad ride from Dolbadarn, past Llangollen and down into the softer vales of the south, and he *was* there, though we left immediately the battle was over. Of course he was there: he told every itinerant priest for weeks beforehand of his intention to make a pilgrimage to the Shrine of the Virgin on St Alban's Day, aware that bait would bring the devil himself, let alone Edmund Mortimer!

Down from Llanidloes into the valley of the Afon Ithon, where we burned Bleddfa Church in passing to distract the residents. Sioned was neck and neck with Elffin's horse the whole way - except on the mountain tracks, where there's no room for two abreast. The sun shone, birds darted from trees, and I wished I had a hawk on my wrist and a day's hunting ahead of me. Great peaks and crags swooped and plunged and soared, great swathes of mist boiled off the escarpments, hidden lakes reflected light, but we had no time for sightseeing.

Rhys Gethin and his band were already there; they spent the night at Mynachdy. Some say it was accident that his group encountered Mortimer's at all, but we knew the Hereford men were coming, and that Mortimer had longbows: a factor that could turn a battle in minutes. Battle-hardened Welsh longbow men who had seen it all and lived, their right arms overmuscled in contrast to the left, their eyes narrowed to their targets. The longbow is sighted by memory and instinct: when the string is drawn past the ear, the bowman is blind, but memory isn't. It's a knack, and thank God I've got it.

Many of the bowmen were disenchanted with their English warlords: some inclined to join Glyndŵr. On long, hard marches or on cold nights beside camp-fires, men talk, and some men can be persuaded. We'd heard rumours of discontent, but we didn't *know*. Not how many, or even if any, of Mortimer's men got the message our agents disseminated. We could only hope.

We arrived before Mortimer. *Tadmaeth*, wearing light armour and his helm with the scarlet plume, reined his horse and sent word to Rhys Gethin, waiting in a hollow to the north of Bryn Glas. We waited on the crest, commanding a view of the valley, waiting for Mortimer to come. I sat Sioned, Elffin beside me, our mounts cropping the grass, the sun warm on our backs, straining our eyes for the glint of sun on steel, or dust rising to betray marching feet.

Around us the plains of Maelienydd undulated and curved in the sunshine of St Alban's Day, the river looping silver. From our vantage point the Holy Well was hidden by the walls of the grey church. I wished there'd been time to visit the Well, first. A bit of a pilgrimage might have helped. A scout galloped up, his horse steaming, and shortly after Elffin touched my arm.

'There!' he said, pointing.

Mortimer's column, banners gaudy in the sun. I gathered Siôned's reins in my hands, hauling her reluctant head out of sweet grass, and held my breath, waiting for them to notice us.

They came into the narrow valley, warriors on destriers; men-at-arms; longbowmen, burdened with armour and weapons, while we waited like birds of prey on the hill above them, lightly armoured and mounted on tough, fast hill ponies, ready to strike. It was late June, but the valley floor was swampy, and the over-laden English force staggered and slipped along the northern bank of the Lugg, reluctant to cross the river and leave themselves vulnerable to attack from both river-banks. Why didn't Mortimer send out scouts? We watched from Wigmore onward, yet they were unaware of us until they were almost under our hooves.

I remembered Hyddgen, when we were trapped in the hollow, a thousand Pembroke Flemings on the ridge above, yet we won the day. Here, we had the advantage of height, and still my stomach churned. Once the battle begins, I'm ice-cold, launching arrow after accurate arrow, and even in the middle of hacking and slashing and stabbing there's a core of coldness inside me. But waiting is awful. I wonder if I'm a coward, or if others feel this way. I shifted my grip on my sword, glanced sideways at Elffin and noticed a line of sweat trickling from under the rim of his helm.

He saw me looking, and pulled a face. 'I hate the waiting,' he muttered, as if he'd read my mind. But then he looked away, as if ashamed, so perhaps he was speaking the truth and was nervous too. The droplet ran down his shaven cheek and inside his neckband, and I was grateful to him.

When Mortimer noticed us, perhaps he thought a single charge would rout us. We appeared few, and despite the advantage of height his great army and crack archers should finish us. Perhaps he thought he could take Glyndŵr alive to Henry and end this "rebellion". Christ, it rankles to be called rebel, when all we've done is fight for our rights.

There were two thousand of them, according to Elffin's estimate, and I trust his judgment. My own in matters of numbers isn't good: there could have been half that number or ten times it, for all I knew. They massed below us, men-at-arms interwoven with wedges of longbowmen, mounted men at the rear, and Mortimer, God knows why, ordered a charge uphill. His men obeyed, but they stumbled and fell up the slope, their armour deadweight. Bryn Glas is deceptive: it looks like a gentle slope, pleasant exertion for a walking man. But these men were mail-clad and running, hefting great swords and lead-filled clubs, shields and maces. Their horsemen were off balance, riding uphill, and their archers not yet in position - not that there is ever a good position for firing uphill.

From our vantage point we fired a few arrows, brought a dozen men down, made a show of fighting when the leaders reached us.

Then, pretending we were overwhelmed by their numbers, we gradually withdrew, retreating slowly over the crest of the hill, inexorably drawing them after us. They, imagining an easy victory, fell in their *Sais* arrogance for the same simple trick that gave us de Grey. They followed us over the crest of the hill, where Rhys Gethin waited, slavering. As Mortimer's weary army crested the ridge, Rhys Gethin's fresh force surged against them, up the small slope, terrible in their savagery, and our band parted like the Red Sea and let them pass between us. When they were through, we turned and joined battle on our own account.

I remember the battle in flashes frozen in time: Elffin, his face contorted, his sword arm high above his head. The terrible, sick sound that steel makes cleaving a man's skull. The stink of shit, the screams of dying men and beasts. The whistle of arrows too close, and the sparking clangour of sword on sword.

For all the element of surprise we might still have lost. Mortimer's army outnumbered us, they were better armoured, but that made them slow, and they were bone-weary. What sealed our victory was what we had hoped and prayed would happen.

Each man drawing a longbow for England remembered he was Welsh (many of them Maelienydd men fighting on their own ground), and turned against his masters. Attacked from both sides, Mortimer's army was finished, more than half the English dead or dying. Mortimer we captured, and others important enough for ransom, and then *Tadmaeth* and our band rode away with the hostages, leaving Rhys Gethin to finish the business.

Edmund Mortimer was our chief prize: Hotspur's brother-in-law, and his nephew the Earl of March Heir Presumptive to King Richard. Mortimer would fetch a fine price, as would Rob Whitney of Whitney Castle, Thomas Clanvow, Mortimer's tenant at Cusop; de la Bere of Kinnersly, and Walter Devereux, all of whom graciously surrendered and were taken with us when we left.

We left Pilleth at a leisurely pace, Glyndŵr making amiable conversation with Mortimer, who, knowing he was safe and ransom certain, responded in kind. So civilised, so civilised, and all the while...

We rode past the moated mass of Huntingdon Castle at Gladestry, looming over the Welsh border, the river bounding it and sheer cliffs behind it. Perhaps we should have attacked it, since we were there anyway. But we were too weary and elated to bother, so we left it for another day. Mind, we had the presence of mind to acquire a field-full of fat lowland cattle and as many sacks of flour from Huntingdon's mill as we could carry, then burned the mill, so Huntingdon wouldn't feel neglected.

We made pilgrimage to Pilleth, but forgot to worship at the Holy Well and shrine.

Rhiannon
June, and I'm still here.

By day I play the dutiful stepmother, and by night I lie on my back and grit my teeth. I am terrified of another baby, but how can I prevent it? Perhaps if I hate enough it will poison my womb so that nothing will live inside me. A child would trap me for ever, and I must get away.

Since de Grey's capture, ap Hywel is at home more often: he isn't popular at Ruthin Castle at the moment. De Grey's agents knew exactly who passed on the information. When de Grey is finally ransomed (ten thousand marks is apparently proving hard to raise) Rhys is likely to be even less popular, so he's busily making himself - and his son - as invisible as possible whilst still husbanding de Grey's lands alongside his own. De Grey will probably punish him somehow, though, and if he suffers, I imagine so shall I, because all his misfortunes are my fault, being Glyndŵr's foster-daughter. Twice *Tadmaeth*'s men have raided us, taken sheep and cattle, torched crops and burned buildings, which makes Rhys doubly angry, first because of his losses, and second because despite being married to me we're still attacked!

I want to tell him that if he'd followed Glyndŵr in the first place, he'd be better off now, but I don't dare. He must know he's chosen the wrong side. Glyndŵr's star is ascending: de Grey is his prisoner, and that's Rhys's fault. For myself, when ap Hywel is on top of me, gasping and grunting, I clench my fists and imagine the smell of burned buildings and the crackle of flaming thatch and hope they come again, soon, and burn the rest of the place, and the house too, as long as Angharad and Gethin and I are out of it. Oh, and Beti and the servants, I suppose. They've done nothing. But I'd like to see Ifan burned. I'd enjoy hearing him screech.

Rhys caught me washing in our chamber this morning. I thought he and Ifan were out of the house, and I'd stripped to scrub away the stench of his attentions. He burst in through the door, and I grabbed my shift to cover myself.

He stared. He doesn't see me naked if I can help it, and his nightly fumblings are always in darkness, as if he's ashamed.

'What do you want?' I asked.

He raised his eyebrows. 'My house. I go where I want, when I want.'

'Of course.' I backtracked, hastily. 'You startled me, that's all. I thought you'd gone out.' I hoped he wouldn't want me, not in daylight. If Rhys was at home, then perhaps so was Ifan, and I couldn't bear the thought of him eavesdropping as he did at night.

Ignoring me, he stripped off his tunic and tossed it onto the floor, took a clean one from the press and shrugged it on, ruffling his thinning hair. He'd be completely bald soon.

It's unlike Rhys to change clothes in the middle of the day - or even in the middle of the week. Prodded by the uncomfortable silence, I asked the question.

'De Grey's agent has sent for me,' he mumbled, kicking off his muddy boots and tugging on clean ones.

'Is Ifan going with you?' I clutched my shift tightly around me.

'Why?'

I shrugged. I could hardly say that if he was I could relax for a few hours, out of danger and un-spied upon. To his father, Ifan was innocent as the Lamb of God. 'No particular reason. I just wondered.'

'Yes. He'll go into the household when de Grey is ransomed. Ifan would have been a squire long ago if his mother had lived.'

Would de Grey take Ifan? Perhaps, but I doubted Ifan would enjoy it much. I hoped Ifan would be sent away: if he was at Ruthin and *Tadmaeth* attacked he might be killed. They knew what he'd done, and since Tomos escaped, they wouldn't let Ifan go. Especially since Llew and Elffin knew what he'd done to me.

I watched them clatter out of the yard, Ifan pale green with nerves. I sent my thoughts to his horse, urging it to buck, to shy, to throw him off and jump up and down on him, but horses are obviously not sensitive to mental suggestion.

I ate breakfast with Beti: her shrill voice continuous as toothache. The sun shone through the open door onto the flagstone floor, and I longed to be outside in the fresh air. Angharad cleared the table, Gethin fast asleep and bound to her body with a shawl.

She saw my face and said 'Beti, why don't you stay with me today? We could start sewing your new kirtle.'

'It must be very full around the hem,' Beti demanded, indicating the desired width with her arms at full stretch 'and have a frill. And a different colour under-kirtle, and ribbons, and -' Her voice tailed away as she followed Angharad.

I finished clearing the table, putting butter and cheese into the cool, slate-lined larder and covering them away from dust and flies. I wanted to ride, but Jack had been so strange lately that I didn't want to ask him, for his safety as well as my own. So far, Ifan hadn't said anything, but somehow he knew Elffin and Llew had been here, and that knowledge was over us like a sword.

I left the house and took the path through the woods, meaning to visit Ceridwen. I hadn't thanked her for her kindness, and I needed to talk to someone sympathetic or burst. Besides, her cottage was well away from Pentregoch, and that was good enough for me.

It was warm, even in the shadow of the trees, and light spackled the path ahead of me. The bluebells had long gone, but there were other wild flowers, pungent wild garlic, celandine like gobbets of butter, purple clover heads, and I picked a bunch of the more fragrant ones for Ceridwen.

Her cottage door was closed, and I knocked and opened it. She was out, so I decided to wait until she came back. I didn't think she'd mind. I surveyed the small room. There I had sat, Gethin on my lap. There, Llew had embraced me, and there - oh, there - Elffin had hidden in the shadows of the hut. And here, on this spot, he had held me tight. I still felt his kiss, light on the top of my head. For days afterwards I felt as if I should have a glowing mark on my scalp where his lips had touched, but when I looked in the mirror there was nothing.

I waited a while, sitting on the settle lost in dreams, but Ceridwen didn't come, and I'd been away too long. What if Rhys came back? They should be away most of the day, but Elin and Gwen gossiped, and Ifan seemed to hear everything. I got up, preparing to leave, but as my hand touched the latch the door swung inward, and Ceridwen stood on the threshold, stooped like an old woman.

I hardly recognised her: the dark eyes were blackened with purple bruises; a graze marred her cheekbone and her lower lip was split and puffed.

'Ceridwen!' I put out a hand and then drew back, afraid to touch her. 'What did you do?'

'Do?' The battered mouth twisted. 'Not much. Gave shelter to two young men who wanted to visit a girl.'

'But - what happened?'

'Your step-son paid me a visit.' She touched her mouth, gently. 'He knew you'd been here, but not why. So he asked me. He's not gentle, when he asks.'

'Ifan hit you?'

'Oh, aye.' She grimaced, disclosing the gap of a missing tooth. 'He hit me all right. Fists, like he'd hit a man. Except he wouldn't hit a man, being a coward.'

My stomach clenched. 'Did you tell him?'

She gazed at me levelly. 'Tell him what, Rhiannon? You brought Gethin to me for balm to help with his teething.'

I sagged with relief. I was safe. Then I felt guilty.

'I knew Ifan had found out that Jack and I'd been here, but God, Ceridwen, I couldn't have been so brave.' She slanted an eyebrow, and winced. 'Brave? What was I going to do, confess I'd harboured two *Meibion Glyndŵr*?'

I began to understand. 'But he beat you, and still you didn't tell.'

She shook her head. 'I'll have him for it, some day, mind. I swear I will.'

Elffin

Rhys Gethin the Fierce: well-named, but what was done with his consent after we left turns my stomach. It was against humanity. I'm glad Llew was with us. He's seen action, but he's still idealistic enough to dream of chivalry and honour, and at Pilleth there was none.

Maredydd blusters and shouts that in war such things happen, but what Rhys Gethin did was evil, and I hope his acts don't turn the Almighty against us. I wish I'd been there to prevent it, although I doubt even I could have stopped it.

The battle was done: Mortimer was prisoner, and the remaining English had been beaten back down the hill. Rhys Gethin should have withdrawn, taken his men and allowed our enemy to collect their wounded and bury their dead. Instead, they stood between the English and their dead, while women, Welsh women, if they can be called women, for they bear no resemblance to the gentle souls I know, fell upon the dead - aye, and the dying, they say - and ripped and horribly mutilated their bodies.

Maredydd says that the women were camp followers who had lost their menfolk and their homes to marauding English. Some, he said, had been raped and beaten like old Huw's niece at Croesau, and they say she's been witless ever since. Perhaps they had been, and were entitled to their moment of savagery, but all the same and whatever, Rhys Gethin should have stopped it.

The English stood helpless while their wounded and dying were attacked, and despite the day's triumph I feel only sadness and sickness and a stain on my own soul, even though I wasn't there.

Rhys Gethin wouldn't let the English bury their dead until long after the battle was ended, and only then on payment of ransom for the bodies. Our own fallen were buried half-way up Bryn Glas, in sight of the square tower of the Church of the Blessed Virgin, sprinkled with water from the Holy Well beyond the Church, and prayed over, and thank God they were comparatively few. The English retrieved their dead and buried them only when Rhys Gethin and his men had left the field.

I was with *Tad* when he was told, and he said nothing. But today his face is grey with lack of sleep, and his beard has more white in it these days. Even in victory there's defeat.

Edmund Mortimer is our prisoner, treated as an honoured guest. He's older than I, at twenty-six, and pleasant company. If he weren't English, I could love him as a brother, I think. My sister Catherine, our Catrin *fach*, is taken with him, and my brothers and I laugh when she loiters where he is, and smiles up at him in that winning way she has.

Catrin, mind, she's beautiful. She'd be a catch for anyone, but father wouldn't ever let an enemy marry her, so Catrin will have to pine for him, I am afraid.

Though... he gave Rhiannon to ap Hywel, who is also an enemy, though *Tad* didn't know it then. I lie awake at night remembering how she felt in my arms, and how she looked. Despite almost two years with Rhys ap Hywel, she still loves me, I know she does, and I long for her, and I'm sickened by the futility of it all. Useless to tell myself she's another man's wife. I want her. How old is she now? She must be seventeen, a woman grown, who's carried and lost a child and is beautiful to bring birds from trees. In my eyes at least.

When I stop thinking of Rhiannon, I think of Gethin, and there's another ache. Handsome and bonny, my son, my *babi braf*, and I can't own him because his mother's a servant in our enemy's house.

If we could see into the future, how differently we'd behave!

CHAPTER TWENTY-SIX

Llewelyn

My brothers constantly argue the question of "right" and "might". Gruffydd, like *Tadmaeth*, is shattered by what was done at Pilleth in Glyndŵr's name. Siôn sided with Maredydd and Madoc, who were pragmatic: justified by the circumstances, they said, the circumstances being war. Desecration of corpses? Torture and mutilation of wounded? Justified? Never! Arguments rage even in the kitchens, where Bron shrieks at Crisiant, fat arms waving, round faces sweating and red with temper. Bron says those who did it will burn in hell. A mother's son, every one, *Sais* or not, she says, and pity, respect and a decent burial their right. Crisiant, closer to the family, disagrees, and our stomachs suffer as a result.

Rhys Gethin let women cut off men's private parts and stuff them - well, never mind. My balls shrivel at the thought. They say some of the English were still alive. What if I should fall, and a horde of English women... Perhaps English women are different. Welsh women are fierce. Men don't get raped, mind, men don't sit at home wondering if their womenfolk are alive or dead in some muddy field somewhere.

I can't imagine Mali doing things like that, and Rhiannon - well, now I think about it, Rhiannon might. God help those who cross her. Mind, I don't think she's quite so brave these days. Living with ap Hywel has changed her, made her cautious, and her fear of Ifan must make her feel helpless as a child. As helpless as she was when Lady Marged married her off, I suppose. God, I'm glad I'm not a woman! No wonder they occasionally take revenge on men - though amputating their cocks is a bit drastic.

I think sometimes of Rhian in that woman's hut: holding Elffin's son, so unlike my scrawny sister. She's not bad looking, now, and Elffin - well, I saw his face when he held her. I saw him kiss her hair. He loves her now it's too late.

I mean, what can he do? Rhian and Gethin are trapped with a man who cares nothing for either of them. I'm wiser now than when she was sent away, though I don't have much experience of women. My Mam died when I was little, and Lady Marged was always distant. Bron hugs me and fusses, and if I make her angry she's likely to give me a thick ear or a bloody nose. Wish there was something I could do, though.

We raided Pentregoch a few weeks back: burned crops, stole cattle and sheep, and set fire to a couple of outbuildings, though we stayed away from the main house for fear of endangering Rhian and Gethin. Mind, I was praying Ifan would come out and fight so I could have a chance at him. I'm going to kill him, and damn chivalry. Traitors don't deserve mercy. But one day, I swear... I hope he's afraid. I hope he's constantly looking over his shoulder.

Pilleth - which when all is said and done was a great victory, regardless of the aftermath - is over, and we're riding south. The Prince needs to visit Gwent and Morgannwg to assess support there. It won't harm to remind the Marcher lords that he is Prince of all Wales, and not just Prince of the North.

I've never been south: they say it's different down there, and they speak a strange sort of Welsh, but I still want to go.

Rhiannon

Ceridwen's potion contains rue and other unidentifiable things, and the taste makes me retch until my stomach aches, and my throat burns with bitter fire, but she says it will stop a child taking root. I gulp it every morning after Rhys leaves, even before I wash away his stink. Better drink poison than be pregnant again.

There's been a battle at Pilleth. A thousand English died, they say, and Edmund Mortimer was captured, though he'll be well treated because of who he is. Not so sure about de Grey, though. He's probably quite comfortable, but if I had my way, he'd be in the foulest, darkest dungeon in the world, and kept there for ever.

Rhys told me about Pilleth but Jack had already brought me the news: I did my best to look sad, but inside was wicked joy. When *Tadmaeth* has taken all of Wales, then I can leave. When he's properly Prince of Wales and the English have scuttled back over the borders where they belong, he surely won't make me stay here any longer. Even Lady Marged might pity me.

Being in the same house as Ifan is sickening. He hit Ceridwen with his fists! I've seen her ribs, covered with great bruises: some perhaps even broken, because she still can't walk upright.

I'm ashamed to say - no, actually I'm not - I took some revenge. Not much, considering what he did. I put the juice of - no, I won't say what - a plant in his food, and an hour later he was green, clutching his guts and vomiting. He wailed and spewed almost without stopping for three days. Ap Hywel sent for an apothecary, but his brew wasn't as powerful as mine! A small evil for a greater one. I'm still afraid of him, but I'm not entirely powerless. I may not be able to protect myself entirely, but I can take revenge if I want!

I can't leave yet, not now. Without Gethin life would be unbearable and I can't leave him. Angharad trusts me with him, and she lets Jack take him, sometimes. Gethin's face brightens when Jack appears; he yells to be lifted and perched on Jack's broad shoulders and carried around the yard, squealing with delight. I wish it was Elffin he reached out to, Elffin's shoulders he rode, Elffin's ears he pulled.

Jack and I are friends again. After Llew and Elffin came, he was strange and seemed to be avoiding me. That was hard, because he's my only friend here. I need him. Oh, I need him.

Eventually, I plucked up courage to face him. Rhys and Ifan were away: I pulled a shawl over my head to protect me from a sudden summer downpour, and splashed through the puddles in the yard. He was sitting on an upturned keg rubbing mending harness.

'Oh,' he said. 'Rhiannon.'

I shook rain off my shawl. 'Yes. Me. What's the matter, Jack? What have I done?'

'Done?' His face was impassive.

'I hardly ever see you, and when I do you don't speak. I miss talking to you, Jack. And Gethin pines for you.'

'He'll get over it.'

'I won't.'

'What?' The careful mask slipped, and there was emotion, at last - but nothing I could read.

'Jack,' I touched his hand. 'You're the only friend I've got. Don't leave me?'

'I'm not going anywhere,' he said shortly.

'What have I done?' I repeated.

He shrugged. 'Nothing. Nothing you can change, anyway.'

'I don't understand. Tell me, please? I'll put it right, I promise, if you'll only tell me.'

'You can't.'

'Try me, Jack. What can I do?' But he shook his head.

I couldn't give up. 'Whatever I've done, please forgive me. I want to be friends. I need you. If you fail me, I can't go on.'

He shoved his hands through his thick hair, making it stand up in tufts. 'Ah, Rhiannon, don't, *cariad*. You're like a terrier with a rat. I won't let you down, I promise. But it's difficult, you're ap Hywel's wife, and -' He stopped. 'It could be dangerous for both of us.'

'I only ever come when I know it's safe. Angharad won't tell, and Elin and Gwen are at the other side of the house.'

'It's still dangerous. But if you need me, Rhiannon, I'm here.'

'Oh, I need you.'

He shrugged, helplessly and picked up the bridle he'd been cleaning. 'Never mind. There, then. All mended.' His smile didn't reach his eyes.

It still wasn't right. But I needed someone to bring news, or take an urgent message. But beyond that I valued Jack. I changed the subject.

'I saw Ceridwen a while ago,' I sat beside him on a feed-bin.

'Oh, aye.'

'Did you know Ifan beat her? Blacked her eyes and split her lip, and I think he might have broken some of her ribs. She shrugs it off, but I can tell she's in pain.'

He put down the bridle, slowly. 'Ceridwen?'

'He wanted to know why we'd visited her. She lied, told him Gethin was teething and we wanted balm. She lied to protect us.'

Jack's eyes narrowed to furious slits. 'I swear, Rhiannon, if it's the last thing I do, I'll make that little bastard suffer. One day -'

'Get in the queue, Jack,' I stood, brushing straw off my skirt, 'it was me he tried to kill, remember?'

'I'm not likely to forget. But don't give him any more opportunities, Rhiannon.'

'Easier said than done - but I'll be careful, I promise.'

Elffin

What a land this is. Undulations of green, forests of dark trees, roaring, gushing, trickling waterfalls and rivers, silver fish dimpling the pools. In woodland, bright petals of sunlight dapple our path, and the loudness of birds is a joyous welcome - almost as loud as that from the people.

There's not a man against Owain Glyndŵr, anywhere! In every hamlet and town, men, women and children rush out to bless us and shout welcome: they wave hats and throw flowers. Cynical Maredydd says the louder a town cheers, the less likely the town is going to burn, but their cheers seem genuine enough.

There are still English that need to be ratted out, and in the southern valleys the Marcher lords try to hinder us. We hit Abergavenny so hard the Lord's ears are probably still ringing. The Castle squats sinister on its mound overlooking the town: it makes a man unwilling to walk in its shadow. It was built centuries ago by the Norman, William de Breos - who could teach even the English a lesson in treachery. He invited his Welsh neighbours to the castle, told them to leave their weapons aside and sit in peace and eat. When they were mellow, relaxed - and unarmed - his men set about slaughtering them all. Long ago, mind, but so what? We have long memories, we Welsh. Perhaps we've evened the score a little.

Usk, Caerleon and Newport (which we took), Cardiff, where we beat down the city gates, sacked the castle and frightened De Spenser out of his wits. At Llandaff we spared the cathedral, because the clergy support us, but scorched the Bishop's mitre in his palace. We razed towns and looted - always with the enthusiastic assistance of the Welsh citizens, all for Owain Glyndŵr. Our numbers increase daily: English reprisals have hardened the population, and Henry's heavy-handedness drives more and more Welsh to us.

We left Cardiff on the old, straight Roman road, the Portway they call it, and rode through lovely Cwm Morgannwg, our dragon's tail of supporters growing with each town. We attacked Penllyn, Llandochdwy, Flemingstone, Talyfan, Llanblethian, Llangeinior, Malafont and Penmark, and destroyed their castles.

Gruffydd wanted to press on up to Gower and beyond, where they say the coastline is as beautiful and as any in the North, and reach Carmarthen quickly. But *Tad* refused to travel there, which was strange. Then I heard the reason and understood.

Tad believes in omens and portents: as well as Crach Ffinnant he consults other wizards. Hopcyn ap Tomos ab Einion for one, who warned Owain that between Carmarthen and Gower he would be captured by a man riding beneath a black banner: *Tad* declined to put this prophecy to the test, and therefore we avoided the straight road. Cynical Maredydd suggested that probably Hopcyn had crops there that he didn't want burned, and livestock he preferred to keep for himself, and so he would say that, wouldn't he - but I think *Tad* was wise.

These valleys are beautiful, but I miss the mountains. I dream, sometimes, of when I climbed Eryri, once. It was a long, hard climb, but at the top, eagles floated on clear air, and vapour boiled off the edges of great rifts and escarpments, hiding the secret lakes - until the mist parted like a drawn curtain to reveal, like a gift, the silver depths mirroring the sky.

Tad has little time for small-talk with his sons these days. Llew hasn't had more than a few words with him for weeks. He's Father to his country now, and his sons must take second place, I suppose.

One night he came to the fire. I didn't hear him, but Llew saw movement in the shadows and sat up, relaxing when he recognised the tall, spare figure. At least, I relaxed, but Llew leapt to his feet to greet his hero.

'Down, Llew,' *Tad* flapped a vague hand in his direction. 'Elffin doesn't jump up in respect for his father, why should you? How goes it, my sons?'

Llew was tongue-tied. Now there's a rare occurrence if you like.

Tad reached out a hand to the warmth. Although it was July, the nights were cold. 'How fares your sister, Llew?'

Llew glanced at me, uncertainly. Slowly I sat up, and met his eyes, hoping he'd understand and speak out - for both of us.

He took a deep breath, perhaps seeking courage: his reverence for *Tad* is greater, I think, than that for Christ, if that isn't blaspheming on his behalf.

'She's unhappy, *Tadmaeth*. She doesn't love ap Hywel, not one bit. She might have, if he'd supported you and been a bit kind to her, but he spied and betrayed you to de Grey, and she'll never forgive him for that. Rhiannon was going to have a baby, my Lord, but her step-son pushed her down the stairs and she nearly died. The baby did die, which was just as well, because she didn't want it anyway.'

Tad blinked, taken aback. He'd probably expected an anodyne 'Well, thank you Sire'.

'Some wives don't love their husbands, Llew. But not many have murderous step-sons! Are you sure? Rhiannon always was an imaginative child.'

'It's true, *Tad*,' I put in. 'If ap Hywel's man hadn't fetched a local wise-woman to help her, she'd have died.'

His mild gaze fell full on me, now. 'And Angharad, Elffin? And my grandson?'

I gulped. 'Gra- Grandson?' I stammered.

'Gethin, isn't it?' His face was unreadable.

I nodded, dumbly. 'How - how did you know?' I managed to croak at last.

'Your mother told me the girl was breeding when she left Sycharth. Elffin, when a man beds a woman - which I seem to remember you did to Angharad once or twice -'

My face went hot, suddenly.

'- she's likely to produce a child. How did I know? I asked, and learned that I have another grandson.' There was almost a smile, but I might have imagined it.

I wondered how far I dared go. 'He's wonderful, *Tad*, you'd be proud of him. He's got teeth, and he's remarkably intelligent.' I plucked up my courage. 'I wish I could bring him home. And Llew's sister, too.' I couldn't let him suspect why I wanted Rhiannon to come home.

He sighed. 'If ap Hywel ever learns he has my grandson in his hands, he'd have a hostage to fortune none of us could afford, bastard or no. And as for Rhiannon, she's still his wife. He might agree to part with Angharad and your son, but your mother won't accept Angharad. Mind, the poor girl wasn't entirely to blame for her condition. Eh, Elffin?'

I opened my mouth to argue, but shut it again. My shoulders slumped. Gethin couldn't come without Angharad, and Mam wouldn't have Angharad. Rhiannon was another man's wife, and that was that. Stalemate.

Then Llew spoke up, his voice wobbling. '*Tadmaeth*. You said, when I saved Elffin's life that time -'

Owain's mouth twitched. 'I remember, Llew. I called you my son.'

'If I'm your son, then Rhiannon must be your daughter,' Llew gabbled, 'and if one of your daughters was desperate with unhappiness and living with a man she loathes and a step-son she is afraid of, wouldn't you bring her home?'

Tad sighed. 'You're a hard man, Llew, putting me on the spot. If she were my daughter, Llew, I'd move heaven and earth to bring her home. Given an opportunity, that is.'

'You mean -' I couldn't keep the hope from my voice, and *Tad* frowned.

'I mean that *if* an opportunity presents itself, and Rhiannon can leave ap Hywel, she may come home. Perhaps Angharad will let her bring Gethin.'

I doubted that, but it was hope. A small, faint hope, with little chance of becoming reality, especially if Mam got to hear of it.

But hope, where before there was none.

CHAPTER TWENTY-SEVEN

Llewelyn

The King has ordered the Sheriffs and their armies to Chester, Shrewsbury and Hereford, and all along the borders troops are mustering. Armed men from Lancaster, Derbyshire and Shropshire mill about with baggage carts, and Stafford is at Hereford mustering their men and those from Gloucester and Worcester. We expect the King to attack from Shrewsbury, and his son from Chester: Warwick, Arundel and Stafford will strike south from Hereford. By early September we must be ready, though we've no army equal to theirs. We can't afford it, and anyway, however many we are, we'll be outnumbered. But as the old saying goes, there are more ways of killing a cat than choking it with cream.

We won't face the King in battle, but wear him down with small, swift attacks. We've infiltrated Henry's armies: our spies mingle in taverns and lurk behind doors - but then, so do the King's. Yesterday Madoc found a "friar" on the Machynlleth road who wore habit and tonsure, but that was all that was priestly about him. Later a man arrived claiming to be from Caernarfon, but all he knew was that it had a castle! When questioned (though to my disgust in quite a gentle manner) he earnestly informed us that the

King's army numbers tens of thousands, enough to annihilate Wales and every "rebel" a hundred times over, without straining a muscle.

We know that captured English spies are under orders to exaggerate the size of their army - so we divided by ten and probably got a truer picture. The King's spies have sounded out local people, and of course every Welshman lied in his teeth and declared for the King. Do they think we're daft?

Men like William Whitford, mind, - there should be a special level of Hell for those like him: Welsh, but promising to lead Henry to Glyndŵr. He says he knows every bush, tree, hollow and cave that *Tadmaeth* has ever walked past and if the King desires he will deliver Owain, Welsh traitor and rebel neatly parcelled and tied with rope. We'll remember William Whitford.

The English burgesses are hurting - the King's demanded mountains of supplies, hordes of men - probably harder to prise the supplies from them than the men: plenty of men, but supplies mean hard cash somewhere along the line.

The King has local guides: sometimes Welsh like Whitford - paid traitors. Whatever: they won't find us. We drift like smoke throughout the Marches, only Elffin and I with Glyndŵr, and Maredydd and Gruffydd when they aren't leading their own bands.

When they started out, we sat near Hereford and watched them come. We hid in the hills as they trudged the valley, their professional soldiers in front, then the lumbering baggage carts, complete with outriders to protect their provisions, the horses nose to arse, the ranks of foot-soldiers close together, not to leave spaces for wicked Welshmen to slither in and steal the King's supplies.

I feel sorry for the pressed-men: they know they're likely to end up dead and never see their homes and families again. The poor sods are herded at the rear of the column, beaten into line if they straggle, and there's one man I've been watching particularly. My gaze kept returning to him, and by the end of the day I felt I knew him, aye, and pitied him.

He's tall and ungainly, his feet splayed, with a pendulous little belly that says he's no soldier and is fond of his ale. He's invariably out of step and stumbling; his boots don't fit and one of the outriders seems to have taken a personal dislike to the poor sod because at every stumble he's clouted, thumped and kicked back into line. He'll probably die in the first skirmish. I hoped that I shouldn't have to kill him at all.

At night the professional soldiers, used to marching all day and sleeping in the field, made themselves as comfortable as they could on bare ground, but the pressed-men just slumped exhausted where they stopped, my man amongst them, and woke up next day stiff and sore to begin the long march again.

Henry was prepared for everything. Carts were laden with food, drink, cooking pots, tents, armour, armaments, great planks of wood and long poles: everything had been taken into consideration. Everything, that is, except a Welsh Autumn.

Wales is a green country. A country is not green unless it is regularly and generously watered, and September is often a wet month. This September, however, was a masterpiece of wetness, a wetness to end all wetnesses, a triumphal downpour from beginning to end. No sooner did Henry cross the border than the heavens cracked open.

Cart tracks became mud-wallows; roads became impassable, rivers rose and the banks of the Usk, the Wye and the Severn disappeared underwater, wooden and sometimes even stone bridges crossing the smaller rivers swept away as gentle rivulets became great battering torrents. And we sat our horses on higher ground and watched the poor bastards drown as they tried to cross them.

We sheltered under trees, waterproofed with tight-woven, well-oiled and hooded wool, homespun and leather, and watched men struggle to unload great poles and ropes and planks of wood from the hopeless, helpless, staggering carts. We watched riders plunge into the rivers, driving stakes into the riverbed, hoping to string ropes from the uprights to make supporting handrails, but the stakes were washed away as soon as they were set. They made bridges, and as fast as they built them they collapsed, so in desperation they formed two lines of mounted men, those horses upstream panicking, struggling to keep their feet against the current, while their riders fought to make any kind of breakwater for the poor bastards battling to cross the river. A second body of horsemen, downstream, fought to hook out foot-soldiers washed away, but the rivers were so fast-flowing that often they missed their grip, or were themselves pulled off their mounts by the those they tried to help, and rescuers and victims died together. Apparently a lot of Englishmen can't swim: they were floating down river like dead sheep for days after, tangled in half-submerged trees, pushed and pulled into whirlpools and eddies. Even the odd horse drowned, too, the currents were so strong.

And I watched my poor scarecrow struggle in shin-deep mud, his flannel clothes so sodden with rain that they probably weighed more than he did. I watched him stumble and fall and get beaten back into the ranks. I knew when his feet got so numb that he couldn't feel them, and when he lost his ill-fitting right boot in the mud and had to walk with one naked foot. I saw the misery on his face and the droop of his shoulders. His belly and his heart were empty and hurting, and I knew that if I were to kill him, he'd probably bless me with his dying breath, so sick was he of Wales, the Welsh and rain, rain, rain.

Their Lordships didn't get off entirely, either. Destriers stumbled, their great feathered hooves clogged with mud, so the horses were miserable and ill-tempered. Armour rusted fast, so riders moved with creaking difficulty. Rain seeped down inside the metal, soaked their wool and flax undergarments and chilled them to the bone. Lightning was an almost constant, blinding sear of icy light. Thunder boomed and roared, terrifying the horses so that they plunged and reared and fell on floundering men and broke their bones, which brought the columns into confusion and deposited their riders on their arses in the mud where they got wetter and more miserable still.

They lost supplies: ale-casks were jounced off lurching carts unnoticed by miserable, sodden men (and we acquired them later) and when they stopped for the night it was too wet for cooking fires, so no hot food was forthcoming, and besides, their cooking pots were all at the bottom of the river. Their provisions were sodden, rotten or missing, so as well as all their other miseries, they were hungry.

And always, a small band of Welsh followed them, picking off those too weak and ill to keep up, and another small band patrolled the hillside above the English column, longbows bringing further chaos to the already devastated armies.

As well as rain, thunder and lightning, hail, snow - I ask you, snow in September! - and the cold, there was also the wind. Hurricanes blew down church steeples, ripped thatches from roofs, and icy winds battered into the faces of miserable men who could hardly see to walk.

Rumours spread by our spies took hold in the English ranks: Owain Glyndŵr can even command the weather (this they were more than happy to believe!). Glyndŵr (they said) carries a stone spit from a raven's beak that makes him invisible. They were afraid of shadows in case this magical, all-powerful enemy was already among them, unheard, unseen - and deadly.

And so they suffered and died, without ever encountering a Welshman. Rain fell, the heavens battered them, and man by man, we picked them off. They died of exposure; drowned; starved; and the foot soldiers had hardly a boot between them when at last they crossed the border back into England, my scarecrow man amongst them, I was pleased to see, because by that time I felt I knew him like a brother, even if I couldn't love him as one.

We lost only Gareth One-Eye, who took a chill when he fell into a puddle, and died.

Rhiannon

I've been on my knees for days. I'm so afraid. The king invaded in September, and Ifan and Rhys rubbed their hands and crowed, anticipating victory. Not, I thought, if I've got anything to do with it. De Grey's steward summoned them to service in de Grey's army, and I hurled myself to my knees, grabbed my rosary, screwed my eyes shut and prayed as I've never prayed before, gabbling *Ave Marias* and *Pater Nosters* like a demented nun. Sometimes I only managed *oh, please, oh please, oh please,* but hoped God would understand. I *know* he did, because I'd been praying barely an hour when the rain began.

It rained for twenty days, by which time the rivers were cascading over their banks, the thatch was leaking in a hundred different places, the yard was a sea of mud and I believed most whole-heartedly in the power of prayer. I'd like to think I persuaded God to send the weather, but pride is a sin and I'd better try to be virtuous, just in case.

Ap Hywel and Ifan were away for more than three weeks, praise God. It was wonderful to have my bed to myself, to stretch out and not encounter an alien, hairy leg, not to be woken a dozen times a night by thunderous snores: and not to have to drink foul stuff to prevent conception.

Beti was distraught because her father had gone to war and might be killed (how I hoped!), but wasn't at all concerned by her brother's absence. Understandable: he's cruel to her, poor scrap. I often see fist-sized bruises on her small body when I help her to dress, and once he tore out a clump of her hair by dragging her off a bench when she irritated him. I suggested that God might see fit to aim a thunderbolt at Ifan, since He's throwing so many of them about anyway, but either He didn't hear or He chose to ignore it, because Ifan came home, as did his father.

This will be a long winter: October is as wet as September was, and then there'll be nothing but cold and wet and snow and misery until March or April. But I can look forward: perhaps next year I'll be able to run away. Next year, Gethin will be big enough to travel. If Angharad comes with me, I'll try to find her a place close to Sycharth or Glyndyfrdwy, wherever we are, so she can see Gethin sometimes. Gethin, of course, will be with me and his father.

Rhys is home, so I'm drinking the potion again. He was exhausted at first, depressed by England's defeat, but now he's at me again and I must put up with it, except when my courses come, which thank God they do with great regularity. I can sometimes steal an extra day each side so that they last from five days to six and sometimes seven, before he notices.

I splashed across the yard to the dairy yesterday, and reached it in time to hear Elin yelp. I opened the door. Ifan, his back to me, had her wedged across the table. Her skirts were up, her hair dangling in the cream-pan. His free hand was busy fumbling with his breeches, and without thinking twice I picked up a handy cream-skimmer and cracked him with it. He crumpled and fell. Elin, her face streaked with tears, the white marks of his fingers across her mouth slowly turning red, stared at me in horror.

'Oh, Mrs Rhiannon, what have you done?'

'Stopped you getting raped,' I said. I tossed the skimmer aside and bent over Ifan's prone body. He was still breathing, unfortunately, but he had a lump like an egg on the back of his head. 'Quick,' I said, 'find Jack.'

She was out of there in a flash, returning with Jack in tow. He stopped on the threshold and groaned.

'Jesus Christ, Rhian, have you killed him?'

'No, unfortunately. He'll live, but he'll have a headache. God's bollocks, Jack, that felt good!' I grinned up at him, my hair straggling over my face, and the words didn't feel like blasphemy.

'It won't last.' He hoisted the unconscious body over his shoulders and, after I'd checked the yard, carried him into the stable and dumped him behind his horse.

'He's still breathing,' he said, loosening his jerkin. 'Rhian, go. When he comes round, I'll tell him his horse kicked him. He won't believe me, but he won't dare tell his father. Ap Hywel thinks the sun shines out of the little bastard's arse.'

I sent Elin back to the dairy and splashed across the yard. I knew I'd have to pay, but fighting back felt good!

Elffin

England will think twice about invading Wales again. God, what it must have cost Henry to have to go back having never fought a battle, having been harried and bothered and sniped at, cursed by the one thing that even His Gracious Majesty Henry of England couldn't control. I almost feel sorry for him. Almost.

They say one night he was asleep, and the wind was so strong that trees were bent double, and his tent was wrecked. But for the fact that he was sleeping in full armour he would have been crushed by the heavy tent-pole falling across his body. It must be hard for a King when even his God is against him!

We didn't forget William Whitford, either. He suffered an unfortunate "accident" soon after Henry tottered back to Hereford. He turned up dead on his own doorstep, which, incidentally, had set itself on fire.

I wish I could talk to Rhiannon. I wish I could tell my son: sons should be told such stories. The hope *Tad* gave me is diminishing, because time is passing. I haven't forgotten what he said, but perhaps he has. He has so much on his mind, after all.

If I could even write to Rhiannon - but I daren't, in case it's intercepted. I'm desperate for news, but there's none, and no way of getting any. I dream of her, but she's always out of reach. Sometimes I dream she's at Sycharth again, a great-eyed, scrawny child, and I wake and wish I had that time again. She could push me into the river any time she wanted. I'd gladly get soaked three times a day if only Rhian could be here to shove me in.

Edmund Mortimer is here at Glyndyfrdwy, and he's a good man, for an enemy. He's honest and charming, and his wit makes him more than likeable. The King still won't ransom him. He thinks Mortimer deliberately lost at Pilleth because he secretly sympathised with *Tad*, and persuaded his archers to turn their coats. So Mortimer will be here for a while, unless Hotspur can change the King's mind, but Henry won't even let Hotspur try to raise the ransom - he named Edmund traitor. This is not the way to keep a warrior like Edmund's father loyal.

Bored, frustrated and fearful for Rhian, I went to find Edmund to see if he was in a mood to talk, play chess, anything to relieve the tedium, but he wasn't in his quarters. I met Crisiant half-way up the stairs, and asked if she'd seen him.

She wouldn't look me in the eyes. I ducked my head so that she had to.

'Come on, Crisiant. Where is he?' The women loved Edmund - I hoped they hadn't helped him escape...

She shrugged, and tried to get away.

'Cris?' I wheedled. 'Come on, where is he?'

'Can't say, Master Elffin,' she said and scurried down the stairs, almost upending Llew in her hurry to be elsewhere.

'You so desperate you're groping Crisiant?'

I feigned a punch at him.

'I can't find Edmund, and Crisiant won't say where he is. You'll do instead. Come and play chess.'

'No. You always win. I know where he is,' he said smugly.

'Where?'

'Haven't you got eyes? Where he always is.'

I refrained from throttling him. 'You going to tell me, or not?'

'He's with Catrin.'

'*Catrin?*'

'Yes, Catrin! They're daft about each other.'

I knew she'd taken a fancy to him, but he's an enemy, for God's sake! A likeable one, but an enemy for all that. Has she no pride? I entered my sister's chamber without knocking (why not? I was looking for our prisoner!) and my little sister scrambled off Mortimer's lap, looking pink and guilty. I was about to speak my mind, when Llew, who'd followed me upstairs, began to laugh.

'Oh, Elffin, you should see your face!'

Catrin gathered her skirts, put her nose in the air and stalked out, leaving me with an hysterical Llew and a shamefaced Mortimer.

'For God's sake, Edmund,' I managed at last, above Llew's howls of amusement, 'what's going on?'

'Your head's permanently up your arse, Elffin.' Llew commented.

'Shut up, Llew,' Mortimer and I said in unison.

From the conversation which followed I learned that not only was Edmund unlikely to be ransomed, he didn't particularly want to be. He was keen to marry my sister and swear fealty to Glyndŵr, who had agreed, and more to the point, Mam was entirely in favour of the match. So, in November, Catrin Glyndŵr will marry Edmund Mortimer. Now there's an alliance!

Delighted as I was, I was even more delighted when Jack arrived on the first dry day we had in October.

CHAPTER TWENTY-EIGHT

Llewelyn
Neither Elffin nor I had expected news of Rhian this side of Christmas, and the two of us got wedged in the doorway trying to get to Jack first. Elffin beat me to the stairs, but then, he's bigger, and shoves harder.

Bron (who took one look at Jack's broad shoulders and battered face last time he came and turned weak at the knees) refused to let us near him until he was by the kitchen fire with hot broth in his hands and a dry robe around his shoulders. Women are strange. Apparently they all love a man with scars and a nose that's been rearranged a time or two. Perhaps I should try to acquire some interesting scars - as painlessly as possible, of course - and see if they attract the girls. I've about given up on Mali, thanks to Bron.

Jack gulped broth, his eyes closed, his face grey with exhaustion, while Elffin and I waited impatiently.

'What's happened?' Elffin burst out eventually, 'is Rhiannon all right? And Gethin?'

'Rhiannon's fine, and Gethin's thriving. He's cut four teeth now, and found his feet. He's driving his Mam mad - she says she needs eyes in the back of her head with him.'

'Did Rhiannon send a message for me? Or Llew?' he added hastily.

Jack shook his head. 'She doesn't know I'm here. It seemed best not to tell her. She's low-spirited, though, which isn't surprising.'

'She's not pregnant again?' Elffin's question tugged at my heart.

'No. Ceridwen's given her something. It makes her vomit, but it works. Listen. If I can get Rhiannon, Angharad and Gethin away, will Glyndŵr take her in?'

'Not Angharad, no shifting Mam there.'

'Angharad won't part with Gethin, and Rhiannon won't leave without him.'

'Can't you make Rhiannon come alone?' I was irritated with my sister. She and Elffin can have their own children, once she's free.

'You don't know your sister as well as you think, Llew. I could never make her leave Gethin. She's determined,' he said with feeling, 'some might say stubborn. Which is why I'm here.'

I felt like smacking Rhiannon very hard, to make her see reason. Didn't she understand what was best for her? Women!

Elffin leaned forward, anxiously. 'What's happened?'

'She caught Ifan in the dairy, trying to rape the servant-girl, and clouted him senseless with a cream-scoop.'

'Did she kill him?' I hoped so.

'Fortunately - or not, as the case may be - no. I lugged him out of the dairy and dumped him in the stable, tried to convince him his horse had kicked him. When he came round he had a lump on his head, but his memory, sadly, was perfect. He knows what he was doing, to whom, and where. He suspects Rhiannon was responsible for his lumps, and he'll make her pay somehow.'

I was half torn by admiration for my sister's action, half frantic with worry for her.

'I told him if anything happens to Rhiannon he'll answer to me, but his father thinks the sun shines out of his arse. And if Ifan should find out I've been here I'll be dismissed - or worse - and no help to Rhian any more.

'How did you get away?'

'A fictional sick aunt. 'I've no family hereabouts, but ap Hywel and Ifan don't know it. I told Rhiannon I was off to Machynlleth market, so naturally she produced a shopping list.' He sighed with exasperation. 'Which means I'll have to go back that way. If I don't take her what she wants there'll be hell to pay. Or she'll guess where I've been, and there'll be hell twice over.'

'We've got to get her from there, Jack.' There was desperation in Elffin's voice. 'How can we talk her into it?'

He laughed. 'Talk her into it? I could talk grass into growing purple, or birds to fly arse-first, but no one will persuade Rhiannon to do anything she doesn't want to do.'

'But she doesn't want to stay with ap Hywel?' Elffin pleaded.

'Of course not. But she won't leave Gethin. Look, we're going round in circles.' He gestured, helplessly. 'What can I do? You know what she's like! All I can do is tell her Glyndŵr will take her in - despite Lady Marged.'

'And if she will leave, will you bring her, Jack? She shouldn't travel alone.'

I couldn't read the expression on Jack's face. 'Of course,' he said.

And we had to be content with that.

Rhiannon

My wrist still aches from clouting Ifan, and so does a muscle in my shoulder: I can't lift my arm to comb my hair, but *Duw* it felt good, that solid *clunk* of wood on skull! Ifan knew his horse hadn't kicked him, and it hadn't been Jack who hit him: Jack would have killed him, not just knocked him out, and therefore it had to be me. It wasn't long before he cornered me in the kitchen.

'You think you got away with it, you and your stable boy, but I won't forget. You'll pay, and so will he.'

I told Jack, who warned me to be careful, but Ifan won't dare do anything while Rhys is in the house, and he'll be here at least until after Christmas, because the weather is deteriorating. Besides, Winter, as always, has put a stop to war.

Jack went to Machynlleth market today. I gave him a list of things that I need, but he said he doubted he'd be able to find them. I told him not to be ridiculous, Machynlleth would have everything I needed, and he had plenty of time, so he reluctantly took the list and left. It occurred to me later that perhaps he wasn't going to Machynlleth at all. But if he were going to Glyndyfrdwy, he would have told me, wouldn't he?

I was waiting for him to come back as soon as the mid-day meal was cleared away. He'd left early, and should be back long before dark, especially if he was only going as far as Machynlleth.

It was a grey afternoon, and the sky threatened snow before nightfall. I hoped he would be safely back by then.

Ifan went off shortly after Jack, and Rhys closeted himself with his accounts in the small room off the kitchen, so I spent the afternoon sewing, playing with Gethin when he woke from his nap, and waiting for the sound of Jack's horse in the yard.

The snow began just as the candles were lighted. Elin was setting the table for the evening meal when I heard hooves clattering on the cobbles. But it was only Ifan.

By the time we'd finished supper, the snow was piling on window-sills and heaping in drifts in the yard. Wind moaned in the eaves, and I shivered. It would be a terrible ride in such weather, and I began to worry in earnest.

At bed-time, when Rhys snuffed all the candles except one each for himself and Ifan, Jack was still not back. Rhys went upstairs, leaving me to follow or be left alone in the dark. For once he fell asleep straight away, but I couldn't rest. My ears strained for hoof beats that never came, and as the hours wore on I became frantic.

I fell asleep from exhaustion in the early hours, and woke with a start, hoping Jack had returned while I slept. But the strange snow-light grew brighter in the morning sun, and somehow I knew, even without looking, that he hadn't.

I slipped out of bed and dressed myself, crept noiselessly downstairs and opened the back door. Snow filled the yard, heaped into corners where the wind had driven it, and still it tumbled from the sky. Perhaps the snow had muffled the sound of his horse, and his hoof marks had already been filled and he was safe after all. I wrapped a shawl around me and went out, shivering. His horse wasn't in the stable. I returned to the house and knocked the snow off my clogs. I glanced back, looking at the tracks I'd made, and hoped the snow would fill them quickly and hide where I'd been.

I almost died of fright when a voice spoke behind me. 'Looking for someone, stepmother?'

Ifan, his lanky body clad in a nightshirt, leaned against the door. His thin mouth stretched in a wide grin.

My stomach lurched. He knew something.
I busied myself with my shawl. 'Like who?'

'Someone who made you leave your bed and go out in the snow.' He dropped his voice to a roguish whisper. 'Were you hoping to meet your lover?'

'I don't have a lover,' I said wearily.

'You're always whispering to Jack, though, aren't you? Now, even to an innocent like me, Rhiannon, that's suspicious.'

'If you were ever innocent, Ifan, so was Judas Iscariot. You scuttle around like a rat, hiding in corners. You torment people who can't fight back -'

'If you mean Elin, she enjoys it.'

'Enjoys it, does she? That was why you had to hold her down?'

'Some women enjoy rape. You might, too, stepmother. Perhaps I'll find out one day.' The smile was gone.

'Find out what?' Neither of us had heard ap Hywel come barefoot down the stairs.

Ifan swung round, the smile back in place. 'Good morning father. What it is that makes people wake early when it snows.'

'Mmph.' He squinted at us blearily. 'Since I'm awake, thanks to your noise, I'll get Jack out early, or I'll have half my stock under the snow. Bloody half-wits always lie under hedges and get buried.'

Ifan's voice was bland. 'Jack didn't come back last night.' His eyes were bright with malice. 'Perhaps he stayed with his aunt.'

Ap Hywel opened the back door and peered out. 'Been out to check, have you, son? I see your footprints.'

Ifan smirked, looking straight at me. 'Aye, *Tad*. First thing.'

'Ah, he's either with his aunt or at an inn somewhere, waiting this out. I daresay he'll be back later.'

But he wasn't. All day I listened for him, though it was still snowing and travel would be difficult. It was evening and getting dark again when at last the muffled thud of hooves in the yard made me rush to the door to peer out into the snowbound yard. It was Jack's horse all right. But it was riderless.

Ap Hywel went outside, thigh deep in snow to catch it, soothing it when it tried to rear up and strike at him with its hooves.

'There now, settle down, settle down,' he cooed, more gentle with the horse than he ever was with me. He led the trembling beast into the stable and called Ifan. 'Rub her down, Ifan.'

Ifan crossed the yard with bad grace, and tied the horse to a ring in the wall. Rhys loosened the saddle-girths.

'There's blood on the saddle,' he said, holding out a reddened palm. 'Looks like Jack's been hurt.'

Already half out of my mind with worry, I gasped and put my hand to my mouth. If Jack was out there, he'd been there all night. If he hadn't bled to death, he'd have frozen. It was fully dark now, but ap Hywel took a lantern and searched near the house (accompanied by a complaining Ifan), while I waited in the parlour, trying to concentrate on sewing, to keep Beti occupied with stories. But my mind was out in the snowbound night, and Beti had to keep prompting me back to the story I was trying, unsuccessfully to tell.

'Time for bed, Beti,' I said at last, bracing myself for the inevitable pout and fuss. But she got up obediently, patting my face with her small, hot hand.

'Don't worry, Rhian,' she said. 'Jack will be all right. Dada will find him.'

But he didn't. 'No sign of him. Looks like he's had a fall. I doubt he'll survive in weather like this. Picked off by one of Glyndŵr's rascals, no doubt.'

Ifan smiled.

Elffin

I gave Jack money for Angharad, and a wooden toy I'd whittled for Gethin, a simple thing with twirling wheels and a square shape easy for small fat hands to grasp. I wanted to write to Rhiannon, but didn't dare. I sent her my love, though, and trusted Jack to deliver it.

When the snow began to fall in great untidy flakes, I wandered out into the courtyard, thinking of the lone man riding to Pentregoch. He wouldn't be back before dark.

'Forget Machynlleth, Jack,' I advised as he was leaving. 'Looks like there'll be snow.'

He looked up at the sky, yellow as a bruise. 'You're right. I'll go straight back and damn Rhiannon's shopping list!' He rode through the wicket gate and set off down the hill.

Inside again, I took a bench close to the fire, thinking of my son and Rhian, idly tossing splinters of wood into the flames where they spat and hissed as they burned. I felt someone slide onto the bench beside me, and glanced up.

'*Tad*!'

He took the great iron poker from the hearth and jabbed at the logs, making them fall in a shower of sparks.

'Now we'll have to build up the fire again,' I complained. 'If you hadn't done that it might have lasted for a while longer before I had to get up.'

'Idleness is your special talent, Elffin, especially when you're close to a warm fire. Your nurse always knew where to find you when you were small - by the fire, fast asleep in a heap of smelly, hairy dogs.'

I grinned. 'I spent as long as you did up a cold mountain last year, and while I'll gladly do it again if necessary, I reserve the right to enjoy firelight and warmth while I can.'

'Fair enough. Elffin -' He stopped. 'What do you think about Mortimer and Catrin?'

I shrugged. 'Bit of a shock, if I'm honest, but I like him. He's honest for a *Sais*, and he loves my sister. And she loves him, as anyone with half an eye can tell.'

'Edmund thinks he'll be old and wizened before Henry ransoms him. He's sensible to throw in his lot with us, and marry Cat. He'll be good for her, and a useful ally. And from my own selfish point of view, it's always easier to lose a daughter to a man she loves, *Sais* or not!'

I opened my mouth to say something, then shut it again. My father, however, reads minds, mine in particular. Perhaps I have a face like Llew's, as transparent as glass when he's thinking.

'You're thinking of Rhiannon,' he said softly. 'Ap Hywel was a mistake, and I'm sorry. But your mother insisted. She knew - God knows how, but your mother knows everything that happens in her household - that the child wanted you.'

Mam seemed to have a finger in every pie. I fumbled for words, but there was no need.

He sighed deeply. 'Your Mam has a spy network that puts mine to shame. When she makes up her mind, nothing will shift it. If my captains had half her steel we'd take London in two hours - even with the wind against us!'

I laughed. For all that he loved Mam, he never underestimated her. 'Is she still set against Rhiannon, *Tad*?'

'She would be, if she knew. But you're a man, and old enough to know your mind. If you can bring the lass here, you shall have her. There're enough needy priests around to sort out an annulment, whatever it costs. Aye, you shall have her, son.' He pulled a mock-fearful face, 'but don't for the love of God tell your Mam I said so!'

His expression made me grin, and I went to bed happy - or at least happier. Jack had completely slipped from my mind, which was filled with plans to rescue my bride - and my son.

CHAPTER TWENTY-NINE

Llewelyn

Elffin is driving me mad. He's up in the clouds one minute, miserable as sin the next. He'll tell me what's up when he's ready, I suppose and asking questions only rubs him up the wrong way, so it's no use pestering him.

While the snow-storm lasted every man with sense stayed indoors. But then, the weather cleared, and after oppressive skies and bitter winds came unseasonable sunshine and blue skies. At night, the air was frosty to set the teeth on edge and the stars so clear and close that I felt I might hear them sing if I listened hard enough. Then the thaw began, and with it, at last, the freedom to move around, at which time Glyndyfrdwy became a good place not to be. Lady Marged was planning a wedding, and in self-defence Elffin and I slipped away to hunt.

Horses don't like snow, and Sioned was skittish, pecking and shying, but Seren, Elffin's mare, was steady enough for two, settling to a steady pace, which encouraged Sioned to do likewise. We kept an eye out for quarry - and predators, both human and animal. Wolves had been seen near Glyndyfrdwy, slinking close because of the cold, and even in this weather there was always a chance of a de Grey raiding party. We were out, so might they be.

I shot a rabbit, but it would be poor eating, being winter-thin. When I'd retrieved it and my arrow, we reined in to watch a stoat, whose dinner we'd probably stolen, snaking perfectly camouflaged across the snow, a dark smudge of tail his only visible part.

'Llew,' Elffin said, and at the studiedly diffident tone I didn't look up. I had a pretty good idea what he was about to say, but wasn't going to let him off the hook so easily.

'Mmhm?' I murmured, watching the stoat freeze at the sound of his voice.

'Something to ask you.'
'Mmhm?'
'You're head of your family. I want to marry your sister.'
I looked up, feigning shock. 'The only sister I have is already married, Elffin!'

He scowled. 'I know that, stupid. But if I can get her away from ap Hywel, and if she can get a divorce from ap Hywel, and if she'll have me, and if -'

I frowned. 'Awful lot of ifs, Elffin, where a sister is concerned.'

'Yes, but - you bastard, Llew. Are you laughing at me?'

'Of course I am, you fool. You didn't have to ask. You're welcome to her. God knows she's worshipped you long enough, although for the life of me I don't see why, and now she's grown breasts you've obviously noticed her too -'

He scowled. 'It isn't like that, Llew. I love her for who she is, not because she's beautiful.'

'Funny, that,' I said. 'You only realising you loved her for her soul *after* she stopped being so scrawny.'

He aimed a clout at my head, and I ducked. 'Now, now, brother. Beating up your future brother-in-law is not the way to cement family relations.'

'So you don't mind?'

Time to be serious. 'I'd be honoured to have you as a brother-in-law, but you've still got to get her away from ap Hywel. He won't let her go willingly.'

Elffin looked grim. 'Then he'll do it unwillingly, if he knows what's good for him. She's in danger, thanks to that brat of his.'

'Do you know, Elffin, I have such a score to settle with that one that it's like nettles in my under-drawers. I'll have him eventually, just you wait and see.'

'Behind me in the queue, Llew. She's my future wife.'

'And my sister, remember.'

Once the formalities were over and done, we picked up the trail of a deer and followed it until we came upon a doe, half-hidden in the bushes. We made sure she wasn't pregnant, for only a brute slaughters a pregnant beast, and dispatched her swiftly. She dropped where she stood, and we butchered her and slung her across Elffin's saddle to carry back to Glyndyfrdwy, our contribution to the wedding feast.

I tightened my grip on Siôned's reins, since she was skittering again. 'How will you get Rhian away, Elffin?'

'I could just ask ap Hywel, but I doubt he'd agree. I may have to kill him -' he stopped at the expression on my face - 'oh, in battle, Llew. I'd not base a marriage on a murder - unless it was Ifan. I'd make an exception for him. *Tad* has forbidden me to go and get her: she has to leave of her own accord.'

'Christ, your Mam'll be biting ankles, Elffin!'

'Then she'll have to bite ankles. I'm having Rhian if it's the last thing I do. Hope it won't be, mind,' he said hastily, looking heavenwards. 'I'm a man grown, and won't be ruled by my mother.'

'What about Gethin, Elffin?'

His face changed. 'I want my son. But bringing him home will be difficult for a different reason. Angharad won't let him go, even with Rhiannon. If she could come too - but Mam won't hold still for it. I just hope God will let me have him in time. It's hard to have a son and not see him grow.'

I understood that, though memories of my own father are dim, now. He'd loved me, I knew that, and taught me the things a father should teach his son. Elffin needed to do that for Gethin, tell him who he is, and where he's come from, about the heroes who live in his past. Gethin, when all's said and done, is the grandson of Owain Glyndŵr, bastard or not, and by the old laws of Hywel Dda, will inherit an equal share of his estate with the legitimate sons and grandsons.

At the gates of Glyndyfrdwy I said a silent prayer on Elffin's behalf. I know marriage vows say that whom God has joined, let no man sunder, but I don't think God had quite so much to do with the joining of ap Hywel and Rhiannon as Lady Marged. Perhaps God will redress the balance when He has time to think about it.

Rhiannon

I'd depended on Jack, he was my friend, and now he's gone. I was frantic with worry for the first few days, and in despair once I'd accepted his death.

Ifan knew. He was always watching me, a slight smile on his pallid face. By the third day I was tempted to wipe it off with a rolling pin. Anger held me together.

Gethin helped keep me sane. Angharad left him with me to occupy my mind, although she, too missed Jack. When Gethin's around there's no time to think about anything else. He's an imp, and into everything. Not a cupboard or a chest remains uninvestigated, and he's developed a passion for the hearth and the fire-dogs which means we daren't take our eyes off him for an instant. He's too big now for Angharad to carry in a shawl: awake he's battling to get free, asleep he's heavy as a millstone. So one of us watches constantly as he hauls himself on to his fat little feet, comical concentration written on his face, and tries to take the one or two steps he can manage before collapsing onto his backside. He's so like his father it amazes me ap Hywel hasn't noticed. He ignores him, and we hustle the baby out of the room if he comes in, but it won't always be like this.

Better ignored than the way Ifan is. Sometimes he sits watching the baby like a cat watching a mouse, and my flesh creeps. I'm more afraid for Gethin than myself. I make sure Ifan can't harm me, but Gethin thinks the world is his friend, and is too small to understand that there are those who would harm even him.

Beti, Gwen and Elin are mourning Jack, too and it's pitiful to see how Gethin looks up hopefully when the yard door opens. Ap Hywel misses him, I think, but only as right-hand man, because he's already looking to fill the vacancy Jack left.

He's gone, but we have no body to bury, and lacking that finality, hope still stirs at the sound of hooves on cobblestones. But that tiny smile on Ifan's face bothers me. I dreamed of it the other night, and tossed and turned until I woke Rhys, who of course - but then, I'm used to that now. I close my eyes and try to breathe evenly and wait for it to be over. And drink my potion.

He lay beside me one night, afterwards. I lay tense, wishing I could get out of bed and wash myself clean, although the water in the ewer was probably frozen again.

'How can you conceive once and not again?' he asked, suddenly.

'How should I know?' I lied, into the darkness. 'Perhaps the first baby damaged me inside. Perhaps I'll never have another baby.' I wondered if it might be true. Perhaps it wasn't Ceridwen's medicine. Perhaps it was me. Perhaps now I'm barren. Now it seems important that I'm not. I want to have Elffin's babies. First I'll give him a son, to make up for him missing so much of Gethin's babyhood, and then a daughter to twist him round her finger, and once I've managed that, a dozen more of any variety he wants.

Rhys sighed. 'Your fault, then. You lost my son, and now, damn it, you're barren.' He grunted. 'My God, a barren cow, foster daughter to Glyndŵr! What a bloody bargain!'

'My fault? Ifan -' I spoke through clenched teeth and I cursed inwardly, wishing I had governed my tongue.

Rhys ap Hywel sighed. 'He didn't touch you. You imagined or invented it. You killed my son. No one else.'

I bit my tongue. What good would it do to antagonise him? I'ms miserable enough already. Why make matters worse?

Elffin

Duw, but it's hard, seeing the preparations for Cat's wedding, all the time wishing it could be Rhiannon's and mine. Edmund and Catrin will marry at the end of November and though it won't be the celebration it might have been, there'll still be plenty to wish them well. Catrin's so happy, and Mortimer gazes at her like the village idiot. He's even learning Welsh, so he can coo in our language too.

Bron, thanks to the web criss-crossing Glyndyfrdwy, in which she and Crisiant sit like fat spiders garnering gossip, knows perfectly well that I've asked Llew for Rhiannon, though God knows how. I haven't said anything, and neither has Llew, he swears. But she's a soft touch for a love story: she smirks when she sets eyes on me, and she feeds me titbits whenever I sit down. I was enjoying one such when I heard the commotion from outside. A woman's voice, pleading, and men's voices, shouting, and then the woman again, the pleading note gone, anger taking it to fish-wife level, louder and more furious by the second. I abandoned my lunch and went into the yard. The gate-keeper leaned across the gate, blocking someone from entering, and that someone had completely lost her temper.

I peered over the gatekeeper's shoulder: it was Ceridwen, and she was spitting like a cat.

'I know her,' I said, tugging the man's jerkin to move him aside. 'Let her in.'

'So you might, friend,' he retorted, shaking himself free, 'but she ain't comin' in. Wanting Elffin, indeed. What would Master Elffin want with a trollop like that? She's nobody.'

'As you will be, *friend*,' I said ominously, 'if you don't get your arse out of my bloody way.'

He spun round, scowling, ready to exert his authority as keeper of the Prince of Wales' gatehouse, and just in time recognised me.

'About time, too,' Ceridwen said, shoving tangled hair back from her face. 'Held up by this bloody *twpsin* when I've come so bloody far is like trying to get into heaven on a bloody broomstick. Well-nigh bloody impossible. And there's me hearing Glyndŵr has a welcome for everyone.'

'He does,' I said, giving the gatekeeper a filthy look. 'This fool has ideas above his station. Ideas,' I said, frowning at the man, 'which will be changed. And quick.'

'Sorry, m'Lord,' he muttered. 'She don't look like nobody much to me.'

'But she is. Which goes to show you can never tell, can you? I'll see *you* later,' I threatened. His face said, 'not if I see you first'.

I took Ceridwen's arm and led her towards the house.

'For Christ's sake take me somewhere warm,' she said, her teeth chattering. 'I near froze my bollocks off getting here to see you.'

I thought of pointing out that bollocks were in short supply in her gender, but the look in her eye said otherwise. Bollocks, occasionally, are more a state of mind than anything else.

'How in God's name did you get here in weather like this?'

'Hitched a ride on a cart for part of the way, and rode pillion behind a travelling friar for a bit. Ditched him pretty quick, mind. Wandering hands.' She scowled. 'I couldn't think of anywhere else to turn for help.'

'Is Rhiannon all right?'

'Jesus Christ!' She rolled her eyes exasperatedly. 'Does that bit of dangling gristle between your legs blind you to everything else? Yes, she's all right, as far as I know, though I haven't seen her since the snow started. Probably worried out of her head, though.'

'Why?'

'I've got Jack at my place, half dead. He should have been all dead, except he managed to drag himself back onto his horse and get himself within shouting distance of me. Moaning distance, more like. He was raving for a week. Rhiannon still doesn't know he's alive, and is probably mindless about it.'

'What happened?'

'Someone - and I've no proof, but I'd stake my eyes it was Ifan - put an arrow in his back the night of the storm. A poor shot, thank God, but he bled a lot, and the cold near finished him.'

'He was here that day!'

'Aye, I know. And I know why. I think Ifan waited for him along the way. Just like him to shoot an enemy in the back.'

One more thing to chalk up against Ifan. His sins were mounting, and I'd punish him, God willing, one day.

'Is he all right?'

'Oh, aye. He lost a bit of blood, and he's still in pain, but he'll live. Chewing rocks, mind, wanting to tear Ifan apart.'

'Can't say I blame him. I'd do it myself if I could get my hands on him. And I will.'

'I can't keep Jack much longer. No one knows he's there, but if Ifan gets wind of it I wouldn't give much for our chances.'

'He must come here. Llew and I'll come and get him.' And then perhaps I could see Rhiannon, and my son...

'You won't. You get caught and you're dead. Ap Hywel might turn you over for ransom, but he might just kill you, you being only the youngest son. He might kill Jack, too, and then all my hard work patching him up'd be wasted.'

'Then I'll send people. Disguise them as - what?'

She pulled a face. 'God-botherers is best. They get about without too much trouble - whether they're genuine priests or not, there's not many who'd risk offing one, so rumours of hell-fire might do some good, I suppose.'

'All right. Now. Something warm to eat and drink, rest, and I'll organise a horse and an escort to take you back. And thank you.'

Her eyes rested on my face. 'I can sort of see what she fancies in you, Elffin.' I blushed. 'But she's as blind as her husband.'

I was still trying to puzzle that one out when, wrapped in one of Crisiant's old cloaks, she went off, pillion behind one of our men.

Next day we dressed two of our men in habits and despite their howls, tonsured them in the interests of authenticity, and sent them for Jack. Without him Rhiannon was in more danger than ever. There were times in those days before Catrin's wedding that my brain felt thick, and thinking got me nowhere.

When he arrived, slung in a litter between the two mules, he looked like death had visited, inspected, and rejected him: his face was ashen and stubbled, and he seemed smaller.

Bron put him to bed in the second-best guest chamber (Mortimer was in the best) and looked after him like a mother hen. He lived on the fat of the land (or at least of the Glyndyfrdwy kitchens). His recovery, once Bron and Crisiant got their hands on him, was rapid, possibly in self-defence, because a man can take only so much female attention.

He remembered nothing of the attack but a hard punch in the back, and icy earth hitting him in the face. How he managed to catch his horse and remount, he couldn't recall, and neither was he conscious of aiming for Ceridwen's cottage. Perhaps horses have more sense than we give them credit for. He remembered falling off a second time, the horse loitering for a while and then disappearing, but nothing else until he came to in Ceridwen's hut.

'What'll you do now?' I asked. He was out of bed and perched on an upturned barrel in the courtyard, partly for the fresh air, partly to escape Bron and Crisiant.

'Go back to Pentregoch,' he said.

'You can't. Ifan will kill you.'

'No one will see me except Ceridwen.'

'Why risk it?'

He stared at me, raising an eyebrow. 'You ask that? You think I'd leave Rhiannon unprotected? Ifan's tried to kill her once, and had a go at me, and damned near succeeded both times.'

'You go back, I go with you,' I said. 'She's going to marry me as soon as I can get her away from ap Hywel.'

'Is that so? Well, even so, you can't come. Until she can leave of her own free will, you're better off here. I'll look after her, Elffin. Don't worry.'

But I did.

CHAPTER THIRTY

Llewelyn

Catrin and Mortimer married in a flurry of tears, silk and candlelight. Elffin, wallowing equally in sentiment and misery drank too much, got revoltingly maudlin, and I had to put him to bed. He moaned for a while then threw up, which made the room stink worse than usual and since there were already seven men sharing it, I took my blanket and opted for the stables.

I settled to sleep in the moonlit hayloft, lulled by the quiet, companionable shifting of horses. Horses smell far better than snoring, farting men. Then I heard the loft-ladder shift and knew I had company. I silently disentangled myself, groping for my knife. A head appeared and I grabbed it, hauled its owner upward, and knelt straddling the body, my knife prodding its throat.

It squeaked, and I realised the throat was slender and the body soft. I felt around in the darkness and found items not usually found on males.

'Don't kill me, Llew! It's only me.'

'Who's me?'

'Me!' she repeated indignantly. 'Mali.'

So it was. Fired by romance after the wedding, fuelled by stolen wine, Mali had evaded Bron and followed me out to the stables. She wriggled again, and I slipped down to lie on top of her. My body had already begun to welcome her, and she arched her spine in response.

I don't love her, but on the other hand she was there, willing, and it had been a while. It wasn't until later I realised that I hadn't followed Dewi's advice. I'd taken a drink or two, Mali was eager and - next morning I remembered, and a jolt of panic hit me.

When did a girl know she was pregnant? I had a rough idea of the mechanics: they bleed once a month, Mali said, and if the bleeding doesn't come for two months, there's a baby coming. In two months, God willing, I'd be far away in South Wales with *Tadmaeth*. Bron would crucify me on the kitchen door if Mali got pregnant, which was nothing to what Lady Marged would do.

I'm ashamed to say I avoided Mali for the next few days, and I steered clean of Bron until she got suspicious, since Elffin and I tend to spend a lot of time in the kitchens, being usually hungry. But then one day Mali caught me when I wasn't paying attention.

'You don't love me no more. You been avoiding me.'

'No I haven't, honest' I blustered.

'Haven't been looking for me, though, have you?'

Oh, but I had. If she only knew how hard! 'I've been busy.'

'No, you been avoiding me. Got no time for me, now.'

'I just -' My voice tailed away, helplessly.

'If you're worried about a babby, you don't have to be. My monthlies come the day after the wedding, so I can't be. So will you talk to me now?'

My knees fairly buckled with relief. 'Of course I will.'

She slid her hand up my jerkin, and I jumped at her cold fingers. 'If you was to go and sleep in the barn again, Llew, I could come and visit you.'

I grinned like an idiot. 'I don't see why n-'

A hand on the end of a fat, freckled arm reached through a doorway, grabbed Mali's hair and yanked. Mali shot backwards and Bron's grim face appeared. 'I warned you, young Llew. Family you may be, but keep your breeches fastened, or I'll have you with my filleting knife. Understood?'

I started to say something manly to put the impertinent cook in her place, but I couldn't think of anything. Instead I heard myself squeak, 'Yes, Bron. Sorry Bron.'

'Oh, you will be, my lad, if this one falls pregnant.'

Some men say that they find forbidden fruit an aphrodisiac. All I can say is, they never met Bron. And I've seen her filleting knife. But memories of the night of Catrin and Edmund's wedding warmed me on many a cold night huddled round a campfire in the middle of nowhere.

Jack, now fully recovered, left Glyndyfrdwy the day after the wedding, planning to hide in the mountains near Pentregoch.

Elffin watched him go as if his torn heart travelled with him. Soon, I told him. Soon we'll have her back. But he looked so miserable that I stopped talking and passed him the wine jug. There's times when wine's more use than talk, and this was a fine French one. It had travelled from France to Bristol, and from Bristol to the quay below Caernarfon Castle, destined for the grand tables of Harlech, but we got there first and saved the carter the trip.

Rhiannon

Damned weather! If it wasn't snowing, hailing or raining, it was blowing a gale, which meant ap Hywel and Ifan stayed home. Wil, the man Rhys has taken on to do Jack's work, was constantly out after snowed-in or half-drowned sheep. He's a sullen, wall-eyed oaf who communicates in grunts and smells worse than the midden.

Ceridwen's potion was almost gone but I couldn't go and get more. I haven't seen her since before Jack disappeared. I wonder if she knows he's dead. I reduced my daily dose, not taking it unless ap Hywel had been at me, but even so, by the time the weather cleared enough to let me out of the house, I was down to a single dose. The sun was shining, but the ground was still sodden underfoot, and the path through the wood would be thick with mud. I dared not take a horse, because ap Hywel would insist that stinking Wil go with me, but I had to go alone. I didn't want to put Ceridwen at risk again.

I was conscious of Ifan's presence every second he was in the house, and at night I imagined I could hear his breathing. It amazed me how normal his ears looked, given that he spent most nights pressing them to the wall. Knowing he listened while his father rutted made it worse still.

I waited until no one was about, then hid behind a tree and watched and waited to make sure no one was following me. Then I scurried through the woods, turning every so often to look and listen. Ceridwen was home, thank God: I don't know what I'd have done if she hadn't been. I wouldn't have dared wait for her. I was so anxious to be inside out of sight that I didn't knock.

'Rhiannon! Thank God for some sunshine, eh?'

'I've been stuck in that damned house so long,' I said, feelingly, 'I've forgotten what fresh air smells like.'

She opened her wall cupboard and brought out a small bag. 'I expect you've come for this,' she said, 'I knew you'd be running low, but I didn't dare risk bringing it to you.'

I fumbled for my purse.

'I don't want money, Rhiannon,' she said softly. 'We're friends, aren't we?'

I stared, taken aback by her kindness, then burst into tears. She gathered me into her arms and held me until I stopped bawling. She smelled of herbs and wood-smoke, and her arms were as comforting as my mother's had been.

'I'm sorry,' I wiped my eyes on my sleeve and sniffed. 'It's been so terrible, and I've got terrible news. Oh, Ceridwen, Jack's dead.'

A shaft of sun filtered through the small window. She shook her head. 'No he's not.' She smiled.

Oh, God! She didn't know. 'He is, he is. He's dead.'

'He's not, he's not, he's alive,' she mimicked, laughing. 'He should be, mind, after getting a crossbow bolt in the back. At least, he was when a couple of Glyndŵr's men took him away for the fat cook to fuss over.'

My knees gave way. 'He's alive? Honestly?'

She nodded. 'I found him outside my house. When I knew he'd live, I went to Glyndyfrdwy - mind, I nearly didn't get past the bloody gatekeeper - and they sent men and a litter to get him. Don't tell anyone. Not even Angharad. '

'A crossbow?'

'Yes. And you know who fired it as well as I do,' she said. 'Rot his soul.'

'If I were a man, I'd kill him.'

'Women can kill, too.' Ceridwen smiled oddly.

I grinned. 'I know. I put something in his food, once. It made him horribly ill. He vomited for days, but he didn't die. I didn't want to kill him quite so much then. I just wanted to make him suffer a bit for hurting Beti. Anyway, poisoning's too good for him. I'd like to get a big knife and torture him and kill him and cut him up into small little pieces, and find some pigs and -'

'I get the general idea,' Ceridwen said. 'Rhiannon, love, you aren't alone any more, and you're tougher than you think. I saw you birth your baby, and I know you won't put up with something you can't change. You're going to run away, aren't you.'

My mouth fell open. 'How did you know that?'

'Because you're in love, and not with your husband. When you run, make sure you choose your time well, and make sure you run in the right direction.'

She was talking riddles. 'He'll be at Sycharth or Glyndyfrdwy,' I said. 'I'll find him, wherever he is.'

She sighed. 'Anyway,' she said briskly, 'get out of here. You've already been away too long.' She opened the door. 'Go on. It's safe. Take care, and remember - while I'm here, you aren't alone. You won't see Jack, but he'll be around.'

I went home, my feet squelching in mud. The skies were cloudy again, but I didn't care. I had a friend, and Jack was alive.

Elffin

Christmas at Glyndyfrdwy again this year. Sycharth would be better, but at least we won't be half-way up a mountainside. It's been a long and frustrating winter, with nothing to do but brood about Rhiannon. It hasn't helped having Edmund and Catrin under my nose, either, me being unrequited and them not. It's bloody hard to look at those two twittering at each other, and I was glad when they left for Edmund's estate at Maelienydd.

At least Jack's watching out for Rhiannon: I must find some way of thanking him when at last I have her. It's a strange feeling loving and being loved back, but we've never even kissed!

I was probably insane to try, but after Cat's wedding, when the

Whole household oozed romance, I plucked up courage to talk to Mam. I know *Tad* said not to tell her, but she's my mother, and she loves me, and she ought to want me to be happy. Besides, Rhiannon's her foster-daughter: she must have some feelings for her. *Tad* and Edmund were closeted in an ante-room, and Mam was in the solar with Crisiant, sitting in a shaft of winter sunshine filtered through the blue gown of a stained-glass maiden. She seemed to be wearing a halo, like a saint.

'Can we have a word, Mam?' I said, hoping Crisiant would take the hint and bugger off. I was disappointed. Crisiant put down her needlework and paid attention.

Mam glanced up. 'What is it, Elffin?'

'Private, Mam?'

Crisiant's face fell as Mam dismissed her. I listened for the sound of her feet on the stairs, but it didn't come. I crept to the door and opened it; sure enough Cris was bent double, her ear jammed against the key-hole.

'Back trouble, Crisiant?' I asked. 'Need help down the stairs?'

Scowling she retreated to the kitchens to share her disappointment with Bron, and I turned to Mam.

'Mam,' I began, 'I -' I was at a loss to know what to say. I tried again. 'Mam, I want to tell you something.'

She stitched a petal on a flower. 'That I have another grandson?'

I gasped. 'You know?'

'Do you think I'm blind? I know.'

I was stunned, but I rallied. 'No, Mam, not that. Rhiannon's unhappy and in danger and I want her away from Pentregoch now. Please, Mam, may she come back? Llew's in a state,' I added, suddenly losing my nerve. 'He's worried sick about her.'

'No.'

'What?'

'No. No, she may not come back. She's ap Hywel's wife and Llew must accept it. I'm sure she's in no real danger.'

'But Ifan's already tried to kill her, Mam!'

'Rhiannon was always an imaginative child, and the tale is second-hand.'

'But Mam, I -'

She frowned. 'No, Elffin. That is my last word on the subject. Rhiannon stays with ap Hywel.'

'What about my son?'

'The bastard?' She shrugged. 'If you want him, yes, he can come, but not his mother. And certainly not Rhiannon. Send Crisiant to me, please, Elffin.'

I was dismissed. 'Mam, I - it's not Llew that wants Rhiannon, it's me. I love her. I didn't know it until too late, but she's all I want. I want to marry her, Mam. Please, Mam?'

She was utterly implacable. 'I would never allow such a match. She has no prospects and no breeding. And I would remind you that she is married. No. Absolutely not. You may go, Elffin.'

'But *Tad* said -'

'Elffin. You are irritating me.'

I slammed the door behind me, realising at last that it was my mother's plotting that had caused this. If I'd ever imagined that she acted in kindness when she married Rhiannon to ap Hywel and sent Angharad away with my son in her belly, I didn't any more. She'd never once considered Rhiannon's happiness, or my son's future, only the smooth running of her own domain. Somehow she'd known Rhian had feelings for me, long before I did. Her meddling has caused such pain. I can't believe that Mam would act so coldly - perhaps with hindsight she's sorry for what she did but can't admit it, even to herself. No. Not true. She's implacable. I've never seen her so unmoving, so unmoved before.

Yet next day she was a normal, loving mother and wife, busy with the smooth running of her household. I love her, she's my Mam, but I've had a chilling glimpse of her ruthlessness. Of my two parents, she is the harder and less merciful.

That damn Crach Ffinant is here, lurking in corners. He can see the future, or so he says, though he's never too specific in his predictions, which are masterpieces of vagueness. His language is so convoluted that what he says could mean anything. "When the moon turns to blood, and the magpie flies into an oak tree stripped of its leaves, then beware the berries of winter". What sort of a message is that, for God's sake? Personally, I'd tell the old fraud to bugger off, but *Tad* listens to him and others like him. Look how he refused to travel between Usk and Carmarthen! Mind, I suppose if it were my death being foretold, I probably wouldn't have risked it either. Who knows if he's really a wizard, or if any of them are? All I know is, they all talk in great loops and whorls of language, and trying to understand their meaning is like trying to catch a handful of smoke. If they'd just say, "now look, my friend, don't go into

Denbigh, or Rhayader, or Cardiff at noon on the second Tuesday in June next year because you'll likely get flattened by a runaway skewbald horse ridden by a man with one leg and a squint", a man could understand and take the necessary precautions. No confusion about the latest word from London. In December Henry married Joanna, daughter of Charles of Navarre. He's unlikely to bother with Wales before Spring, since he's busy being a doting husband and will want to get her pregnant first, since young Henry is of an age to get himself killed in battle, with luck. And I wouldn't mind being the one to do it, please God, if you're listening. Anyway, while the weather was hammering Henry's armies, Hotspur was crossing the border at Dunstanburgh to have a go at the Scots. They met them in pitched battle from a hilltop, apparently, and the wind and sun were behind them. That must have been a relief after Henry's experience of the invisible armies of Owain Glyndŵr. There were Frenchmen with the Scots, but 500 English bowmen carried the day. The Scots sat and watched them set stakes against a cavalry charge and bend their longbows undisturbed. The Scottish archers attempted to return the fire, but their short bows were no match for a Welsh longbow (and they are Welsh, even if the bloody English have taken to them) and they panicked and ran.

The Douglas, in whose family run both red hair and short tempers, lost the latter and led a mad charge at the English, who calmly notched armour-piercing arrows to their longbows and systematically perforated the oncoming Scots in a lot of vital and uncomfortable places. Douglas lost an eye and was wounded five times through his armour, although he'd been assured it was arrow-proof. I'd've asked for my money back, if I'd been Douglas. The English gave no quarter, and afterwards countless common soldiers were dead, and Douglas, together with four earls, eight barons and knights of rank, and thirty French knights were all taken prisoner and held for ransom.

The King has still not ransomed Edmund Mortimer, which has rankled with Hotspur, especially since de Grey got let out on 11th November with a payment of six thousand marks and a promise of another four thousand from his son, but then, de Grey is de Grey, and as Madoc says, cream and bastards always rise.

Possibly Henry's refusal to ransom Edmund was behind Hotspur's refusal to hand over his prisoners to the King. There's a lot of money in prisoners. There's trouble brewing in that quarter, and maybe *Tad* can profit from it somehow, now Edmund Mortimer is with us.

Catrin's marriage has been advantageous already: news of Hotspur's victory at Humbleton Hill was brought to Edmund by his own squire, Gwilym Lloyd of Denbigh.

Additionally, shortly after Edmund married Catrin he wrote to Sir John Greyndor, Hywel Vaughan and other important people of Maelienydd and Presteigne, leaving them in no doubt of his loyalties.

"Very dear and well-beloved," he wrote, *"I greet you much and make known to you that Owain Glyndŵr has raised a quarrel of which the object is, if King Richard be living, to restore him to the crown; and if not that my honoured nephew, who is the right heir to the said crown, shall be king of England; and that the said Owain will assert his right in Wales. And I, seeing and considering that the said quarrel is good and reasonable, have consented to join it, and to aid and maintain it, and by the grace of God to a good end, Amen. I ardently hope and from my heart that you will support and enable me to bring this struggle of mine to a successful issue.*

Written at Maelienydd the 13th day of December. EDMUND MORTIMER."

Not only that: in marrying Catrin he's pissed all over Henry's laws against Englishmen marrying Welsh women!

The King now has three separate wars going on, and nothing empties an Exchequer faster than war. Since the English Parliament is inclined to monitor his extravagances, I doubt he's too happy except in his marriage. If in that: there's more expediency than passion in most royal marriages.

Which brings me back to Rhiannon.   Perhaps by Spring, we'll be together, despite Mam. Perhaps by the end of 1403 we'll be married, and *Tad* will have all Wales under his banner, and the English will be gone from here forever.   Perhaps.

CHAPTER THIRTY-ONE

Llewelyn

At last we were able to move and in the optimism of the new year we attacked Harlech and Aberystwyth, both still in English hands, and Shropshire in the Marches chaining the borders of Wales.

Shropshire's burgesses were terrified and begged the King for protection, which was most satisfying. From Llyn and the Northern districts our men have infiltrated Flintshire, which supports *Tadmaeth*. Dyffryn Clwyd is ours, and we've garrisoned the castles at Trefaldwyn and Fflint. Not bad for the "barefoot Welsh doggis" scorned by the English parliament.

The King's son is now lieutenant of the Marches, with permanent levies from the counties of Gloucester, Hereford, Worcester and Shropshire, though he's barely fifteen, though he's no ordinary fifteen-year old, being battle-hardened since he was twelve. The King must value him less than *Tadmaeth* does Elffin, who was kept safe until there was no choice (despite Elffin's complaints).

North Wales, except for the castles at Beaumaris, Caernarfon, Harlech and Aberystwyth, is ours, and we'll take them soon. Their supplies arrive from Bristol via the Menai Straits and not overland, so these strongholds are better situated to resist. Occasionally, however, envoys from Chester tiptoe across the border bearing supplies to aid the garrisons, but we usually intercept them. We make good use of the King's liberated goods.

Tadmaeth is treating with Hotspur. Gwilym ap Robert Lloyd of Denbigh is acting as intermediary, and we hope the Percys will join us. Together with Hotspur we could chase bastard Henry from England, let alone Wales, aye, and his boy-soldier with him.

We've heard nothing from Jack recently, which has been hard on Elffin. I worry about Rhiannon too, but Elffin groans and mopes and is driving me demented. I've given up trying to cheer him: if something can't be changed, then it must be borne until it can. My Mam used to say that.

It was a relief to go and bother Aberystwyth: Mali was caught sneaking into my chamber, once by Bron, once by Crisiant, and if Lady Marged hears about it Mali will be gone. God protect me from Lady Marged! I'm safer attacking Aberystwyth Castle. I tried to warn Mali, but she wails that I don't want her any more, and oh, God, I hate to see a girl cry. It makes me feel guilty even when I haven't done anything. I've done plenty, mind, but the risk isn't worth the pleasure.

Anyway, Mali was only a diversion. I was a boy then and now I'm a man. Now there's Hafwen, beautiful as her name, who came with Isobel and Adda to Edmund and Catrin's wedding. I sat beside her during the wedding feast. She was lower down the table but I changed my place when no one was watching. She wouldn't even look at me at first, but I persisted, and I saw her blush, and at the end of the evening she smiled at me.

She left with Isobel and Adda afterwards, and now I must miss her until we meet again at Glyndyfrdwy or Sycharth - which will probably be next Christmas. Still, plenty to occupy my mind until then, so I shan't miss her too much.

I was wounded in the attack on Aberystwyth. Luckily I was on Sioned: if I'd been on foot the arrow would have hit my chest. I was turning to face an attacker when I felt a punch in my leg that rocked me - the shaft sticking out of my thigh. Lucky it wasn't from a longbow, which would have gone through my armour, pinned my thigh to the saddle and injured Sioned into the bargain. There wasn't much blood until it was drawn, and thank God it came out clean. Painfully, but clean. It's a deep wound, and my leg is sore and stiff, thanks to the surgeon, who isn't the tenderest of souls. I drank poppy juice to dull the pain, but it doesn't dull it so much as detach it: I still felt pain as the wound was cleansed and stitched, but couldn't summon the enthusiasm to yell. Elffin says I turned purple and left finger-shaped bruises on his wrist.

Thank God it healed well - some lose legs to a minor scratch if infection sets in - then I found myself a stick and hobbled about, fussed over by Bron and Crisiant, though my brothers weren't at all sympathetic. Madoc even told me I was limping on the wrong leg, and I should at least be consistent. He said he knew men who'd had both legs and both arms amputated and made less fuss, but I ignored him. It's a good wound, and I got it in battle. The scar is purplish-red now. I hope it doesn't fade too much. I want to have something to show Hafwen: girls like a scar. A good scar is worth a hundred love-notes, according to Gruffydd, who knows. He has scars all over.

A priest arrived yesterday with news: Prince Henry is mustering his armies at Shropshire, so I've discarded my walking-stick. I don't want to be left behind.

Rhiannon

The weather's improving, the first snowdrops and celandine are bustling through the earth, birds are loud in the mornings even though it's only February, and around the house the hedges are taking on the pale green mist of budding leaves. I'm counting the days until I can get away from here, because life gets more unbearable each day, and warmer weather is a promise of escape.

Ap Hywel is getting suspicious: no matter how hard he tries, I don't conceive. He asks difficult questions, and the lies I tell him cause more lies, and one day they'll trip me. With Rhys's questions and Ifan's malevolent presence, I'm so nervous I jump at shadows.

Rhys caught me in the still-room one morning, just as I'd downed the foul medicine. Thank Holy Mary I'd hidden the potion. I steep the herbs in wine to make them drinkable, but whenever I smell and taste the stuff I retch. If I hold my nose while I drink it helps, but then it's hard to swallow, and the filthy stuff shoots down my nose instead of my gullet, which makes it even worse. Some days, not to vomit, I dig my nails into the palms of my hands until they bleed, because vomiting day after day makes my throat raw. Sometimes the vomit is streaked with blood. It is rotting my teeth, too: I'll be toothless by the time I'm twenty at this rate.

His voice startled me. 'Are you ill?' No hint of sympathy: but then, why should there be? He loves me no more than I love him.

I shook my head, my jaw clamped shut, and swiftly rinsed the cup in my washing-bowl.

'What were you drinking?'

'Water. I was thirsty.'

'Water makes you vomit?'

'My stomach is upset, that's all. Perhaps last night's mutton...'

'It tasted all right to me.'

'Then it was something else.'

He was staring at me, his limp, thinning hair flopping over his forehead, the scalp pink at the crown and temples.

'Are you pregnant?'

'No,' I said, too fast. I softened my voice. 'At least, I don't think so. My courses aren't due for another week. Perhaps I am.' Stupid to antagonise him by being too sure. Let him - and me - have that week's grace before he begins to nag me again.

'Perhaps you aren't. Have you stitched nettles into my under-drawers?'

'That's an old wives' tale.'

'But something's going on, isn't it, Rhiannon? You conceived once, why not again?'

'It's not for want of trying, is it, Rhys?' I said tartly.

'I try. You lie stiff as stone. A wife has duties, Rhiannon.'

'And I perform them.

'But you don't conceive.'

I said nothing, silence being safer.

'Ifan thinks the witch has given you something.' He picked up the cup and sniffed it, but thank God I'd rinsed it.

'You discuss our marriage with your son?'

'He's anxious for a brother.'

'So he can kill that one before it's born, too?'

Rhys raised his hand to hit me. I managed not to flinch and after a moment in which we glared at each other, neither of us backing down, he stamped away.

It will be March, soon. In May, I'm leaving. I'm going home to Sycharth, and Angharad and Gethin are coming with me. If Lady Marged will take me back, I can put up with anything. It's bound to be better than staying here. If she won't, we'll manage somehow, Me, Gethin and Angharad. But I can't stay where Death walks. That sounds melodramatic, I know, but sometimes even the stupidest person senses things. And I *know* that Ifan will try again some time, somehow.

Two days later, I went to Llangollen market, escorted by wall-eyed, silent Wil. The market was busy as an ants' nest. Stall-holders shouted their wares, pedlars strolled bellowing their wares between the wooden trestles, small boys stole anything they could lay hands on, housewives idled along lifting and touching and pinching and weighing, and over it all the strong stench of unwashed humanity and the cleaner stink of the cows, chickens, horses and other beasts penned for sale or slaughter. Ceridwen was there, her flannel-covered stall spread with herbs and potions. Her face lit up when she saw me.

Ignoring my escort, I approached her stall. She waited until Wil's head was turned away, pretending to show me herbs and vials. I lifted the cool, gritty jars and put them back.

'Have you seen Jack?' I whispered, and she nodded. I weighed a small sack of dried thyme in my palm, sniffed an open jar, tasted a syrup with a dipped finger.

'He's back. Your brother's sent news - and Elffin too.'

My hand closed on a packet of herbs, and I felt leaves crumble. She had news. 'Oh, how is he? Tell me?' I pleaded.

'Jack? Fine. Almost completely recovered. Your brother was wounded in the thigh, Jack says, but he's fine.' Ceridwen grinned and removed the ruined sack from my fingers. 'He sends his love.'

Llew, thank God, was safe then. 'And Elffin?

'Good news.' She glanced past me. 'Take care, your handsome escort -' she pulled a face and crossed her eyes '- is watching. Glyndŵr is more sympathetic than your *mamaeth*. If you're unhappy with ap Hywel, and if he'll let you go, Glyndŵr will take you in, despite his wife. Lady Marged says no, but Glyndŵr will over-rule her. She'll take the boy, however, but not Angharad. She must give up her son or keep him and forget whose son he is.'

I was pitched between joy and despair. 'I can't leave Gethin! And I know Angharad won't let him go, not even to Elffin.'

'Then you're in a tangle, little sister,' Ceridwen said softly. 'Does the Lady who Gethin's father is?'

'Oh, she knows,' I said, bitterly. 'She knew long before Elffin, and she won't change her mind. Ruthless as de Grey in her own way, is *Mamaeth*.'

'So what will you do?'

I raised my hands, helplessly. 'What can I do? I've no one but Glyndŵr to turn to, nowhere else to go.'

'There's always Jack,' she said softly.

'What can Jack do? He's supposed to be dead. I don't even know where he is. Or how I can contact him.'

'He's safe in the mountains. He'd take care of you.'

'What, two women and a baby in the mountains? Gethin would die of the damp and cold and Angharad and I wouldn't be far behind.'

'Then you've no choice, have you? Stay with ap Hywel until Gethins old enough to survive, then take your chances either with Jack or Lady Marged.'

I saw the years stretching ahead of me, and my shoulders slumped.

'Beggin' yer pardon, Mrs Rhiannon,' Wil said, eyeing Ceridwen and sniffing wetly. 'On'y the Master said you was to be back 'ome before dark, so we better get going soonish, look.'

I bought a few packets of herbs from Ceridwen, for the look of it, since I'd spent so long at her stall, and took the opportunity also to get further supplies of my morning potion. I grasped Ceridwen's hand, quickly, as she counted coins into mine, and squeezed it in gratitude and friendship.

'Remember,' she whispered as I turned to go, 'there's always Jack.'

Yes. There was always Jack.

Elffin

Prince Henry is mustering at Shrewsbury: let him come. We're more than a match for a boy. *Tad* says that he was always strange: Henry seemed to have no time for childhood.

My brothers and I kicked pig-bladders about the courtyard and wrestled and did what boys are supposed to do, like stealing apples and tripping the maids and baiting the men-at-arms, Henry, so *Tad* says, studied battle formations and siege warfare. He may know the technical side of warfare, but he's still a boy. We're men and my father rules Wales and always will. God willing.

The early months of the year were spent attacking English-held castles, though we gained none. They'd been fortified against us, but at least we reminded them that we hadn't gone away, nor are we likely to, until we have Wales again. Oh, and we killed a few men, as well, and burned a couple of houses and stole some livestock and emptied a few barns, just to keep our hands in.

Tad is determined to have a Welsh Parliament at Machynlleth, where our people can bring their grievances and problems and be treated fairly and honestly, unlike the English Parliament, where a man is insulted and cheated if he is Welsh. There's no justice for a Welshman in London: my father's experience proved that.

Tad speaks of other dreams for his Wales: Universities in the North and South so that Welsh students don't have to go to England. His rule needs lawyers and clerics of our own nationality to draft our laws and treaties. A Welsh bishop at St David's instead of one imposed by the English - can you believe that, in the place where our own Saint lived, an Englishman sits fatly lording it over Welsh clergy? My father wants a Welsh church free of English Bishops, and all manner of wonderful things for Wales and the Welsh. Owain Glyndŵr, by the Grace of God True and Rightful Prince of Wales, will see to it. I believe.

I believe in dreams coming true. I must, because if I don't all my hopes for Rhiannon will be lost, and my life is worth nothing without her. I wonder if she still has the silver fox? I wish now that it had been pure Welsh gold, set with emeralds and diamonds. The only thing I've ever given her, and I gave it so lightly, so carelessly. If I'd known, then, I should never have let her go.

I don't know if *Tad* has spoken to Mam about Rhiannon yet. She hasn't said anything, but then, Mam is close as a cockle and knows more of what's going on than all the rest of us put together.

She knew I was bedding Angharad, and said nothing. She solved the problem in her own efficient way, and as a result my son is hostage in my enemy's house. I squirm, sometimes, wondering what she thought. It's amazing, the power of a mother. Here I am, almost twenty years old, over six feet tall and strong enough to heft a broadsword, and still she can give me a look that numbs me from nose to toes and back again, chastising all the way. She doesn't say much, Mam - but she's fearsome. *Tad* is the gentle one.

How will she treat Rhiannon if - when - I bring her home? If she's difficult, if she hurts her, then I'll take her away, married or not, and we'll live our lives away from her. And please God I'll have my son, too. I wonder if he's walking yet.

And if he can talk: if he can he should be talking to me, his father, and not a stranger, not to ap Hywel. Sometimes I dream of him, his sturdy, resilient little body, his clutching hands, his round little face. And I long for him.

CHAPTER THIRTY-TWO

Llewelyn

Beaumaris, Caernarfon, Harlech and Llanbadarn are still in English hands, tight as limpets, and no stone big enough to smash them off. Successes elsewhere, mind: each day another town rises to *Tadmaeth's* banner. Men come, proud Welsh, for their Prince.

Tadmaeth is credited with the ability to be everywhere at once. The English claim he's at every battle, and every English soldier has seen him, has personally been savaged by him - when he's not invisible, that is.

They don't know that when the east wind rakes the mountains and the cold penetrates a man's soul, my poor *Tadmaeth* suffers. He's stiffer, slower, more reluctant to move from the fire at night; but by day he's our Hope, leading us, cheering us on, guiding us.

The Shropshire burgesses are begging Henry for men, money, arms, food, but they've no chance of getting it. Henry's tight with his gold. His son will need money to fight his father's war: will the old man be as deaf to him as he is to his Marcher lords?

Winter warfare is a miserable business, but in winter attacks aren't expected, and *Tadmaeth*'s persistence has paid dividends. On 22nd February we attacked Hope, near Chester, and it burned despite its sweating townsfolk with bucket-chains and beating brooms. I remember a fat English miller, his face scarlet with rage under its coating of flour, dancing and shrieking while his mill burned.

And while we were burning and looting, hand-picked Llyn men with the gift of persuasion infiltrated the county: lurking in alehouses, marketplaces and back alleys, persuading, gentling, suggesting. Each day more men come to support Owain, and slowly, stealthily, by the back door, Flintshire is becoming ours.

Yesterday men from Dyffryn Clwyd defected from the English garrison with news that Henry has strengthened the garrisons at Montgomery and Fflint. Too late for Fflint. We'll have it soon.

Just as well we were busy, or Elffin might have gone mad with frustration; he'd have been hatching mad plans to fetch Rhian and Gethin, but at the end of a day's skirmishing he wants nothing more than hot food, ale and a place to sleep.

He got an arrow in the arm at Hope. It's not serious, but he'll fret all the more because if an opportunity arises to rescue Rhiannon, he's helpless. Still, he'll be fine in a week or two. It was only a little wound, and nothing like as bad as mine was.

At Hope I was racing, sword in hand, through the town's narrow streets, mud and filth splashed to my thighs. Town people don't seem to care where they hurl their shit, and it disgusts me. Men were ahead of me and some behind, but suddenly I found myself alone beside a door, dark wood strapped with iron, well-kept, and the prospect of loot made me push it open. The house was empty, the owners having exercised discretion and disappeared long since.

It was so strange, being in that neat home: I wandered through the three small downstairs rooms idly lifting cups and trinkets - aye, and acquiring some, I admit. A woman's needlework stretched over a frame, the colours glowing in the light of candles that had burned almost away, the needle stuck hastily into the fabric, a snake of crimson silk trailing. A bowl of winter fruit, apples and late pears on a table, and beside it, an apple with a single bite taken out of it, the white flesh turned brown.

I took a candle and went upstairs: neat beds piled with comforters and feather mattresses; polished presses, fresh straw scattered, even a wooden doll sprawled on a small stool. Normally I should have ripped the comforters in a cloud of feathers, smashed the crockery, set fire to the hangings, wrecked and ruined these people for their mere presence in Wales. But this place had a familiarity, a comfort, a sense of long-standing affection, a happy home life briefly paused, and I couldn't bring myself to harm it. Elffin would have laughed at me, but - perhaps you understand. Perhaps not. It doesn't matter. I know what I felt and I am glad I did no harm.

In the last of the three linked bedrooms up the steep stairs, in what was obviously the room where the master and mistress of the house slept, I turned to see a man watching me, and flung up my sword to protect myself. I felt foolish when I realised it was only a mirror standing in the corner, its dim surface reflecting the gleam of the candle. I went closer, and stared. It was so long since I'd seen my reflection that I hardly recognised myself. I saw not a boy, but a man, broad-shouldered, stubble-faced, my hair in need of a cut, caught behind my neck with a leather thong. Somehow, while I was busy elsewhere, I'd grown up and become - immodest to say it, but it's true - handsome. I rubbed my jaw and grinned. No wonder the maids follow me about!

A shout from outside sent me scurrying downstairs. Caradoc, his dirty face dark with sweat, beat my back, making me stagger. 'Did you torch the place, Llew?' he bellowed, and pounded me again when I said that I had. I'm only ashamed that I lied, I'm glad I spared it, so that the people who lived there could return to it and continue their lives, master and mistress to sleep and love in the bed, and the child to play with its puppet. If Elffin had found out, mind, he'd have thought I'd gone soft in the head, but I remember that place, and wonder about the family that lived there. I visit it sometimes in that time between wakefulness and sleep, and the thought of it brings me peace.

Rhiannon

Ifan is home. I check rooms before I enter them, to make sure that he's not there - or if he is, that someone else is, too. He stares at me across the supper table, his eyes narrowed, his thin lips set, and

Glyndŵr has torched Hope, infuriating Rhys, who has part ownership of a business there which is probably destroyed, rooftop, cellar and contents. Good. Glyndŵr's coming. Wales will soon be his, thriving beneath Uther Pendragon's banner: red, gleaming Welsh gold, the dragon rippling as if it were alive. And the English - aye, and the traitor Welsh like my husband and his rat-faced son - will be dead or driven out or subjugated as we Welsh have been for so long. Soon, please God, soon. I am desperate.

I woke this morning at the tail of February, and the sun was out: one of those rare, brief winter days when spring is poised despite mud and bare branches. I flung open the upstairs shutters to let light and air into musty rooms, and decided then and there to escape outdoors despite the chill air and attack the weeds in the herb-garden before they choked my plants entirely.

Angharad was helping Beti, and Gethin was asleep on Angharad's pallet, fat arms flung above his head, round face turned aside. His hair was slightly damp, and though when he's awake he's far from angelic, now, with that great concentration that only sleeping babies have, he looked like one of the small angels that Lady Marged embroidered on the wall-hangings for the chapel at Sycharth. I stroked his soft face, smiled and softly closed the door behind me, taking with me into the sunlight the feel of smooth, damp baby skin, the remembered sound of his laughter.

Wearing wooden clogs and an old skirt and shawl because of the mud, I took a willow trug, a bit of flat wood to kneel on and an old knife, and went forth to do battle with dock and dandelion, nettle and bindweed. Strange how self-respecting herbs and flowers die back in winter but weeds flourish.

There's something good about grubbing in mud, especially after a long winter trapped indoors. The sun was warm on my back and exercise meant I wasn't cold and oh, I was grateful to be free of

Ifan's presence. He was about somewhere, but I didn't care. I was busy and away from him, and breathing clean, cold air.

I'd worked for an hour, perhaps less, when I heard Angharad. The sound brought me upright, grubbing-knife held like a weapon, trug of weeds scattered. She was screaming wildly, frantically, hysterically, no form to her screams, no words.

Stumbling, I rushed indoors, kicking the clogs off as I crossed the threshold. The screams were coming from upstairs, and I scrambled up, panting for breath, tripping over my mud-stained hem. She was sitting on the floor, her back to the window, both hands pressed over her eyes, and still she screamed, a wordless battery of noise. I grabbed her hands, trying to pull them away from her face, but she shook her head wildly and struggled.

'Angharad! Stop it! Tell me what's wrong!'

Sobbing great wrenching sobs, she waved her hand at the window and slumped sideways to lie limp and weeping on the floor. And then I realised that Gethin was not there. My heart rose in my throat. Leaning across Angharad's prostrate body, I looked fearfully out of the window.

In the cobbled yard, limp as a thrown rag, lay the light of my life, his fat arms spread in macabre imitation of the way he had lain in sleep, and from beneath his head came a slow seep of scarlet.

I spun on my bare feet, picking up a splinter I scarcely felt, hurled myself down the stairs, praying, begging God, making wild promises, if only, only, Gethin was alive, had somehow, miraculously, survived the fall.

I reached the small figure at the same time as Wil, his one eye skyward, his other trying to focus on the baby. He put out a foot, tentatively, and I struck out at him with my fists. No one should touch him except me, and I screamed that I'd kill him dead if his filthy foot touched my baby.

I lifted the little head, the face still warm, the eyes closed, dark lashes soft on white skin. My hands were bloodied, and when I lifted him, my clothes, too, but I didn't care. I held him, laid my palm along the soft neck where the pulse should have beaten steadily, evenly, strongly - and felt nothing. The even rise and fall of the small chest had ceased, and I knew he was dead though my mind could not begin to accept it. Gwen was peering out of the window, wailing in concert with Angharad, but Elin, for once showing some common sense, caught Beti's skirt and stopped her rushing to investigate the commotion.

I carried him into the house and sat on the settle, holding him close, feeling the awful bonelessness of the small body. My mind was blank as a clean sheet, and for a minute I feared my wits had gone entirely. And then 'Wil!' I rasped, 'fetch Ceridwen!'

He shifted from one foot to the other, looking uncomfortable. 'I ain't goin' near no witch, Mrs Rhiannon. Not me.'

Gwen, having come downstairs, flung her shawl over her head. 'I'll fetch her. Oh, Mrs Rhiannon, is the *babi* dead?'

'No!' I muttered, but I knew he was. But still, there was a mad spark of hope that perhaps Ceridwen might do something - anything, black arts or not. I would willingly sell my soul to all the devils of hell if only Gethin could be alive again. 'Gwenny, go, please. And *run!*'

Gwen took off like a rabbit, brushing past Elin, who had shut Beti in her room with instructions to stay there. Angharad had fallen silent, at last, but the echo of her terrible screams hung in the air like shards of ice.

'Oh, Mrs Rhian,' Elin wept, 'oh, what can we do?'

'Gwen's gone for Ceridwen. Go and sit with Angharad.'

'I don't know what to say to her, I don't,' the girl wailed. 'How can I tell her the *babi* is dead, Mrs Rhiannon? I can't tell her that!'

'Then don't tell her anything. Unless she asks, and I don't think she will. I think she knows.'

Gwen was quickly back with Ceridwen, her face red with exertion, although Ceridwen was her usual calm self. She gently took Gethin from me, laying the small figure on the kitchen table, blood smearing the scrubbed wood, and laid her hand on the small throat, bent her cheek to his parted lips and shook her head. 'I'm so sorry, Rhian, he's gone. It must have been quick, if that helps.'

It didn't, not at all. I couldn't accept that there was no more to be done except believe something too terrible to contemplate. 'There must be something you can do!' My voice cracked.

'Nothing but help you bury him, my poor little sister.' She stared down at Gethin's body. 'How did it happen?' she asked, and her voice seemed to come from far off. I saw myself blithely flinging open shutters, leaving the sleeping child in a room with open windows, not thinking for one second that -

My fault. I'd killed him.

'I opened the shutters,' I muttered. 'He was asleep. He must have woken and climbed - oh Christ Jesus, Ceridwen. I killed my baby.'

Ceridwen shook her head. 'I've been upstairs in this house, and I know what the windows are like. It's a strange, tall house, this one. The ceilings are high, and so are the windows.'

She was right. I stared at her. 'How...'

'I don't know. Where is Ifan?'

We stared at each other. 'In the stables, I think, with Wil. But Wil came running when he heard Angharad.'

Ceridwen turned abruptly and went across the yard. She returned in minutes. 'Ifan wasn't with Wil.'

'Looking for me, Rhiannon?' The voice was silky, innocent. I looked at my stepson and knew the truth.

Elffin

Duw, this wound hurts. My right arm, too, so I'm useless for just about everything. Llew, naturally, is calling it a "little scratch" and reminding me of the massive crater in his own heroic thigh. When my arm is healed, the very first thing I am going to do is beat the daylights out of the smug little bastard.

Still, it was got in a good fight. Bloody archers in upper rooms. Nothing I could have done to avoid it, and luckily he was a poor shot. One in the arm is better than one in the throat! Once it had been yanked out and our surgeon had cobbled up the flesh, it began to heal almost immediately. But because it's muscle, whenever I move, even to cut my meat or do anything, it reminds me. Bron's fussing over me and I'll be stuffed as a Christmas goose before long, and too fat to move at all.

When I can ride again, I'm determined to see Rhiannon and my son. I don't know how, mind, since we're mostly harrying the north-east and Shropshire, and I don't want to miss any of it, and we're a long way from Pentregoch. *Tad* looks tired and his rheumatism gives him hell, but he won't rest despite Mam's pleas to let younger men lead occasionally.

Torching Hope brought satisfaction totally out of proportion to the size of the town sacked and the amount of loot acquired. Hope, you see, is the English borough where, the year before *Tad* became Prince, they made a charter banning Welshmen from holding markets within three leagues of the town, or brewing ale, and all Welshmen in the valley around Hope must bring their produce for sale at Hope. English running the market, so Welsh prices were driven down until wares were hardly worth selling, and honest traders suffering and starving because of Hope's damned charter.

We were forbidden to hold assemblies of any kind within the town walls, either: but Owain Glyndŵr assembled the following year to take back what was rightfully his, and so the righteous citizens of Hope can stuff their charter up their collective arse.

My spirits would be a lot higher but for this damned wound. Any other time I'd have appreciated being indoors when the rain hurls down and the winds howl, but now I have too much time to think of Rhiannon and Gethin. And they brought me to Sycharth when I was wounded, because it was closer, and I'm lonely. Mam and Bron and a few of the other servants are here to fuss over me, but I miss the companionship of *Tad* and my brothers - God, even Llew, who drives me mad when he visits. Still, I'll soon be fit and able to join them.

Last time Llew came, he told me that the King has made his son lieutenant of Wales and the Marches, so he can call upon the sheriffs of the border counties for supplies and troops. He's only a boy, Henry, but he has huge powers and a burgeoning reputation. But still a boy, and we're men, and Wales is rising. All Wales. We sent his father home soaked and miserable, and we'll do the same for the son if he comes visiting without being invited.

CHAPTER THIRTY-THREE

Llewelyn
Glyndyfrdwy is all upside-down with Catrin, Edmund, Isobel and Adda all here. Servants run everywhere with pots, pans and pillows, Lady Marged fusses over her daughters and sons-in-law, with much talk of pregnancies and childbirth and speculation about who is, who has, and who isn't, as always when women are working together. God, do men talk about their testicles with such intimacy? Of course not, more important matters occupy us, unless our testicles are in immediate jeopardy. Which God prevent, amen.

Edmund and my brothers are constantly with *Tadmaeth*. The household speculates and everyone has opinions, but no one knows anything. Elffin says there's to be a great council to discuss what's best for Wales. More and more Welshmen believe that Owain

Glyndŵr is our true Prince, and only he cares what happens to Wales and the Welsh. He doesn't put the profit wrung from Wales before the welfare of her people. Welshmen are willing to surrender their lives to ensure that Glyndŵr's vision of Wales endures.

On a more personal note, since Isobel and Adda are here, so is Hafwen. When they arrived I hurried to lift her from her saddle and set her safely on the cobblestones. I was gratified to see her blush when - eventually - I took my hands from her waist. Some of her companions giggled, and Elffin rolled his eyes, but it was worth it to feel her under my hands.

Mali, however, has a face like a slapped arse. Good thing she isn't helping Bron in the kitchen any more, or Hafwen might end up poisoned. Mali's looks are enough to kill, but making beds and emptying chamber-pots doesn't give much opportunity for revenge.

Mali was all right to practise on, but Hafwen is different. Anyway, Bron's beady eyes have been on me if I've been anywhere near Mali, and on Mali if I've been elsewhere, so no chance of her slipping away to meet me. But work this out if you can! I haven't looked at Mali since Hafwen came back, and yet Bron's still nagging! Mid-morning yesterday I went to liberate some cheese and Bron went for me with a ladle as I stuffed it into my mouth.

'Bron!' I protested, half-laughing, hunching my shoulders to protect myself. 'Pity, please, I'm starving to death!'

'Good job too,' she sniffed. 'Playing fast-and-loose with that poor child. You should be ashamed of yourself. You'll get no sympathy here when you come scrounging for food all hours of the day and night, no, nor no food either.'

'Fast-and-loose?' I was mystified.

'Breaking poor Mali's heart. Fickle, you are. You should be ashamed. Poor girl is demented with it, and all your fault.'

At least she'd stopped hitting me. 'But Bron, you said don't go near Mali! You said you'd take your filleting knife to me if I even breathed on her! I haven't touched her!'

'That was then. This is now. Fancy piece turns up and poor Mali's forgotten, is that it? Shame, Llew, shame. And her working so hard to better herself to be worthy of you.'

My jaw dropped. 'But you said -'

'Never mind what I said. Shame, Llew! I just hope you haven't put her in the family way, or there'll be hell to pay, I promise you that, when Lady Marged gets to hear of it.'

'Family way?' I gave a rueful laugh. 'Chance'd be a fine thing,' I muttered, earning myself another clout from the ladle. 'What am I supposed to do, Bron? She's only a chamber-maid.'

'Only a kitchen maid when you first had her, Llewelyn,' she said sharply. 'Wasn't beneath you then, was she?'

Damn my sense of humour. 'Well, yes, actually,' I said, grinning, and the ladle went up again.

Bloody good thing I can run. And I got the cheese, too. But women, eh? First I'm threatened because I'm after a girl, then I'm beaten black and blue because I'm not! Where's the logic, eh? But then, women are illogical, Elffin says. He says women and logic are total strangers, and I agree.

But Hafwen, my Haf, is different. She's perfect. She's tiny, barely up to my chest, and her hair is dark, her eyes brown and soft, and her voice is musical as birdsong. She is intelligent, too, for a girl, and when I happened to mention we were to attack Hawarden she clutched my arm and begged me with tears in her eyes to take care! I've kissed her, once, and I'll do it again, often as I can.

Not, however, forgetting Lady Marged. Respectful as I am of *Mamaeth, Duw*, she terrifies me! Last thing I want to do is stir her up, so I meet Haf in secret. Difficult in the middle of winter in a place like Glyndyfrdwy, as you can imagine. Ears and eyes everywhere, and Lady Marged's more than most.

Rhiannon

My step-son glanced disinterestedly at the small body. 'Is it dead?'

I stood up and opened my mouth to scream at him, but Ceridwen caught my wrist. I drew a deep, shuddering breath, and closed my mouth.

'Yes,' Ceridwen said, ice in her voice. 'He's dead.'

'Ah well. Sad. Children die. So many things can go wrong: they take a chill and die in a day. Cut themselves and the wound becomes infected; they can fall and kill themselves. So easy, so easy. Little, little lives, so quickly snuffed.' There was almost a smile at the corner of his mouth. 'No use getting fond of them.'

'And sometimes they are killed,' I said softly. 'And trust me, Ifan, will be avenged.'

'Killed? Avenged? Rhiannon, you're mad.'

'Sometimes people can be thrown from windows, just as they can be pushed downstairs. But they are not forgotten.'

'Such an unimportant life. Bastard child, whore-mother. Who cares?'

'I care, Ifan. And so, when he learns of it, will his father.'

'He has a father? You amaze me, Rhiannon.'

'He has a father. And his father will spit you and gut you without thinking twice.'

Ifan widened his eyes. 'Who? Some stable lad? Some servant? You terrify me. Oh, look. I'm shaking!' Laughing, he turned on his heel and left the room.

Ceridwen shook the wrist she held. 'For God's sake, Rhiannon, watch your tongue. If Ifan finds out who Gethin is, you'd be in even more danger. Can you imagine what Elffin will do when he finds out that Ifan killed Gethin? And the easiest way of preventing Elffin from finding out is to kill you, Angharad and me, too.'

She was right. But I mourned my baby, and didn't care.

Elin and Gwen put Angharad to bed dosed with poppy juice, but even in her sleep she moaned and sobbed. My heart ached for her.

Then Ceridwen and I turned to the soul-wrenching task of burying Gethin. My heart breaking, my teeth sunk bloody into my lip, we undressed and washed his rounded, lovely body, clothed him in a clean gown and wrapped him in the sheepskin from his own bed. I cut tendrils of his soft, curling hair to save for his father, mother and myself, then kissed him. I had no tears. Ceridwen carried a spade, and I held him close, the light of my life, his small face peaceful in the mocking warmth of the sheepskin, to a place where, later in the year the bluebells would seep in a blue tide from the woods. We took turns to dig down into the brown loam and laid him in the ground. I pulled the sheepskin up to cover his face, and we shovelled the rich earth over the tiny body. I prayed, and we left him.

I pray Jesus, God and Holy Mary that I never have to do such a thing again in all my life, because it is certain I should die of grief. Walking away from the raw brown mound, leaving Gethin behind, hurt almost beyond bearing. I couldn't stand upright: my back curved to protect the pain roaring inside me. Only fury stiffened my soul, kept me from going back and flinging myself on the grave to weep and weep. That and Ceridwen's strong arm about my shoulders.

When ap Hywel returned, Ceridwen was gone, Angharad was still drugged and sleeping, and his meal was ready. All was normal except for my reddened eyes and trembling hands, and Beti in her bed, having sobbed herself to sleep, crying for her playmate.

When he came in for supper he stared at me. 'Are you ill?'

I shook my head.

'Then what is it? You look like death. Are you queasy?' He made a short, humourless noise that was almost a laugh. 'Surely you aren't pregnant.'

No, praise God, I thought. 'No. But Angharad's child -' I could not bring myself to speak his name '- fell from the window today and was killed.'

He shrugged. 'Sad. Pass the butter, Ifan. Buried?'

I nodded, knowing that if I spoke I'd never stop. I served my husband and my stepson, and excused myself.

I ached in every limb, and my face felt like fire. Was I taking a chill? I couldn't stop trembling, and there was a lump in my throat as big as a boulder. I wanted to die: every breath hurt. But behind the grief, sustaining me, the anger was as tangible as rock, so strong that I knew I must control it somehow. But I would make Ifan suffer. Some day, somehow, I would see him suffer and die, even as Gethin died. Better, perhaps God would let me kill him.

I lay rigid in my bed, unable to sleep. My husband came up much later and still I lay awake. Thank God he did not touch me. If he had laid one finger on my body I would have shattered into a million pieces, screamed until I had no breath left.

I watched the moon creep round the room, and heard the first bird of sunrise. Some time during the night I realised that there was one thing - and one thing only, and I felt guilty for even thinking the thought - that was good about Gethin's death.

Now I could go whenever I wished, unencumbered by Angharad, who would never have left Gethin, and I just as certainly would never have left without him.

As soon as breakfast was done, and Rhys and Ifan had gone I left Gwen and Elin to look after Angharad and Beti and slipped away from the house into the woods, first making sure that Wil was not watching.

Ceridwen was barely awake, her hair tangled about a face creased from sleep when she opened the door of her cottage.

'Rhian? What is it?'

I pushed past her, wanting to get inside before I was seen. 'Now Gethin's dead there's nothing to keep me here. I have to get away, get to Sycharth, to Elffin. If I stay Ifan will kill me, somehow.'

'He will. There aren't many purely evil in this world, Rhiannon, but he is one.'

'I'd poison him before I leave, but then Rhys would have reason to follow me and bring me back. I must tell Elffin. He'll punish Ifan somehow. Oh, Ceridwen, I want to see Ifan torn apart by hot pincers until he is dead, and then kill him all over again.'

She touched my hand, calming me. 'I'll miss you.'

'Then come with me.'

She shook her head. 'My home's here. Besides, someone has to care for Angharad. When the grief eases things may be different.' She shrugged. 'Perhaps I'll come later.'

I felt guilty at leaving Angharad. Perhaps I should stay.

'Whatever you're thinking, Rhian, you're wrong. Go as soon as you can. Glyndŵr will take you in and Elffin will protect you, whatever his bloody wife says. You can't stay here any longer.'

'Will you tell Jack what's happened, tell him I'm going to Sycharth. Say he doesn't need to worry about me now. Once I am with Elffin I'll be all right.'

Ceridwen turned away, busying herself with rekindling the fire in the centre of the room. 'Oh, he'll still worry about you, Rhian, safe with Elffin or not. When will you go? And how?'

'Soon as I can. I won't tell Angharad. What she doesn't know can't be beaten out of her. Tell her I'm sorry, but I couldn't stay?'

She nodded. 'Of course. May the Mother watch over you.'

'The Blessed Virgin isn't interested in me,' I said bitterly, 'or she'd have taken pity on me by now.'

Ceridwen raised an eyebrow. 'My Mother is an older Goddess.'

I heard her, but was too distraught to think about Goddesses and Virgins. 'I'll sleep under a hedge if I have to, but I won't spend one more night under that roof, or share that man's bed ever again. I'll get word to you, somehow, to tell you I'm safe. And for God's sake, Ceridwen, be careful of Ifan! He might kill you next time.'

I hugged her, and cried a little, for she was my friend and sister, then scurried back through the forest, looking constantly over my shoulder for fear of Ifan.

Elffin

Edmund's here and Adda, and naturally Isobel and Catrin are with them, and there are women chattering like magpies all over the place. Catrin is anxious to see me wed, it seems, and has been bleating about Adda's sister, who is fourteen and apparently looks and sings like an angel. But my heart is Rhiannon's and always will be, although no one could accuse her of being angelic.

Edmund and Adda, of course, are here for a reason, and on Wednesday of this week John Hanmer arrived; my Uncle Tudur and my cousin; Rob Puleston, and many other North and Mid Wales *uchelwyr*. My brothers and I were summoned, and we joined them at the great table (now shifted into the solar, to my mother's annoyance, since she believes that the solar is for relaxation, not business). However, it is the largest room at Glyndyfrdwy, so she must put up with it. As she'll put up with other things, if I have my way. And I shall.

We took our places at the table, *Tad* formally welcomed our guests, and when wine had been poured, he spoke.

'This rising came from small beginning, friends, from such small embers, blown into the great fire which is engulfing Wales. Please God soon North and South, West and East will be united against England. We shall be free and Wales will be whole once more.' He moved his clenched fist in a slow circle on the table-top, as if he were grinding the King's face into the gleaming grain. 'So close, my friends,' he said. 'We have Flintshire, and most of mid and South Wales, and some of the West and East. We have had little rest this winter, knowing that we must strike while the flame is hot. When the weather improves, who knows what will happen? I'll not rest until we have all Wales. Brecon and Carmarthen, and in the north Beaumaris, Caernarfon and Harlech. We control their supply network, and God willing, we'll have them soon. Once Henry's strongholds are taken, nothing can stop us.'

My uncle Tudur raised his beaker of wine. 'My lords,' he said, 'Owain Glyndŵr, by the Grace of God, True and Rightful Prince of Wales. God bless and protect him.'

The toast was drunk with low rumbles of assent by all there, old battle-scarred warriors, younger men like Edmund Mortimer, my brothers and myself. I glanced around, seeing leather jerkins and rich velvets reflected in the polished oak, all the men who had placed their lives in my father's hands, in his service.

Tad replaced his goblet on the table. 'A united Wales, our own great Parliament to govern it. There will be justice and honesty, and not only for the rich and powerful. When we are free, when we have driven out England once and for all, then I have other plans, my friends.' His eyes brightened. 'Universities, north and south, fine as any in England, for Wales needs scholars. A true Welsh Bishop in our Cathedral and a Welsh church free of English corruption. When Wales is free and Henry of England licking his wounds in London.' It was hope that lit *Tad*'s tired face, hope and belief, but somehow, despite his grand words and *hwyl*, I knew that there was little joy in his soul. The gentle man who had made Sycharth and Glyndyfrdwy stately and boundlessly welcoming, content with his family and his music, is long gone, and in his place is a man I hardly recognise, although he is my own father.

Rob Puleston, a crop-headed, droop-moustached, wary lank of a man, nodded assent, but accompanied it with a furrowing of his forehead and a word of caution. 'And young Hal? As Henry's lieutenant in Wales he won't stand by and give you free rein. Your ambitions won't be worth a rat's fart, Owain. For all his youth, Monmouth Harry is a force to be reckoned with.'

Father laughed. 'Aye, Rob, he is. But his father's close with his cash, and my informants say that young Harry is already pleading for money - more money than skinflint Henry will ever release. An army without funds is a reluctant army. Soldiers must have food in their bellies, and weapons in their hands, shoes on their feet, to say nothing of horses and armour - and they have none of these. The Marcher lords have been squeezed until they squeak, but I guarantee old Henry won't open his purse. Besides, there are few places in Wales young Henry could sleep well of nights, and - well, that leads me to another matter. My son-in-law will explain.'

Mortimer poured wine and sat back. He's gained weight since marrying Cat: contentment, probably. They were still cooing in corners like sweethearts, and she has a child in her belly already.

'Gwilym ap Robert Lloyd of Denbigh, squire to my brother-in-law Percy, has been carrying messages between our Prince and Hotspur.'

Hotspur? The name made me sit up straight, and my brothers did likewise.

Edmund sipped, and continued. 'Hotspur is disenchanted with his King, and is of a mind to throw in his lot with us. To have the Percys at our backs would bring Henry to his knees in short order.'

'Percys at our backs might leave us with knives sticking out of them. Can we trust him?' Rob Puleston leaned forward, cupping his wine between large hands, frowning.

'He's honourable,' Edmund said, 'but disenchanted. Henry's mistake was not letting him ransom me.' He smiled into his wine cup. 'Though ransom was the furthest thing from my mind.'

'Then we should treat with him,' Puleston said, squaring his shoulders against the high back of his chair. 'Commit to nothing, mind: but at least hear what he has to say.'

Minor objections were raised by some, but after discussion which continued late into the evening, a plan was proposed to put to Hotspur, dividing Wales and England in a way that was acceptable to both sides. If he was of a mind to burn his bridges and join us, and terms for an alliance could be agreed, then, Glyndŵr and Northumberland - what a force that would make!

The great table of the solar was abandoned for another in the great hall, and we dined at length and in good spirits, all of us rejoicing in the fact that there was no way in which the rise of Owain Glyndŵr could be prevented, now. It was only later, lounging beside the fire after almost everyone else had tottered to their beds, that I learned the rest of it from my brothers. The shadows in the Great Hall wrapped around us and we were warmed and content with heat and wine, and such conditions breed slow conversation and confidences.

Gruffydd leaned forward, resting his elbows on his knees. 'Hotspur, yes. He'll bring us nothing but advantage, but what about the rest of it? *Tad* believes he can do it, but - I'm not convinced it's right, or that it will work.'

'What? Universities and the Bishopric? Why not?' I prodded a log with my foot and it fell in a cascade of spitting sparks.

'No, not that. There's more. He's going to treat with the Scots and French.'

I sat up, slowly. 'I knew about the French, of course. But the Scots? Bloody hell, Gruffydd, he's fought them most of his life!'

'Aye, but then he was England's. Now he's Prince of Wales, and reasons that they're Gaels and we're Celts, and we've a common enemy.'

'It's hard work swallowing the Scots, let alone the French! I met a Frenchman once - little, greasy fellow. Smelled of garlic. I couldn't stand to be near him. Besides, they eat snails!'

Madoc laughed. 'My much-travelled little brother. One Frenchman doesn't make a country, and there are plenty of Welshmen who stink.'

Maredydd was more nervous about the Scots: barbarians and savages he calls them, but Madoc is enthusiastic.

'But God, Madoc, the garlic! What if they're all like him? What use will they be as allies if we can't get near them for the smell?'

'Trust me, little brother, they aren't. With Scotland and France, we could dictate our own terms to Henry. If he's lucky, we may let him keep some of England - though with the Percys on our side, not much of the north of it!'

I considered the idea. I'd imagined the struggle was confined to England and Wales, had never dreamed that we might actually involve other kingdoms. I tried to imagine Owain Glyndŵr, treating as equal with the King of France - but then, why not?

My father is the Prince of Wales.

CHAPTER THIRTY-FOUR

Llewelyn

When all the guests had gone, Isobel and Adda went, too, with tears and hugs from *Tadmaeth* for Isobel: families are precious when each meeting may be the last. With them went my Haf, her lips trembling - as indeed were mine as I watched her woebegone face recede until the small train disappeared down the valley, but misery was soon forgotten when we rode South to Llandovery, Llandeilo, Carmarthen, to show the people their Prince.

But first *Tadmaeth* consulted his sorcerer. 'My Prince,' he said, hands thrust into the sleeves of his robe, 'what you desire you will achieve. Your Welsh Church, Universities, Parliament. Owain Glyndyfrdwy, in six hundred years and more you will be remembered with honour. While stars burn and fall, while centuries turn, Welshmen will speak your name with pride. Owain Glyndŵr, by the Grace of your God, True Prince of Wales.'

Tadmaeth was content, but as always I was uneasy in Ffinnant's presence and his words which said so much - and also so little.

I missed Elffin, who was still at Sycharth because his wound had become infected. Madoc and I were there collecting supplies when he took a turn for the worse. He was delirious: sometimes he thought Rhiannon was with him and Gethin, and my heart ached.

The surgeon thought the wound had been clean, but something, a flake of rust or some filth had got into it, and the small cut was red and puffy, the wound like an evil little mouth, and his arm swelled and became dark and shiny. It had to be lanced and cleaned, and ointment applied to keep the wound open, and then poultices were heated and slapped on the gash to heal it. Oh, and Bron, who was looking after him, concocted a brew of tansy, nettles, raspberry and cabbage and forced it down his throat three times a day. The only comfort, according to Elffin, was that at least it was boiled in ale which made it slightly less poisonous than it might have been. By the time we left, however, he was on the mend, though furious at being left behind. I patted his head and told him to be a good boy for Bron, and I'd see him when he was well.

Good thing he was weakened by fever and I'm fast on my feet!

Our numbers grew on the journey, and it was slow going for a while as men and weapons poured from every town to join us, rich and poor, each determined to fight for his Prince. We took the road south, our motley army straggling out behind us. Then over the sound of hooves and gruff voices, the clatter of feet and the million other sounds of an army on the move, I heard shouting. I turned in the saddle and saw a figure on horseback, riding hard. Jack, looking as if he had ridden hard and long.

I hauled Siôned's head round and rode back to meet him, my stomach churning. His urgency could only mean trouble. 'Jack? What is it, man?'

He hauled his sweating horse to a standstill. 'Where's Elffin?'

'At Sycharth - a flesh wound turned bad, but he'll live. Why?'

'Your sister's run from ap Hywel.'

'Jesus! Did she take the baby, too?'

'Gethin's dead. Angharad's mindless and Rhiannon's run.'

'Gethin dead? Christ's bloody bones, Jack! How? Fever?'

Jack shook his head, struggling to control his breathing. 'He fell - or was thrown - from an upstairs window. Smashed his head on the cobbles. And before you ask, yes, Ifan was there.'

Rage hit me. I gripped my reins as if I could strangle Ifan with them there and then, swaying in the saddle with the force of my feelings. 'Where's Rhian now?'

'Christ only knows - she left yesterday morning. Ap Hywel only realised she'd gone half way through the day, and he and his son and their man are out looking for her. She'll be heading for Sycharth, but if Ifan finds her first she's dead. He's tried to kill her once: he won't fail again. We have to find her before he does.'

'Jesus wept, Jack!' I rubbed my face with my hands. 'She could be anywhere. They might already have found her. What in God's name am I to do?'

'Find her first, Llew. Glyndŵr will understand. Ask him. But for Christ's sake, hurry!'

Tadmaeth was at the head of the column, deep in conversation with Gruffydd. Both men turned at my shout.

'Llew? What?' *Tadmaeth*'s face was concerned, and he and Gruffydd swung their mounts out of line, and reined in beside me.

I was shaking. 'Rhian's run away and ap Hywel and his son are looking for her. *Tadmaeth,* if the son finds her first...'

'And Gethin?' Glyndŵr asked. Could he really care about a bastard child when he had so much on his mind?

'Dead. Thrown from a window, his skull smashed. Angharad is mad with grief, and Rhiannon has run away. *Tadmaeth*, she's my sister. I can't let her -' My voice choked and I fell silent.

Grief was plain in his eyes. For Rhiannon or the grandson he'd never held? 'Find her. Take her to Sycharth. Tell my wife - no. Give her this.' He tugged off a ring and gave it to me. 'Tell Marged Rhiannon is my daughter as you are my son. My exact words, mind, Llew.' He'd left no room for *Mamaeth* to manoeuvre: this was an order, not a request.

'*Diolch i ti, Tadmaeth*. When she's safe, I'll be back.'

He gripped my arm then spurred his horse to the head of the column. I swung Sioned round and rode back to Jack.

'When we find her, I'm to take her to Sycharth. Lady Marged will take her in - on Glyndŵr's own orders.' Jack grinned his relief, his teeth flashing white against the dark stubble on his cheeks. I kicked Siôned's flanks, and Jack made to follow me, but I stopped him. 'You take the valley road. If I take the other, one of us will find her. If you do, take her home. I'll meet you at Sycharth, sunset tomorrow. Pray we find her before that bastard Ifan does.'

There's a lot of country between Corwen and Pentregoch, and a wandering girl is hard to find, especially a girl with - and I knew this for a fact, having grown up with her - a lamentably poor sense of direction. But if she had any sense at all she'd keep off the main tracks and stick to the hidden roads, which might keep her safe, but would make finding her twice as hard. I rode back along the way Jack had come. She'd obviously had the sense to take to the woods, so it was likely Jack would find her.

But as the afternoon wore on and the sun slithered behind the hills, I began to worry that perhaps she was lying injured somewhere. There was no sign of her. I took the most likely paths, hidden from the main tracks, and searched, straining my eyes to see between the massed trunks and new-greening vegetation, searching for hoof- or footprints in damp places. I wanted to shout her name, but didn't dare, fearing hostile ears. At the sound of approaching hooves I hid myself, but it wasn't ap Hywel or Ifan: nor, sadly, was it my sister. I would have asked the rider if he had seen a solitary girl, but he was heading at a full gallop the way I'd come, and was gone before I could attract his attention. I wondered who he was and where he was going, but soon forgot him in my concern for Rhian.

I searched the road to Pentregoch all that day and half the night, slept under a tree and began again next morning. I wished I'd made a better arrangement with Jack. I couldn't stop looking for her without knowing if he had found her. But by mid-day on the second day she was still missing, and despite my misgivings, I had to give up and hope Jack had her. I could hardly go to Pentreoch and ask. I set off towards Sycharth. Elffin should be told what had happened. Wounded or not, he'd never stop searching until he found her. Jack *must* have her. She would have been trying to stay hidden, so it was understandable that I hadn't found her. But still fear nagged. What if Jack hadn't found her, and I'd missed her?

Rhiannon

I didn't sleep last night. My head buzzed with exhaustion and grief, anxiety and joy, because today I would escape. I wanted to leap from bed at dawn, but I tried to act normally so that Rhys and Ifan wouldn't suspect. When the sun was up, I lay with my eyes closed, and when Gwen crept into the room and shook my shoulder, I pretended I'd been asleep, rubbing my eyes and yawning.

By the time ap Hywel came to breakfast I was in agonies in case either of them stayed behind, but at last they left.

I sent Elin to the dairy and gave Gwen orders to turn out the bed-chambers at the front of the house, which would keep her occupied and away from the back door. I packed a few things, nothing I hadn't brought with me, and pinned the silver fox to my cloak. I wandered casually to the stables, hoping desperately that Wil would be elsewhere and I could take the mare and go, quickly, without any further delay. Ap Hywel owed me at least a horse for all he and his son had done to me.

Unfortunately, Wil was in the stable, comfortable on a feed-bin, mending an old harness and whistling through his teeth. I racked my brains trying to think of some message he could take somewhere, anywhere, but I couldn't think of anything credible, and the last thing I wanted was to rouse his suspicions.

Disconsolately I wandered back into the house: I could hear Gwen's voice murmuring, coaxing, gentling, and supposed she was talking to Angharad.

I sat with Angharad for hours last evening, watching her weep until there were no tears left in her. She lay motionless and pale, holding Gethin's small tunic. I didn't know what to say. I was going to leave her, and guilt seared me, but I had to go to save my life. I couldn't take her with me. She couldn't speak or think in her grief, and if I didn't go now, I might never get away. With all my soul I longed for Elffin and Sycharth. If I stayed, I'd fall into the same wordless, helpless misery as Angharad, and I'd die, either of misery or by Ifan's hand.

The sun arced higher and still Wil sat, a stolid barrier between me and safety. I began to panic. Suppose Rhys came back, or Ifan, before I could get away? If necessary I wouldn't wait until I could steal a horse but would go on foot. Could I manage to walk? It was only a few hours ride Sycharth. How long would it take me to walk it? Twice as long? Three times? Four? But I had only house shoes, and none fit to walk any distance in.

Then Wil stuck his head through the front door. 'Beggin' your pardon, Mrs Rhiannon, but I got to go to the village. This old harness do need a smith, aye, not cobblin'. If the master'ud pay for a new one we'd all be happier, 'specially me, wasting my time, look, but he won't loosen his purse strings and that's a fact, so I must go and get the smith to do what I can't and hope the master will pay the bill.'

'Go, Wil,' I said, as calmly as I could. 'I'll see that the bill is paid.'

I waited until he was out of sight and then flew to the stables, saddled the mare in a flurry of fumbling fingers, flung the saddlebag containing my few possessions across her rump and mounted. Keeping as close to the house as I could I walked the horse round towards the back gate. I was almost through it when Beti appeared.

'Where are you going, Rhiannon?' she asked. 'Can I come? '

'No.' Tension made me snap and the child's face drooped, tears welling..

'I don't want Gethin to be dead, Rhiannon,' she whimpered. 'I'm lonely. I want Jack, but he died too. I want to come with you. I don't want to be here where everyone is sad. I'm afraid. Please can I come? Please?'

With an effort, I softened my voice. 'No, sweetheart. I have to go out, and I must ride fast and you can't come. But -' I searched my mind for something to say to her to pacify her, something to distract her, to occupy her mind while I got away '- I want you to make a tisane, with honey and mead and feverfew, you know, I showed you how, remember? - and help poor Angharad drink it. Will you do that? She's so lonely without Gethin.' The thought of Gethin made my voice catch and the tears well. Somehow I must tell Elffin...

'Will you bring me a present when you come back?'

I wasn't coming back. Ever. 'Of course I will, Beti,' I lied. I'd send something to her somehow - when I was safely at Sycharth. I hated her father and brother but had grown fond of Beti despite her incessant chatter. Her thumb in her mouth, the child turned disconsolately on her heel and wandered indoors. I put my heels to the mare's flanks and leaped forward and through the gate.

I knew, roughly, the way to Sycharth, though I'd never travelled it without an escort. *Where's Jack when I need him?* I thought grimly, and tried to think. The road lay straight ahead for about ten miles - but that was the road that ap Hywel and his son had taken, and the last thing I wanted to do was meet them on their way back. Through the woods, into the valley and to Sycharth that way. Further, but safer - if I kept my eyes and ears open.

Despite the sun, the wind was chill for May and I pulled my cloak and hood close about me, bent over the mare's neck and rode into the woods, crouching to avoid low branches. My mare splashed through streams, slithered through mud and clattered down hillsides, but I managed to keep away from the main road. Once, I had to haul on the reins and pull the horse back into the trees when a lone rider hurtled past, but it wasn't ap Hywel or Ifan and as soon as he'd disappeared I carried on. I wished I had some sort of a weapon, but I had nothing except my wits and the sharp pin holding my hood to my hair. Fat lot of good that would be against a sword. Like spitting at a dragon!

The hours passed, and I had no idea where I was. I knew the sun set in the west, and that Sycharth was that way, so I followed the red glow as it slipped lower in the sky. And then it became too dark to ride, too dark to see and the trees were darker shadows against the darkness. Branches lashed at my face and tore at my clothes and eventually, I had to stop. In the morning I'd watch where the sun rose, and go in the opposite direction. I'd be bound to reach Sycharth eventually. I tied the mare to a tree and huddled nearby, wrapped in my cloak against the cold. After a while, I took the cloth from under the mare's saddle and wrapped that around me as well. Although I was sheltered from the wind, the air was bitterly cold, and even in the darkness I could see my breath clouding on the air. The horse stamped and blew, and I wished it would lie down so I could huddle into its side and take warmth from its body, but it seemed not to want to sleep. Did horses sleep standing up? I didn't know. They stood in the stable, but perhaps at night, in the open, they lay down, like cows. I only knew I was cold and getting colder by the minute.

Periodically I got up and stamped my numb feet, waved my arms, jumped up and down, anything, to keep from freezing. It would almost be better to try to keep travelling rather than sit still and freeze, but when I untied the horse and mounted and moved off through the woods I rode into a low branch, making me see stars. I'd have to stay put and try not to freeze until at least first light. Disconsolately, I got down, and looked for another tree to tie my mount to.

Then, through the darkness, I saw a small red glow. A fire! Warmth! Light! Swiftly I tied the reins to a low branch and crept as silently as I could through the woods, feeling my way from tree to tree, praying I wouldn't step on a twig and betray my presence. There was no one on guard: a solitary slumped figure lay sleeping beside the embers of the fire. What if it were Ifan or ap Rhys? Whoever it was, was bundled so tight in warm blankets that his face was invisible. Perhaps I could creep closer, just warm my hands a little, without waking him.

Slowly, slowly, I crept forward and then was grabbed and lifted off my feet from behind. I didn't scream. Instead, both my hands flew up, one to rake my captor's face with my nails, the other to pull the bodkin from my hood. I reached it, and stabbed it downward, sinking it deep into my captor's thigh.

'Ow!' he yelled, and, 'Jesus!' and dropped me.

I held the pin ready to strike again, backing, trying to move towards my horse, praying he wouldn't draw his sword and kill me, because a cloak-pin isn't much of a weapon against a sword.

Then I realised that the voice was familiar. 'Jack?'

'Rhian?'

I lowered my makeshift weapon: Jack rubbed his thigh, scowling. The pin had sunk in deep: I'd had to tug hard to get it out. He glared at me.

'Did you have to stab me, Rhian?' he complained, 'as well as nearly taking out my eye with your fingernails? Don't you know a friend when you see one?'

'I couldn't see you, could I? What did you expect me to do?' I snapped, 'you grabbed me from behind. You could have been anyone. You could have been Ifan.'

'And if I had been, how much good would a bodkin be? He'd have slit your throat before you had time to scream.'

'You didn't,' I retorted. 'It caught you off guard!'

'Aye, but I'm not Ifan.'

'Just as well. If you had been, my next stab would have been into your heart. Even a bodkin can kill if it's put in the right place.'

I turned and stretched my hands to the fire. 'I'm frozen,' I said, fiercely, 'but I'd rather freeze to death than go back to ap Hywel, so it's no good you trying to make me. If Lady Marged won't have me, then I'll live in a cave if I have to. I won't go back to .'

Jack bent and threw some more wood on the fire. 'You don't need to. Glyndŵr will take you in. Lady Marged won't disobey him, though he won't be at Sycharth when we get there.'

'Where is he?'

'Riding south at the head of an army. The news is good: all of the north is his and they say there are thirty thousand men with him to persuade the south to rise.'

My hopes collapsed. 'And Elffin's with him?'

'He should have been,' Jack replied, his face lit by the glow of the fire, 'but a flesh wound in his arm turned rotten and he had to stay behind at Sycharth.'

I flew at him, grabbing his arm. 'Is he bad? Dying? Tell me!'

Jack shook off my hand. 'No, no. He'll do. His mother and Bron have been dosing him. He'll live, I tell you, stop fussing.'

I could feel the smile break across my face. 'He'll be there when we get to Sycharth?'

'Unless he's made a miraculous recovery, aye, he'll be there. According to Llew, yesterday he was weak as water.'

Then I remembered, and my stomach turned. 'I have to tell him Gethin is dead. Ifan killed him, I know it in my soul - even though I can't prove it.'

'I know. Ceridwen told me, and that you'd run. Why do you think I'm here? It was hours before anyone realised you'd gone, but she came to tell me. I knew if Ifan reached you first you'd never see Sycharth, so I went after Glyndŵr. Llew is looking for you, too. He's taken the other road, and we agreed to meet at Sycharth at sunset tonight in the hope that one of us found you. Anyway, we must leave here: the sun's almost up. Where did you leave your horse?'

'Over there. Somewhere. Not far.' I hoped I had tied it tightly enough and it hadn't wandered off.

'Can you find it again?'

'Of course.' I strode away, leaving Jack stamping out the fire and rolling the bedding.

I stumbled through the undergrowth. Where was the damned horse? Surely I hadn't left it quite so far away? It was hard to tell: last night it had been pitch black, but now sunrise was imminent.

And then I saw it, still securely tied to a tree. I was busy congratulating myself when I was once more grabbed from behind. This time, I knew it wasn't Jack, and this time I was helpless, since my captor pinioned my arms to my sides so that I couldn't reach the bodkin in my cloak. He forgot my voice, however, and I let out a piercing scream before he remembered, and clapped his hand over my open mouth. I recognised his smell: it was my husband. I tried to bite him.

He was alone, thank God. Ap Hywel put me down, still gripping my arms, his face florid with fury. He shook me violently, my hair flying wildly about my face, my head jerking. 'Bitch! Thought you could run, did you? And steal from me into the bargain. Where did you think you could go? Who'd have you, whore?'

'I didn't steal anything. I only took the horse, and -' But he'd lost interest in me.

He stared past me, his jaw slackly open.

'Jesus Christ!' he stammered. 'You're dead!' He released my arm to draw his sword.

'Wrong,' Jack said. 'No thanks to your son. How does it feel to sire a murdering coward who kills babies and attacks from behind?'

Ap Hywel shoved me aside, and the two men faced each other. They were matched in size, though ap Hywel was older. He was an experienced swordsman, but Jack was better. The fight was short and fierce, and at the end of it Jack, his shoulders heaving, had his foot on ap Hywel's chest and his sword poised to thrust.

I wanted Jack to kill him. If it had been Ifan he'd have cut his throat without a second thought.

But it wasn't, and Jack, unlike Ifan, would not kill in cold blood. Instead, he took ap Hywel's horse and let him walk home unhurt, if humiliated.

Then we set off towards Sycharth.

'I wish you'd killed him, Jack,' I said after a while. 'He deserved to die.'

'No he didn't. I can't blame him for wanting his wife back, if only to save face with his neighbours.'

'I wasn't his wife.'

'Yes, you were. Whatever you say, you still are.'

'But I love Elffin.'

'Yes,' Jack's voice was weary. 'You love Elffin. I know. Be quiet, Rhian. Just ride. Consider how you're going to tell Elffin that his son is dead.'

I lapsed into silence then. It was a long day, but pleasantly warm after the chill of the previous night. If we'd taken the main track to Sycharth we could have reached it by mid-morning, but because I'd detoured the day before, we were approaching it in a great loop, and by the time we neared it, the sun was sinking, turning the clouds crimson.

We were no more than three miles away when we saw a rider approaching, riding fast. Recognising the Pulaston livery, we spurred forward, and the rider waited for us to draw level.

'In a hurry, friend?' Jack asked. 'Yesterday you were riding as fast in the opposite direction. What news?'

The rider glanced at him, and then sideways at me. 'Who's asking?'

'Rhiannon ap Hywel,' I said, before Jack could speak. 'Wife to Rhys ap Hywel of Pentregoch and *maethferch* to Owain Glyndŵr.'

The rider blinked. *'Iesu Grist!* Cover both sides, *ferch*, don't you! Where you heading?'

'Sycharth,' I said, the name joy in my mouth.

'Ah no. Not there, lady,' the rider mopped sweat from his face with his sleeve. 'Young Henry visited Sycharth yesterday, and will surely be at Glyndyfrdwy today. Nothing left of Sycharth but ashes. Head south, lady. Follow Glyndŵr. Safer there.'

I opened my mouth to speak, but Jack spoke first.

'Sycharth, gone?'

The man nodded. 'Not a stone standing.'

'And the people? The household, the tenants?'

The man shrugged. 'Warned. If they heeded, then they're safe. If not, then -' His silence was eloquent.

When he'd gone, I sat my horse like a corpse, coldness seeping over me, unable to think or move. 'What shall we do, Jack? Where can I go? Glyndyfrdwy? Perhaps Elffin is wounded -'

'Or captured, or dead.' Jack's voice was harsh.

'Don't say that!' My voice cracked. 'He can't be dead!'

Jack shrugged. 'Either way, Glyndyfrdwy is the last place we should go.'

'But if Elffin isn't at Glyndyfrdwy, and Sycharth is gone, then where will he be? Where can he be?'

'Riding after Glyndŵr, wound or no wound, I imagine. Look, Rhiannon, we can't stay here. We must follow Owain. I'll take care of you, I promise. If Elffin's alive, I'll find him for you, I promise.'

I had no one else to trust. And so we turned our horses away from home and rode south.

Elffin

The awful bastard luck that makes an apparently healing wound suddenly boil and suppurate, bringing fever and more pain, leaves a man wobbly as calves-foot-jelly and totally at the mercy of mothers and other bloody women who are on this earth to torment a man and dose him up with foul concoctions that make him heave, and slap poultices on a wound that stink and burn worse than the wound itself. Even harder when a man's father and brothers go off to war without him, and leave him behind like a woman. Still, I'm out of bed today, and soon I'll be away.

Mam is fussing. Three times this morning she's brought possets to nourish me, unsalted beef broth or pappish stuff with bread soaked in milk and honey, when what I crave is red meat, though when it comes I can't swallow it.

I managed to totter upstairs to the solar, where the warmth and jewelled light made me feel better. I'm glad I was here when my wound inflamed. I was bored with Glyndyfrdwy, and Sycharth is home. I sat in *Tad's* chair, stretched out my legs and closed my eyes, wondering where he was, and my brothers, and if they'd encountered the enemy yet, and wishing I was with them.

I was woken by shouts from the courtyard, and was halfway to the window before I was awake. A rider had come in, fast, straight over our gatekeeper, who was picking himself up from the mud and reaching for his sword. Recognising Rob Pulaston's livery, I flung open the casement and stuck my head out.

'Hold off, man,' I bellowed at the gatekeeper. 'Don't stick him, at least until we've heard what he has to say.' The rider's face turned upwards, and I beckoned him upstairs, going to the door to greet him and to shout for wine and food.

His face was grey with fatigue.

'What is it?' I asked, knowing that Rob Pulaston was with my father, riding south, and thinking it was he who was in trouble.

'Bad news, Master Elffin,' he said, slumping onto a stool. 'The King's brat's on his way to Sycharth.'

I stared at him. 'Here?'

'Aye, torching and looting as he comes. You must get out, you and your household. I'll warn as many of your father's tenants as I can. Go, Master Elffin, and fast. He's no more than an hour or two behind me, and I must warn Glyndyfrdwy, too. He'll go there when he doesn't find Glyndŵr here.'

Mam came into the room, followed by Crisiant bearing a tray.

'What is it, Elffin? Is your father -?'

'*Tad*'s fine. But Prince Henry's crossed the border looking for him. He's on his way here.'

'You have to leave, Lady Marged, quick as you can,' Rob Pulaston's man urged.

Mam looked uncertain, almost panic-stricken, which frightened me almost as much as the thought of Henry's approaching army. My mother was always calm and certain. She would be calm and certain at the Last Trump, my Mam, and probably order God about. Or so I'd thought. I took charge.

'Crisiant, get the household together and tell them what's happening. Tell them to take whatever they can carry that won't slow them down, and wait in the courtyard. Tell them to dress warmly, and wear stout shoes if they have them. There aren't enough horses for everyone, but the old can ride in carts and the children can go in carts or pillion on horseback. Mam, send someone to warn the village, and then go and pack what you need.' Still she dithered and for the first time in my life I shouted at her. 'For Christ's sake get on and do as you're told, Mam!' Amazingly, she obeyed. Jesus, ordering her about *and* blaspheming, all in one day. There's rebellion!

I flung on a cloak and went downstairs, wound forgotten, to organise the household. I wanted to stay and fight, but I was one wounded man with a household of women, children and old men, and I had no choice but to run. Much as I wanted to meet Prince Henry face to face, and swipe his arrogant *Sais* head off his shoulders, I was a realist, and in my current state of health more likely I'd lose my own head or get myself captured, which would only hamper *Tad*.

When we were all packed, and the horses and baggage carts were heading across the moat away from the house, I lingered behind and looked around. The stately buildings, the stained glass of the chapel, the white-painted dovecote, all my childhood was here, and here I fell in love with Rhiannon.

As my horse clattered across the wooden drawbridge, a thought struck me. Henry had generously bestowed both Sycharth and Glyndyfrdwy upon Beaufort. On the whole I'd rather see them burned than in his possession, but I doubted Beaufort would be much impressed by his Prince's abuse of his possessions!

But still, my eyes pricked and I couldn't look back.

I delivered Mam like a complaining package to Isobel, and apart from Bron and Crisiant who stayed with her, allowed the rest of my charges to scatter to places of safety.

My wound, thank God, was healing fast, and after a few days rest I gratefully kissed Mam and my sister, and rode, laden with clean hose and loving messages, to join *Tad*. It was a long ride, for they'd been travelling as fast as an army can, but a lone rider travels faster, and I soon saw the dust rising from the column, and then the straggling tail of the army. There were thousands, marching, and at the head of the procession the golden standard of Uther Pendragon snarled and cracked in the sun.

Despite the grim news I carried, my grin stretched from ear to ear, and the wind was cold on my teeth as I dug my heels into Seren to reach my father and brothers. They were all there, my brothers and comrades, and men turned and cheered at my approach. And Llewelyn, my brother, who turned Sioned out of the line and rode to meet me.

Llewelyn

Half a mile from Sycharth I smelled the strangeness in the air. I reined in Sioned and sniffed. Wood-smoke? Burning, anyway.

The smell grew stronger the closer I got to Sycharth, and uneasiness crept up my spine. Then, as I left the trees I saw smoke spiralling up over the hills. Filled with dread I put my heels to Sioned and rode for Sycharth, knowing, but afraid to admit even to myself what I suspected.

Sycharth, my golden place, my home, my childhood haven, was gone, and only a blackened pile of ashes and rubble remained. But Elffin, my brother? Lady Marged, fat Bron, the rest of the household? Where were they?

The drawbridge was scorched but intact, and I rode across it, my stomach tight, my heart thudding, my mind raging with pain and fear. The moat was thick with floating ash, and what water was visible reflected the crimson evening sky. The main building, the family chapel, the guest quarters, their wooden frames easily combustible, had been torched, and the stone foundations were cracked and blackened. Shards of jewel glass scattered the cobblestones, crunching under Siôned's hooves, and she shied at the stench of smoke and the strangeness in the air. White doves wheeled homeless above a dovecote gone forever, and a wolfhound slunk from behind a wall and trotted at Siôned's side, grateful to see a human in such strangeness.

I dismounted and forced myself to look closely at the ashes. There were no bodies, no twisted remnants of humanity, praise God. There'd been no slaughter here. Though my beloved Sycharth had gone, it looked as if Elffin had somehow led the household to safety. Perhaps they were already safe at Glyndyfrdwy, and Jack and Rhiannon with them. I would look there.

And so I rode down through Owain Glyndŵr's lands, and all along the route towards Glyndyfrdwy I passed the smoking ruins of his tenants' homes and farm buildings, but met not one soul until the next day, when a rider approached from the west. I drew my sword, but sheathed it again when I recognised Rob Pulaston's messenger. 'Sycharth is gone,' I said, 'all burned.' Saying the words made them true, and the pain was physical.

'I know, lad. And Glyndyfrdwy will be gone by nightfall.'

'And the household?'

'Safe, hiding until Glyndŵr returns. Henry's brat is sharpening his teeth on property since he can't find the Prince. Who is half way to Carmarthen by now.'

I rubbed my face, weary to the bone, not knowing which way to turn. 'I have to follow Glyndŵr, but my sister's missing. I know my duty, but how can I abandon my sister?'

'Are you Glyndŵr's ward, the boy who first called him Prince?'

I nodded.

'Then your sister's safe. I met her on the road, with an escort, and turned them back. She's probably with Lady Marged by now. Don't worry. Follow Glyndŵr.'

Thank Christ and all His Saints. She was safe. Gratefully I put my sister out of my mind and rode south to rejoin my Prince. And as I rode I tried to remember Sycharth as my childish eyes had first seen it, flooded with amber light from the sun sinking over the hills, long shadows casting secrets, violet shadows and mellow evening light.

I could not find it.

To be continued...

Author's End Note

The temptation to write a novel about Owain Glyndŵr emerged over a considerable time. It stemmed originally from a gradual realisation that the Welsh history I had been taught in school had been an English version of Welsh history – history written, as it generally is, by the conquerors. To put it another way, I didn't know as much about Welsh history as I thought I did.

When I began the research for this book, which would eventually lead to the award of a PhD from the University of Wales, I was already the author of several novels for children. I could have continued writing them (and indeed have) but my fascination with history - not the dates, the treaties, the blue bloodlines, but the real lives of the people who made it – won the day, and I launched myself upon what was to prove the most daunting, time-consuming and frequently depressing undertaking of my writing career. It took me two years to undergo the research to give me sufficient confidence to begin the book, and to find the way in, the "handle" that let me inside the characters' heads, two more to produce a first, skeletal draft of the first part, and two more to complete the entire novel.

I've taken some liberties in telling this story: I've given poor Iolo Goch a thoroughly bad character, and my assassination of Lady Margaret Glyndŵr's good name will never be forgiven by any descendants who may be Out There. But I hope that they, and you, the reader, will forgive me ~ and also my temerity in giving her an extra son, Elffin. Madoc, too, died in a way that aided my tale.

My characters don't speak 15th Century Welsh ~ or even English ~ so here again I've taken liberties ~ and hope I haven't included any 21st Century howlers! All errors are mine, and I claim pardon for them in advance. I'm a writer, not an historian, and early in my extensive research I coined a collective noun: "A disagreement of historians". But I've done my best and hope that I've given some idea of the nature of Owain Glyndŵr, whose dreams and deeds are the pride of Welsh history. He never surrendered to the English, although the fight for Welsh independence withered and died in the course of too many years until its revival in the Twentieth Century.

The legend, of course, is that Owain sleeps, awaiting the call...

Long live Owain Glyndŵr, True and Rightful Prince of Wales!

BIBLIOGRAPHY

During the ten years it has taken to complete "*Silver Fox*" I've consulted a vast number of books: the following is a note of those I found particularly useful.

Title	Author
The Marcher Lords	A C Reeves
A Mirror of Medieval Wales	Charles Kightly
The Towns of Medieval Wales	Ian Soulsby
Wales Through the Ages Wales Vol. II	A J Roderick
Owain Glyndwr - Prince of Wales	Ian Skidmore*
The Revolt of Owain Glyndwr	R. R. Davies
OG and the War of Inde--pendance in the Welsh Borders	Geoffrey Hodges*
Owen Glendower	Sir J E Lloyd*
A History of Wales	John Davies*
In Search of Wales	J V Morton
Owen Glyn Dwr	J D Griffith Davies*
In Search of Owen Glyndwr	Chris Barber*
Welsh Academy English/Welsh Dictionary	Bruce Griffiths & Dafydd Glyn Jones
Castles of the Princes of Gwynedd	Richard Avent
Wild Wales	George Borrow
The Herbal Remedies of The Physicians of Myddfai	Trans. J Pughe*
A Dictionary of Plant Lore	Roy Vickery
700 Years of English Cooking	Maxine McKendry
Food in History	Reay Tannahill
OG and the Last Struggle for Welsh Independence	A G Bradley
Owain Glyndwr	Glanmor Williams
Norman Usk - the Birth of A Town	A G Mein
Wales, Castles Historic Places	Cadw

Pamphlets

The Pennal Letter   -   National Library of Wales, Aberystwyth
Denbighshire, People and Places - Dr Charles Kightly
Enjoy Medieval Denbighshire - Dr Charles Kightly
Rhuthin   - Clwyd Library Service (Access No. L3161186/G)
Exploring Ruthin - Ruthin Community

*These books were the most frequently and gratefully consulted!

For more good reads from the prolific keyboard of Jenny Sullivan, especially the very many books for children she has written log onto

www.robsullivan.clara.net

and make your choice.

OR

try

www.wugglespublishing.co.uk
(who published this book), for all sorts of stuff.

AND

Log on to www.pdemitchell.com
(who produced the "Silver Fox" illustration) for some excellent Gothic-style reading containing mystery, horror, adventure, violence and anything else you can think of in a really good yarn.